Unmasqued

Unmasqued

An Erotic Novel of the Phantom of the Opera

COLETTE GALE

A SIGNET ECLIPSE BOOK

SIGNET ECLIPSE
Published by New American Library, a division of
Penguin Group (USA) Inc., 375 Hudson Street,
New York, New York 10014, USA
Penguin Group (Canada), 90 Eglinton Avenue East, Suite 700, Toronto,
Ontario M4P 2Y3, Canada (a division of Pearson Penguin Canada Inc.)
Penguin Books Ltd., 80 Strand, London WC2R 0RL, England
Penguin Ireland, 25 St. Stephen's Green, Dublin 2,
Ireland (a division of Penguin Books Ltd.)
Penguin Group (Australia), 250 Camberwell Road, Camberwell, Victoria 3124,
Australia (a division of Pearson Australia Group Pty. Ltd.)
Penguin Books India Pvt. Ltd., 11 Community Centre, Panchsheel Park,
New Delhi - 110 017, India
Penguin Group (NZ), 67 Apollo Drive, Rosedale, North Shore 0745,
Auckland, New Zealand (a division of Pearson New Zealand Ltd.)
Penguin Books (South Africa) (Pty.) Ltd., 24 Sturdee Avenue,
Rosebank, Johannesburg 2196, South Africa

Penguin Books Ltd., Registered Offices:
80 Strand, London WC2R 0RL, England

First published by Signet Eclipse, an imprint of New American Library,
a division of Penguin Group (USA) Inc.

First Printing, August 2007
10 9 8 7 6 5 4 3 2 1

SIGNET ECLIPSE and logo are trademarks of Penguin Group (USA) Inc.

LIBRARY OF CONGRESS CATALOGING-IN-PUBLICATION DATA

Gale, Colette.
   Unmasqued/Colette Gale.
      p. cm.
   ISBN: 978-0-451-22137-7
   1. Phantom of the Opera (Fictitious character)—Fiction. 2. Paris (France)—Fiction. I. Title.

PS3607.A412U66 2007
813'.6—dc22   2006036396

Set in Adobe Garamond
Designed by Spring Hoteling

Printed in the United States of America

*For all the women who thought Christine
should have stayed with the Phantom*

Parisians are always at a masked ball.

—GASTON LEROUX, *The Phantom of the Opera*

Biographer's Note

*M*any versions of the Paris Opera House and its alleged "Phantom of the Opera" have been told in the last century and a half. Gaston Leroux's tale has often been considered the most accurate because it was based on official reports filed in Paris at the time of the events in question.

Hollywood, in its turn, has interpreted the book in different ways, taking dramatic license where and when the producers and directors wished. The most famous version, the wildly successful stage musical by Andrew Lloyd Webber, subsequently adapted for film, promoted yet a different version of the story.

It was not until this author received the personal diaries of Miss Christine Daaé (and validated their authenticity) that the true story became known: the story that appears in this volume.

Initially, this author's intention was to keep the diaries private in deference to Miss Daaé's family, and that of the Chagny brothers, but upon further consideration, I came to feel that in all fairness to Christine and Erik, the truth could no longer be obscured.

For decades, as the romantic, horrific legend of the Phantom of the Opera has been told, Erik has been portrayed as a murderous villain, Christine as the helpless, manipulated ingenue, and Vicomte Raoul de Chagny as the brave, love-struck swain.

In fact, the actual events of those months at the Opera House are quite different from the official version promoted by Monsieur Leroux and the Parisian officials (most likely, in this author's opinion, in order to protect the reputation, and influence, of the Chagny family).

Much of what is purported to be fact by these sources apparently came from a mysterious individual identified only as "the Persian," who claimed to be an intimate of the Opera Ghost. In fact, in all research and in the documents that make up the basis of this author's studies, there is no such person or entity either described or alluded to. It can only be construed, then, that this mysterious personage was merely a figment of the imagination of Leroux and the Parisian officials, created in their attempt to clear all blame from the Chagny brothers.

Thus, the story that appears in this volume is taken directly, and in all explicit detail, from the diaries and journals of Christine Daaé. I have also included details from her personal letters from the ballet mistress Madame Maude Giry, with whom Christine apparently developed a deep friendship after the events described herein.

This, then, is the entire story of Christine, Erik, and the Chagny brothers—the truth, once and for all.

—Colette Gale
August 2007

Part I:

The Phantom of the Opera

ONE

Paris, 1887

Christine Daaé closed her eyes as the heavy, sumptuous silk billowed down over her laced form. She'd never dreamed she'd wear a costume of such finery, with the glitter of so many gems and the gushing fall of lace from every edge and flounce. The silk was pale rose pink and the jewels a rainbow of crimsons, fuchsias, and peridot green. Lace of all tones of white—pure snow, blue white, eggshell, aged ivory—dripped from the sleeves and brushed the floor. Tiny rosettes of pink and red silk grew in the holes of the lace pattern.

The costume was heavy and smelled like Carlotta's cloying rose perfume, and when it surrounded her, it clogged Christine's nose and caused her eyes to water. The aroma was not the pure scent of roses sent by her *Ange de Musique*, the scent that she gladly buried her nose within and drew deeply from. The smell from Carlotta's discarded costume was rank and overpowering, just as Carlotta herself was.

Yet, and yet . . . Christine would wear it, for tonight she was to take the prima donna's place in more than her gown. She would sing the aria of Juliet, from Gounod's *Roméo et Juliette*, in front of the entire Opera House because Carlotta, the Opera House's star, had stormed off in a great snit earlier today.

During rehearsal, one of the backdrops had fallen from its moorings a bit too close to the very costume Christine was now donning, but which at that time had been worn by the diva Carlotta. She had just had the pleasure of meeting the Opera House's two new managers, Messieurs Moncharmin and Richard, when the wooden pole clattered to the stage. It brushed the edges of her gown, landing in a loud thump at her feet.

Carlotta bolted away as quickly as her generous form would allow when the length of heavy canvas tumbled to the ground, her bosoms and jowls bouncing and her outraged screams echoing in the sudden silence. She clapped her hand to her chest, sending off a puff of white powder from her bosom. "How dare it! How dare it!" she shrieked, yanking off her tall, feathery headdress and tossing it at one of the costumiers. "La Carlotta is ill! La Carlotta *shall not sing*!"

She stalked off the stage and disappeared in a froth of skirts and feathers, the new managers staring after her in shock.

Horrified whispers skittered around the stage and pit in her wake.

"It is the Opera Ghost!"

"He has done it again."

"She could have been killed!"

"It was he who stole my powder puff," hissed one of the dancers.

"He moves like a shadow," added another.

"An evil creature he is," chortled Joseph Buquet, the chief stage-hand, bugging his eyes out to frighten the young dancers. "His eyes are like coals! His teeth blackened and rotted. His face is stretched tight, and yellow, and his black clothes hang from his bones. He will hunt you down and eat you for dinner!"

Madame Giry, the mistress of the corps de ballet, silenced the gossip with a sharp snap of her fingers and the glare of her jet-bead eyes. "Do not speak of what you do not know," she ordered, look-ing sharply at Buquet, who had not troubled to keep his voice to a whisper. "Now, to work! You also, Sorelli. You might be our star dancer, but you must still focus on your practice!"

She directed the dancers behind the steel curtain that separated the ballet foyer from the rest of the stage. Mairie, the lead choreog-rapher, bade the performers to continue their practice. If whispers and undertones continued, Madame Giry did not hear them . . . or, at least, did not acknowledge them.

It was surely a most unfortunate occurrence to happen on the very day the two new managers took over the reins of the famous Paris Opera House. The outgoing managers, Debienne and Poligny, had been respected and feared by the performers. But these new managers, Messieurs Richard and Moncharmin, who came from the trash-removal business, looked merely wide-eyed and full of consternation.

"Opera Ghost?" Christine, who had been standing near enough to hear their conversation, overheard Monsieur Moncharmin ask his companion. "Debienne and Poligny mentioned nothing about such a thing when they turned over this Opera House! What can be meant by this?"

Monsieur Richard, the taller and more dapper of the two men, tucked his hands in his waistcoat pockets and tipped onto his toes, murmuring in response to his companion, "Likely it is nothing but some bizarre legend, Armand. We are now in the theater business! They have many superstitions and stories and we shall learn of them as we progress. I'm sure it shall prove to be quite entertaining, in more ways than one." He chuckled indulgently, then sobered. "More importantly, how shall we replace La Carlotta for tonight's gala performance? There is no one else who can sing with such grace."

"We cannot cancel the performance," Moncharmin muttered. "Chagny shall be attending and everything must be in order."

Then, before Christine could blink an eye, Madame Giry had whisked over from her management of the dancers and pulled her forward, thrusting her in front of the managers. "Miss Daaé will be a more-than-adequate replacement for La Carlotta this evening. Her singing has improved enormously in the last three months."

Monsieur Richard looked down at Christine, arching one brow as he scanned her simple chorus costume, patched where it had been burned by a careless hair-curling iron, and frayed at the skirt's hem. Christine's palms dampened as she clasped her hands together, uncertain whether to dread or hope. It was the chance she'd never thought she'd have. "One of the dancer girls? I do not see how—"

"Come, Richard, it cannot hurt to give the girl a chance," Moncharmin prodded. "After all, who else is there?" He made a sweeping gesture for Christine to step forward onto the main part of the stage, then turned to the maestro and snapped an order for him to play.

Her throat so dry she wasn't sure any note would come forth, Christine walked to center stage, her full, calf-length skirt bouncing with each step. The platform, which pitched at a gentle slant from the back down toward the gaslights along the edge, seemed vast and frightening, despite the fact that the seats in the stalls were completely empty.

A few awkward notes as the violinists found their chairs again, and the cellist readied his bow, for the orchestra had left their seats when the accident with the backdrop occurred and had to get re-settled . . . and then, as if she had waited an eternity, the melody.

She knew the music, and opened her mouth to sing, pushing her breath out as her angel had taught her, keeping her mouth rounded and her notes long and true until the end. As her song poured forth—hesitant at first, then a bit wobbly, then soft, then louder and clearer—Christine basked in the wonder of the most exciting moment of her seventeen years.

She closed her eyes, every detail of the beautiful Opera House printed on her memory, but in her imagination, she added people filling the rows of stalls that curved in an easy arch in front of the pit, and in the gallery beyond. The high, domed ceiling of the auditorium was painted with Lenepveu's colorful rendition of the Muses, dancing gracefully in a circle of clouds. In the center of the painting stretched a long chain from which hung a magnificent crystal chandelier.

Boxes with crimson interiors adorned the walls of the auditorium, the closest ones near enough that Christine would be able to see the detail of any female spectator's gown. Massive gold columns separated the boxes, and the front of each balcony was decorated with an ornate design of flowers, fleurs-de-lis, and cherubs. Above Christine's head, over the proscenium, trumpeted more angels with their elegant instruments.

Even if the managers did not let her sing tonight, she was standing on the stage and *doing it*: doing the thing she had dreamed of, fantasized about, since she was young.

If this was to be her only chance, *he* had prepared her well for it, and she would enjoy every moment of it. Christine had learned that things changed much too quickly in life, and to seize joy when it was offered . . . for it was much too rare and precious.

When she finished singing, Christine could not resist making a grand curtsy, though there was no audience to see her. When she straightened up, she glanced first at Madame Giry—whose stern face held the barest sketch of approval—and then at the skeptical Monsieur Richard.

He was smiling.

Now, as they prepared for the evening performance that was to celebrate the Opera House's two new managers, as well as its new patrons, Madame stood behind Christine and surveyed her in the floor-to-ceiling mirror.

"You look beautiful, Christine," she told her, critically examining her from the fall of the gown to the pile of dark hair at the top of her head. Their eyes met above the three busy costumiers that poked and prodded at Christine's headdress, her shoes, her flounces. "He will be very pleased."

At the mention of *him*, Christine felt the air stir in her small dressing room. It became warm, suddenly, yet the tip of her nose cooled; the hair on her arms lifted. Her cheeks burned while the shift in the air felt like a caress over the back of her bare shoulders and neck. If only her angel would show himself to her . . . come to her in person, instead of just in that hypnotic, pulling, beautiful voice he used when tutoring her in her singing.

"It is my greatest hope that I shall do so." She was looking at the mirror directly in front of her, the item that dominated the small, narrow dressing room. The room *he* had insisted she use now that she was no longer in the chorus, according to Madame Giry.

"Come, now, you have done with the fussing!" Madame snapped at the frithering girls, who seemed to have noticed a change in the air and were casting about in fright. "Out!"

She shepherded everyone out and, with her hand on the door, turned to look at Christine. "He wishes a moment with you before you sing."

Christine was startled. Their lessons, where he taught her to master her untutored voice and to feel the music throughout her entire being, occurred in the chapel, where she prayed for her father and mother, and where he had first spoken to her, or in the conservatoire. But never had he communicated with her at any other time. Would he speak to her now?

Madame was gone, and Christine stood in front of the mirror, looking at herself and the long expanse of empty chamber behind her. The light burned low and warm, yet the shadows loomed tall into the curved ceiling.

She felt him. He was there, her *Ange de Musique*, her Angel of Music.

The air trembled and the gas lamps blinked out with a soft *pop*. Her heart fluttered in her chest; her palms grew damp just as they had done this afternoon. Yet she did not move, but watched as what had been her reflection in the grand mirror slid into nothing but glinting shades of silver, gray, and black.

And then . . . something light and warm, heavy and gentle, brushed over the back of her shoulders, along the curved edge of the back of her dress. She released her breath, and the warmth closed over her skin. Her heart beat rapidly; he was there! He was in the room with her!

Leather—smooth, cool, pliable—fingered over her skin, the dip of her delicate bones, brushing the long bareness of her neck. Heat rushed in the wake of his touch, sending sharp pleasure down into the depths of her belly. She closed her eyes, drew in a shudder, and reached out for the cold glass of the mirror in front of her. Her hand imprinted on its unyielding chill, an anomaly from the warmth that burned against her back.

He breathed, standing behind her, and she felt his height, strength, darkness wrapping around her. "On the stage, you will sing for me this night."

As always, the timbre of his voice frightened her with its intensity, warmed her with its smooth cadence, teased her with its hint of mockery. It embodied the beauty of the music she loved so, with its rhythm and tone and its cool, unforgiving command. And tonight, instead of coming to her from some disembodied location, it was there, behind her, next to her. Touching her.

"I will." She started to turn, to face him, desperately wanting to see him . . . but his hands on her shoulders stopped her. Firmly.

"No."

She had never seen her *ange*, had heard him speak to her only in darkness such as this, or even in the low light of the conservatoire when she visited there alone to practice . . . in the chapel, when he sang in a low, ghostly murmur whilst she prayed for the soul of her lost father, and that of her mother, who'd died so long ago. Perhaps once she had felt him touch her, as he did tonight, but she had been sleeping and was not certain if it had been a dream.

This—his leather-covered hands smoothing over her shoulders and around to cup her neck, curving around her throat, leaving delicate shivers in their wake—was no dream. She'd often wondered if he was a spirit or a ghost. But the warm solidness behind her answered her question: He was no ghost.

He was a man, perhaps more . . . but he was no specter to dissolve into thin air. The Opera Ghost was an angel, with a darkly rich voice.

When he sang, a tenor.

When he coaxed, velvet smooth.

When he raged, cold and cutting as a stiletto.

"Christine . . . ," he breathed in her ear, his mouth close and warm. The syllables of her name were a deep, ringing well of elegant, coaxing tones.

The fingers of her right hand, splayed on the glass of the mirror, slipped a fraction from the nervous moisture beneath her palm. Her other hand reached up behind her head, collided with soft, sleek hair that did not belong to her. She dug her fingers into the heavy strands, felt the shift of his scalp under her finger pads as something behind her moved, pressing into the back of her hips. Hard, solid, hot, he was, and she felt it even through the layers of silk and crinolines. It caused a burst of warmth to flood to the place between her legs and Christine removed her hand from the mirror.

Her fingers were cold and moist, and they sought back behind her, brushing over the top of his head as her left hand had done . . . and then slid down over his temples, and touched something smooth and unexpected where his forehead would be—lifeless, cool, and yielding. Not flesh, not hair—

He shifted away from her touch, grabbing her hands and pulling them down behind her, between them, trapping them at the base of her spine, where the folds of his cloak billowed about. "Your boldness surprises me, Christine."

"Why can I not see you?"

"When it is time." Something hot and warm, faintly moist, touched her neck and sent shivers down to the base of her belly; she tried to turn toward him, but his hands gripped her wrists too tightly. "When it is time," he repeated, his mouth against her delicate shoulder. "Now . . . you sing for me tonight. And if you please me, you shall be rewarded with my devotion."

And then he was gone.

The lights fluttered back to life, and Christine was alone in her room. The only sign of what had occurred was the streak of finger-prints on the mirror . . . and a glistening trail of moisture along her neck.

The sea of faces, the heat from the hooded gas lamps at the edge of the stage, the strange constriction of the heavy costume . . . the blur of light and sound and the deep breaths that she needed to take . . . the mosaic of sensations swam in Christine's mind as she sang. She felt the music tear from her body as if released by some pent-up energy. She heard the reverberation as the clear, high notes swelled and filled the stage alcove. And then she drew in her last breath and expelled the last note, and the sea of rapt faces turned into a mass of thunderous applause, cheers, shouts.

L'Ange de Musique would be pleased.

And over the shouts and whistles, she heard it, deep in her heart. . . . "Brava . . . *bravissima* . . ."

And in the wings of the stage, she saw Madame Giry, nodding and beaming with clear, studying eyes.

Christine was left in the midst of the stage to make a care-ful curtsy in her heavy, formfitting gown, over and over. Flowers, gloves, even hats, were tossed onstage at her feet.

From the box in which they were sitting, the Comte and Vicomte de Chagny watched Christine Daaé's bowed head as she made her third curtsy. Still the crowd roared and applauded.

"Quite a lovely woman. Very lush," mused Philippe, the *comte*, settling back in his seat. "It is no wonder the dancer La Sorelli never cared to introduce her to me during our attachment. Miss Daaé is her name? I wonder where she came from and how long she has been here. I have never seen her in the dancers' lounge, nor in the singers' lounge. I wonder where she has been hiding."

"Her father died some years ago," replied Raoul, his younger brother. "I do not know how long she has been here at the Opera House. I only learned she was here this week. I have not spoken with her in years."

"So it is no wonder that you insisted that you would attend tonight, without your regular companion of Mademoiselle Le Rochet."

Philippe noticed that Raoul had not taken his eyes from the dark-haired figure below. "I met Miss Daaé at the sea near Perros-Guirec some years ago. . . . Do you recall that summer? You were there too, that first day I met her and her father."

"I am sure I would not forget such a lovely form if I had seen it before." No, indeed. He was not accustomed to passing by such lovely womanhood without finding a way to sample it. And an actress, of course, would be simple and easy for the picking . . . despite the growing strength of the bourgeois, who believed that with the Third Republic and the rise of their class, the actresses had miraculously become modest and moral.

A laughable assumption.

"We were younger then. She was but a girl. I saved her scarf from being blown away by the surf—oh, look at her! She looks as though she might faint!" Raoul stood from his seat as if to rush to her side.

Philippe grabbed his arm and pulled him back. "Sit, dear brother. It is not fitting for a Chagny to make a fool of himself over a singer or dancer, even one as beautiful and gifted as she. And see, the others have caught her. She is not about to crumple to the floor in front of an entire opera house without someone else noticing." Indeed, several of the dancers had rushed to her side and caught her as she began to sag. Her face did look pale. Philippe turned and considered Raoul thoughtfully. "You appear quite taken with her."

"I've never met a more lovely, endearing woman. It was an unforgettable summer, and I spent a great deal of time with them. You were too busy with your own affairs to notice. I met her father, a great violinist, who would play for us . . . and she would sing. Only passably then, but with great promise. She sings more beautifully now than she ever has. Before Monsieur Daaé died, he would tell us wonderful stories about the Angel of Music and Little Lotte . . . tales from Sweden, where they were from. He never came to love it here in France, and often told us stories from their homeland, for which he was strongly homesick." Raoul seemed lost in his memories, a fact that greatly annoyed Philippe, who preferred to live for the moment.

Philippe stood. "Then I would imagine you must hasten to congratulate Miss Daaé on her lovely performance. She will be delighted to renew your acquaintance, whilst I make my way to the dancers' lounge, where La Sorelli is waiting to renew mine." A smile played about his lips. This could be quite interesting, Philippe thought.

When at last she came offstage, Christine was surrounded by the girls of the ballet corps, of which she had been a member until just this afternoon. Even if her new role was only temporary, the entire day had been like a dream. The girls squealed and clapped and bore her like a hero in their midst back to her dressing room, for what she had accomplished was in the heart of every one of them as well.

Still light-headed from her experience, her fingers trembling and her knees weak, Christine nevertheless felt as though she could be no happier. She'd sung perfectly, clear and true, dressed in the heavy, gorgeous gown that looked as though it belonged to a queen. The applause had been for her, and her alone. The enraptured faces, rows after rows of them, had been in her honor.

It was as if she'd traveled back in time to the moment when as a very young child, she'd seen the beautiful lady . . . dressed in a glittering golden gown, seeded with pearls and rubies, her honey-colored hair coiffed in whorls and braids and little puffs around her ears, with more jewels and slender golden chains woven through-out . . . and she, little Christine, gazed up at her in adoration.

She would never forget that beautiful woman opening her lovely pink lips, so soft and plump and shiny, and the incredible sound that came from them. She remembered how her voice made Christine's little heart expand in her chest, and how she wanted to touch the lady's skirt where its scalloped hem brushed the stage directly in front of her eyes. How, looking up in awe, she had wanted to be up there herself, like a splendid bird, capable of making such sweet, pure sounds, and looking like a faery princess.

And she was certain that standing on the stage, in the midst of all the adoration, garbed as richly as a queen, the woman was happy. Joyous. Loved. She had to be. One could not be that beautiful and that adored and not be happy and secure.

Eventually, young Christine somehow convinced herself that the beautiful woman was really her mother, who had died when she was five. She used the memory as a talisman, as an aspiration and an escape from a life that was as colorless and bland as the woman's gown was brilliant and warm.

Her lonely life, spent with her father, who still swam in his own grief for the loss of his wife, had few pleasures. Master Daaé was a famous violinist who traveled and took Christine with him everywhere; thus, she had no home, nor friends, and merely saw city after city from coaches and small hotel rooms. It was not until that long-ago summer by the sea at Perros-Guirec that her father decided to stay in one place. But that was years after Christine had seen, and fallen in love with, the beautiful lady.

And tonight, with shaking knees and churning belly, she'd *become* that beautiful lady of her dreams.

And now all would be well. She would be happy and loved and safe.

Now, as Christine reached her dressing room, a deep, masculine voice penetrated the high-pitched tones of her girlish companions. "Miss Daaé?"

The voice, not the disembodied one of her *ange*, but an earthly one, was close behind her and drew Christine from the task of unlocking the door of her room.

As she turned, his name came to her ears, hissed in the undertow of voices from the excited girls. . . . "The Vicomte de Chagny! It is he! The new patron's brother!"

She turned and saw him, recognition following immediately. "Raoul!" she exclaimed without thinking, for he was a friend from her childhood, one whom she'd come to know for a short, happy time during that summer by the sea.

How handsome he had grown, how tall and chiseled and elegant he was, from his slender fingers to his small, clipped mustache. His long blond hair, clubbed at the back of his neck, gleamed golden and tawny in the light. Clear blue eyes smiled at her, taking her back to those days when they'd played together and listened to her father's stories about the Angel of Music. She recognized that he was wearing a naval uniform and was not surprised, for he'd loved the sea, even all those years ago.

She wondered what Raoul would say if she told him she'd been visited by a true *ange*, and that he'd been tutoring her for months. And that it was because of his tutoring that she had become the beautiful lady.

He stepped forward and the sea of girls parted before him like he was Moses. He removed the tasseled key from her hand. "Allow me, Miss Daaé."

He unlocked her dressing room door, sending it open with a flourish. She brushed past him, noticing how the heavy gown dragged against his shiny boots and cuffed jacket.

He closed the door and they were alone.

Lamps glowed, and the shadows that seemed so often to be dramatic were now low and brown, and did not lurk in the corners as they were often wont to do. Flowers had already been brought into her room, and vases rested on every surface—the floor, the dressing table, the tea table, even the sitting stool. Roses, daisies, gillyflowers, lilies . . . filling the air with their perfume.

"Christine, you were magnificent." Raoul came to her side, clasping her hand with his and drawing it to his perfect lips.

"Raoul, how lovely to see you again," she replied, slipping her hand from his and brushing her fingers over his fine cheek. It was warm and smooth.

"You have grown up so. I could not believe it was you, my little Christine, singing like an angel."

An angel.

Christine stepped back, suddenly nervous. "Raoul, I am no angel."

But he did not seem to notice her apprehension. "You are, you are, beautiful angel. I shall have to make a point of returning to the opera every night, now that Philippe and I are the patrons and now that you are to be the new star."

"I hope that I shall see you often," she replied, and felt a change in the air. It was *him*. For some reason, she didn't want *him* to know about Raoul, that she had an admirer. "Raoul, shall we leave here? I must speak to Messieurs Richard and Moncharmin, and I am hungry, and we have so much to talk about. It has been so many years."

"Yes, indeed, I would be happy to escort you to dinner."

She opened the door, and was greeted by a throng of admirers clutching flowers and waiting eagerly. "Oh, my," she said, pleased and warm, but very, very aware of a barely tangible shift in the room's mood behind her.

Raoul pushed past her. Blocking the door, as if to keep the others from seeing into the room, or, perhaps, seeing much of Christine, he turned toward her. "I shall bring my carriage around and come back for you shortly. Shall I call someone to help you change?"

"No . . . no, thank you, Raoul. I shall be able to take care of it myself."

He closed the door and she was alone.

And then she realized that she wasn't. "Madame Giry?"

"You did well tonight, Christine. But *he* will not be pleased if you neglect your rest in favor of social activities." Madame Giry had moved behind her and was working quickly at the buttons that lined her spine.

The heavy costume fell away, and Madame's warm hands moved over her shoulders and down her arms to push the silk to the floor. "Take care not to anger him, Christine. His wrath is not to be borne. Are you certain it is wise to go with the *vicomte*?"

So Christine's worry that her angel would not be happy to know she already had an admirer was correct. "But . . . I must eat, madame. And he is nothing but an old friend, and the brother of the new patron. It can only be good for the success of the theater if he wishes to dine with me."

Madame's face, aged but still beautiful, turned hard with concern. She bent close to Christine's ear, her breath warm and moist, sending prickling shivers along the edge of her neck. "Have a care, Christine, for as his pupil, you have the chance to be great, with or without the favor of the patron's brother. If you please him, you will be cared for beyond your imagination. If you displease him, his wrath will be immense. He is brilliant and kind, but he is selfish and would not be willing to share you. Note well what I say, Christine. With *him* as your tutor, you need not worry about finding a protector, as the other girls do."

Did she mean that her angel would be her protector? Or that he merely wished to be certain that she did not forget about her lessons?

Instead of asking, for Christine felt a strange squiggling feeling in her middle at the thought that *he* might hear, she twisted the subject. "A protector? Raoul? I do not think he has such an idea in his head. He is only an old friend, pleased to see me again. Nevertheless, I will heed your warning, madame," Christine replied earnestly. She did not forget that it was her *ange* who had tutored her to this wondrous night. "It is only a dinner, to celebrate my debut."

"I hope that you shall remember that, my dear. And it is fitting that you should celebrate. Now, quickly, let us change your clothing and get you prepared for dinner. It must be a short meal, so that you sleep well tonight. Look, I have brought you a gown to wear."

Surprised, and embarrassed that she hadn't thought for herself of what she would wear to dinner with a *vicomte* and the theater managers, Christine turned. "It's beautiful. Where did it come from?"

It was striking, and very stylish, and nothing like any gown Christine had ever owned, or even seen up close. Certainly the opera costumes were all beautiful and bejeweled and ornate—the better to be seen from the boxes and the stalls—but they were too heavy and fancy to wear in the real world.

"I bullied Tiline into letting you borrow it," Madame explained. "Her Monsieur Boulan has gifted her with many lovely gowns as of late."

It was a dinner gown of deep garnet satin trimmed with gold lace that gathered in soft folds at the tops of her arms. The lace made a narrow vee from shoulder to shoulder in front and back, and where the dark red bodice gathered over her breasts, more gold lace hung along its lower edges.

The skirt was nearly as heavy as the costume Christine had been wearing, and fell in generous folds that were gathered up into a bustle at the base of her spine. A wide swath of gold satin draped from each side of the front of the skirt and was fastened over the bustle with a huge bow made from more gold lace festooned with white and red satin roses.

When she saw herself in the mirror, she hardly recognized herself as shy, lonely little Christine Daaé.

"Thank you, madame," she said as she left the room at last.

Outside of her dressing room, the passageway was empty. Still, shadowed, silent . . . so unlike what Christine was used to, with the comings and goings of actors and costumiers and musicians, prop hands and stagehands . . . it was quiet and lonely. As she had been, it seemed, forever.

But now, tonight, she was a star. Everyone wanted to see her, speak to her, be with her. No longer the shy mouse of a girl, she was sought after by a *vicomte*! Even if he was an old friend, he would not have sought her out if he did not wish to see *her*.

She was no innocent girl. Madame Giry had seen to it that none of her little dancers—called *rats de l'opéra* for the fact that they often came to the theater young and straggly, and were seen as always being underfoot—were innocent ingenues, though they might appear to be. She instructed them in more than simply ballet. Madame felt each of the young rats was her responsibility, for many of them had chosen the profession over being a schoolmistress or working in manual labor, upon being orphaned or because their family became destitute.

The theater was a profession, Madame told them, that allowed a woman quite a bit of control over her life, including her choice of lover or protector—if she was young and pretty, or at least if she was talented both onstage and in the boudoir. Thus Madame had ensured that none of her charges were waiting to be deflowered and left with nothing to show for it. Her rats were taught how to take advantage, rather than be taken advantage of. She instructed them how to attract and select a good protector who would not be physically cruel in the boudoir and who would otherwise treat them well.

But Christine could not fathom that Raoul—good, handsome, polite Raoul, who had dashed into the surf to retrieve her scarf when it blew away—would dare have the thought of being a protector. It made her warm to even think of it.

Raoul did not fit the image of one. Christine had met the older gentlemen that took care of the two former dancers Tiline and Régina when those two began to have solos of their own and thus attracted attention to themselves. Their protectors had bloated cheeks, were pompous, and had squinting, beady eyes that seemed always to be looking right through the girls' costumes—yet they patted the girls on the heads and brought them gifts and trinkets whenever they visited. If one did not look in their eyes, one might think they were no more than a father or favored uncle. But of course, that was not so, and Christine, who had not been a virgin since her sixteenth birthday, recognized all too well that the looks in their eyes were anything but paternal.

Now the two girls, who hardly had time any longer for the other dancers in the corps de ballet from which they had so recently graduated, complained of having to juggle the attentions of the older men, who paid for their costumes and jewelry and for their own small flats, with their interest in younger, more attractive and virile men who did not have the pocketbook . . . but had other amenities.

Christine herself had never been in a position to attract the attention of a possible protector. Even if she had, she would have taken care before doing so, for she was known as one of Madame Giry's most virtuous girls. She was one who did not flirt, who did not make promises with her eyes, who took care that her bosom didn't show and her ankles didn't flash.

But perhaps tonight had changed everything. Now she had attracted great attention! Perhaps that was why Raoul had made his way so quickly backstage, and barricaded them in her dressing room. Perhaps he was merely trying to protect her from any other men who'd found her sudden, triumphant debut of interest.

No, she did not place Raoul in the same category as those pudgy, false-fatherly gentlemen who scanned the dancers and singers and actresses as if they were clusters of horseflesh . . . but neither did she dismiss him. Not at all. For he had been handsome and charming, and quite obviously pleased to see her.

Now, Christine should have been hurrying along the passageway toward the back door that led into the side alley, where Raoul would be waiting for her . . . but instead, she found herself moving back toward the stage. The place of her triumph.

She had rarely had occasion to be on the stage when the room, with its vast rows of seats and high, domed ceiling, was empty of everything but . . . echoes. Echoes of performances past, echoes of smoke from the doused lights, echoes of perfume and applause.

She wasn't sure what drew her, but she heeded the innate call and walked out onto the stark wooden-planked stage. Her footsteps, nearly silent in slippers, took her to the monstrous stage's center, and Christine stood, facing the invisible audience.

A whisper of air stirred, raising the hair all along her arms and at the base of her neck. She resisted the urge to look behind her; instead, she smoothed one hand up along her arm, then down, over her long glove, and then back up again. Waiting.

A sudden beam of limelight shot down from above, circling her in its white glow, cutting her off from the darkness around her. The sphere was compact, just large enough that she might walk two small steps before moving out of it and back into the empty black if she chose. It was warm; even though it had not pounded on her for long, the heat from the light above played across her bare shoulders and bosom, and over the upper parts of her arms that were not covered by her gloves.

The light dulled her eyesight as it did when she performed. She could not see the shadowy seats in the theater, nor could she see the red velvet curtains swagged at the edge of the proscenium. All she could see was the white beam of light; all she could feel was its increasing warmth.

"Christine . . ."

The sound of her name, faint, hollow, erotic, came from behind. Or perhaps above. She wasn't sure.

"Ange?" she managed to ask. Her heart was suddenly thumping madly.

Before she could turn to look, she felt him behind her again, just as he had been in her dressing room. He had spoken to her, taught her, sung with her . . . but he had never appeared to her before. And now twice in one day.

His hands closed over her shoulders, the supple, tacky leather of his gloves grabbing at her delicate skin as he moved his palms down over her arms, pulling at the low, sweeping neckline of her gown. The fabric tightened over her breasts, uncovering her suddenly hard, sharp nipples, baring her skin to the heat of the light above.

"You pleased me greatly tonight," he murmured in that low, melodious voice. It burned in her ear and sent waves of sharp prickles along her neck, down her arms, over her breasts and nipples, to her belly, and lower.

Christine dared to look down, and she saw black, gloved hands dark on her white shoulders and the deep, dark vee between her breasts lifted and pushed together by her corset, and the hint of pink from her areolas above the dark crimson gown. "Thank you," she breathed, reaching up to cover one of his hands with hers. She felt the faintest tremor in his fingers, beneath her own, and wondered suddenly . . . was it from anger?

Or was it the same sudden trembling she felt over her body?

Now her white-gloved fingers splayed over his wide black ones, and she could feel the heat from him burn into her skin beneath. His free hand moved, threading fingers up into the back of her coiled hair, combing gently through it and then grasping to pull her head back. The beam of light struck her gaze and blinded her; she closed her eyes as sudden tears stung them.

From behind, his face moved against her; she felt warm flesh brush against her right jawline and then hot, soft lips press against her skin. Her head held immobile, her eyes closed against the searing light, Christine struggled to draw in a breath and succeeded only in shuddering and faintly sobbing as pleasure burned where he kissed her, drawing on her flesh, slowly, insistently.

His lips, warm, moist, gentle, inched along her jaw, down the side of her taut throat. Her neck ached; her lips parted; her knees weakened. Her fingers closed around his hand at her shoulder, while her other hand reached up to touch him behind her. She needed to feel him, to know him.

"No," he snarled against her skin, and, releasing her hair, snatched at her questing fingers and pulled them away from his face. He moved quickly and imprisoned both of her wrists in one leathered hand, above her head.

He moved. She could feel him reach up, behind her, and then suddenly she felt something wrapping around her wrists. She gasped, and tried to pull her arms free, but he was too strong. Before she knew it, he'd secured her hands above her head, wrists crossed, elbows bent gently.

"Did you not know that curiosity killed the cat?" he murmured gently into her ear, his sudden anger seeming to have defused. He circled around so that he stood just next to her, but still slightly behind so that she could not see any part of his face . . . only the gloved hand and the long, black arm to which it was connected, the strong black leg that crossed in front of her skirt, and the shiny black shoe that stepped in the pool of light below.

She tried to move her hands down from the top of her head, but something held them there, something from above. She could do nothing but tug and pull and feel the sway of the rope as it swung from the catwalk above. Her heart beat faster; she could not seem to draw in a full breath.

"Now . . . ," he sighed, moving close to her, one hand in a vee at the front of her neck, cupping her throat, the other at her nape. "I shall show you how well your performance pleased me tonight."

"*Ange,* please . . ." She could scarcely form the words . . . and for what she was pleading, she did not know.

His chuckle was quiet, but he did not respond with words. Instead, she felt his hand moving down her spine. The heavy weight of her gown loosened, gapping and falling away in the back where his nimble fingers undid the buttons Madame Giry had fastened only a short time ago.

His other hand slipped under the steel ribbing of her corset, sliding under her left breast and to lift it from the cup of her stays. His leather-covered thumb moved over her stark, hard nipple and she felt a jolt of pleasure spear into her belly, and then to the place between her legs. It flooded moist and hot there, and she pulled, trying to bring her arms to touch him, forgetting that she could not. The rope held, and she succeeded only in straining her arms and causing her *ange* to chuckle again.

"Relax, *ma voix*," he murmured, his voice rougher than before. His thumb continued to rub across the sensitive part of her nipple, while the other hand slid down beneath the open buttons of her gown, down and around her buttocks.

Christine jerked when that hand found its way under her che-mise and down into her drawers, cool leather fingers slicking down stickily, spreading the cleft of her rear. She tried to buck away, but he only pressed harder, his fingers sliding to cover the underside of one round buttock while his front hand slipped to the vee of her legs. His palm pressed there, into her sex, through her gown, and moved in a circular motion over the silk and lace that covered her.

Wrists bound above her, she was trapped between his hands, one set of fingers pushing her skirts down and between her legs, and the other urging her forward from behind, into his palm that cupped her. Her breasts were tight, her nipples painfully hard. Her arms were cold and prickly from lack of blood. The beam of light burned down on them and sweat dampened her face and shoulders and breasts, making her skin slick and heavy. She bucked her hips, trying to get free, or closer, or away—anything to relieve the pres-sure building inside her.

As he massaged her with his hands, pressing her between them, one warm leather finger slipped from behind, sliding through the wetness that pooled between her legs. Christine moaned when that finger, impersonal in its black case, slid inside her. He pushed her back, his other hand still in place at the juncture of her thighs, massaging just where the edge of her mound was. . . . How could he feel it, through all the reams of cloth?

Such thoughts fled when he removed his hand from her front and yanked hard at her corset, pulling it down and away from her heavy, tight breasts. She was poised, balanced, on the finger deep inside her, and her breasts were bare in the hot white light, pink nipples hard and pointing, aching when he brushed his hand over one, then the other. *Mon Dieu,* what if someone came upon them?

He pinched, tweaked, rubbed, and she moved her hips, swimming on that leather finger, trying to find something, some relief, some end. "Ah, yes," he breathed into her ear. His voice was thick and deep. "You open yourself to me. . . . Yes, *ma voix,* yes, you may shudder and moan. It is a beautiful music you make now, on this stage. Performing only for me."

Christine was no innocent when it came to pleasure of the body, but she had never felt the hot rush of lust combined with the inability to move as she wished, touch as she needed to. She'd never felt this rage of need she now felt, standing—no, dangling, for her knees sagged and she could no longer hold herself upright.

When he bent his dark head and closed his mouth around the nipple nearest him, Christine could hold back no longer. She cried out, felt the weight of her body straining on the rope above, dangling with her wrists held high and helpless. Wetness, moisture, liquid everywhere . . . between her legs, on her breast, sweat from the heat of the light—she was dripping, throbbing, panting.

She cried out, unable to hold back the frustration that built inside. His lips sucked at her nipple, drawing it so tightly into his mouth that she thought she must scream from the pain, and cry from the pleasure.

The finger inside her slipped free, rubbing over her engorged pip, straining between her nether lips, as she circled her hips, trying to move it closer, harder, faster, in the rhythm she needed. He lifted his mouth. "Come for me, Christine. . . . Come . . . *now.*"

His other hand again pushed back on her, holding her hips in place as that nimble finger worked from behind, round and round, slipping and gliding through her, until at last the pleasure peaked and she shuddered, crying out her orgasm from deep within.

Then there was only the aftermath: silence, but for their twin breaths, harsh and needy. The dull throb between her legs; the ache at the breast where he'd sucked so hard. His warm leather hand as it glided up and over her ass, bringing her wetness along with it over the round swell of her buttocks. He drew away from her breast, moving back behind her before she saw more than the gleam of dark hair. His hands settled on her shoulders and he pressed into her from behind.

She felt his erection; it pushed into the base of her bare back, through his trousers, insistent and promising. Hard, and it sent a renewal of lust through her middle, stabbing into her stomach.

"I trust that your pleasure was as great as mine," he murmured, back at her ear again and safely out of her view. His voice was not smooth; it was uneven but low, as though he struggled to keep it steady. He moved his hands up along her arms, moving from her bare skin to the fine cotton gloves that stretched from elbow to wrist.

"I believe mine was the greater," Christine replied, her own words shaky. "But if you will untie me, *ange*, I would like to touch you . . . and see you."

"My name is Erik. You may call me that, but now is not the time. Behave yourself this night, *ma voix*, and I will come to you again soon. Your tutelage has only just begun." She felt his chest lift and press against her from behind as he drew in a long, deep breath, held it, then released it.

His gloves, fingers spread, ran down from her wrists, over her face, jaw, and neck, smoothly over her bare breasts, pausing to massage them . . . then close and hard over her belly and to her throbbing sex. Heat followed the leather, and she sagged again under the weight of desire, closing her eyes and tipping her head back into the blare of light.

And then suddenly, he left. He left her burning and aching for more, her nipples hard and pointed, one redder than the other from his mouth, and sore. Her sex throbbing again, in memory and need. Her back cold without him behind her, her gown sagging from her uplifted arms.

And then, before she could fathom that he'd left her stranded and half-naked on the middle of the Opera House stage, something fell from above. Her arms dropped, still tied, to her waist, the rope slapping onto the hard wood at her feet.

Two

Christine was still struggling to untie the rope around her wrists when the limelight above blinked out and left her in total darkness, half-clothed and in the middle of the stage.

She heard the whisper of movement above and knew that it was her *ange*, Erik, who was making his way along the jittery catwalk above, which was normally the dominion of the tale-spinning Joseph Buquet.

Then all was silent, except for her ragged breaths.

She pulled at the ropes, her breasts jiggling against her loosened corset, her sensitive nipples rubbing against its lacy edge.

"Christine?"

Mon Dieu. Raoul! She'd forgotten him.

"Christine, are you back there?"

She struggled harder, and at last felt the rope loosen from her gloved wrists. It snaked to the floor, and she felt it nudge against her skirt. Quickly, she began to pull the corset up over her breasts, shimmying and shrugging to fit them back into their confining cups.

"Christine!"

His voice was closer now, and she could hear the footfalls of his boots. Her stays were in place, but there was no way she could tighten them without assistance, and certainly no way she could button up the long row of tiny pearls down her back.

"Raoul, I am here. On the stage."

"On the stage?" His gentle laugh reached her ears. "Reliving your moment of triumph, are you, little Christine? Let me get a light."

"No! No light, Raoul, please. Just . . . come here."

Erik was gone; she knew he had left, for she could not feel his presence. And she needed assistance to button up her gown. How dare he do that to her . . . and then leave her to fend for herself?

At least he had not left her hanging. That would have been quite difficult to explain to Raoul or anyone else who might find her.

"Where are you, Christine?"

"This way. I need your help."

When she heard him on the edge of the stage, she started toward him. It was purely black, so that she didn't realize how close he was. She walked right into him and he caught her, sagging gown and all.

"Christine!" His voice betrayed the surprise at the bare, warm flesh his hands felt at her back. "What is happening?"

"I need help fastening my gown," she said, her hands moving up and over his solid shoulders. Were Erik's as broad? Was he as tall? How could she not know such simple things when he knew so much of her . . . had taken so much?

"Your gown feels as though it is about to fall off," Raoul replied in a strangled voice. Yet his hands made no effort to move from their spot on her bare back.

"It is." Her voice was husky. It was Erik's fault for leaving her wanting more.

The timbre of her words must have seemed like an invitation for Raoul, for suddenly he tightened his arms, crushing his mouth down over hers.

Christine tipped up her face to meet his lips, and felt her breasts surge and her tender nipples tighten against the sagging confines of her stays.

After the initial rough impact, Raoul tamed himself and gentled his mouth. He tasted, sipped, slicked his tongue over her lips and slipped it around and along hers as she drew in her breath, deeper and harder, pushing her nearly bare breasts up against his shirt.

"Oh, Christine," he groaned, pulling away yet holding her hips firmly against his. His erection raged against her, through five layers of clothing, sending her own sex to throbbing again. "We cannot. . . ." He drew in his breath, steadying it. "My brother, the *comte*, and the messieurs Moncharmin and Richard await us. . . . We cannot be much longer. We must go."

Christine pulled away reluctantly, feeling the ache of unsated lust. Any guilt she might have felt for her response to Raoul's feverish kisses so soon after her intimacy with Erik was quickly dismissed. After all, *he* had taken from her, and *he* had left her wanting more. Of Erik, she wanted more, but Raoul was tall and handsome and elegant . . . and Raoul, she could see and touch.

But his kisses were different from Erik's, and the way he moved his hands over her body was too tentative, as though he was afraid to touch her. Erik was bold, and knew how to pull and coax forth and peak her desire . . . just as he did her music.

"*Oui*, let us go. I am famished," she told Raoul, turning in the dark, presenting her backside to him. "Finish my buttons, my dear *vicomte*, and we shall be off to eat." And then back here to rest, she promised herself.

She would sleep well; but tonight, she feared, her dreams would be filled with more than the memory of a disembodied voice. Tonight, she would dream of his touch as well.

Erik moved along the catwalk like a starving panther—fast, silent, smooth. Hunger gnawing.

He knew the upper workings of the Paris Opera House like he knew every other area, from the high, flat roof open to the moon and sun alike, to the backstage, to the dormitories so vast they were nearly a city unto themselves . . . to the cavernous tunnels and sub-terranean lake that snaked deep below.

The Opera House was his domain.

Music was his language.

Christine was his obsession.

True . . . he'd hardly noticed her at first. Until recently, he'd barely paid attention to the comings and goings of the dancers and singers. The dark, silent theater had been his bailiwick. After all had gone home in the early-morning hours, he'd roamed the backstage, the catwalks, the stalls, even the boxes and the grand marble foyer.

But one day, perhaps six months ago, when it was still summer and the nights were short, he'd not returned to his little cottage in time. Or else she had been up early.

He'd seen her come onto the stage just as she had tonight after her brilliant performance, alone. In the silence.

She had done nothing so very unusual to capture his attention;

surely Christine Daaé had not been the first young woman to stand on an empty stage and wish for the chance to make it her own. But that was what she'd done.

Her long, dark hair was caught back in a simple ribbon. She wore her battered chorus girl costume; perhaps she'd been wearing it all night. Since then, he'd been close enough to see it and notice the darned slippers and the ladders decorating the backs of her stockings.

She'd sung, there, by herself, on the empty stage. Not brilliantly, not even with much emotion, but Erik heard the promise in her amateurish voice.

And then when she turned and he saw from his place in the wings the full force of her heart-shaped face, his heart—which had been protective steel for so long—softened. She looked so sad.

Lonely.

He wondered if she'd been alone as long as he had.

Now, his breath ragged, his heart thudding, his erection excruciating, Erik finally allowed himself to stop, rest, leaning heavily against the rough brick wall that edged the very top of the massive space that included the stage and backstage. He was tucked up and behind the upper proscenium. In this dark, remote corner, the ceiling was only inches above him. His fingers trembled, and he stripped off his leather gloves, and they snapped softly in the quiet . . . broken only by his harsh breathing.

At last, after months of watching, teaching, loving Christine from afar, he had touched her. *Touched her*.

Touched her, and she'd *welcomed* it. There'd been no revulsion, no crying, no struggling.

She'd had pleasure, had responded. Deliciously.

What it had cost him to slip away. Let her go.

Bringing the collection of empty leather fingers to his face, he breathed, smelled her on them, and tipped his masked face against the brick. His mask. Barrier to peace and satiation.

He'd fashioned several of them of leather, tanning and tooling them as if he aroused a lover, until they all were smooth as skin. He had one of black, for when he wished to move about unnoticed at night, and one of cream, which blended with the color of his flesh. If he was to wear it, it must be comfortable, pliable, sensual. He must not be aware that it was on; it must become such a part of him that the only way he could tell it was there was by touch.

Or sight.

He rarely looked in the mirror, even when he wore the mask.

The pale leather mask, more supple than even the gloves he held to his trembling mouth, covered just half of his face. One mangled eye. One scored temple. One ravaged nostril. One mottled, slashed cheekbone. And it curved around to sweep at the corner of his mouth, leaving his wide, sensual lips bare. It tied over his thick dark hair, at the back of his crown.

A faint sound drew his attention; he pulled away from the wall and, holding the rail, looked down.

A pale, ugly face gleamed up at him from the next catwalk below. Buquet, the ape.

"Quite a show you put on down there," drawled the man, looking boldly up at Erik. "A nice piece of pussy, and you managed to find your way down into it. Not that you're the first, you know."

It was nothing for Erik to launch himself from the narrow, rickety catwalk and flip himself onto the one below. He landed, flatfooted and steady, and turned face-to-face with Buquet.

"You are a coarse, stupid man," Erik said, fury cold and steady through him. He might burn for Christine, but he had learned long ago to control his other emotions into efficiency. He did not rage; he acted with decisiveness.

Buquet had the balls to laugh, yet Erik saw that he stepped back. Fear glinted in his eyes, displayed by the low lantern the man carried. "I'd be happy to keep what I saw to myself, if you allow me to watch——"

Erik's hand shot out and closed around the man's throat. His fingers tightened over his windpipe, and lifted his weaselly bulk from the narrow wood planks. "If I find out you have even breathed the same air as Miss Daaé, if you even *think* to come within twenty yards of her, I will make your miserable life *even more hellish.*"

The man choked and gasped beneath the same fingers that played the piano with such elegance and beauty. Erik constricted, then loosened them, and allowed the man to collapse at his feet. One leg dangled off the narrow walkway.

"Do not let me see you or hear you again, Buquet."

He turned to stalk away, the frustration that had been centered in his cock now vibrating throughout his being. Rage and desire were a monstrous combination.

"You'll never have her, scuttling rat." Buquet's words were so soft, perhaps he did not mean for Erik to hear them. The coward. But Erik did hear, and he whirled back around just as the man leaped at him.

Buquet's lantern rested on the walk, leaving his hands free. One held the flimsy rope railing, and the other a glinting silver knife. "You're naught but a sick devil, scurrying about in the dark," he said boldly, brave now that he brandished his weapon. "You must hide your filthy self——"

Erik kicked out, and Buquet dodged on the narrow footbridge, continuing to taunt him. "You bury yerself in the dark, and yearn for what you will never have. She won't be looking on the likes of you, no matter that she spreads her legs when you force her. She'll not spread 'em for your cock, for the——"

Erik stopped the mocking voice with both feet, slamming into the man's face as he lifted himself with the weak rope railing on either side. Buquet tumbled to the boards and, grasping at the rope with one hand, pulled himself up, the knife raised in the other.

As he brought the knife down, Erik ducked and lunged, and knocked the man off-balance . . . and then felt the footbridge tip as he slid to the edge. Before Erik could turn, the walkway righted with a jerk, swaying mightily as Buquet tipped off and he hurtled through the air.

He caught, tangled in the ropes from the backdrops and lights, hanging there as he frantically tried to claw himself free. Erik watched, and saw what was going to happen before it did . . . before he could move to try to stop it.

Rope snagged around Buquet, and as he struggled to free his hands, one of the lines looped around his neck. As the last part slipped free from his arm, Buquet fell freely until that rope tightened its deadly grip.

His neck broke with an ugly snap that echoed in the dark chamber.

Erik turned impassively, picked up his gloves, and, leaving the lantern and the knife, walked off the catwalk to the iron ladder that lined the wall.

They would find Buquet in the morning, and it would be yet another evil attributed to the Opera Ghost.

The tussle with Buquet had eased some of the rampant lust coursing through his body, but as Erik climbed silently down the iron ladder, it all came flooding back. Images swam there, haunting him in the dark as he forced himself to count the rungs. Anything to keep his mind steady.

But the counting could not keep them away. The open curve of Christine's white neck. Heavy, walnut-colored hair brushing the part of his face that was bare, he imagined it falling in long waves down her pale back. Plump pink lips, wet and full like the lips of her sex, open and inviting. Panting, as she writhed on his finger. Hard pointed nipples, shooting up, jiggling and jerking with every shuddering breath she took.

The vibration of her beneath his hands, between his palms. Her scent . . . roses and lavender and whatever it was that made her Christine. Slickness everywhere, the musky smell curling into his nostrils as he played her. Played her.

His throat was dry and crackling and his erection surging, straining with need. Buquet's words haunted him.

She will never spread her legs for your cock.

You will never have her.

Nothing but a sick devil, scurrying about in the dark.

Buquet's taunts mingled with memories of his youth, of those dark, horrid days with his brother, where the girls would scream at the sight of Erik's face. And his brother would shove them at him, make him touch them. So he could watch them scream, and fight.

Erik stepped onto the wooden floor of the backstage and turned. Someone was there.

Madame Giry stepped forward, holding a lantern that sent stark shadows over her aging face. "Erik . . . did you kill Buquet?"

"He killed himself," he replied. "Though it was fortunate for me that he managed it on his own, for I sorely wanted to help him along."

Maude, known as Madame Giry to everyone else in the Opera House, moved closer to him. She smelled like lilies, an erotic scent for a woman nearing fifty. She was the same age his mother would have been, had she lived a full life and not died when he was merely twelve.

The two women had been the best of friends, close as twins from their childhood in the south. They moved together to Paris to pursue dancing careers. His only portrait of his mother was one that Maude had given him of the two women together, and they could hardly have been more different. The young Maude was fair-skinned and fresh-faced, with generous curves, while Erik's mother had the lithe, exotic beauty of her Persian mother and French father.

Ten years ago, when Erik was in trouble and had nowhere else to turn, he came to the only friend he knew. Maude had been his protector ever since.

"Buquet was a filthy man who did not know to keep his mouth shut. I have caught him spying on my girls more than once. He is no great loss."

"I will be blamed."

She nodded. "Yet another tragedy attributed to your legend. This will only serve to protect you further, Erik, and you know how important it is that you remain a mysterious, shadowy figure. As long as you remain a half-believed legend, you are safe. With a little prompting, the new managers will be inclined to keep you happy in exchange for a peaceful house."

"And you will continue to ensure that they do."

"I will ensure that they have every reason to comply with your requirements. I consider it my duty to keep them satisfied . . . on all levels." In the low light, her face transformed with a meaningful smile.

Maude loved sex, and she did not confine her lustful appetites to one partner, or even many. She had slept with legions over the years, and prided herself for hiding her great appetites behind a rigid, proper persona. "I'll make myself acquainted with them first before I introduce them to some of the girls." She looked at him thoughtfully. "Something I would be most happy to do for you, Erik. There are one or two who could be counted on to remain discreet. Or I'll see them thrown out on the street."

"No," he managed to say calmly, though his cock shifted beneath his trousers. "I'll wait."

With a sideways glance, Maude raised an eyebrow and shrugged. "You are becoming as chaste as Christine is."

"Your girls might be discreet, but they will still gossip. And La Carlotta, though out of your chaperonage, has the loudest lips of them all. It is best if I remain the shadowy ghost I've been for the last nine years so that none can identify me."

Yes, nearly ten years of his life—one-third of it!—had been spent hovering in the shadows of this Opera House. Hiding and lurking and pretending to be nothing but a specter. Would he ever be free to live in the light?

"As you wish, Erik," Maude told him, with a gentle bow of acquiescence.

After she left, and Erik felt the rage of his cock refuse to subside, he wondered at his instant refusal. He could have taken her up on her offer. It would be easy and quick.

But he'd resolved years ago he would force no one to see his monstrous self. He wanted no more of the fear, of the revulsion, he'd seen in the girls he'd been forced to touch.

He wanted none of them.

None but Christine.

THREE

*C*hristine sat next to Raoul at the restaurant where they supped. In a quiet corner, at a table surrounded by a large, curving sofa, the five of them ate a late meal and discussed that evening's successful performance.

Raoul sat so that his thigh lined hers and the pointed tail of his coat flipped up over the back of her gown. He was solicitous and charming, ensuring that her wineglass was always filled with the deep golden Bordeaux and her plate had the choicest pieces of roast fowl.

Next to Raoul sat one of the Opera House's new managers, Monsieur Armand Moncharmin, the one who had urged his counterpart to let her sing.

He was shorter and stouter than his partner, with soft, puppy-dog eyes and little jowls that added to the canine impression he presented. A shy man, he appeared too nervous to look at Christine for long, although his gaze continued to dart back to her person when he did not expect her to be looking. This was the type of man, she thought as she slipped a grape into her mouth, who would be afraid to unbutton his nightshirt for his wife and would insist on making love with the lights off.

Next to Christine, leaving a greater distance between her gown and his trousers than Raoul had done, was the other new manager. Monsieur Firmin Richard was the elder of the two partners, and he sported a neat, slicked mustache that did not dare to showcase any of the gray that winged his temples. His eyes were sharper and more considering than Armand's, but Christine had already heard that Moncharmin was the one who handled the money, and Richard, the dandy who actually understood music, was the one who managed the personnel.

Directly across the table from her was Raoul's elder brother by a decade, Philippe, the Comte de Chagny. Later, Christine was to realize he had deliberately chosen that seat for the advantage it gave him. A more mature version of his younger brother, the *comte* exuded power and control from the condescending flare of his aristocratic nostrils to the thin, settled lips that curved in the faintest of considering smiles.

In his shadow, Raoul seemed little more than a handsome, earnest boy who wanted desperately to gain his big brother's approval.

"I see from your uniform that you are a graduated member of the École Navale Impériale," Monsieur Moncharmin commented to Raoul.

"Indeed," replied the *vicomte*, offering a smile to Christine, then returning his attention to the short manager. "I recently graduated from my training upon the *Borda* and found myself with little to do until I was invited to join my brother at his patronage of your Opera House. I cannot but think it was a serendipitous occurrence that of all nights, he should invite me to this evening's gala."

"Raoul graduated near the top of his class," added the *comte* as he set his wineglass down with a smart snap, "and then embarked on a journey around the world. His sisters and I are pleased that he has chosen to return for a brief furlough before leaving on his next journey."

"Where shall you be heading off to next, then?" asked Monsieur Richard. "I myself cannot stomach the sea, even a short journey, for it makes me ill."

"My brother wields enough influence that I was able to be assigned to the mission of the *Requin*, which will not leave for several weeks yet." Under the table, he squeezed Christine's fingers as though to let her know he would not forget her.

"Is that the ship that is to search for the survivors of the polar expedition?"

"Yes, indeed. The *d'Artois*. But I shall not be called for a month, so I will have plenty of nights to return to the Opera House."

"Our Miss Daaé was quite a triumph this evening." Moncharmin braved a look at Christine, then reapplied himself to his potatoes.

"Yes . . . but whatever happened to that Spanish singer? Carlotta?" spoke the *comte* suddenly. "Although our Miss Daaé turned many heads with her beauty and her voice, I am curious as to how such a young girl managed to snare the stage from the Opera House's star. Unless it was part of your scheme as the new managers? Out with the old and in with the new, perhaps?"

Philippe's gray blue eyes rarely left Christine's person, even as he spoke to his brother or the managers. They were heavy, calculating, and disturbing. When she moved closer to Raoul, pressing her arm against his as if to melt into the protection of his person, Philippe's mouth tipped up at one side in a sardonic grin as if he understood and was amused by it.

Richard replied, "Carlotta was overset by an accident on the stage today, and it was decided she should rest her nerves this evening."

"An accident?" Raoul asked, concern in his face as he looked at Christine. "Somehow I had not considered the opera to be so dangerous."

"It is no more dangerous than crossing the street, unless one is foolish enough to believe in the stories about the ghost who haunts the theater," Richard grumbled.

"An opera *ghost*?" The *comte* was clearly amused. He drank again from his garnet-colored wine, and refilled the glass with a flourish.

"It is a foolish superstition," Richard replied. "Sorelli has insisted on placing a horseshoe on the table of the *foyer de la danse* for each performer to touch before setting onstage. She claims it is a talisman against the evil of the ghost. A ghost which does not exist." He shook his head, the cord from his monocle wagging in time.

The *comte* raised his eyebrows. "One does not consider La Sorelli as endowed with much common sense, although the dancer certainly is not lacking in other areas of endowment." He watched Christine over the rim of his goblet.

She looked away, focusing her attention on Raoul's warm thigh brushing against hers, and the fact that his face and hands were much more elegant and comforting than the intense expression on his brother's face. She realized, suddenly, that it was fortunate that she had caught the eye of the younger brother before that of the elder one.

"Theater folk are mad—*pardonnez-moi*, mademoiselle—they have too many of these absurd superstitions. It is ridiculous. We nearly had to cancel the plans for *Faust*, which is to open next week, because of the scenery." Moncharmin began to rapidly chew his bite of bread as though agitated or embarrassed.

"The scenery?" Raoul was mystified. "Was there a fear that it should fall? Is it not merely a painted backdrop?"

"Oh, no, no . . . did you not notice, my lord, that the scenery has real doors and windows? And corners and alcoves? It is the new style, to make the set more realistic, and we spent twenty thousand francs to build the Heaven set for *Faust* in order to keep our theater ahead of its competitors . . . and they refused to even rehearse with it." Moncharmin's bread was being ravaged. Crumbs sprayed. Crust dangled. "I cannot begin to understand this business."

"It is the blue," Christine ventured to speak. Everyone looked at her, even Moncharmin. But then he flickered away. The *comte*'s attention did not. "The blue on the scenery—the sky. No one in the theater will perform with a scenery that is blue, for it brings misfortune. Death or loss of money."

"Death? Is that so?" The *comte*'s gray blue eyes swept over her in that arrogant, calculating way that made Christine think of the protectors. But there was not one hint of fatherliness in his whole attitude.

Raoul did not seem to notice. "How did you resolve it, then?"

"It was insisted that we add silver ornamentation to the set— another cost, of course." Moncharmin reached to mangle the loaf of bread in the center of the table. "Another five thousand francs."

The *comte* smoothly changed the subject. "I did not mention how delightful it is to see you again, Miss Daaé. I am told we met briefly some years ago, when you and my little brother romped at the beach in Perros-Guirec. Not a very fashionable place, but one near my aunt's home, where Raoul was raised."

"You remind me of a bittersweet time, Comte de Chagny," Christine replied. That summer in Brittany was the last summer she had with her father. "My father died that following winter, when I was ten."

"It was Madame Valerius who raised you then, was it not?" added Raoul.

"Yes, she and her husband, the professor of music at the National Academy of Music in the Opera House, were friends and admirers of my father, who was a great violinist. They were kind enough to keep me with them until I was able to enroll at the conservatoire." From then, it was an easy path for her to find her way to the chorus and ballet corps, all the time hoping for the chance to advance further.

To find her place.

Had she found it now?

"That day you met her at the seashore, I rescued her black scarf from the surf, Philippe," Raoul added. "Do you recall being there, now that I have reminded you?"

"Indeed I do," Philippe replied, his attention focused on Christine. "I do remember the girl, who has now grown to be such a beautiful young woman. It is no surprise, Raoul, that you have determined to reawaken your acquaintance with her. If I did not already have a countess, I would be so inclined." He gave a brief nod, meant to imply tribute to Christine. But she saw the look in his eyes and knew better.

From the time she was twelve and joined the chorus for a mere eight hundred francs per annum, she had lived in the dormitory at the Opera House, sharing a room with the other dancers. Living in such a casual, communal environment, she'd been exposed early on to the sexual interactions between men and women through whispered conversations, spying in dressing rooms, and her own clumsy, groping experience with one of the props boys that eventually led to her own deflowering.

And then of course, there had been Madame Giry, who spoke frankly of such liaisons and experience, and urged her girls to make their own decisions and taught them how to utilize their feminine power to the best of their ability. And how to be certain they were not gotten with child, and what to do if they should be.

Christine had witnessed the coquettish ways dancers and singers of all ranks—both men and women—teased and flirted with the admirers who came backstage to the *foyer de la danse* after the performances. She saw the hungry way the men looked at the dancers, at times with admiration, as Raoul did with her . . . and at other times with a condescending desire. As the *comte* did now.

She looked at his ungloved hand holding the wineglass, three of his fingers bearing heavy, jeweled rings, and imagined that hand on her flesh. It would be cold, and demanding, she knew; it would not allow her to shrink away, to flinch. Christine watched as he trickled his fingers, blunt tipped and thick, over the side of his glass as if to call attention to them.

She tore her gaze away, and it skittered upward and was trapped. By calculating grayish blue eyes. He nodded once, then turned his attention to the others at the table. He spoke no more to her that night. He did not even acknowledge her presence with anything but an occasional searing stare. After the meal was finished, Raoul excused himself and Christine and sent for his carriage.

When they returned to the Opera House, Christine found herself looking at the huge marble theater in a different light. Since joining the corps de ballet, she'd hardly ever seen the facade of the famous columned building, for most often, her comings and goings were relegated to the back, where the dormitories were located. But now, as the sun was rising over the creamy Paris skyline, Raoul drove his carriage around the front of the Opera House, to the side rotunda where he would normally enter the building. Christine looked up at the colossal sculpture of Apollo, holding the globe of the earth up toward the sky, and she suddenly felt as though she were just as high and powerful as he.

When Raoul realized he had made a mistake, he sent her a rueful smile and drove the horses around to the back of the building. It was a long walk to the dormitories, and at last Christine realized how exhausted she was.

"When shall I see you next?" asked Raoul, stopping at her door. Although he had dragged her up against him only hours ago, and ravaged her mouth as though starving, he seemed to have shed that intensity and now looked upon her as something delicate and breakable. Something out of reach, something to be worshipped.

"When do you wish to?" she asked.

"Now. Tonight. Tomorrow. The morning." He took her hands, his eyes soft and luminous in the low gaslight in the hall. "Forever."

Christine laughed lightly and pulled gently away. "Such strong words, Raoul, and we barely know each other."

"I have known you for years, Christine, and I have never forgotten you. . . . It was only fate that pulled us apart and brought us back together. If my brother had not become the Opera House's new patron, I should not have been here tonight to see you sing and to have renewed my acquaintance with you." He tilted his head gently, as though to better look in her eyes. "Do you not feel you know me? Don't you feel the connection between us?"

"Yes, I do feel a connection: the memory of a lovely summer all those years ago. From such a happy time in my life," she replied. "I feel as though you are an old friend. Someone comfortable, familiar."

Not someone who unsettled her, or burned her. No, not Raoul.

Raoul did not burn her.

"You see?" Raoul broke into a beam of a smile. "I feel the same, Christine. I shall speak to my brother—"

"The *comte*?" The warmth that had begun to swell in her filtered away. "Why must you speak to him?"

"Because if I wish to court you"—he smiled, wide and brilliant, like a young boy—"I must ensure he will approve."

"But you are a Chagny! He will never allow you to court me. I am not . . . you cannot."

"I shall court you anyway, in secret if I must," Raoul told her fiercely. "I am the younger son. I do not need to wed for my family. It is becoming more accepted for actresses to marry well. And you are no Blanche d'Antigny." He spoke of the Parisian actress who had been driven from the Russian stage because of her immorality.

Perhaps he was right. Perhaps it was becoming more accepted. More possible. Could she ever aspire to being the wife of a *vicomte*, little Christine Daaé, daughter of a violinist?

She thought of Marie Bière, the singer who had not had the benefit of Madame Giry's mentorship, but had found her way nevertheless. Marie had been freed after her arrest for attempting to murder her rich lover, when he had left her pregnant and destitute. Even the courts had found in her favor, she, an actress! Perhaps times were changing.

But Raoul was still speaking earnestly, holding her hands and looking at her with his blue eyes. "My brother *will* approve. He spoke of your beauty and grace, and I saw that he found your company quite enjoyable at dinner. He would never have spoken to you so informally if he had not."

Christine felt a chill over the back of her neck. There was no doubt that the Comte de Chagny found her attractive. And his informal comment had felt more like a bearbaiting than conversation. Still. Raoul made her feel comfortable and happy, and he was the personification of a rare memory of happiness.

She was the beautiful singing lady now, wanted and loved by all. There would be no more loneliness.

Perhaps someday, she would even enter the Opera House auditorium through the huge, sweeping staircase.

"Monsieur Moncharmin," called Madame Giry, seeing the flare of his dark cloak as he disappeared around the corner early the morning after Christine Daaé's maiden solo performance. "Please wait for a moment."

When she caught up with him, she saw that his little round cheeks had turned apple red, and that he avoided looking her in the eye. However, his attention seemed to be caught and trapped by her generous bosom, covered modestly by her high-necked gown, but jutting out like a wide shelf, nevertheless.

Bien. This would make her task much easier. She gave a large, shuddering breath, sending her breasts jiggling mightily.

"Yes, Madame Giry?" he asked in a choked voice.

"I have something for you, monsieur. It is a letter." She handed him the stiff parchment, folded over and closed with a bloodred seal. Armand Moncharmin's name was written on it in sharp, bold black ink.

"What is this?" Armand was peering at the seal, no doubt trying to discern the intertwining initials on it. "O.Q.?"

"It says *O.G.* For 'Opera Ghost.' "

This statement garnered her the first full-faced look from the portly man. "Opera Ghost? *Mon Dieu,* what lunacy are you speaking of? That imbecilic rumor that caused Carlotta to run out on us last evening?"

"The Opera Ghost. Surely Messieurs Debienne and Poligny

told you about their contract with him when they turned the house over to you?"

"Contract?" Armand had broken the seal and was scanning the letter. As Madame Giry was well aware of its contents, she refrained from speaking. "Salary? Box Five? What is this?" He appeared to have no problems looking her in the eye now that the subject of finances had been broached.

"It is very simple. The Opera Ghost wishes to have his monthly salary paid, which, for this month, you owe him approximately twenty-three thousand francs. Debienne and Poligny did pay him for the first ten days, as I believe he noted.

"The Opera Ghost also insists that you continue to keep Box Five—you know it, the one just next to the stage—available for him at all times. He was quite annoyed last evening when he attempted to enter the box and learned that you had let it out. In turn, he will keep his end of the bargain by keeping out of your way. In other words, you will need to continue the contract he had with the previous managers in order to be left in peace, which, I must say, he sorely wishes to do."

"We cannot—twenty-four thousand francs? Box Five? We cannot afford to do that!" Armand sputtered.

"But I do not see how you cannot," Madame Giry told him gently. She really was looking forward to getting him out of those trousers. He was no more substantial than a plump teddy bear— even with all of his bluff and bluster. She could not hold back a smile at the thought. Perhaps . . .

"Shall I take you to see Box Five?" she asked. Erik would not mind; he normally did not come up from his underground lair during the morning hours. Madame Giry slipped her arm under Armand's and gently but firmly turned him in the proper direction. She was taller than he was, helped by the heels of her shoes and also genetics, and the top of his head came just to her chin. That would be a lovely change, to have a man with such easy access to her very sensitive breasts. Perhaps, in order to give the poor man some warning of the delights to come, she would endeavor to trip and stumble against him when they walked down the steps from the managers' offices, where they were now, to the foyer of the Opera House.

After all, she had not obtained the coveted position of the Opera House's ballet mistress by being shy and retiring. Indeed, she had been a magnificent dancer in her day and perhaps could have gone on to be as renowned as La Sorelli if not for the unfortunate injury to her left ankle fifteen years ago.

She could still dance, of course, but her ankle could not hold her weight as well, and Maude would do nothing if she could not do it perfectly. Thus, partly because of her talent and her reputation for hard work and perfection, and partly because she had grown up helping her mother at the ballet school, she was able to attain the position as the ballet mistress at the conservatoire. And when the Opera House was inaugurated a decade ago, Maude brought some of her rats with her to the new theater. Of course, it had not hurt that she had demonstrated her other . . . skills to the messieurs Debienne and Poligny for years. They had had quite a comfortable arrangement.

"I am quite certain I know which one is Box Five. It is the one that has always been reserved by Debienne and Poligny," Armand replied, but he did not sound convinced. Perhaps it was the massive shelf of her jutting breasts that had distracted him. But, no, to Maude's annoyance, he was back on another topic almost immediately. "And what is this about Christine Daaé? I can barely read the creature's writing."

"Miss Daaé is the Opera Ghost's protégée, and he merely *suggests*"—she put gentle emphasis on that word—"that she be afforded the same types of roles and attention as La Carlotta has had. In fact, that was why he was particularly annoyed that his box was occupied last night. He wished to see her debut performance."

"Miss Daaé, his protégée?" Armand repeated as Maude steered him down the wide sweep of marble steps that led to the main salon of the Opera House.

"Of course. The ghost is quite a musical genius, and he has been tutoring her for the last several months."

"Tutoring her?"

Maude resisted a sigh. His continued repetition of every phrase she uttered was becoming tiresome. Best to fill that mouth with something other than confused words, and the sooner the better.

"Now, Monsieur Armand," she said patiently. "Let me explain to you, as I am certain that you are wondering even though you have not asked . . . how I've come to know so much about the Opera Ghost."

He looked at her in surprise; apparently, he had not thought to wonder any such thing. Maude sighed. Apparently, the man's head was filled with numbers and nothing else. Well, she would quickly change that.

"*Oui*, madame, I should like to know."

"I have been given the responsibility by the Opera Ghost to steward his box—Five, of course—and to make certain it is always ready for him. He prefers me and no one else to enter the box. Ah. And here we are, Monsieur Armand."

She opened the door to Box Five with a flourish.

Armand stepped in hesitantly, and Maude followed him. The box was more of a circle than a square, for the balcony edge was round, and it curved around into a small room. The only wall of the little chamber that was straight was the one from which they'd entered.

There were six seats in the box, the last row set back in the shadows to provide privacy for the occupants. Behind the last row, between it and the door, was a narrow strip of floor, just wide enough to accommodate a person who might wish for a horizontal surface, as Maude had occasion to know.

The box was dark except for the faint glow of light that eked into the theater from the narrow stained-glass windows, one on each wall of the building. The filtered light showed only the suggestion of rows of humped seats and the bare curve of the other eleven private boxes. The stage was dark as a tomb; it was too early for any of the rehearsals or stagehands to be moving about.

Theater was a night business.

She and Armand were perfectly alone.

"Now, Monsieur Armand," said Maude, taking matters into her own hands without hesitation, "let us dispense with that letter and discuss what is really important." She plucked the parchment from his fingers and let it flutter to the floor.

"What . . . what is it that you mean. . . ." Armand should have ended the statement with a question mark, but instead, his voice trailed off into nothing as Maude closed her hand around the front of his trousers.

"Why, this, Monsieur Armand." Ahh, yes. His little john was quite interested in becoming the really important topic of conversation.

"But . . . Madame Giry!" Armand's voice cracked like that of a boy turning to man . . . but he did not move from her proximity. No . . . he did not move away, but he did not move closer. His breathing sharpened, however, and Maude recognized this as progress for her shy teddy bear.

"Now, monsieur . . . do not think I have not noticed how you have admired me," she murmured, her hands quite busy with the buttons of his trousers. She stood much closer to him now, close enough that her breasts touched his collarbones.

He had grown full and hard in her hand. What his cock did not have in length, it made up for in girth . . . and then some. Both sets of Maude's lips grew wet at the thought of him filling her to stretching.

And it was all in the name of duty. Duty to Erik, duty to her little rats . . . a duty meant to keep everything moving smoothly at the theater. She smiled. She loved her job.

Armand's trousers slipped to his ankles, and she knelt before him, wanting to spice things up a bit, get him comfortable before she let him play with her. She had to stretch the sides of her lips wide to fit him in, and it was a pleasure to suck a cock that did not gag her with its length, but that filled her from cheek to cheek with hot, pulsing flesh.

Her underdrawers were soaking now, and her nipples hard and pointed like little cannon. If he would just *move* a little, she could rub them against his knees. . . .

Losing patience, she reached up and grabbed his hands—which had been fluttering aimlessly at his waist as she worked his cock— and planted them firmly over the front of her breasts. The mere contact sent her aching nipples tightening further, and as she pulled away from him, stopping just at the head, she sucked harder as she massaged his hands over her breasts.

She couldn't hold back a groan as she felt the tension building; Armand seemed to catch on, for he began to move his hands of his own accord. Maude slicked her tongue over the underside of his cock, and felt him shudder and shiver in surprise. *Mon Dieu*, had the man never been pleasured thus? What would happen if she stuck her thumb up his ass?

But she could save that little experiment for later.

The buttons that confined her melon-sized breasts came undone easily, and when her bodice opened and they spilled from their restraint, the release was almost orgasmic. But she needed more. Maude reached behind her and found one of the seats. She let Armand's erection slip out of her mouth as she pulled herself into one of the chairs.

"Come here," she said, but he was already scrambling after her. She urged him into place, straddling her, his thick cock pushing into her stomach.

And she rested her head back, exposing white shoulders and two huge white breasts, tipped with rosy nipples that were so hard they hurt. She slid her hands under them and jostled their beautiful weight, offering them to him.

Armand appeared to have lost any remaining shyness; he surged forward and grasped and grappled with them. Pinching the left nipple, he hefted and jiggled her other breast and then leaned forward to take it into his mouth.

When his moist, hot mouth closed around her entire areola and *sucked*, hard, Maude jerked and groaned as pleasure speared down past her belly. She nearly came right then, but pulled herself back from the edge.

His thumb teased her other nipple; his full, soft lips pulled on the right in a rhythm that matched the way she was running her hand up and down his cock. Faster, tighter, he sucked and she stroked, and the pool of wet between her legs grew larger and hotter, her sex growing and throbbing painfully. She moved her hips beneath him as he switched breasts, sucking on the left one, tweaking and thumbing the right. Pleasure built and grew, and still he sucked, and still she stroked, and held back.

And when she felt his cock moving, the surge of liquid racing

along toward the end, she loosened her grip, stopped the rhythm. . . .
Not yet, she thought. Not . . . yet . . .

Armand groaned against her nipple, and if possible, it felt as
though his erection grew larger; but then Maude wasn't thinking
about anything but the tugging at her breasts. He was moving back
and forth between the two of them, sucking and flicking with his
fingers. Her hips moved; her breasts were so tight a coin would
bounce off them. . . . She grasped his head and held it at her left
nipple, and he sucked, and it got tighter, and her pip pounded and
swam, and suddenly she exploded, shuddering beneath him.

"*Mon Dieu . . . mon Dieu . . .* ," he groaned, the words forming
around her areola as he jutted his cock insistently into her stomach.

"*Oui, oui, mon petit ours*, my little bear," she breathed, rolling
him off of her lap, over the arm of the chair, and onto the seat next
to her.

Just as she began to hitch up her skirts, and find the sopping
hole in her drawers, illumination burst from the stage below.

"*Mon Dieu!*" Armand started, jerking beneath her as she straddled him. He struggled to sit up from the slouched position that left
his cock standing straight up like a lovely, hard column, but Maude
pushed him back.

"*Non*, my dear. No one can see us. . . . Just do not make any
noise. See?" She smiled her most wicked smile as she slid herself
over the head of his upstanding cock.

Armand flinched, sighed, eyes half closing . . . and then they
popped open when she slipped him inside her like a pickpocket's
hand into a purse. It felt as though she could not open her legs wide
enough. The sweet, familiar feeling of a hard cock, moving inside,
slipping and sliding against her, sent another shudder through her,
and Maude snatched in her breath in surprise. How lovely that it
had happened again so quickly!

She would have to keep her little teddy bear.

His little moist mouth was a round O and she leaned forward to kiss it in thanks as much as for him. Maude thrust her tongue into his mouth just as she had thrust him inside of her, and she rocked on his hips, felt his hands come up and grab at her ass, and felt the constant pleasure of her raw nipples scraping against his coat. A silver button was in the perfect position to snag it with every rhythm, and she leaned closer, wanting more of the pleasure-pain there.

She throbbed and slipped and slid, and he rocked frantically beneath her, his eyes as circular and wide as his mouth. It built and built, and she felt his erection change, shift under her, knew he was close, and just as he burst inside her, someone screamed.

It came from the stage.

Four

*J*oseph Buquet's body had been found, tangled and gently swaying, in the stage lines that he had manipulated for nearly twenty years.

If anyone noticed that Monsieur Moncharmin's trousers were buttoned up improperly, it was not deemed important enough to mention. There was too much commotion and apprehension permeating the Opera House for anyone to worry about anything but the Opera Ghost.

For, as Erik and Maude had expected, the blame was immediately attached to him.

"But look at how the cords are wrapped around his neck," protested Madame Giry. "What an imprecise way it would have been to try to strangle someone. Surely it was an accident."

"The ghost frightened him and made him fall to his death,"

shrieked one of the girls. Madame whirled upon her with frightfully sharp black eyes.

No one, not even Monsieur Moncharmin, would have recognized her as the wanton with the spilling breasts and groaning, openmouthed exertions from only moments before.

"You do not know of what you speak," Madame told the girl sternly. "You had best learn to hold your tongue; else you might find *yourself* a victim of the Opera Ghost."

After the police had been called and the stage was cleared, the managers stood off to the side. Monsieur Firmin Richard turned to Monsieur Moncharmin and showed him a thick parchment note with his name written on it. "I have received this letter," he told him.

"And I have received one too! This Opera Ghost requires that we pay him twenty-four thousand francs per month or he will not allow us a peaceful existence."

"And my letter states that we must allow Christine Daaé to perform Marguerite in *Faust* tonight."

"But that is Carlotta's role! She did not sing last night, because she was angry about the backdrop falling . . . but certainly she has heard of Miss Daaé's success and will return tonight to retake the stage." Armand sounded ill. "What shall we tell her?"

"Of course Carlotta will sing tonight," Firmin replied, tearing the parchment into two long strips. "Madame Giry is right; Buquet likely had too much to drink and fell off the catwalk. Do you not remember Poligny warning us about him? The Opera Ghost is nothing but a foolish person trying to scare us into paying him blackmail. Well, it will not work in my Opera House!" He dropped the parchment and watched it flutter to the floor.

"And what of Box Five? The Phantom has insisted we leave it empty for his use. Madame Giry has explained it all to me."

"The ghost, specter that he is, does not *need* a box to sit in,"

Firmin replied with disdain. "He is a phantom, and he can fly about the stage if he wishes to watch the performance. We shall let the box for this evening's performance."

Late in the morning after her grand performance, Christine was in her dressing room. The masses of flowers from the night before had been organized onto one small table and the floor next to it. The mingled scents of rose, lily, gardenia, and gillyflower were cloying and sweet.

Three heavy gowns—rose, lavender shot with silver, and sapphire blue—lay carefully arranged over a chair. They were gowns that she never would have been close enough to touch if La Carlotta had not stomped petulantly out of the Opera House.

If the backdrop hadn't fallen and startled the diva, Christine would still be sharing a dressing room with the other chorus girls. There would be no floor-to-ceiling mirror of her own, but instead, a long narrow one, around which the twenty girls would push and shove and gather as they dressed.

If the backdrop hadn't fallen.

She gasped.

He had done it. He had made the heavy canvas drop to the ground, knowing that it would send La Carlotta into hysterics . . . certain that it would cause her to stalk away, to act the prima donna and refuse to sing.

Carlotta had expected to be soothed and coaxed back. She had not known that the Angel of Music had made other plans.

Christine had heard about the death of Joseph Buquet, and felt a tremor of fear. Her *ange* was a strict and demanding tutor, but he had never given her cause to be frightened of him. Even the first time the angel approached her, she had not been frightened.

She had been praying in the small chapel, tucked beneath the grand stone staircase of the Opera House. It was the only place she felt close to her father, even though he was buried in a graveyard near the Bay of Perros. Even after nearly eight years, she grieved for him, missed his absentminded smile and faraway eyes, missed the way his fingers were always moving, always playing something on an invisible violin—even when he hugged her, or sat reading in his chair, or riding in a carriage.

Papa had entertained her, and for a time Raoul too, with stories about the Angel of Music. "Every musician, every artist, who is worthy shall be visited by an angel," he would tell them. "Perhaps only once, an infant might see his angel . . . and then grow to be a child prodigy. Or perhaps the angel would come more than once, and tutor one who has the promise of talent. But to be sure, if the angel blesses one with his presence, the musician is sure to be a success." And then he would pick up his violin and play soft, haunting melodies like *The Resurrection of Lazarus* with such beauty that Christine was certain her father *had* been visited by an angel.

When he died, she'd lost her music.

It was only because of Professor Valerius's influence that Christine had been allowed to join the chorus at the National Academy of Music, there at the Opera House, when she was twelve. He insisted that she'd shown great talent in singing, but that grief from the death of her father had suffocated it, and that it would return in time if nurtured.

But the five years she'd been in the chorus, Christine remained a shadow of the quiet, melancholy girl who'd had the angelic voice her sponsor remembered.

Until that day in the chapel.

That day, as she often did, she spoke to her father, talking with him about her memories of their life and travels. She reminded him again of his promise to send her an Angel of Music when he died, so that she might find a way to express her grief in losing him. So that she might find her music again.

And then, she'd heard him call her. "Christine . . ." Soft, haunting, barely audible. She looked around the small damp room, but saw no one. Her knees pressed into a thin rug, feeling the stones beneath, as she turned back and forth, looking up and down.

And then she heard it again. "Christine . . . I am your angel. . . ."

And she knew her father had kept his promise.

Now, three months and many hard-won lessons later, and the morning after her *grande* performance at the gala, she smoothed her fingers over the velvet petals of one red rose, thinking of what Raoul would say if he knew.

Should she tell Raoul about the Angel of Music? Would he believe her?

And then, suddenly from out of her silence, on the faint note of a sweet violin, she heard, "Christine . . ." Just as she had that first day.

"Ange." She bolted to her feet to close the door, then moved immediately in front of the tall mirror, watching behind her image. But she saw nothing in the reflection.

"You returned quite late last night," came his rich voice. "It will not do for the new opera star to forgo her rest and practice in favor of social obligations."

He was there, but she could not see him. Of course, she felt the way his voice slipped around her, embracing her, and she recognized his breath, moving in the stillness of the room, matching her own. In that way she could feel him. But she yearned to see him.

"I am sorry, angel," she replied. "I did not mean to anger you."

"Anger me you will, if you continue to go about in the company of men until all hours of the morning."

The warning edge in his smooth voice frightened her. "I understand, angel."

"My name is *Erik*."

"Erik, *oui*."

"Last night I gave you pleasure, did I not?" The coaxing timbre of his voice set the hairs along her arms to rising.

"Yes, you did, ang—Erik." So much pleasure that she had dreamt of it, twisting and turning in her sheets, and awakening damp and panting with the memory. Her fingers trembled as she clutched them into the gauze of her dressing gown.

"I wish to pleasure you in that way again, and more, Christine." There was a wisp of roughness in his words.

"I wish you to as well," she replied, stepping automatically toward the tall, glinting mirror, as though she would find him there. Alas, she saw only herself: wide-eyed, her oval face pale but for the pink of her lips, and her long hair falling loose to her hips. She touched the cool glass with one hand, as if reaching for him. "Angel . . . Erik . . . I wish to see you, to touch you, to pleasure you too. Please . . ."

The room was silent. Still.

"Angel?" Christine asked, suddenly terrified that she had frightened him away. Had she been too bold?

She strained her ears for the sound of his music, the beautiful tones of violin and flute—and, of course, his melodious voice—that would fill her ears and her being.

Silence.

"Angel?" she called again. "Erik?"

Then she felt it again: felt him, his presence. Bold, strong, encompassing. "Christine," he replied. His voice hesitated on the last syllable, then became smooth again as he continued. "When the time is right, we shall be one. But until then, you must practice patience. And you must work hard. And you must remember that I am your tutor, and I am the one who can bring forth your music."

"Yes, angel." It was true. She had been able to sing, certainly, before the Angel of Music had come into her dressing room and into her life three months ago, but under his tutelage, she had blossomed and grown like a late-blooming flower unfurling itself under the intense heat of summer sun.

"Now, I wish to hear you sing Marguerite's aria. Carlotta will not be singing it tonight. You will."

Christine drew in her breath and felt her breasts straining against the corset that lifted and pushed them together. Her nipples were hard, stabbing the light lawn chemise she wore, pushing against the firm boning of the corset.

The music came from nowhere, and everywhere. It filled the tall, narrow dressing room, simmered in her ears, and pounded through her veins. As she began to sing, the lights dimmed somehow. . . . The edges of her image in the mirror, her mouth wide, her eyes bright, her cheeks flushed pink—all became gray as the illumination faded. Her arms, clad in the sleeves of a pale yellow dressing gown, rose gracefully as though to help express the notes, and the yellow silk slid back, down to her shoulders, baring her slender arms. She became the beautiful lady once again.

True, clear, smooth . . . she sang, and Erik's music whorled about her, his presence filled her . . . and then his voice joined hers. His dusky tenor mingled with her pure soprano, and she felt as though she were flying.

Soaring.

She closed her eyes and sang, felt Erik's presence and the gift of beautiful music that he awakened within her. She knew then, in the deepest part of her core, that she could never be without him.

She could never lose him.

For he brought the best of her forward. He prodded, pushed, annoyed, and demanded the very best of her music from the very deepest part of her being. Somehow, he knew her. Somehow, he knew how to draw it forth, to make her feel this way. Exquisite. Powerful. Heady.

The hair on the back of her arms, on the nape of her neck, and on the crown of her head rose, tense and sensitive, and still she sang. And he with her.

Tears shimmered at the corners of her eyes; she felt them, warm and heavy, and then the trail they left down along her cheek. She felt her corset tighten with each gut-level breath, and then loosen as she held on to the highest, longest C note until she thought her vision would fade away, and still she drew in another breath to follow the C with an E.

When the last of her notes faded and there was nothing left but her heavy breathing, and the ending swell of music, Christine opened her eyes.

The room was still dim; not dark, but dim. One gas lamp glowed on the wall next to her, casting just enough light that her form showed clear in the mirror. The rest of the chamber held only shadows and the faint aroma of rose.

"Christine . . . you have pleased me to no end."

"Thank you, angel. You are my inspiration."

"If you sing like that this evening, you will inspire the entire Opera House to love you."

"I will, angel. Erik." She had thought of him as her *ange* for so long that it was easy to forget his name.

"Now . . ." His voice took on a gentle purr. "Now I wish to see you, Christine. All of you. So that when you stand onstage tonight, and I am sitting in Box Five, I will see you in a way that no one else can. And I will know that you sing for me."

A sharp shot of desire pierced her middle at his words. She felt the tingle, the curling pain of lust, low in her belly and then down between her legs. Just from his words. From the image he'd placed in her mind.

"Now . . . take off your dressing gown, Christine."

Her fingers trembled as she unknotted the tie just below her breasts, and she allowed the ruffled, silky robe to slide from her shoulders and crumple to the floor. She stood in front of the mirror, and saw herself dressed in the loose, light chemise fitted to her curves by the corset over it. Her feet were not bare; thin silk stockings covered them and stretched up past her knees, under the hem of the chemise.

"More, Christine."

She took the top edges of the corset over each breast and wrenched them toward each other, twisting to release the top hook. Her breasts rubbed against the fabric covering them, brushing her fumbling fingers, and they swelled, aching for something more.

The hooks released, one by one, and she was able to breathe deeply, more freely. Christine dropped the corset, and it fell at her feet with a soft thud. She stood in her chemise, with its low, rounded neckline made of fabric thin enough to see her nipples thrusting through. Her hair had fallen half over one shoulder, and half down her back, so that she could see the ends of her curls just coming from around the back of her hip. Her cheeks were flushed, her pink lips parted and moist from a quick lick of her tongue.

"Christine . . ." His voice coaxed, but there was an edge there . . . one that hovered just beyond her hearing, but was ready to lash out if she did not comply.

She reached down, grasping the hem of her shift, and pulled it slowly up and over her head, and then she was free.

Tall, slender, pale, with a dark thatch between her legs, two dusky spots at her breasts with curving shadows beneath them, and a swath of curling hair falling behind her shoulders to whirl around her hips.

She could feel him breathing, felt herself breathing faster, more harshly. Yet she stood there, proud, bare, ready.

Ready for him.

"Step to the mirror."

Christine's heart pounded; she could see the mad pumping in her throat. Her eyes fixated on the sign of her racing pulse as she walked slowly toward the tall silver length of mirror. She stopped when she was close enough that her breath left hot circles of condensation on the glass.

"Closer."

She did.

Now her panting left larger circles. Her ten fingers, each pressing against the smooth, hard surface, squeaked softly as she positioned them. Her nipples just brushed the ice of the mirror, as cold as the Seine in January. The tips of her silk-clad toes touched the bottom of the heavy, ornate frame.

Her nipples hardened further, and the contrast between the heat of the rest of her body and the chill at her breasts sent another trail of lust skittering through her. She shifted, rubbing the very tips of her nipples against the cold, making them harder, pointier. Aching.

"Closer." The command was nothing more than a breath.

Christine moved, and now she pressed against the cold mirror as if she were lying on it, turning her head to one side. It was unbearably cold, stamping her warm skin against the silvery glass . . .

but she did it, breathing hard and concentrating on the feeling of stark cold versus the heat of desire. Little bumps erupted over her body and she had to close her mouth to keep from crying out at the amazing cold. Incredible that such a smooth, clear surface could cause such discomfort, such shock.

She rested her cheek flat, so close that her eyes could not focus on the image she made.

Her breasts pushed against the chill, two icy circles seeping into her hard, aching nipples.

Her hips thrust forward, the bone of her pubis trapping the mass of tight black curls between it and the silver glass.

The tops of her thighs; then her knees, slightly bent so that she could press against the looking glass.

The tender, sensitive inside skin of her arms, forming L shapes on either side of her head.

"How does that feel, Christine?"

She could not form the words, but she felt it. The hot core in her belly and the gathering moisture between her legs. The torture of her hard nipples against the glass, still so cold.

"Now, straighten your arms; grab the edge of the frame."

She did, sliding her damp hands along the freezing glass, leaving a trail of moisture behind them while her breasts crushed against the silver. She could barely reach the edges of the frame, but at last her fingers closed over the bumps of a rose on the left, and something she could not identify on the right. She curled her fingers around the edges, and felt the muscles in her arms relax, felt the pleasure of stretching her limbs.

And then, something closed around her right wrist, locking it into place from the back side of the mirror. She didn't have a chance to react before the left one was confined. Caught, tied, trussed to the edge of the mirror frame.

Her breath left her in a whoosh, a gasp, and she twisted her head against the glass, turning her face to the other side as if she thought she might get a glimpse . . . of something. Her cheek, her nose and mouth, her lashes . . . her other cheek, trapping a thick lock of hair. Pressing against the warm mirror.

"How do you feel, Christine?"

Her sex was throbbing; her nipples were in agony; her breath was coming so fast that she steamed a huge, moist circle on the mirror. She licked her lips, tried to swallow. All she could think of was how the smooth, cold glass felt against her skin.

"Angel," she breathed.

"Erik. My name is Erik."

"Erik. Please, Erik . . ."

Pressed against the glass, she could see nothing that was not directly in front of her face, only the wall—two, perhaps three feet away—a gas lamp, the corner of a small table.

But she heard something, and then she began to breathe harder. Her breath came in short, sharp gasps, because she knew he was there. In the room with her. Somehow.

She tried to pull away from the mirror, but her arms were extended so far that she could barely turn her face from side to side. When she struggled to raise her head, her sex pushed against the glass, the coarse hairs crushed beneath it. She could not pull far enough to see anything but the small distance to her right side . . . or to her left.

Christine was not frightened. But she was . . . aware. So completely, painfully aware of every hair on her body, every muscle, every heartbeat, every breath . . . of the growing moisture and heat, her need . . .

When he touched her, she jerked, slamming her hips into the mirror before she could stop herself. His hand—no, a finger . . . just one finger trailed, bumping, down her spine as the other hand lifted her hair away, baring her back, without touching her skin.

A bare finger. Not a gloved one.

Flesh to flesh. Warm, roughly padded, firm and sure, his finger moved down to the curve of her buttocks, slipped quickly into the top of the cleft . . . then disappeared.

Two hands gathered the mass of her hair; she felt them pull it together, lift it, and twist it into a loose coil. . . . Then something slid into it, a comb across her scalp holding her hair in place, and he removed his hands. Her nape and shoulders and back were bare.

Christine closed her eyes, waiting, trying to slow her breath, to release the coil of lust that was so tight it was painful.

Then she felt him at the back of her left leg, two hands deftly rolling the silk stocking down her thigh, over her knee, and to the floor. She lifted her foot without hesitation, and felt the rough wool of the carpet under it when the stocking was removed. He did the same with the other, and then she was completely naked. Totally bare. Hidden only by the mirror against her.

"Erik . . . ," she moaned. She didn't know what else to do. He wasn't touching her anymore; he wasn't speaking. "Please . . ."

She felt rather than saw his shadow as he stepped closer; his figure blocked the direct light from the gas lamp, so all she could see in the close mirror was the dark shape of a head and shoulders looming behind her.

Then a hand pressed flat against the center of her back, just between her shoulder blades. Fingers curled gently around the nape of her neck and delicately held her there as another hand slid down along the right side of her body. His hand traced her ribs and over the swell of her hip, then cupped one side of her rear.

Nothing but that, nothing but that bare touch, and she was trembling beneath it. Panting. The stinging between her legs grew, and she felt wetness surge as she throbbed and pushed against the mirror.

"Spread your legs."

His fingers dipped low from behind, and slid into the lower vee between her legs, up, and into the pool of her moisture. His thumb fit in the valley between her buttocks, and his fingers began to circle around her inner lips, tracing the slick opening, rolling through the wetness, and spreading it over her plump labia.

Through the roaring in her ears, she could hear his breathing rough behind her. She felt the way his talented hand, prisoning her neck so gently, trembled and flexed over her skin. But most of her attention was focused on the hard, throbbing nub of her pip as his fingers slipped around it, and next to it, and then, finally, cupped it from behind. Flicked it. Once, twice . . . she moaned, pushing back, away from the mirror, into his hand.

"Christine . . ." His voice shook.

Now he was close behind her; his forehead rested on the mirror next to hers so that she couldn't turn to look at him. She felt the bare brush of his sleeve to the left of her shoulder, and down, near her knees, where his trousers touched the back of her leg. He moved again, and then she was trapped between his tall, powerful body and the cold, hard silk of glass.

His arms traced hers, spread far from her body, his hands closing around her wrists; his legs pushed into the backs of hers. His hips, his cock, pressed into the small of her back, the buttons of his trouser fastenings stamping on her skin.

His hands slid from her wrists along the length of her arms, down over the underside of her shoulders, and alongside her breasts. She arched back from the mirror as far as her taut arms would allow, and he laughed softly against her head, his breath hot at her temple.

"Impatient, are you, Christine?" But he slipped his hands around the front of her, closing over her hard nipples, still cold from the mirror, and covered them with his warm palms. From behind, he pushed her hips into the mirror and massaged her breasts with long, flexible fingers. She moaned, and rolled her pubis into the glass, and he followed her rhythm, rolling and shifting with her. She was trembling and pulsing all over, her entire being focused on the need he aroused within her.

Christine tried to turn her head, to put her face next to his, but he hissed and pulled his head away from the mirror before she could come face-to-face with him.

"You are impatient, aren't you?" There was that edge again, lacing his erotic voice, the edge that told her he was not pleased with her impatience. She tipped her head back to the mirror, pressing her cheek again to the moist spot she'd left, and closed her eyes.

"Please, Erik," she whispered.

He pulled on her nipples, one after the other in a fast, tortuous rhythm that caused her breathing to grow rougher, more ragged. Spikes of desire shot down to her pip with each tweak. It felt as if it was growing, swelling, and could take no more before it would burst. . . .

Then he slid his hands down and captured her hips, one on each side, and held her firmly against the mirror. She could not move from the waist down, and barely from the waist up.

He'd moved away and only his hands were touching her, planting her pubis and hip bones on the glass.

Then she felt his mouth on her shoulder, hot and moist and scoring into her skin. He was not gentle, or featherlight. . . . He nipped and teethed and licked, all the while holding her hips so that she could not wriggle, until she was shaking and shuddering with need.

He sucked on her skin, trailed the delicate tip of his tongue all the way down her spine. She felt him kneeling behind her, braced herself as his tongue slid along the cleft of her buttocks, sending her squirming and shivering, half sobbing, and gasping to catch her breath.

Oh, please . . . was all she could think. She could not even form the words. Her pip was throbbing so hard, it was painful; she could feel a trickle of wet as it trailed down the inside of her thigh. Then his tongue was there, licking it, following the trail back up to her hot, wet quim, and she thought she would scream.

He pulled the sides of her bottom apart, leveraged her hips away from the glass so that she was half-leaning, half-hanging from her wrists; her face, shoulders, breasts, arms, shoved up against it. She felt him moving close behind her, and suddenly his tongue was just where she needed it.

She gave a soft scream, jerking uncontrollably against the mirror as he flicked his tongue over the hard nub of her tickler, faster, faster, harder, side to side, until she let go and sagged into a mass of quivering, shaking, shuddering muscle and bone and wetness.

Her mouth was open, planted against the glass, screaming silently into its silvery silk as she came, and came, and convulsed against it. Her body, damp and hot, slid helplessly against the mirror, leaving chaotic streaks over it.

"Now," said Erik into her ear, "you will remember this when you sing tonight, won't you, Christine?" He sounded ragged, out of breath, strained. "I'll be watching you from Box Five, and remember . . . you sing for me. And me alone. No one else can give you what I give you."

And then he was gone.

And moments later, her wrists loosened from behind the mirror, and Christine collapsed in a heap on the floor, landing on the silk of her discarded robe and the taut boning of her corset.

FIVE

*M*eanwhile, in a well-appointed flat not so far from the Opera House, Carlotta shrieked and tore the parchment paper that purported to be a note from the Opera Ghost into two long strips. "*Impossible!* Impossible! He cannot!"

"But what is it, *ma chère?*" Guy looked up from his pose upon her pillow-laden bed.

She cast a glance at his sleek, bulging muscles, arranged just the way she liked them, tan and perfect against the light bedding. He was propped on an elbow and his long, muscular legs were crossed at the ankle. His cock, at half-mast in its bush of tawny hair, enticed her, just as the classic beauty of his mouth did.

But then she recalled the letter, signed *O.G.*, but more likely to have been written by a friend of Miss Christine Daaé. "*Imbecile!*" she cried, her feigned French or Spanish accent (depending upon the day) dissolving into her gutter London voice. "The cur thinks to keep me from singing! He says if I sing tonight, a horrible catastrophe will occur."

"But who would not want La Carlotta to sing?" asked Guy, running a hand artfully through his thick golden hair and placing his luscious lips in a pout. "He is foolish. And not worth your time, *chère*. Come here. . . . Let me distract you from this foolishness."

"The Opera Ghost! He does not want La Carlotta to sing. He wishes for his student Christine Daaé to take my place on the stage." Carlotta's chest felt tight. She should never have bowed out of the performance last evening. The papers had been filled with praise for the young bitch, whose freshness had surprised and delighted them. "The exaltation of a voice and the rapture of a pure soul," raved *L'Opinion Nationale*, which had only days earlier sung praises for Carlotta's own clear, glass-shattering soprano.

She was only thirty-five—much too young to be replaced by that snippet of a girl.

"Opera Ghost?" Guy sounded confused . . . but that was not unusual. He had muscle and stamina abounding, but what he had between his legs seemed to seep every bit of sense from his brain. Not that Carlotta cared much about the brains of a young buck like Guy. She had money enough, and brains of her own, and found she needed little from Guy or his ilk but a strong, on-command performance. Which he was most inclined to give.

"That bloody ghost!"

"But there are no such things as ghosts, *chère*. And you do not take orders from anyone but the managers, do you not?"

"No, that is true." Perhaps she was becoming a bit too sensitive. Messieurs Richard and Moncharmin had said nothing to her about not singing. The vile note had to have been written by that little snip, or one of her supporters.

"Please, *ma chère*, you will upset yourself. Why don't you come over here and let me ease your worries?" He patted a pink satin pillow, jostling its tassel.

Carlotta eyed him speculatively. He settled back flat on the mattress, placing his hands behind his head. The bulge of muscle filled the triangles his arms made, and his stone-hard pectorals gleamed smooth and tan in the sunlight streaming through the window. She smiled coyly, stepping toward the bed as she dropped the strips of parchment at her feet.

How glad she was that she had graduated from the grasping hands of Monsieur Contriste, her first protector, to this stage in her career, where she need not sacrifice anything for money, and where she made her own choices—in bed and otherwise. She had Maude Giry and her own talent and hard work to thank for her current situation. She was not about to let a wisp of a girl—or an Opera Ghost—take it away from her.

She had heard, for she had spies in the theater, that the Chagny brothers had dined with the bitch last evening. If Christine Daaé had such backing as from the *comte* and his brother, that would not bode well for Carlotta. But her spy said it was the younger one, the *vicomte*, who appeared most taken with her usurper.

And the *comte*, who had recently interrupted his attachment with La Sorelli, might very well be looking for a replacement.

How convenient. She felt her lips curl into a smile.

And then she returned to the matter at hand.

"You cannot move," she told Guy sharply, the Spanish lilt back in her voice.

"As always, I await your every command."

She reached out and trickled her fingertip over the ridges of his hairless belly, bumping, one, two, three, from the curve of his rib cage down toward his groin. He shivered under her touch, but he did not move.

Except for his cock. It flinched and grew.

"I said you were not to move," she reminded him mildly. And slapped at it.

He grunted and his cock grew larger. Carlotta felt his eyes fastened on her as she bent forward to take the tip in her mouth. She circled her lips around it, slipping her tongue over the velvet skin, and then pulled back to look down at him.

He had not moved, but his eyes were dark and focused on her mouth. His beautiful chest rose and fell a bit faster. She liked it best when it was covered with droplets of sweat, when he had to fight for control.

Carlotta yanked at the tie of her dressing gown and let it fall to the floor. She stood in front of him and let him look his fill. Her breasts were generous and had barely begun to sag, and her hips were round and voluptuous. Her waist nipped in, leaving her a perfect hourglass form. She had no bush tangling over her quim; every hair had been plucked away, leaving her smooth and white.

"Now," she told Guy in a cool voice, "we shall see how well you will distract me."

She clambered onto the bed near his feet and crawled so that she straddled his massive thighs. Sitting her bare rump on his knees, Carlotta spread her legs wide so that he would have a clear view of her sex, and rose up on her knees.

Taking her breasts in her hands, she began to play with herself. She teased her already tight nipples until they were puckered tight as her anus, flicking them with her fingers, sending shoots of desire down to her sex. She lifted and squeezed and massaged, all the while watching Guy watch her.

He did not move, but his chest rose a bit faster; his eyes narrowed a bit farther. When she slipped one hand down to cover her mons, his attention followed her. She was wet and she slid her fingers between her labia, drenching them and bringing her juices up to wet her nipple. The feel of her slick fingertips swirling over the very front of the tight nubbin made her pip throb and swim.

When her areola was hard and shiny with her moisture, Carlotta eased herself forward, sliding her dripping self over his cock, letting it slip through the juices of her lips to rest in the crack of her ass as she moved up closer to his head.

"Taste," she told him, bringing her wet nipple down to his mouth. She felt the jerk of his body as he reacted, but then he quickly subdued the urge to remove his hands from behind his head and reach for her.

When his hot mouth closed over her entire areola, Carlotta closed her eyes and thrust her chest toward him. Pleasure drove down to her belly with every hard suck of his lips, and she rocked her hips over his strong, flat belly, rubbing her juicy sex into his skin. It swelled and burned, and when he released her nipple to slide his tongue over it, slipping over the most sensitive area, another rush of liquid dampened her sex.

"Harder!" she ordered, grinding herself down, rocking her hips faster as he fastened his teeth around her nipple. "Suck me harder!"

He sucked; she could see the cords in his neck stand out as he fought to keep his hands in place behind his head, and the movement of his jaw as he sucked and licked and at last drew the whole front of her breast into his mouth. Inside that hot, wet cavern, her nipple strained and he swirled his tongue, that thick, strong muscle, up and around and under her jutting nib.

Carlotta slid a hand between her legs and found the kernel of her sex, jimmying it around as she rocked and he sucked and she came closer to the end. The orgasm vibrated through her, and she moaned, keeping the rhythm of her finger strong until every last bit of pleasure had shuddered through her nerves.

Guy released her nipple as she pulled away, and he was breathing hard. His eyes were dark and unfocused, his mouth open as he drew in circles of air. But his arms had remained behind his head as ordered.

"Very good," she purred, leaning forward to kiss him. She planted one hand on each side of his head, resting on his bulging forearms, wrapping her small white hands halfway around the tan muscles, and bent her lips to his.

She tasted the bare musky scent of herself on him, and thrust her tongue into his mouth to get every drop. He began to kiss her back, his lips fighting with hers, but she pulled away.

"I did not give you permission," she reminded him sharply, sitting back on her heels, her hot quim warm on his belly. "You shall have to be punished quite thoroughly."

His eyes flared dark and his pupils grew larger, and for a moment, she thought he was about to beg. But he did not, for he did not have permission to speak.

"Good, very good," she told him, acknowledging his restraint. "Now you will eat me." That ought to get him to the edge.

She slithered up his hot, muscular torso, taking a moment to suck, *hard*, on one flat nipple, before arranging her widespread legs over his face. Gripping the ornate iron decoration of the headboard above him, she positioned herself just above his mouth, making certain she was high enough that he would have to lift his head to reach her.

The first swipe of his strong, hot tongue sent a wave of renewed lust spreading through her. He swept it over one thick labium, up, around, and down the other one. His tongue was flat and wide and wet and it made a delicious slapping sound as it dipped around her lips. Carlotta stifled a moan and tipped her head back, her breasts pressing against the cold iron scrollwork. Her nipples were tight again, hurting in their pleasure, and her knees began to tremble.

She could see the red silk that draped from the ceiling in a sort of canopy above her and she focused on its burning hue, bringing the sensation of pulsing, red heat from her vision down to the throbbing of her sex. Guy slid his tongue into the slit between her inner and outer lips, tracing it around and back, around and back again. He had not touched her pip, not even slipped inside her vagina. Just stroked and teased over her hairless lips, sending her hips to rocking again above him.

"Eat me!" she ordered, and felt the trembling of her knees and thighs, trying to keep herself from settling down over that luscious mouth. She would make him work for it. Beg her for it.

But he wasn't begging yet; he was nibbling at her labia now . . . ignoring her nib, ignoring that wide-open sex of her rumpled inner lips . . . just nibbling with gentle, hard teeth. Teasing. By God, he was teasing her!

His tongue slipped away from her outer lip and swept over the delicately wrinkled skin between it and her inner thigh, down and over the shivery sensitive skin of her inner thigh, and then back to allow his lips to suck on the lower edge of one swollen labium. Right where it folded into her skin. She was dripping, and she felt her juices running down her thigh, heard the erotic wet sounds as his tongue lapped through them.

"Eat me!" she ordered again, her voice husky.

And then, without warning, Guy reared his head up and fastened his mouth around her hard, swollen pip and *sucked*, drawing the little nib harshly into his mouth, and pulling on it as though he were trying to swallow it.

The sharpest, most intense arc of pleasure burst through her, radiating in a blast from the center of her body. Carlotta screamed and came, shuddering so hard that she lost the battle with her muscles and collapsed over his mouth, where his tongue and lips still worked, still did their job, as she dissolved into a mass of shudders and sweat.

When she fell away, onto the bed next to him, she became aware of the manner in which his chest was rising and falling: fast, as though he'd been running. And she saw that his hands were still behind his head.

"Very good," she told him, and reached for the column of his cock. It was purple and thick and the vein that ran down it looked as though it were ready to burst. When she closed her fingers around it, Guy jerked, his eyes fastening on her hand as though he could will her to move it. Up and down, up and down . . .

She did not, of course. She held it, purposely still, barely touching it, not nearly as tightly as he wanted her to.

"Is there something you wish to say?" she asked.

"Please . . . may I come?"

She did not answer; she gave him a delicate stroke that sent tremors rippling over his stomach. He closed his eyes and let his head fall back onto the bed.

"Please . . ."

She tightened her fingers around his cock. Warm velvet it was, and she wanted to feel it inside her. Her sex was awakening again, even after the intense orgasm. Her breasts tightened. Saliva pooled in her mouth.

She stroked him, twice, hard and fast, and then released him when she felt him get ready to let go.

"No, you may not."

Carlotta straddled him and slipped his cock up inside her slick inner lips, her mouth opening in a silent moan of pleasure. She moved, rocked, once, to settle his length, then looked down at him.

He stared up at the ceiling, eyes focused on it as though it held some great secret of immortality. His handsome face was set, unmoving, his nostrils flared as though to draw in greater amounts of air. The vein in his neck contracted madly and she saw that . . .

"I did not give you permission to move your hand."

Guy drew in a harsh breath and closed his eyes. He replaced the hand that had moved from behind his head back where it belonged. His lips moved; Carlotta thought perhaps that they moved to form the word "please."

"Open your eyes," she ordered. "Watch me. If you take your eyes off me, your punishment will be boundless."

He obediently opened his eyes and she shifted her hips deliberately. She saw the way his lids flickered and twitched and his breath hitched . . . but he did not look away. His eyes did not roll back into his head as she was certain they wanted to.

"Very good," she purred. And twitched her hips again, harder, and tightened her inner lips around him. This time his lips moved involuntarily and his breath stopped, his chest full . . . then, after a moment, started again.

She gathered her breasts in her hands and began to pluck at her hard nipples, sending those delicious sensations down to her sex. She licked her lips, watching in delight as Guy mirrored her by licking his own lips.

She rose up on his cock, and back down, and up again, and watched him struggle to maintain his composure . . . and congratulated herself, not for the first time, on her student. This find of hers . . . this lustful man who was little more than a boy willing to be molded and taught . . . and tortured. Would the Comte de Chagny be so pliable?

Somehow, she thought not.

She rocked on his cock, not up and down, but back and forth, making certain the head of his cock stroked the special spot inside her vagina, and pressed against her nib. Her own breath was coming faster, and she heard his even when her eyes were closed.

She opened them, and saw to her delight that he was still watching her, a desperate expression blazing in his eyes. His mouth gapped; his arms strained behind his head, muscles bulging.

Carlotta lifted herself up and began to work up and down on his cock. He gasped, and shuddered, and begged, "Please, please, let me fuck you. . . . Let me . . . fuck . . . you. . . ."

"No," she told him. "No!"

She worked harder, watching his face, judging when he was coming close, and stopped in time, settled on him. Felt the huge cock inside her and the beautiful throb of her pip pushed against it.

She smiled. He groaned. She pinched her nipple. He watched.

She leaned forward and offered one to him, and he sucked on it like he was starving. It hurt and it sent a ripple of need down to her sex and she pulled away, causing a loud smacking sound from his lips.

"Guy." She said his name gently, and it took a moment for him to focus on her eyes instead of her breasts. He did not appear to have the energy to speak. "What do you want?"

He stared at her . . . dragged in his breath, exhaled the words, "Fuck . . . you . . ."

"Say it, say it louder," she coaxed, arching backward to place her hands on his thighs. Her breasts jutted out in front of her and he focused avidly on them.

"I want . . . to fuck . . . you. . . ."

"Fuck me, then. *Fuck me.*"

And then suddenly, she was on her back, and Guy was rearing over her, using his knee to keep her legs apart as he gripped her shoulders. He slammed inside of her, slammed into her quim, into the top of her vagina, harder and harder, faster and faster. Carlotta moaned as he hit that inner spot, ramming against it, until she quaked with an orgasm from the inside out.

She reached up behind and grabbed the iron scrollwork, felt her breasts jouncing and bouncing with his desperate rhythm. Her orgasm went on and on; she lifted her hips, met his, violently, with every thrust. It was hot and wet and they slid together, in and out, in and out. . . . He groaned, cried out, jammed himself inside her one final time, and she felt him coursing inside the long hot tunnel of her, and she shuddered too.

He collapsed on her, his heavy, sweaty body deliciously hot, his chest ramming against her breasts.

Carlotta slapped him on the bare ass. "We will discuss your punishment tomorrow."

And, knees trembling, she rolled from the bed, grinning, determined to sing tonight . . . and to snare herself a *comte*. Ghost or no ghost.

Raoul crossed the stage rapidly, resisting the desire to duck when he heard a particularly loud crash behind him. Only hours before the evening's performance, it was a madhouse in here! However could they be ready in time?

The chaos was deafening. He tightened his fingers around the huge bunch of stems he carried. This was even worse than being on a ship's deck during a violent storm, trying to secure the lines and keep oneself from being washed overboard.

Someone was hammering nails onto a piece of scenery with great vigor; a backdrop was being lowered from its high rigging and had been caught on something, so it was now being shaken with a violence that caused Raoul no little concern. A piece of glass was being fitted into the hole in a wall of scenery; someone shouted to "Watch out!" and another person yelled, "Behind you!"

All in all, he wished he'd chosen a different route to the backstage dressing rooms than through the front doors of the Opera House, down among the stalls, up onto the stage, and behind it. Particularly during the day, when there was a cacophony of preparation for the performance of *Faust* that night, these halls were difficult to navigate.

He stepped around a flat being carried from the seemingly depthless wings, and, adjusting his hat so that it sat straight on his crown, he hurried along between more flats, tables, costumiers, carpenters, wigmakers, and scenery docks, finding his way only by chance because, of course, he'd been to Christine's dressing room only one time.

But as it turned out, Raoul did not need to find his way to her private room, for as he passed along the hall, one of the dancers, whose name he had no reason to recall, attracted his attention. "Are you looking for Miss Daaé?" she asked. But she gave him a look from under her lashes, complete with dimple and tucked chin, that suggested she would prefer he was not.

"I am indeed. Do you know where she is?"

"She is in the *foyer de la danse*," she replied.

Raoul picked up his pace. The dancers' lounge was the place where the performers met their admirers after performances, and at other convenient times. He did not wish to imagine Christine—for he could not think of her as Miss Daaé, having known her as a young girl—meeting any other admirers but himself.

By the time he found his way to the lounge, after making two misturns, he had worked himself into a bit of a state. Why did his pulse race so when he thought of her? Why did the thought of another man even looking at her make his fingers tighten?

When he opened the door—flung it, really—he found a scene much worse than he'd feared.

There was Christine, seated on a lush pink velvet sofa, in a room that looked too much like the boudoir of a courtesan for his comfort. Everything was plush and stuffed and velvet: chairs, sofas, large cushions on the floor, even three large square fabric cubes topped with glass that acted as tables. The colors burned sensually: rosy pink, crimson, royal purple, and saffron.

Wine bottles, platters of cakes and *fromages* and bread, bowls of glistening grapes and bright oranges and dusky brown pears, empty glasses, filled glasses—all of these trappings of entertainment littered the tables and hung in the hands of the men . . . the nearly dozen men . . . who fawned over his Christine. There were other dancers in the room, and two girls that he recognized, vaguely, as singers, but they did not hold the attention of their guests as did Christine.

She looked up when he came in, and it was not merely vanity that caused him to see the pleasure and true delight in her face. She smiled. Her fair cheeks became rosy and her blue eyes sparkled.

Raoul was not a Chagny for nothing, and never had he worn the mantle so well. "Good afternoon, Miss Daaé. I apologize for my tardiness in coming to call for you, as I'd promised last evening. Shall we go?"

He walked over to her, making his way through her admirers, and extended his arm to her. Their eyes met, and he couldn't help but catch his breath at her glorious beauty. She looked so innocent, so young, so pure.

And he had loved her for so long.

Christine rose, and his heart swelled, for until she did, he was not altogether certain she would support his presumption.

"For me?" she asked, smiling, looking at the massive bunch of hothouse roses he still held.

He'd forgotten them; but even in the midst of that little embarrassment, he did not mind. For she was coming with him. "Of course, mademoiselle. Pure white roses, tipped with the blush of pink . . . only for you."

If Christine's other admirers were affronted at his sudden whisking away of the object of their affection, Raoul did not notice. He had a goddess on his arm, and he knew nothing else.

Even though it was a winter's day, he wanted to take her outside . . . away from the dark busyness of the theater, away from the clamor of her other admirers. He settled her comfortably in his carriage, tucking fox- and rabbit-fur blankets about her legs and then wrapping the softest of ermines around her shoulders.

A fresh snow sparkled and would have blinded him if he'd not had his top-hat brim down low over his eyes. "Where shall we go?" he asked, turning to smile at her.

"Wherever you wish."

He glanced at her as the carriage started off, the horse's hooves clip-clopping smartly as they turned along the busy rue de la Paix. Her ivory cheeks had blossomed pink in the chill air, and even the tip of her perfect nose had reddened. He thought she looked delectable.

But while he was watching her, she was watching everything else. It occurred to him that she probably did not often have the luxury of taking a carriage ride through the streets of Paris. If she left the Opera House, it was likely rare, and on foot.

Raoul turned his attention to the *rue* and looked at it as she must see it, with its occasional closed carriages and caped men in tall hats driving them. Women and men walked along the brick streets too, both garbed in subdued, but fashionable, clothing for the messy winter months, holding umbrellas as they did in nearly every season—to protect them from sun, rain, or snow.

Raoul noticed the street vendors calling out to sell *fromages* and fruits and bread, dressed in clothing not much better than what Christine herself wore, and dodging a trio of scruffy dogs that bothered them underfoot.

When they turned along the Left Bank, the icy Seine lay unbroken in a long stretch of white. They were flanked on the other side by a rough wall that separated the street from the road, and the river. And then he saw the spidery, wrought-iron atrocity that was just beginning to take form on the riverfront ahead of them.

Christine must have heard his snort of disgust, for she turned her attention away from the sights to look at him. "You do not like this new tower that is being built?"

"Indeed not," he replied. "Monsieur Eiffel will destroy the Parisian silhouette, with this tall, gangly monstrosity. I have seen drawings of what it will look like when it is finished, and I cannot believe the mayor has allowed such an affront to take place in our beautiful city."

Christine gave him an innocent smile that eased some of his annoyance. "But it is for the celebration of the centenary of your Great Revolution. And there is no intention that they shall leave it standing after, is there?"

"I certainly hope not, but we will have to look at it for at least two more years. And you might recall that it was not my revolution," he chided gently. "My family were some of the ones who lost more than our land during the Reign of Terror. But being Swedish, perhaps you are not as well versed in our history. At any rate," he said, determined to steer the conversation away from such unpleasantness and toward something more personal, "I hope you aren't angry with me for taking you away from your admirers."

"No, of course not, Raoul. I am pleased that you would care to be seen with me in public."

"Of course I do, Christine. I told you that I intend to court you."

She looked away. "I know that's what you said, but . . . well, that was last evening."

"You think that I might have changed my mind overnight? When all I could think of last night was you?"

"I was not suggesting that *you* would have changed your mind, but that perhaps you might have had some assistance."

"You speak of my brother, the one who himself had a widely known attachment to none other than La Sorelli." Raoul laughed, but it felt hollow. He hadn't spoken to Philippe yet, and although he had every intention of courting—and, if the truth be known, marrying—Christine Daaé, he acknowledged that it would likely take some convincing of his brother.

But he would do it. Philippe never denied him anything he truly wished; for he was twelve years older, and had always thought of Raoul as more of a son than a brother, since their mother had died when Raoul was born, and their father less than a decade later.

It was true, however, that Raoul did not like to think of angering or disappointing Philippe. That was why he'd gone to sea: to make something of himself that the *comte* would be proud of.

Christine didn't reply, and they rode along in silence, broken only by the shouts of street vendors and the scrabbling of carriages along the cobbled street.

Raoul struggled to put his thoughts into words; he wanted to talk to her, to find out about her, to *learn* her . . . but one could not just suddenly delve into a woman's life with personal questions. Yet, he felt almost as if he had earned the right to do so, all those years ago, that summer. After all, he wasn't just a young man who'd suddenly noticed her glorious voice and lovely person. . . . He'd known of it for years.

Perhaps he would start there. Where they'd left off. "I didn't realize your father died that winter after our summer together. It must have been terrible for you."

She nodded next to him. "It was the coldest winter I'd ever known. I felt frozen, Raoul. Numb and slow. He was all I had. Father and his music. And then suddenly, it was gone. It was worse than losing Mama, for I was so young and I barely remember her. But Papa . . . but you know. You lost your parents too."

"Yes, but . . . well, it was different for me. I had my brother, who became like a father to me, and my two sisters, who were all so much older than I. And my mother's sister, who raised me. Of course, I have her to thank for living in Brest, for that is how we came to be in Perros and how you and I met." He flashed her a quick look. She had a sad smile on her face. She must be remembering.

"I had no one. No one except the Valeriuses, and they were wonderful to keep me on, but it wasn't the same. For a long time, I didn't want to even hear the violin. Do you still play?" she asked suddenly, taking him by surprise.

"I haven't in many years, but I believe if I picked up the instrument, I would remember what your father taught me that summer, after I rescued your scarf."

"Those were lovely days by the sea, with the gulls calling in the distance behind the notes you and father were practicing."

He chuckled. "I would not have called them notes, Christine. . . . I was only a passable player, not talented like your father. And you."

There was another silence as he considered his next move. He needed to ask; he needed to know . . . but he was afraid. So at last, he tightened his fingers on the reins, looked straight ahead, and said, "Christine. How . . . how was it for you all these years in the Opera House? What I mean to say is . . . Sorelli and my brother have been together, and other singers and dancers have had protectors, and . . . I just wish to know. . . . Have you been treated . . . well?"

When she didn't respond, he gripped the reins tighter, but didn't look at her. This was so much more difficult than steering a massive ship in a storm and planning and executing voyages and training for ship-to-ship attacks. There, one could learn one's way with the lines and the sheets and the navigation, and even use the weather and myriad weapons.

But this was a woman, and she did not have a helm.

At last Christine spoke, her voice barely audible over the soft crunch of hooves on a portion of the *rue* that was still covered with snow. "I was lonely. I didn't fit in with the other girls, because for a long time, I didn't want to sing. I barely danced. When Papa died, I lost the music and I still don't know how Professor Valerius convinced the conservatoire to take me. Perhaps because I was the daughter of the famous violinist, they believed I would rise to the occasion."

"But you have, Christine. You did! You were magnificent last night."

"Last night. Yes, I felt it. But there were many months and years where I didn't belong and I didn't believe I would ever have the chance to be . . . to be the beautiful lady, who stands onstage in the limelight, and garners all of the applause and admiration. I longed for it, Raoul . . . but it was out of my reach."

"You have arrived there, Christine. No one will contest it now." He wanted to reach over and take her hand from beneath those furs and press it to his lips, to comfort her. How he wished he'd been there during her lonely days.

"I made friends with one of the other dancers and Franco, a young Italian man who was brilliant at organizing the props docks. Franco and I . . . Raoul, he made me feel not so alone. We were clumsy and furtive, but we needed each other."

Raoul swallowed. He'd hoped, but he really hadn't believed she might have still been untouched, living in an environment such as the Opera House. "Did you love him?"

When she shrugged, the furs shifted and fell away, exposing her shoulder to the brisk wind. She busied herself, trying to pull the fox and rabbit skins back up over her as she answered. "I don't know. But whatever it was, it did not last long, for he soon had his attention caught by one of the older chorus girls, and they ran off to join the theater in Marseilles."

"And after Franco?"

"Does it matter so much to you, Raoul? Will my answer change anything?"

"No." It was true.

"Then why ask it?"

"Because I want to know that your life wasn't as hard as I think it was; while I was raised in a world of luxury and comfort, I don't want to believe that you were lonely and afraid or . . . or mistreated. All those times I thought of you—and I did think of you, Christine, I truly did."

"Thank you, Raoul. It's nice to know that perhaps I wasn't as alone as I thought I was. And . . . to answer your question, no, I did not seek out a protector. Nor did one seek me out. I was too shy, and not talented enough. I didn't attract their attention, and I was rather glad I did not. And it seemed so . . . false. Practical, perhaps, but false."

"I'm selfish, but I am glad."

"I was lonely. I was surrounded by people all the time, but I was alone. I don't know if I shall ever find my place."

"You will, Christine. You *will*. With me."

Then she looked at him. "That's what I love about you, Raoul. You're a good listener. You help me to put into words things that I didn't realize I felt until I spoke them."

But he didn't want to be just a good listener, just a friend. He wanted all of her.

And he would have it. All of her.

Erik dreamt.

He dreamt of her, of her long, swirling dark hair, cloaking him . . . of the slender warmth of her body, lining his own, tangling with his limbs.

Of her luscious mouth, red and full, smiling, pouting, coming to him, closing over him . . . of her delicate fingers, narrow and creamy in the dark hair of his body . . . of driving into her, filling her, joining with her . . . loving her.

Loving her.

Of her laughing, singing, dancing . . . even of eating, of mundane things such as dressing her hair and buttoning her gown.

He dreamt of Christine onstage, singing for him, only for him, her blue eyes lifted to his box and her whole being centered on him, on pleasing him.

Of waking next to her.

Of walking boldly into the Opera House to take his seat in the front of the stalls.

Of pushing through the throngs of admirers outside her dressing room door, carrying an impossible armful of lilies.

Of driving with her along the Seine, in an open carriage.

And then the dreams changed . . . from a warm, sun-filled day to a dark, cold emptiness. To pain, searing pain, and scratchy wool coverings and iron chains. To the shrieks and cries and jeers, and the running. Always, the running, and running, and running.

Down dark hallways, through moon-glistening streets, into deep, dank tunnels and underground rivers. With the echoes of life above, permanently exorcised from his own. He could not draw in enough breath; he could not gasp in enough air. . . . He rounded the corner of the never-ending tunnel. . . .

And saw Christine, hanging on the wall, the black and gray and evil blue stone wall, her arms spread, her legs apart, her body white and naked against the dark.

He couldn't get to her . . . couldn't reach her. . . . He kept running toward her, running and stumbling and running, but he could not reach her. . . .

And then strong hands pulled on him, captured him . . . held his muscular arms; something hard crashed against the backs of his knees, sending him crumpling. His legs bound, his arms chained, he was thrown to the floor. The cold, wet, dark floor.

You'll never have her, scuttling rat.

You bury yourself in the dark, and yearn for what you will never have. She will never look on the likes of you, no matter that she spreads her legs when you force her. She'll not spread 'em for your cock.

As Buquet's taunting words echoed in his mind, reverberating in the cavern of his dreams, Erik struggled against his bonds. He had to reach her . . . to get to Christine. . . .

But then . . . she was not alone.

Hands reached out, covering her breasts, and someone bent to her throat, his shadowy shape obstructing Erik's vision from his miserable position on the stone floor. She moaned and closed her eyes, tipping her head back, baring her long, creamy neck.

The man played with her breasts, fingered her nipples, bent to suck loudly on one as Erik was forced to watch. Her hips were moving; she was making soft huffing sounds from full parted lips; she shivered and shifted and moaned as the man sucked on her beautiful breast, leaving it red and moist from his lips.

Erik could see every texture of her ruched-up areola under the thick fingers of the man who manipulated it . . . the jutting red point, the gentle pink wrinkles. It was as if it filled his vision; then the close view of the man's lips, closing over the nipple. Greedy, they sucked, pulling it into the circle as the white flesh around it trembled and shook.

She cried out when the man moved, his hand fingering the black thatch between her legs. Erik saw it then, the red, swollen sex that he would die for . . . the slick, warm velvet of Christine. . . . She bumped and moved and cried and Erik struggled again to pull himself loose and go to her. . . . The man's head bent there; Erik could see only the back of it as it moved, as he licked and sucked and tasted her.

She thrashed against the manacles that held her spread-eagled, her head rolling from side to side, her breasts, now free from questing fingers, bouncing and jiggling. She cried out, cried and struggled, begging . . . and the man pulled away.

He turned, and Erik saw the familiar face of his brother, glistening with Christine. His lips, full and red, dripped with her and he smiled. Mocking. Taunting.

"Don't frighten the girls, Erik. They cannot stand your touch. Hear them scream?"

She spreads her legs when you force her. She'll not spread 'em for your cock.

"But she'll take mine," his brother said to Erik. "She'll take mine."

He turned back to Christine, suddenly naked with her, and somehow her arms were around him as he drove into her. Then Erik could see the cock as though he were next to it, working in and out of her swollen sex, in and out, in and out, the rhythm pulsing within him, his own need building in agony.

Then he saw them from a distance again, writhing, twined, against the wall, Christine's arms around him, her face tilted up, her eyes closed in deep pleasure. She cried out, cried her release, scoring her nails down the man's back, and Erik felt her shudders as though it were he buried inside her. . . .

And he woke.

Panting, sweating, naked, and tangled. His cock screaming with pain, jutting toward the ceiling. His heart racing, his hands clenched.

His unmasked face wet with tears.

Christine.

"Oh, Christine," he cried softly, bringing his hands to his face. One side, smooth but for the stubble that edged his jaw . . . the other, rough and textured as the bark of a tree.

How he loved her.

He wanted her, yes, but he *loved* her.

He had grown to love her. Watching her, seeing the same loneliness in her face that would be etched in his own . . . if he had the courage to look at it.

Listening to her music—music that *he* pulled forth from her, music that they created together.

But she could never love him, deformed and defective as he was. He dared not let her see him, barely allowed her to touch him, though his body craved it. Trembled for it.

Oh, he had hope, buried so deeply inside him that he rarely let it out. Perhaps someday she would love him for himself, in spite of his face. In spite of his past.

From that first morning he'd watched her sing alone on the stage, months ago, Erik had been fascinated. Who knew why Christine should have touched him so, that first day? But she had.

After that, he'd watched her. Lurked. Loitered. Saw that she was not like the other girls—not like many of them, anyway.

There was a purity about her, and a shy goodness. A tolerance. She was kind to the door closer, the lowest of low on the hierarchy of the opera personnel, who had the club foot. Instead of ignoring the half-blind man who worked in the cellars below the stage, she greeted him. And he learned to recognize her voice.

She shared her meager meal of Red Egg and garlic sausage with one of the younger, smaller dancers, who obviously was in need of extra nourishment. She even gave one of her hair ribbons—a lovely scarlet one—to an *ouvreuse* for her daughter's new baby.

Perhaps that was part of the reason he'd fallen in love with her. Certainly, if it were just for her beauty and her singing voice, there were others who'd passed their way through the Opera House. Carlotta had once even been less jaded, more innocent. Beautiful.

But neither she nor anyone else had ever touched Erik's heart and soul the way Christine Daaé had. Lonely, sad, magnificent Christine.

And now . . . anger churned inside him. She was dining and associating with Raoul de Chagny and his brother, the *comte*.

Erik had not known whom she had left with last night after their interlude on the stage until he'd listened in on the *foyer de la danse*, when Raoul de Chagny had swept in and fairly carried her off. Until that moment, Erik had been merely indulgent, watching from his hidden knot high in the wall, as his protégée shyly accepted the attentions of her admirers.

It was nothing more than he'd expected—of course one as gifted and beautiful, but still with that underlying innocence, would attract the attention of the *abonnés*. And Christine had given him no cause to feel any differently, for she was polite, and reserved, but seemed to single none of the men out. They were all the same to her.

Until Raoul de Chagny.

Her eyes had lit up and sparkled, and she swooned up to her feet upon his presence. And immediately took his imperious arm.

And then he'd swept her away, out of the theater, away from Erik, away from the Opera Ghost's stronghold.

Leaving Erik alone, with the darkness of his destiny and the taunts of his imagination.

Six

With the encouragement of the two managers, and her many supporters, Carlotta defied the Opera Ghost's warning, gliding onto the stage that night in full costume and regalia. She had determined that she would sing, and sing she would.

Feathers quivering from her ornate, glittering headdress, the train of her silk gown and yards of ruffles and gathers spilling onto the floorboards, the prima donna took her position in the exact front center of the auditorium as the beaming Moncharmin and Richard looked on from their places in Box Five.

"The ghost is late," chuckled Firmin Richard to his partner. "The performance has begun and he has not arrived to claim his seat."

"I am glad we did not let this box out tonight; I am looking forward to hearing La Carlotta's performance. She is not afraid of the ridiculous jokester ghost."

"I refuse to keep this box unavailable to our patrons any longer. Opera Ghost, indeed."

"And whoever it is . . . he shall not find any salary forthcoming from us," Moncharmin replied, laughing to himself. "We can put those twenty-four thousand francs to much better use."

The second act passed without incident, and during the intermission, the two managers left their box in order to greet La Carlotta backstage.

"You have never sung better, madame," Firmin Richard told her, bowing over her hand. "I am so pleased you did not disappoint your many supporters and comply with the threatening letter you received."

"*Ridículo*. The Opera Ghost is nothing but a story made up by Christine Daaé's friends, trying to frighten me. *Me, La Carlotta!*" She humphed and preened, and the managers, well satisfied with the result of their foiling whatever plot had been hatched, returned to their box for the third act.

When they reentered Box Five, however, they noticed almost immediately that a box of candy had been placed on the railing.

"Where in heaven has this come from?" asked Moncharmin, pointing to the box.

"And these?" Richard produced a pair of opera glasses that had not been there when they had left. "Call the *ouvreuse* and find out who has been here since we left. Someone must have put them here as a joke."

But when they questioned the ushers, they all indicated that no one had come along the staircase leading to the box. No one at all.

Richard and Moncharmin looked at each other uneasily, but settled into their seats as the curtain rose for the third act of *Faust*. It was only an instant later that a strange draft, eerie and unhealthy, began to seep through the box. Moncharmin fancied he could hear someone breathing, just behind him. The managers looked at each other, but remained silent, suddenly very attentive to what was happening onstage.

It was time for Carlotta's entrance. Richard realized he was holding his breath, twisting his fingers into the handkerchief he had somehow pulled from his pocket.

When La Carlotta made her third and final entrance of the evening, a great cheer arose from her supporters in the audience. A triumphant gleam in her eyes, La Carlotta raised her arms and began to sing Marguerite's response to Faust's entreaty.

No! 'Tis a princess I view!
A princess before me!

Suddenly, a most unnerving rumble sounded from . . . somewhere. Above, below, in front . . . later, witnesses were not able to agree on the location of the noise, but it was the sound of an angry growl or grumbling. Moncharmin choked audibly and Richard dropped his handkerchief. It fluttered to the seats below.

After the ominous rumble, Carlotta paused, hitching her breath, casting a wary glance behind her . . . but she was standing far in front of the backdrops, even in front of the proscenium, nearly upon the gaslights that studded the edge of the stage. She picked up and carried the next few notes, even as the grumbling sounded again and a flicker of a shadow blinked over the stage, sending her fuchsia gown into shades of dirty pink.

Faust approached her, and sang his lines.

Carlotta opened her mouth and began to sing her reply:

And a deep languid charm
I feel without alarm
With its melody enwind—

But—it was *horrible*!

The audience stood as one, gaping at the people around them. The managers turned to each other, clasping the other's forearm, their mouths wide with horror, eyes goggling, jowls shaking.

It was inconceivable . . . but the last syllable had come from Carlotta's mouth, not as a beautiful, clear note . . . but as the sound of the croak of a *frog*.

Her face was the picture of a terrified, bewildered woman. Her hands rose to her throat as if to ascertain whether it was still hers. She looked at Piangi, the man playing Faust, who was staring back at her as though she had grown a second nose.

"Impossible," Richard gasped to his partner. "She has just been singing so perfectly. All night."

"It was an inhuman sound. It must have been . . . it had to have been a mistake."

"She has sung the most intricate and beautiful notes. . . . How could this be? She has never faltered, in all of her performances."

They turned back to the stage, holding their breaths. Moncharmin noticed to his dismay that the draft seemed to have gotten colder. More sharp and eerie. And the breathing . . . it was closer. Louder. He swallowed deeply and began to wish quite vehemently that they had not made those jests about refusing to pay the ghost's salary.

The orchestra began to play. The buzzing of the people had risen, and now ebbed back into silence. All waited expectantly.

Carlotta, looking not quite as triumphant as she had appeared earlier, drew in her breath to sing. Richard held his own breath, waiting. . . .

Oh, how strange, like a spell
Does the evening bind me.

"Go on, *go on*," Richard hissed, his heart beating so hard his fingers jolted on the box's railing.

And a deep, languid—CROAK!
I feel without CROAK! CROAK!

The croaks echoed with hoarse ugliness through the auditorium and Carlotta closed her mouth, clapping her small hands over it as if to push the awful sounds back in. Her eyes bugging, she picked up her skirts and ran offstage as the audience erupted in a mass of whispers and titters.

From behind them, the managers heard a low, rumbling laughter. "The way she sings tonight, 'tis a wonder she doesn't bring down the chandelier!" It was the ghost! Behind them, speaking behind them in the very same box!

Moncharmin and Richard dared not turn to look behind them, but Moncharmin glanced quickly up at the chandelier as if expecting it to tumble to the stage. It swayed gently, but did not appear to be in danger of falling.

"What shall we do now? The show is ruined," he said to Richard.

"He wants Daaé to sing. We shall give him Daaé, then," the taller man replied, more bravely than he felt, and hoped assiduously that the ghost had heard him and would leave off. He stood at the edge of the box and called out into the auditorium. "Please, ladies and gentlemen . . . the show will go on. We shall present to you Miss Daaé, performing the remainder of the role of Marguerite for your pleasure."

Thus, moments later, due to some quick work on the part of the stage manager and the director, the newest star of the Opera

House, Christine Daaé, stepped into the circle of light left empty by Carlotta.

She looked angelic and fragile. Her long, dark hair was left unbound and curled in a gentle, delicate swath that hung to the middle of her back. Her pale blue gown was not nearly as ornate and fancy as that of La Carlotta, but it suited her innocence . . . and clearly displayed the woman inside. The neckline plunged to a deep vee between her breasts, lifted high and steady by her corset. Her long, white arms were bare from the shoulders down; only the narrowest band of blue rosettes formed the sleeves that rested just below the juncture of arm and shoulder. The delicate curve of her collarbone, the dip at the base of her throat, were shown in fine relief by the yellow light above.

But her face. It was her face and voice that captivated the audience. A woman had never sung so purely, so cleanly and perfectly in all the Opera House's history. The rapturous expression on her beautiful countenance bespoke of some ecstasy that was beyond the grasp of the audience, but that clearly moved her. She sang as though she could never stop, as though she would never tire, never run out of words or notes.

Indeed, Christine knew she had never sung so beautifully. She felt the music filling her veins, sounding her nerve endings . . . carrying her away. She felt Erik's presence, knew he had somehow caused Carlotta's embarrassment to pave the way for Christine's own triumph.

As she sang, she did as he requested: She sang for him. She felt his hands on her skin, his gentle lips scoring her bare shoulder. Her breasts, lifted enticingly, tightened and swelled as she recalled the gentle, persuasive hands that had fondled them earlier.

She felt naked, bare, warm, and titillated and basked in the heat of the limelight, and she felt as though she and her angel sang together, somewhere, alone. And joined together as one.

They were joined. They would be one.

And when she was done, when she broke from the trancelike state that had enabled her to sing without nervousness or fear, the applause of the audience brought her back to herself. She bowed and curtsied and accepted the roses and lilies and gillyflowers tossed and presented to her. Elation grew inside her as the audience continued to cheer, until her excitement was such that she was hardly able to stand still. She had succeeded! She had never been so happy, so exultant, in her life.

When a large mass of blush-edged white roses dropped at her feet, bound with a crimson ribbon, she looked up and saw Raoul waving to her from the box nearest the stage. Smiling, flush and exhilarated with her triumph, Christine picked up Raoul's offering and buried her face in the beautiful blooms.

And when she ran off the stage and hurried her way through the wings of the backstage, Raoul was already there to meet her. Somehow, he managed to slip an arm around hers and whisk her off into an empty wardrobe closet before she reached the *foyer de la danse* and any of her other admirers could get to her.

In the small, close room, lit by one single lamp, they were surrounded by racks of glittering gowns and feathered headdresses, props of swords and shields and belts and girdles. Lacy corsets, flowered hats, gloves, and silky, beaded skirts pushed them together so that they stood very close in the narrow aisle of the closet.

"Christine, my love, you were brilliant!" Holding her hands, he gazed at her fervently, his shadowed blue eyes gleaming with pride and emotion.

"Thank you, Raoul," she cried, hardly able to contain herself, and dropped the roses at their feet as he drew her into his arms.

His kiss was brief and gentle, sweeping reverently over her parted lips. "You are so beautiful," he whispered against her mouth, drawing her flush against him. "And you sing like a perfect angel. You are perfect, Christine."

She pulled away, resting a hand against his handsome cheek, excitement still raging through her. His skin glowed golden in the yellow light, his butter-colored hair tipped with a nimbus from the illumination behind him. "I am not perfect, Raoul, but it is kind of you to say so. Indeed, my tutor says I still have much work to do." Christine smiled up at him, her attention on his slender, elegant lips. How lovely it was to *see* the man in front of her, to touch him and to look at him. . . . Still exultant and bold, she stepped forward into him and raised her face to kiss his delicate lips.

His arms wrapped around her as though suddenly loosened from bounds, pulling her roughly up against his body. Their mouths fought to taste the other, to sample and lick and nibble. His shoulders, high and broad, felt sturdy under Christine's hands . . . so different from her encounters with Erik, where she had never faced him . . . never felt the length of his body pressed up against her breasts, her mons . . . never fulfilled the need to touch him, to trace her hand over his body.

"Christine," Raoul muttered, and he was moving along her jaw to her neck, his mouth wet on her skin. She arched back, pushing her chest into his groping hands, wanting to feel those fingers over her tight nipples.

Her breasts pulled free and he bent to take one into the warm cavern of his mouth. Christine arched against him as he sucked, her hand trailing down to the bulge between his thighs.

Suddenly, the door just behind Raoul's shoulder opened.

Christine pushed him away as she recognized the erect black figure of Madame Giry. "M-madame," she stammered, hastily thrusting her breasts back into their confinements.

"Christine. You are keeping him waiting." Her black eyes scored over her and then over Raoul as she waited, arms crossed over her middle, for Christine to put herself to rights.

"Of course, madame," Christine replied, suddenly overcome with remorse. How could she have kept Erik waiting? Of course he would want to see her . . . after her performance tonight, he would want to be with her . . . to touch her. To make her *feel*.

As she was making a final adjustment, Raoul had turned politely away, but as she stepped out of the wardrobe closet, he was waiting for her.

Just as Erik was waiting for her.

How could she have forgotten Erik, even for the moment? The excitement of her second debut, the thrill of conquering the audience yet again . . . of being the beautiful lady of her dreams . . . and then Raoul had appeared to sweep her off her feet before she knew what he was doing.

But only her angel could make her feel . . . truly feel. Only with him was she able to leave the grief and emptiness behind her.

It was for him that she sang.

Perhaps . . . perhaps tonight, she would be able to see and feel him at last. "If I've pleased him," she whispered to herself as Raoul took her arm with a proprietary air, following Madame Giry down the busy passageway.

"Pleased who?" he asked, slipping a finger down beneath the edge of her now-in-place bodice to smooth over her areola.

"My tutor," she replied, pulling gently away.

"Tutor? You did mention a tutor. Who is it?" asked Raoul, his brows drawing together in an annoyed fashion.

"Do you remember when my father used to tell us about the Angel of Music? He promised to send him to me . . . and he has. My tutor is the Angel of Music! He will be waiting for me. And if I have pleased him . . ." Her heart raced in anticipation.

"What is it you are talking about, Christine? Waiting for you? Who is this man?"

She stopped in the hallway, pulling Raoul to the side so that the bustle of stagehands, dancers, and musicians could continue unfettered. "He is the Angel of Music, Raoul. He . . . he lives here at the Opera House, and of course he will be waiting for me in my dressing room. It is because of him that I am able to sing as I do."

"He lives here? He's not . . . he isn't this—this thing that they call the Opera Ghost?" Raoul looked horrified. "The creature who ran Carlotta off the stage tonight? Did he put some sort of spell upon her?"

Christine reached for his cheek. "Raoul, he is not a ghost. And he is a friend to me . . . and a teacher." A lover. "He's been my tutor for more than three months, and since he has come to me, I have been so happy. You should be happy for me too. Since I lost Father, I have not been able to find peace . . . until my *ange*."

"But Christine . . . a man? In your dressing room? Why, that's improper!"

Christine smiled fondly up at him. "Improper? I am an actor, a singer. . . . I live in the world of the theater. And you were in my dressing room as well."

"Christine, you cannot see him anymore." Raoul was greatly agitated. "You must tell him that he cannot visit you."

Now she dropped her hand from his face, her heart beating faster. She could never agree to that. "But why? Raoul, I would never do that."

"Because . . . because my future wife cannot be meeting with strange men in her dressing room."

Christine stared up at him in shock, but before she could respond, a strong hand gripped her arm. It was Madame Giry, and she had a most urgent, annoyed look on her austere face. "Christine, you will anger him if you tarry further."

"Yes, of course," she said, and started off down the hallway, bringing Raoul along with her.

"But, Christine . . . you . . ."

"I must go, Raoul. The angel is very strict and I do not want to anger him. It is because of him that I have had the success that I have. You saw what happened to Carlotta tonight when she failed to follow his instructions."

"But . . . you will dine with us tonight, will you not?" Raoul looked at her so pleadingly, his blue eyes as desperate as the grip on her wrist. His hold caused her to stop just outside her dressing room door, and he spun her from her path to look at him.

She couldn't turn him down. "I will. I must speak with the angel first . . . and then, yes, I will be pleased to have dinner with you, if he permits."

"If he permits? Christine, what are you saying? That he is in control of you?"

"Raoul, no, not really . . . but he is a strict taskmaster. I will never reach my greatest potential if I do not follow his instructions. And . . . if I do not follow his instructions, he will cease to visit me. I could not bear that."

"But, Christine, I do not understand. How can you allow this—this creature to control your life?"

"It is simple, Raoul. Without him, I would not be singing as I am today. I would still be simple, shy, lonely Christine Daaé. Under his tutelage, I have blossomed at last. Do not lie and say that you do not find my voice and my talent part of your attraction to me. I have seen it in your eyes."

"Christine, I do not deny that my love for you is even greater with your success. But if you stopped singing tomorrow, I would still love you."

"But I would not love myself. I find the greatest joy in my music, and he has helped me to find this joy. Please understand, Raoul. . . . It is a joy, a freedom . . . a special beauty that I have not experienced since Papa died. I do not wish to talk on it further, Raoul. You cannot change my mind, and it really will not make for a friendly dinner if we are arguing." She smiled at him, and saw his acquiescence. "So, yes, I will join you for dinner if he does not mind . . . but perhaps just the two of us?" she added, thinking of the uncomfortable way Philippe had looked at her the night before.

"I will call the carriage and be back for you right away," Raoul told her, a bit reluctantly. "And I will make arrangements for just the two of us to dine."

When he released her and strode away, Christine turned and found herself face-to-face with Madame Giry. "You are playing very dangerously, Christine," she told her.

"No . . . no, I do not know what you mean."

"He will not be pleased with your delay tonight, and he will be most especially displeased that you have been flirting with the *vicomte*, of all people. If he should find out it is Raoul de Chagny who has caught your attention . . ." She pressed her lips together. "I have warned you. . . . Take care that you do not anger him or you may very well lose him. You saw Carlotta's disgrace tonight. Make no mistake: Though she brought her own destruction upon herself, he helped to manifest it. And listen to me carefully: You must not tell the *vicomte* or his brother *anything* of him, do you understand?"

But she already had. Christine's saliva dried in her throat. "I will heed your advice, Madame Giry. I do not wish to do anything to lose *mon ange*."

"Very good. Now, into your dressing room. He will come to you soon."

But even after Christine had entered the room and changed from her costume into a lace-trimmed dressing gown, Erik did not make his presence known. She sat on a quilted seat in the center of the room, watching herself in the mirror as her face grew graver and more worried while the moments ticked on.

A pounding on her door distracted her momentarily; she cracked it open to find an impatient Raoul waiting for her. "Come, Christine, the horses are becoming restless, and so am I."

Christine cast a glance behind her. The room felt empty; perhaps Erik was angry and was not going to come to her tonight.

"All right . . . give me one more moment to change into street clothes and to get my cloak." She closed the door and started toward the small wardrobe that held her meager collection of street clothes.

But before she had even pulled the doors wide, she felt the air in the room move.

"Erik!" she cried, relief sweeping through her.

She knew his presence; though he had yet to announce himself any other way, she sensed him. The five lamps sputtered, then were doused, leaving only one burning low.

But then, there was nothing. Silence . . . harsh and empty.

"Erik? Angel?" Christine called.

The shadows grew tall, crisscrossing the room, as the half-moon of light left by the single lamp sputtered. The air chilled, moved, and shifted, sending the hair at the back of her neck on edge and her nipples tightening.

"Where are you?"

"Christine? What is it?" Raoul's voice came through the dressing room door, accompanied by his pounding fists. The doorknob jiggled in vain. "Unlock the door, Christine!"

But she had not locked it.

"Erik? Are you there?" she called again, her voice rising. "Angel?"

"Christine!" Raoul shouted, pounding harder, shoving at the door.

"*Christinnnne . . . ,*" her name came at last, on a breath that swept through her.

"Erik. You *are* there! Where are you?"

"Christine! Open the door!" Raoul had resorted to kicking at it, if the low, dull thuds were any indication. "Are you all right? Say something!"

"*Christinnnne . . . step to the mirror.*"

At once, lust surged through her body at the memory of her bare flesh against the cold, silver looking glass. The teasing and the pleasure he'd given her . . . the rising, pounding orgasm he'd brought her to . . .

But when she came near the glass, she saw that the mirror was moving . . . and suddenly, strong arms were pulling her, tugging her into what had been solid, imposing glass, which had somehow melted away. Into the mirror.

She was encloaked in something heavy and black; it smelled like damp wool and sandalwood . . . and then the dressing room and the mirror were behind her and she looked up for the first time into the face of the Angel of Music.

It was shadowed; half was dark and hidden. . . . The other half bore an eye that gleamed, not with gentleness and caring, but with fury and determination. Half the mouth was not shadowed; it was formed as sensually as she had imagined, with full, defined lips that curled angrily above a set jaw.

Before she could say a word, express any kind of relief—but did she even feel relieved, now that she saw the forbidding expression on his half-hidden face?—Erik tugged her harshly away from the mirror, and began to pull her down a dark passageway.

"You can leave your lover to wonder where you have gone," he snapped at the sound of Christine's dressing room door splintering behind them.

"Erik, please, you have misunderstood!" Christine tried to pull away from him, but his grip was too strong. Her heart was jamming madly in her chest, and she regretted those foolish moments in the wardrobe room with Raoul.

"I misunderstand *nothing*," he told her tightly, continuing their mad rush down the hall. She tripped and stumbled and without his hold she would have fallen more than once. "I did not misunderstand that boy's hands down your gown, did I? Or your tongue down his throat? Did I, Christine?"

It was a cool fury that iced his words, and that frightened her more than any blistering rage would have done. The fact that it was so calm, and so measured . . . and the expression in his one visible eye so harsh . . . Christine began to fear, for the first time, what her tutor might do to her.

"Where are you taking me?" she asked.

"You will find out soon enough." He pulled her around a corner and she saw, to her amazement, a white horse standing, bridled and saddled, glowing from the illumination of a single torch. Despite the dim light, she recognized the mount as one of the set animals that had disappeared from the Opera House stable some time ago. Cesar was his name.

Erik helped her up and, taking the reins, began to lead the stallion down another, wider hallway.

Erik remained at Cesar's head, in front of Christine, and all she could see was his tall black figure, with the billowing cape that fell past his knees. She had yet to see him in full light; it seemed as though he was purposely keeping to the shadows.

When the long, sloping hallway ended, after many twists and turns and junctures, Erik helped Christine down—none too gently—and she found that they had left the underpinnings of the Opera House and were on the shore of a small underground lake. A boat waited and, without words, he directed her into it and pushed the vessel off with a long pole.

Her hands had grown clammy and her pounding heart had not slowed; it continued to drum in her chest, sending tremors reverberating through her. Christine wondered what was to become of her. What Erik planned to do with her.

And in spite of the towering, angry presence behind her, the harsh, curt words he'd spoken to her, and the impersonal touch when he'd helped her into the shallow boat, she warmed to him. Her nervous body responded by awakening and wanting him . . . wanting his touch, his teasing lips and his gentle, elegant fingers. Her throat was dry, her cheeks were warm, and her fingers clasped together as Christine realized that, despite Erik's angry distance, she was anticipating his touch.

For surely . . . surely, now, here, wherever they were going, she would be able to see him and touch him.

At last, the boat slid onto the stone boundary of the underground lake, and Christine saw a small structure, a house, that appeared to be built into the side of a wall, or cavern. A low yellow light glowed in one window.

"Welcome to my home," Erik told her unkindly. Yet now he was not rough or rude when helping her from the boat. She noticed he had pulled a hood up over his head whilst they rode in the boat, and it continued to obscure his face, leaving most of it in shadow.

Christine stepped down and found herself in ankle-deep water. It was cold, and it shocked her through her silken stockings and fine leather slippers, eating into the hem of the laced and ruffled dressing gown she still wore and weighting it down. She slogged through the water onto the smooth, hard beach, noticing the gray-

and black-shining stones scattered along the water's edge, painted with the white glow of six torches affixed to the sides of the vast, domed, stone chamber that housed the underground lake.

Inside the small building, Christine was surprised to find that it was outfitted as comfortably as any home.

"It must be . . . terrible living in darkness all the time, Erik," she said, reaching for his arm as he brushed past her.

He nearly flung her away, keeping his hooded face averted as he strode into the structure. "Save your pity," he snapped, stalking away from where she stood in what was the kitchen and eating area.

Christine watched after him, her apprehension growing. What was he going to do with her? Was she a prisoner?

Moments later, she heard his returning footfalls. They slowed, pausing almost imperceptibly as they approached the room where she sat . . . and then sped up as if to get there quickly. Get it over with.

When he walked in the room, Christine saw him for the first time. Out of the shadow, out from under the hood. Black and powerful and intimidating.

Erik stood, hands on his hips as if braced, and glared down at her.

She realized now why his face had seemed to be half-shadowed all the time . . . why, when she had reached back behind her that first time he came to her . . . and when he'd hung her from her wrists on the opera stage . . . why his face had felt . . . strange. Unyielding and leathery.

The mask obscured what surely was . . . or had been . . . or, at least, had been promised to be . . . a perfect face. Smooth, sculptured, sensual. Eyes that sat deeply in their places; one-half of a sharp jaw that curved like the bend in a harp; the deep slash of shadow like dark paint defining his proud cheekbone.

His mouth was uncovered; the mask curved along the bridge of his nose, bisecting the swarthy skin with matte black covering and then following the upper line of his lips, like one-half of a mustache. It extended from the center of his face to just in front of the ear, and up and along the hairline more than halfway across his forehead. She saw the slim black cord stretching from the mask up, over, and into the dark hair at his temple.

But what was under the mask?

She stood, almost without willing it, and reached toward him, but he snatched her wrist in the air.

"Don't touch it." He threw her arm down. She felt his deep-seated fury still radiating from him.

"Erik, please . . ."

"Please, you say? *Please?*" His voice changed . . . took on that low, simmering tone that had coaxed her against the mirror . . . and drawn so much from her. Christine stepped back at the sudden burning in his eyes. Nestled in their deep hoods, they looked at her with the hunger of a lion.

Her chest rose and fell as if she'd been running. Something hot and heavy moved through her, steaming her face and burning inside her body, making her stomach writhe. Her nipples jutted against the light chemise she wore, the only covering under her dressing gown. She trembled, and she saw that his bare fingers trembled too.

"I shall look forward to hearing you say that to me," he said, in an easy manner that belied the intensity in his eyes. " *'Please, Erik.'* Oh, yes indeed, I am quite certain you will find many ways to beg me."

"Erik, what are you going to do?" Fluttering in her belly rose up into her throat, and her cheeks burned hotter. She had a fairly good idea of the answer to that.

His smile mocked her. "We can start by having you take off

your clothes, Christine. And make it quick. I have waited far too long to have you waste my time."

Her fingers were steady as she tugged the buttons and laces of her dressing gown loose. Christine whisked it off her shoulders, feeling his avid stare on her and knowing her own surge of power at the look in his eyes. She didn't have to look down to see her nipples poking through the fine lawn chemise, or the tops of her breasts rounding over the low round neckline.

"All of them," he growled, making as if to reach for her.

Christine stepped lightly to the side as his hand fell back down, and watched him as he stared at her . . . as if drawing in the sight of her gave him breath. And she pulled the thin shift up and over her head, and felt the gust of cooler air over her sensitive flesh.

His breathing became more shallow, more audible. Then as she watched, he drew in a deep, tremulous breath and exhaled long and slow.

"Now . . ." The syllable was ruptured, as though his voice broke when he tried to speak it. But his eyes . . . they remained steady and heavy on her, focused not on her tight, pink-tipped breasts . . . or even on the triangle between her legs . . . but drilling into her own gaze. "Now, Christine, you will see what happens when you allow another man to touch you."

SEVEN

At last Raoul was able to force the door open and he burst into Christine's dressing room. It was empty.

"Christine!" he shouted, pulling the wardrobe doors open. It was impossible! How could she have disappeared? "Christine!"

She'd been talking to someone. Could it have been her tutor, that Angel of Music she spoke of? "Christine!"

There was a noise behind him and he whirled. The stern-looking woman who'd interrupted him and Christine earlier stood in the open doorway of the dressing room. Her hair was scraped back from her face, pulling taut the skin around her dark, glittering eyes.

"May I help you, monsieur *le vicomte?*"

"Where is Christine? She has gone! Where has that madman taken her?" Fear and apprehension stormed through his veins, and he felt a surge of some other emotion replace it. Fury. Bald, burning fury.

"I do not know of what you speak, but it is clear that Miss Daaé is not in her dressing room. And . . . tut, tut . . . the door will need to be repaired before she is to use the room again. Monsieur *le vicomte*, perhaps you are a bit overset. . . . I would be most pleased to show you to the *foyer de la danse*, where you can perhaps have something to drink. You know, these beautiful actresses and singers . . . well, they are prone to fickleness. It is possible Miss Daaé has found herself a new admirer."

He looked at her, and saw a mask of innocence and calm on her face. Either she did not know, or she did not wish him to know. "I shall find my own way," he snarled, and pushed past her, his body trembling with fear and rage.

Despite what had to have been the most mortifying moment of her career, La Carlotta was holding court with a bevy of admirers in the *foyer de la danse* when Philippe entered the crowded room shortly after the disrupted performance of *Faust*.

He cast a curious look in her direction, taking in ink black hair that curled in little whorls around her face as though they'd been painted on her skin; her generous, shivering breasts, barely covered to the nipple by a wine-colored gown; and the luscious lips that looked as though they'd been drawn together in a little bud. Since he had only seen Carlotta before with those lips open wide in one aria or another, he was surprised that they looked so . . . pouty. Rather delicious.

And along with the rest of her lush, curvaceous body . . . well, it was nearly enough to put the visions of Christine Daaé from his mind. Nearly.

In fact, Philippe had found it more than difficult to dispel his own imagination's explicit and extremely erotic images of the Opera House's de facto newest star. Not only was he no longer merely amused by his brother's apparent infatuation with Miss Daaé, but he was now annoyed by it. It would take some careful manipulating to get Raoul to share.

It was not that he didn't believe he could convince his brother to do so—after all, it was only a woman at stake, and Raoul was a particularly biddable person. It was just that it was going to take so much more effort than he usually needed to expend in order to enjoy a woman. He would have to tread more carefully than he cared to, for despite the fact that he had no qualms about manipulating his younger brother, he did not wish to anger him.

Philippe was lost in mental images of rosy-tipped breasts, shiny lips parted by gasps of pain and pleading, and long dark hair wrapped around his wrist when suddenly Carlotta herself was in front of him. "Good evening, madame," he said, transferring his thoughts to the voluptuous woman in front of him.

"Monsieur *le comte*," she purred in imperfect French laced with Spanish, the expression in her eyes unmistakable in its invitation. "Our newest *patrón*. *Muy bien* that you have come."

"I see you have recovered from your . . . mishap," Philippe replied, knowing that he was impolite to mention her mishap, but curious to see how the diva would respond.

Her eyelashes barely flickered. *"Está macabro,"* she responded with vehemence, keeping her low-lashed gaze on him even as she appeared to look down modestly. "It was horrible. But I have seen to it that it shall never happen again."

Philippe had allowed her to maneuver him toward a quiet corner of the room. Her obvious interest was very unlike the Carlotta he had observed, albeit briefly, from a distance. Normally, the woman required the men to come to her—and she did not appear to have any great dearth of male companionship. His curiosity piqued, he waited for her to sit, and then chose a ridiculously uncomfortable cushion near enough to her that they could speak without being overheard.

"And how do you expect to prevent it?" he asked, taking the opportunity to slip his fingers into the prominently offered bosom. The neckline, which plunged down nearly to her navel, was so tight that it cut across the tops of her areolas. When he pulled the boned material away from one melon-sized breast, it pulled taut against the other, flattening her breast even as the other was exposed. "Do you have some influence with this Opera Ghost of which they speak? Or do you simply plan to touch La Sorelli's lucky horseshoe before your next performance in order to stave off the misfortune brought by the Phantom?"

"Opera Ghost! Pah!" Carlotta replied, leaning forward. When his finger and thumb found her jutting nipple, Philippe gave it an experimental squeeze and was gratified to see the response in her eyes. "I do not believe in any Opera Ghost. *Ridículo!* He sabotaged my voice tonic, which I leave in the wings to gargle with between songs. Ghost or no ghost, whoever he is, he wished to embarrass Carlotta, and he traded the tonic for something that made my voice do that—that horrible thing. I recognized it immediately when I tasted the tonic again. It was no ghostly effort, but a man-made one."

"You seem to be in the minority," Philippe said. Her skin was soft and warm, and Philippe tasted it at the juncture of her neck and shoulder. Greasepaint and powder flavored his lips at first, but then he found sweet and salty flesh and sucked hard. Carlotta purred under his mouth, and his hand slipped fully under the band of her neckline and cupped her breast. "Why is that?"

Carlotta pulled away, and he saw the calculation in her eyes. "He is no more a ghost than you or I," she told him. "I have heard things."

Philippe cared much less for what gossip the singer had heard than for the generous mounds of flesh offered beneath that cabernet gown, but in the public eye, he was a gentleman and would wait until an appropriate time. "Things?" he murmured, raising her plump white arm for the simple pleasure of seeing its corresponding breast lift.

"The daughter of the ballet mistress, she speaks of the man they call the ghost. She is a particular friend of Miss Daaé, and somehow, this girl, she knows other things that have been said about him. This ghost who is not a ghost but a man with a horrible face, who hides it under a mask."

It took a moment, but the cant of her words fell away and left Philippe with a shock at their meaning. He paused, his fingers closing over her wrist perhaps a bit too tightly. But when he looked up, she did not show pain in her eyes . . . but only pleasure. And satisfaction. "A man? In a mask?"

Was it possible? Could it be he? Here, all this time?

Philippe sat back and released Carlotta, his mind sifting through the possibility. "What more do you know about this man? How long has this ghost been here? What does he look like?"

Carlotta's face took on an even slier, craftier expression. "There have been rumors of a . . . presence . . . here since the Opera House's inauguration ten years ago, and perhaps even longer, while it was being built. I do not know what he looks like, but he must move with the agility of youth in order to clamber about as easily and quickly as he seems to."

"Indeed. I believe we might have several things to . . . discuss," Philippe told her, his mind still working. It had been nearly ten years ago that all of those disagreeable events had happened, events that he'd taken great care to sweep under the carpet, so to speak. It was fortunate that it had been during the unpleasantness of the war, thus making it much simpler for him to obliterate any evidence of what had happened.

Still . . . Erik had disappeared during that time, and . . . "It took many years for this Opera House to be constructed, did it not?"

"Many years," Carlotta purred, making the words sound like a seduction instead of a mere statement of fact. "And it is my understanding that the construction stopped during the war, when this building was used as a hospital during the Siege of Paris."

"And were there rumors of the ghost during that time as well, do you know?"

"I do not know . . . but I can find out. *Sí*, I shall ask one of those *ouvreuses estúpidas*. All they do is gossip."

Philippe thought privately that it would be gossip enough if the great Carlotta should stoop to speak to one of the lowly female ushers, but he was willing to have her do so.

Just then, he heard the rumble of a commotion across the room and saw his brother enter the salon with a wild look in his eyes. When Raoul saw Philippe, he immediately started toward him, pushing blindly through the clusters of other mingling dancers, actors, and their admirers.

"She is gone!" Raoul said when he was upon them. "Christine, Miss Daaé . . . she is gone. The opera ghost has taken her!"

Philippe raised one eyebrow and looked up at his brother, whose eyes had a half-mad light in them. Then he turned his attention back to Carlotta. God forbid that a woman ever lowered him to such a state. "See that you find out what you can on this Opera Ghost and I shall be most greatly . . . and creatively . . . appreciative of your efforts."

"It shall be my greatest pleasure," she replied, her lashes fluttering and her breasts quivering.

"I hope it shall be mine as well."

She looked at him, all cunning and promise. "I shall ensure it is so."

EIGHT

*E*rik gripped Christine's arm and propelled her in front of him, down a short hallway. He kept her at a distance, as if trying to avoid any accidental brush of her body against his.

If she hadn't seen the way he was looking at her, experienced the heavy, proprietary gaze, she would have thought he found her distasteful. But no. It was definitely not distaste in his eyes.

Down the hall he prodded her, to where it ended in a room . . . a space clearly designed for a working genius spurred by creativity. To her surprise, overhead a small glassed-in dome allowed the night sky to shine through. Apparently, he did not live in complete darkness.

As they stopped, she looked at him again and saw him try to hide the flinch from her direct gaze. Perhaps he lived in a different kind of darkness, intense and complete in its own way. Pity stirred within her—pity and desire. Raoul's touch had been nothing but a poor shadow of the one that sent her emotions reeling . . . and fool she had been to allow it to go so far.

The room was larger than her dressing room, and dominated by a sleek black piano, a mahogany harp, and a viola, violin, and cello. A dais built perpendicular to the instruments held a long, wide table that appeared to be nothing more than a working desk. Papers were scattered over it, and leather thongs to bind them, and pens, inkpots, and books.

She had barely taken in these aspects of the room when he moved up behind her and captured both of her wrists at the base of her spine. Then he slid an arm through her elbows, imprisoning them behind her, and crooked his other arm around her neck, pulling her back against him.

"I saw you with that boy," he said in her ear. His melodious voice didn't sound angry as much as it sounded full of promise. Hard promise. Her throat dried. "Christine, do you not understand that *you belong to me?*"

"Erik, I . . . I—"

"Quiet!" He wrenched his arm tighter around her neck—not enough to cut off her air, but enough that her head snapped back against his chest. She could feel tremors moving through him; whether they were from his bare control or from some other emotion, she did not know. "You will experience the agony I have endured."

He released her arms, keeping her throat in his strong grip, and slipped his hand around to feel her breast. He cupped it, rocked it gently in his palm, flicked a thumb over her nipple. Her body had learned well; it responded by tightening and jutting, and the nervous flutterings in her belly turned into twinges of desire.

She arched her breasts forward into his hand, her hips and rear pushing into his groin. The buttons from his shirt imprinted on the skin of her back as he continued to toy with her breast, and hold her immobile against him. When he pinched her nipple, she sighed from deep within and felt the welcome moisture gathering between her legs. She could hardly wait to feel his thick, hard cock slip inside her, and she relaxed against him.

The arm around her neck loosened so that he could brush his fingers along her jaw from his position behind, combing them into her hair and stroking her earlobe, gentle and sensual. Christine closed her eyes, reveling in his touch, allowing the pleasure to build inside her, simple and unhurried. Unlike the other times they'd been together, when he'd commanded and controlled her, she felt as though they were balanced, matched.

When he drew in his breath deeply, she felt his chest rise against her back, taking her with it, and she tipped her head, letting it fall against his shoulder. The hand that had been rubbing rhythmically over her nipple and sending jolts of desire into the pit of her stomach left its place and skimmed down over her belly to her mound, where she ached for him to touch her.

He combed his fingers through the wiry hair that grew there, teasing and lifting it, lightly tickling over her sensitive skin while he continued to play with the softer hair that grew on her head. Erik shifted behind her and she felt his mouth on her shoulder, warm and full, smoothing along the slope of her skin.

He released her neck, moving his hand to cover her other breast while he kissed her neck, and slid his fingers into the folds of her swollen labia. Christine sighed, and reached around behind her to feel the erection pushing through the front of his trousers. When she touched him through the fabric, he jerked, his breath snagging, and he pushed himself forward, into her palms, rubbing harshly against her hands.

Her pip was throbbing just as hard as his cock, and her wetness caused Erik's hand to move in and out with ease, sliding with soft slick sounds broken only by their tandem breathing. He rubbed her nipple, stroked her nib, sucked on her skin, drawing the pleasure from her so that the rhythm of her breathing surpassed his.

"Erik . . . ," she sighed, rolling her hips back against his cock, feeling his warm breath near her face.

He released her and, with both hands, stroked up from her hips over her breasts . . . pausing to cup and squeeze them . . . and then along her arms, capturing them in place over his cock behind her.

Then, suddenly, she felt something . . . odd in front. She opened her eyes. The harp was there. Somehow, in the turbulence of her pleasure-fogged mind, he'd inched her right up against it.

The instrument was taller than she was, its gilt neck curving as beautifully as a woman's body. The longest strings reached to her cheeks.

"Hold on to it," Erik commanded from behind. His voice was tight and sharp, yet barely audible.

Remembering her similar experience with the mirror, Christine felt a surge of lust as she reached out, one hand toward the tall, straight column, and the other stretching over to grasp the opposite end of the curving neck. Her arms were spread so far that her nipples brushed against the cold strings; then they shifted so that the taut nubbins slipped into spaces between them. The fit was snug and tight, with her nipples jutting between the wires.

"Spread your legs," Erik said, and she complied. Now she was juxtaposed over the front of the harp, her hands positioned at the top, her nipples imprisoned by the wires, and her feet positioned on the floor with the base of the harp between them.

Behind her, she heard the soft swish of movement, but when

she would have turned to look, he snapped, "Don't move." And suddenly, something dark went over her eyes. A blindfold.

"Erik!" She started to remove her hands from the harp, started to tell him he didn't need that anymore . . . but strong hands grabbed her wrists and held them in place.

"Don't move." He tied the blindfold, and a lock of her hair got caught up in the knot, pulling tightly. "And don't speak. Except . . . to beg."

Those last two syllables, hissed deep and low into her ear, sent a sharp pang of pleasure laced with trepidation jolting through her. Christine drew in her breath and her nipples slid up between the harp strings along with her rising chest. They tightened and grew harder at the strange sensation of the narrow openings lined with metal . . . and when she released her breath, letting her forehead rest against the smooth wood of the harp, her clamped nipples slid back down. And grew stiffer still.

Then she felt him . . . behind her. Warm and solid, pressing up against her again, tall and *jutting* . . . his hot, bare cock pushing into the curve of her bottom. His hands on her hips, his mouth—oh, please!—on her shoulder. She moved her forehead against the harp, and the blindfold jacked up enough so that she could see down to his legs lining hers, his feet, bare, long, brown, on either side of her narrow white ones partly obscured by the cuffs of his dark trousers.

But his cock . . . he grasped her hips, holding her, and slid his burning cock beneath the vee of her buttocks and through the juices of her sex, and she saw the red purple of its head just poking from beneath her bush. She felt him trembling behind her, holding her steady; his thighs pressed at an angle against her bare ones, his knees and ankles bumping against the outsides of her same joints. They were locked together . . . yet they were not.

He slid one hand across her belly to finger her sex, dip into her juices, and smooth them around her swollen labia . . . stroking, petting, teasing. Christine moaned and pressed back against him, then up and into his hand, trying to grind herself into an orgasm. But he moved his hand from her greedy pip, taking her wetness to rub it on the underside of his cock while he pushed the top of it through her pool. Its head peeked again beneath her dark curls, and Christine tried to jimmy her hips, to make it hit her nib just right . . . or—*mon Dieu!*—to slip inside her where she needed him.

But he was grasping her waist again, breathing hot and hard into the top of her head, rubbing his cock back and forth in the cradle of her quim, and then finally, he cried out . . . one long, low, agonized groan, and jammed his body against her so hard she slammed into the harp with a twang.

She saw the thick white spurt of his seed as it shot from beneath her lower lips, between the strings of the harp, and onto the wooden floor. Christine sagged against the instrument, aware of the lines marking her flesh, but unable to push away with his solid weight behind her.

Her pip throbbed, her quim burned, and her nipples ached, and she wanted her turn. Her arms were tired of holding on to the harp. . . .

His hands were on her again. He'd recovered, pulled away, and removed the warmth of his clothed body from her back. The sudden rush of cool air . . . and anticipation . . . made the fine hair on her back lift, and when he traced the sides of her body from breast to hip again, she shivered. Smiled into the wires with anticipation.

And then . . . nothing.

"Erik?" Her voice came out breathless and pleading.

"Are you begging? So soon?" he asked, his voice mild and mocking. "If you are not, then remain silent. And . . . let me fix this."

And the blindfold came back down over her eyes, then tightened at the back of her head. The pain of her hair caught in the knot distracted her momentarily from the pulsing between her legs.

She realized she could move her arms; why did she hold them up there?

But again he seemed to anticipate her. No sooner had she thought to move than something powerful gripped her left wrist. "Allow me."

He lowered her hand, smoothing it along the straight column of wood carved with some ornate design her fingers did not recognize, and positioned it at the level of her hips. Tied it there. Then he did the same with her right hand, attaching it to the harp on the other side.

"Why can I not touch you?" she cried, turning her face and grinding it into the wires, trying to loosen the blindfold. "Or see you? Why, Erik, why?"

"You really must be taught how to plead more prettily," he said, and she could hear that he had moved and was no longer behind her. "You must not want it badly enough. Perhaps I can be of some assistance."

Something brushed against her right arm, and then she heard the gentle tinkle of notes near her face . . . the brush of his fingers over one, then the other nipple as the music twanged to a dull halt.

"You are standing too close," he said, his voice deceptively gentle. "Step away so that the strings may still move . . . ah, yes." He leaned closer to her again; she could smell him, feel him, and the brush of air as he played a scale against her.

And this time, when the strings moved against her nipples, their touch was so bare that they kept their tone . . . and brushed against the front of the sensitive nubbins in a rough, scraping way.

Then, quick, questing fingers slipped up her thigh, between her labia, and scooped out her wetness, then slid back in and around in a quick tease over her thick outer lips, sending her hips thrashing and her forehead into the wires. The blindfold jarred loose again at the expense of the hair at the back of her neck, and she found that she could see more of the room.

He rubbed her wetness all over her nipples—"For lubrication," he murmured into her ear—and adjusted her blindfold; then she felt him return to his place at the harp.

Erik played in long strokes, plucking the strings in a sensual, rising melody that made her think of soft blues and violets. His fingers skimmed over the strings, brushing the underside of her breasts, and leaving the lines to score against her nipples in their wake. As he played, and she felt each note sink into her body, her nipples became more and more sensitive. Needy. The back of his hand occasionally brushed against the sensitive bush of hair at her sex, causing needles of awareness to zero in on her pip . . . so close, yet ignored.

It was incessant titillation, the teasing of her breasts in combination with his playing. . . . Lust built, and built, settling hot and throbbing between her legs, where her entire attention had become concentrated. Wetness trickled down the inside of her thigh, tickling and teasing her.

He played as though he would never stop, the tempo of the music rising to a great crescendo, and Christine became one with it, with his music. . . . Somewhere in the confusion of pleasure and discomfort and desire, she recognized his need and his intention to meld her and his other obsession into one sensual experience. One that brought her no relief, no peak . . . but one that pleased him. It pleased him to torture her this way, to see her want and need him. To see her become, literally, one with his work.

She did not know how long it went on, but at last the notes trickled away softly on the air, a lover giving a breathless sigh as the last vestiges of pleasure ebbed away.

Then he moved, silent and swift, and came to stand behind her again. She felt his deep, even breathing as he dipped his fingers into her warm wetness. Christine muffled a cry of hope and need, shifting and sliding her hips above his hand. When he knelt behind and spread her lips and licked her all around, with flat, slow strokes, she gripped the sides of the harp and lifted herself, trying to move . . . needing him to touch that throbbing nubbin that would send release pummeling through her.

But he would not let her; he teased with long, firm licks, designed for him to taste and for her to *need*.

"Erik, please . . . oh, please," she moaned, rubbing her damp face into the harp.

"Are you sorry for letting that boy touch you?" he asked, standing and pinching her nipples from behind. Pinch, tweak, pinch, twist, flick . . . they were tight, sensitive. Shudders of pleasure rippled through her torso.

"I am so sorry. . . . Please forgive me," she moaned hopefully.

"I should forgive you for letting another man place his hands on you? His mouth on you?" His hands landed heavily on her shoulders. Holding her there, biting into her skin.

"Erik . . . please . . ."

"Do you think I would forgive your betrayal that easily?" He jammed his fingers up into her hair, under the blindfold, and tightened them over the back of her scalp. Pushing her forehead into the wood, holding her there, he placed his mouth next to her ear. Warm breath moistened her skin. "I saw his hands on your breasts, Christine. I saw you moaning for him just as you moan for me." He jerked his wrist and her head rammed into the wood. "You touched him, Christine! You touched him and your hands are meant only for me, the Angel of Music. Do you not know that without me, you would be nothing?"

She was sobbing now; her desire still burned between her legs, but fear and frustration had taken the edge off. "I want to touch you, Erik! I want to touch *you* and see *you* and you won't allow it! At least I can see and touch Raoul! How can I be true to you if I cannot *have* you?" she wailed, her voice escalating.

Sudden pain screamed through the back of her head as he yanked the blindfold off. "You shall see me now, then, Christine. Your Angel of Music." Bitterness edged his words.

He came from behind her, angry, striding over to the violin so that she saw his long legs and smooth, powerful movements. Snatching it up, he turned back to face Christine, who was still drawn up over the harp like a set of strings. Integrated with the music that was his life.

Mounting the violin between his shoulder and the side of his face that was masked, he began to play, drawing the bow over the strings slowly at first. His lips parted slightly, wide and dark red, the top shadowing the bottom. His eyes closed, one disappearing into the shadowy mask and the other fringed with thick black lashes. Erik drew in several long, deep breaths as though using the rhythm to calm himself. The music from the violin cried and coaxed, wooed and wailed, and reminded Christine that the man before her was a genius. His long, tapered face settled into something that appeared to be both anguish and serenity, as if the moment was both painful and a culmination of some great desire.

His clothing still covered most of his tall, sleek body, but she saw that his shirt had come untied at the throat, baring a broad, dark-haired chest nearly to the waist. Her attention focused on that part of him, that part she'd never seen, never touched. His skin was golden brown, matching that of his face, as if he had been born with flesh a darker tone than that of most of the foppish men she knew. It made her want to touch him. . . . Saliva pooled in her mouth and moisture gathered between her legs as she thought of spanning her hands over that hard chest and feeling the crisp rough hair and the warmth of his skin. *Touching him.*

He looked up at that moment, snaring her gaze, and the desire and fury that mingled in his expression made her stomach twist and pinch. "Do you like it?" he asked, and at first she thought he meant his chest. "It is part of the opera I am writing."

"It's beautiful," she managed to reply. "Erik, I want to touch you. I have seen you, and now I want to touch you."

A pained smile twisted his lips. "I'm certain you do. But perhaps not quite as much as you wished to touch the immature *vicomte*, eh? I think . . ." Never taking his eyes from hers, he set the violin down and started toward her. "I think I should assist you further in discerning which male person you are more enthralled with. Which one you will yearn for, long after you have left his bed." The last words came out harsh and twisted, and Christine saw great fury lighting his eyes.

Oh, why had she ever kissed Raoul! Erik was the one she wanted . . . *needed.*

He faced her with the harp between them like the bars of a cage, still unwilling to shed all of his protection. Kneeling, he reached to flick his tongue over the strings and over the hint of nipple that brushed them from the other side. Christine moved closer, thrusting her breasts against the strings, anything to get nearer to that hot, delicious mouth. He drew one nipple into his lips, sucking it and half of her areola deeply into his mouth from between the harp strings . . . and she heard the faint, soprano tinkle of a melody next to her ear. The pads of his fingers brushed the strings as he fed on her nipple, rough and relentless, elongating what nature had created. It jolted teasingly from her body with the rhythm of his mouth. She gripped the edges of the harp with her hands and pushed against the strings, pleasure from her breast building and spreading to each of her fingers and down to her toes.

"Erik . . . ," she moaned, pushing her hips against the instrument. He found her swollen lips through the strings, and slid his fingers into her deep, wet folds . . . two, no, three . . . pushing up into her as he moved to suck her other breast.

Christine felt the need, the lust rising; the same finger pads that had played the harp strings tickled her, slid through and around her quim, and brushed past her pip, around it. . . . Her breathing came faster and she realized she was moving her hips, gyrating against the harp and his fingers, trying to get the pressure in the right place. . . .

And then he stopped. Her breasts pressed, wet, against the strings; moisture trickled down her thigh. She throbbed everywhere; she panted; she opened her eyes and found herself face-to-face with Erik. His eyes were so close; his mouth . . . she could feel the heat of his own rasping breath, huffing over her cheeks. The mask reared large and oblique on his face like an insurmountable wall.

"Erik . . . please . . . let me go. . . . Let me touch you . . . ," she begged. "You know you want me to."

"More than you know, Christine," he whispered. He drew in a deep, shuddering breath, closed his eyes. Then opened them again. They were blue, intense . . . rich, lapis lazuli blue, flecked with black and gray . . . one fringed with dark lashes and the other encircled by tooled leather. "I can't bear seeing you with another. You cannot do that to me . . . anymore. Do you understand?" He reached up both hands and grasped the curving neck of the harp as if he was suddenly exhausted and needed to hold himself up.

Or to brace himself for what was to come. His masked face tipped toward her.

"I understand. Erik . . . I understand." Her breath was shaky; her knees were trembling. Would he release her? Would she at last touch him?

From his side of the harp, he slid his hands along its curves, down the straight column and wavy neck, and over her fingers, grasping the wood. The tips of his fingers were rough over her delicate skin, smoothing over the tops of her hands. Suddenly, one was loosened, and her arm fell to its side. And then the other.

And then, just the harp was between them. The harp, the strings . . . his mask.

Erik stepped back from the instrument. Wariness glistened in his expression, yet his face was hard and angry.

Christine moved toward Erik as she would approach a skittish cat . . . slowly and easily, even though her body screamed for her to tear into him. The inner parts of her wet thighs slipped against each other as she stepped, and the pressure on the heat of her sex made it throb even more.

Erik stood straight, his arms hanging uselessly to his waist as though he could not fathom what to do with them. When she came close enough, she reached out and grasped his large, elegant hands, one in each of her small white ones. They trembled and were warm, and she smelled herself on them.

Moving her hands up along his arms, she traced through his shirt the easy curve of solid muscle from his forearms up to rounded biceps, and over square-angled shoulders. And then . . . at last . . . hot, moist skin at the open throat of his shirt. His heart thudded under her hands; his chest rose and fell, hitching at the beginning of each deep breath. She pulled the shirt apart, touching everywhere . . . *mon Dieu,* everywhere, and still she wanted more . . . the hard, tiny nipples, the smooth, firm pectorals, the soft curling hair.

Erik's skin flinched under her hands, trembling as she passed over his belly, yanking the shirt apart and sending buttons bouncing to the floor. His breath came faster and shallower, and at last his hands moved, resting on her shoulders as if they needed to be propped up.

Christine pulled his trousers apart, sending them to the floor in a crumple at his bare feet, and at last beheld his gorgeous, straining cock. Magnificent and powerful, it jutted toward her in a gentle curve of flesh straining purple and red and golden brown.

She grabbed him with both hands, and he cried out. When she stroked him only twice, he pulsed and came, pouring over her hands, his fingers gripping her shoulders.

"Erik," she sobbed, pressing her body along the length of his, her face in his hot shoulder, her arms around his waist, pulling his hips and still-hard cock against her belly. Their bodies were steamy and slick with moisture, his, hers, sweat, tears. The throbbing between her legs was unbearable, painful and huge. "Please, Erik . . . please . . . now."

He lifted her into his arms, and carried her from the music room, the unmasked side of his face toward her. Several long strides later, and they were in another room, and he fell onto a large bed with her.

His hands were everywhere, his mouth too . . . her breasts, her shoulder, the side of her neck, her belly. . . .

"Erik!" she panted, pulling him toward her, on top of her. Her fingers closed around his erection, still long and hard, hot and full, bringing it closer to her crying sex. Settling back on his mighty thighs, propping himself up with one golden arm, he grasped his cock at its base and teased her with its head.

Tracing the lips of her tender, swollen labia, sliding into the folds between them, the head slipped easily through the slick pool. At last, Christine could wait no longer. She reached for it, closing her fingers around Erik's thick cock, and lifted her hips in frustration.

But he pulled back, his strength easily greater than hers. "No," he said, moving her hands away. Before she could protest, he skimmed away, down her legs, and planted his big hands on the insides of her thighs, holding them so wide apart that her knees touched the bed.

Her sex was wide open, and her entire being was centered there, in that throbbing, hot, wet place. Erik's fingers were gentle but firm, holding her still as he bent to her quim.

When his tongue came out, he brought it quickly up from the bottom of her vagina, slipping into the narrow crevice and ending in the space just below her pip. He paused, jiggling under it, and Christine screamed in pleasure and impatience when at last the point of his tongue flickered right over the hard, protruding nubbin.

"*Mon Dieu,*" she moaned, thrashing her head from side to side over the bed. "Erik! *Please!*" she panted, her hips trying to move, but held firmly in place by his hands on her thighs.

He teased her again, and again, his tongue pointed, then flat, then swirling through the juices and swollen lips of her sex. Flicking over her nib, into the deep crevice where she wanted his cock . . . but he never, *never* licked her in a rhythm that would give relief.

It burned and stung and pulsed and she cried and thrashed and trembled. "Erik, I beg you. . . . I beg you. . . ." Over and over and over again . . .

He pulled away, and looked up at her. His hands remained heavy on her thighs. Dark blue eyes bored into her own, flat and harsh. "How do you feel, Christine?"

She could barely catch her breath. "I . . . want you . . . to . . . let me . . . come."

"How does it feel?"

"It . . . hurts. It . . . please, Erik . . . please . . ." She struggled throw off his hold, but he was much too strong, even when she tried to pull his hands away by gripping his wrists with her fingers.

"I know it hurts. I meant that it should. Christine, you have only experienced a sliver of my pain. The pain of seeing you, and wanting you . . . and seeing you with him, touching him . . . baring your breasts for him." His voice was angry, shaking with fury. "Do you understand now?"

She was crying in earnest, the pain in his eyes as forceful as the grip on her thighs, and the screaming need between her legs. "Yes . . . ," she sobbed. "I will never . . . again . . . only . . . you . . . Erik."

He released her, and she braced herself for the deep, long slide of his cock into her . . . but felt nothing but chill.

He stood, pulled away from the bed, and started out of the room.

"Erik!" She scrambled off, after him, her hands grabbing at him. "Erik!"

He turned and she saw an awful, deep need in his eyes. So deep and buried that it nearly sent her scuttling away from its power . . . but she reached for him. "Erik," she said more calmly. "I need you. Please . . . let us become the one we are meant to be."

Everything happened so quickly and roughly after that. . . . Strong hands gripped her arms, propelled her back. She fell on the feather mattress, and felt his heavy weight on her . . . welcome, *mon Dieu*! Nothing had ever been so welcome as his heavy, solid, driving body on top of hers.

He matched her, length to length, toe to toe, shoulder to

shoulder . . . hip to hip. Her legs were wrenched blessedly apart and—*mon Dieu, mon Dieu!*—his long, strong cock slid at last into the beckoning place, filling her. Filling and satisfying her . . . at last . . . at last . . .

Christine had never felt such exquisite pleasure. He slid himself in, became one with her as promised . . . full, hard, long . . . stroke after stroke. . . . Deep pleasure burned, coiled, rose, blossomed, and she screamed, thrashed, bucked, moved with him, as she cried and sobbed her release. Nothing . . . *nothing* had ever been so draining . . . so complete. . . .

They rolled together . . . wet . . . hot . . . shuddering.

"Erik . . . ," she breathed, drawing deep the release, the reverberations of the last vestiges of pleasure as they swept over her, in wave after wave, after wave. "I love you. Never leave me."

"Christine . . ." His tears burned salty and wet into the curve of her neck. His mask was heavy and sticky on her shoulder. "You are mine. You are my music . . . my muse. I will always be yours. Never betray me."

"Never, Erik. Never."

Christine awoke alone.

When she opened her eyes, it took her a moment to remember . . . and then she did. Erik. Strong, golden, passionate. Her angel.

Her body was sore, exhausted, and wholly aware of every one of its nerve endings. She rolled over, taking the heavy feather-stuffed quilt with her in a safe cocoon, and looked around the room.

It was dark. Only one low lamp burned. But the shadows it cast were not evil or threatening; rather the room felt safe and sensual. Red and black brocade hangings covered the walls, hung from the ceiling-high bedposts. A fire blazed in the hearth. One wall was painted with large, splashy murals of dancers in the most erotic of poses.

And music. She heard Erik playing a piano in some distant room, its chords crashing and thundering in a rise of emotion.

Christine sat up and pushed her hair behind her shoulders, thinking about the dangerous, reclusive man who was her lover. He had never removed his mask, through their whole night of passion. Once, she'd reached for it, just to touch it, and he'd wrenched her arm away, furious.

"Never touch this," he told her fiercely, his eyes dark and stormy. *"Never."*

Even now, she felt the cold anger that had poisoned him. How horrible had his life been? What did the mask hide? Scars? What could be so terrible that he had to hide beneath a face fitted of leather?

He need have no secrets from her . . . not after the way they had been last night. Languid, she stretched her arms and realized she had never felt so settled and happy since her father had died. Her Angel of Music had turned out to be more than a muse, more than a tutor.

He was her love.

NINE

Dieu, he loved the way the sleek handle fitted in his hand. The wood had been shaped into a curve that matched his palm perfectly, allowing him to hold it with ease. The feel of it alone was enough to swell his cock.

Hefting it in his left hand, he traced the long, wicked braid that trailed from the handle. The gentle bumps of black leather made a tail no bigger around than his thumb at its widest. It was smooth and supple, ending six feet later in a narrow, slender point with a tiny, hard knot. A tiny knot, just like the little nubbin of a throbbing pip.

A knot that raised the most beautiful of welts.

And elicited the most agonized of screams.

The most desperate of pleadings.

And the most volatile of orgasms.

Thwack!

Philippe cracked the whip, snapping it in the air just behind

Delia's ear, and watched in abject pleasure as she jerked and trembled, pulling at the manacles that held her wrists above her head.

She was already sobbing, and he hadn't even touched her yet.

"Now, my dear countess," he said in his low, rolling voice as his trousers tightened over his swelling cock, "I want you to show me how much you love the taste of my leather. It had better be loud . . . and it had better be real."

Delia, his wife and quite honestly the best he'd ever fucked, which was the only reason he'd deigned to make her his countess, panted and gasped her intention to comply.

Her pale ass rounded plumply over the smooth wooden pole that she half straddled, half hung from. The pole was built for such a purpose, set at a forty-five-degree angle from floor to ceiling. She had clambered up as far as she could go, holding on with her hands and wrapping her legs around it, all the while attempting to dodge the flick of his whip whilst retaining her balance.

When she had climbed as high as she could, Philippe had reached up to stretch her hands along the length of the pole, manacling her to chains that hung from the ceiling. Then he'd pulled her higher. Next, he strapped her knees together beneath the pole, and her ankles above it, leaving her precariously balanced with her ass and juicy pink quim lifted and wide open to his view.

And what a lovely view it was.

Crack!

He flicked the leather thong in the air behind her, and she startled, whimpering. The red lips of her pussy trembled and shivered as she tried to maintain her balance.

She dared not fall, for she knew the penalty if she did.

Crack! Thwack!

This time, the nubbin end of the whip snapped at her buttocks and Delia jerked and cried out.

But not loud enough. Not nearly loud enough.

Philippe stepped closer and sent the leather raining down on her, once, twice, thrice . . . laying pink welts over her buttocks, and one over the backs of her legs. He knew exactly how to wield the leather tail without drawing blood. Pain, yes, of course . . . but no permanent marks. Nothing that would make her unable to perform her duties.

Her sobs were muffled as she tried to contain them. "Did you like that, my dear Delia?" His cock pounded in its confines; he slipped his hand down and loosened his trousers.

"Yes . . . yes." Her words came out in little sobbing gasps.

His cock free, Philippe slid the length of the leather braid between his fingers, all the way to the narrowest part, and toyed with the little knotted nub at the end. Looking over at the sleek black rack on the wall, he considered exchanging this whip for one with six little nibs at the end . . . but decided not to. There was something ironically lovely about flaying a woman with a pip-ended whip.

"I can't hear you, my dear," he growled, twitching the whip and sending the barest brush of it over her ass.

"Please, Philippe, please . . . ," she cried louder.

When he reached forward to touch her with his finger, she started and tensed. He slid his middle finger down from her tight little anus to the full, hot lips of her labia, massaging in deft circular motions through her juices, then brought them back up and around her puckered rear opening. Then back down to the little throbbing pip, where he fingered it just as he had the end of his whip.

Delia squirmed and sighed, her breathing speeding and little beads of moisture forming over her upper lip and sheening on her back. "Please, please, please, please . . . ," she whispered over and over, lifting her hips as high as her trembling thighs would allow, giving him better access.

Then, without warning, he removed his hand and flicked the

whip in one smooth motion, replacing pleasure with pain, and he heard the soft, wet *thwack* of the leather meet her drenched lips.

She arched up, raising her head in a vain bid to pull her arms free, as her hips pushed down to the pole as if to protect her pussy, and cried out louder than ever.

"Very good, Delia, very good," Philippe told her, stepping back to get a good, wide sweep. "Now, let's hear it some more."

And he raised his arm and let the whip fly.

It branded her back, and he sent it cracking through the air and smacking against her skin, more and more, until she was thrashing on the pole. Her hips rose and fell with each blow; her arms jerked and shook, trembling and stretched above her head. Her face, turned toward him, was tear-streaked and wide-eyed. Blond hair fell in one long swath over her neck and one shoulder, shimmering like a curtain with her every movement.

He dropped the whip and seized her hips, straddling the pole behind her, and slammed his engorged cock into her juicy, swollen sex. Delia gasped and shuddered, her flesh trembling beneath his hands.

Bending forward, he reached down around and covered her two dangling breasts, one with each hand, lifting, lowering, squeezing and pinching. Her hips began to move under him, and the pleasure built painfully in his cock. Twisting her hard nipples, he plucked at them as he rammed her full, in and out, thrust after thrust.

She groaned and cried and twitched in agitation beneath him; he could feel her rising to the peak and just before she tipped over, he pulled out, jerking his hot spew all over her ass, and the gentle curves above it. He spewed and shuddered, his eyes rolling back in his head for a moment as he savored the release.

Delia whimpered, continuing to move in a vain attempt to bring herself to orgasm, and Philippe climbed off her rocking body.

He picked up the whip and brought it down over her left buttock, the puddle of come splattering under its force and flying through the air. She shrieked and bucked harder.

"You . . . did . . . not . . . please . . . me." He marked each syllable with the flay of the whip, and Delia struggled under the slicing leather. And when he saw that she was trying to grind her throbbing nubbin onto the pole in search of some relief, he laughed and changed the angle of the whip.

One smack across her labia and she was lifting those juicy hips again, and left off trying to cheat herself into orgasm.

Three more thwacks and he let the whip fall to his side so he could observe. And enjoy the moment.

Delia lay panting on the pole, her bum pink and red with welts, juice from her pussy smeared all over her swollen lips, and his spew shining over her skin.

"See?" he said, turning away from his wife and toward the peephole in the wall. He opened the hidden latch and drew the door open. "I have often spoken of the pleasures of marriage . . . and now you have seen for yourself what mastery you might obtain."

Raoul stepped into the room, his attention focused quite appropriately on the sweating, straining, submissive Delia. "Yes, I see."

"Do not be so hesitant, brother," Philippe snapped. "She is eager for you. Help yourself."

Raoul walked toward his brother's wife, unfastening the buttons of his trousers as he went. Philippe watched as the healthy young cock, thicker and longer than his own, was released.

It was not the size but how it was wielded, Philippe knew. Thus, he did not feel the slightest bit of envy when Raoul slipped it slowly inside that lovely sex. He watched his brother's buttocks tighten and flex as he stroked and thrust, slick with the sounds of her juices, as his rhythm became faster and more urgent.

At last, when he gave a harsh, guttural sigh with one last thrust, Raoul slumped forward over Delia's beautiful hips as she shuddered and came beneath him, crying out in relief.

Philippe, his own cock throbbing again, yanked his brother away and took his place, filling his wife with his member and reminding her who was master. He pinched her nipples, reached around, and tweaked her pip, and rammed into her a mere three times before ejaculating.

When he pulled away, breathing calmly and rebuttoning his trousers, he turned to look at Raoul. "When you have the Daaé wench, she will make a nice addition to our escapades, will she not?"

Raoul was fastidiously wiping the wetness from his still-hard cock. He looked up at Philippe, shock blossoming over his face. "I—I do not want Christine to be like this."

Philippe laughed in delight at his brother's ingenuousness. "Of course you do. Your cock was hard as a pike when you saw the way Delia was whipped. Can you not imagine the two of them together: one dark, one light? It would be most enjoyable—for all of us."

Most enjoyable indeed.

Months ago, when Erik had first called to her, Christine thought that the disembodied voice was her father's, for whose else would it be? He'd promised to send her the Angel of Music, and since he was in heaven, it had to be him.

When she heard her name that first day, kneeling in the small chapel tucked in the corner of the Opera House, at first she didn't know how to respond.

"Christine . . ."

At last she answered. "Who is it?" Her voice quavered, but she wasn't frightened, not really. It was just . . . strange.

"It is your angel. . . ."

"My angel? Papa?"

"Your Angel of Music . . . did your papa not promise he would send him?"

Her heart beat faster and she felt a rush of joy. Her father had not forgotten her! She had waited for years, but he had finally answered her prayers. "Papa!" she said. "I have missed you so."

There was a long silence, so long that she feared she'd frightened him away. Christine felt as though the air crackled with her nervousness. . . . Could she have driven him off? At last, after being alone for so long, was her chance at comfort gone so quickly?

Then, finally, when she felt as though she'd held her breath for hours, the voice spoke again. "I am not your father, Christine. But I am the *Ange de Musique*. And I wish to help you feel again."

"To feel again." She repeated the words dumbly, considering what they meant.

"You miss your music, do you not? You feel lonely, different from the other girls, yes?"

She nodded, and then realized he might not be able to see her. "Yes, angel, I have found little joy in my music since Papa died. Do you . . . speak to him?"

"I do not speak to him, Christine, but I know that he misses you as much as you miss him." The voice was so smooth and calm, lulling, and yet titillating. Elegant. Beautiful. Sensual. It made the hair on the back of her neck and arms lift, and something in the middle of her stomach tingle. "I would like to be your tutor. Would you like that? Would you like to feel your music again?"

"You would help me?"

And so it had begun.

The Angel of Music would come to her at least once a day, at a time when she was alone, and he would sing to her, and with her, and play for her. Christine looked forward to those times, and because she was never certain where or when he would come to her, she was often in a state of expectancy and happiness.

In time, her lessons about music would become more than just lessons. Yes, he had high expectations and he drove her toward perfection, but as the weeks went on, the disembodied voice seemed to relax. He allowed himself to speak of things other than notes and breathing and timing.

Christine found herself becoming more comfortable with her mysterious tutor, and the strange way in which he taught her as well. Perhaps it was because she couldn't see him that she felt better able to talk of things deep inside her, of her opinions and dreams. It was almost like praying, or like daydreaming, this speaking into a room where there was no one's face to frown at her, no stiffening of a body to disapprove.

One day Christine remembered in particular. She had had a horrible day—it started when her very last pair of wearable stockings got a huge ladder along the outside of one leg; it was so wide and long that it could not be hidden, nor twisted around to the back of her leg, for then the two ladders on the other side would show.

Because of that, she was late for dance practice, and had to endure what the ballet girls called Madame Giry's "hairy eyeball" glare along with her silent treatment as Christine attempted to catch up on what she'd missed.

After that, in an effort to return to the dormitories to beg or borrow another pair of stockings, Christine had hurried along the backstage hall and came face to face with La Carlotta. The diva was wearing a monstrously tall hat, a nest of birds and butterflies and flowers, and the panniers of her impossibly wide gown that put her in the fashion of Marie Antoinette blocked the narrow passageway so that no one could walk by.

Christine curtsied and tried to brace herself against the rough wooden wall to allow the other woman to move past, but Carlotta was not to be hurried. In fact, she moseyed along, chatting with a wide-eyed composer, until she came just to where Christine stood . . . and she stopped.

Turning her back to Christine, Carlotta cooed and flirted and practiced a few soprano trills at the top of her powerful lungs, whilst Christine remained pinned between the wire-shaped gown and the wall. There was no way for her to get past without brushing roughly against Carlotta's gown, and she did not dare attempt that.

At last, Carlotta seemed to notice her. She turned, the pannier of her skirt bumping into Christine, and focused an angry look on her. Despite the fact that she was not a bit taller than the younger girl, the combination of her outraged expression and her towering hat made her seem gigantic.

"What you are doing, listening to my private conversations, little rat?"

"I was—I was merely trying to pass by," Christine stammered, trying once again to slink past the obnoxious wire-framed skirt.

Carlotta thrust her face into Christine's, her rouge- and powder-scented face, and rose-scented breath, overwhelming her. "Get out of my sight, you little rat! And you mind your own business!" The diva's Spanish-flavored *r* sounds rolled and spit in Christine's face. "You do not have any business with me!"

Christine fled. As she pushed her way down the hall, she heard the continued outrage from La Carlotta as she waxed angrily to the composer, and anyone who would listen, about "little rats who do not know their place" and other annoyances, at the top of her very capable lungs.

As she scuttled down the passageway, trying to hold back tears, Christine heard giggles and whispered comments and some outright laughter. Instead of going back to her dormitory room, she turned blindly down the corridor that led to the small grotto used as a chapel. The place she prayed for her father's soul, and the place where her *ange* had first spoken to her.

There, the tears of frustration and humiliation came, soaking the sleeve of her ratty practice costume, and dripping down onto the flimsy, floppy skirt in her lap.

She had not been there long when she heard his welcome voice. "Christine . . ."

"Angel," she replied tearfully. Wiping her face and swallowing her tears, she looked up and round in the small cavelike chapel, lit only by seven candles in small alcoves in the wall.

"Do not trouble yourself with her, Christine," he told her. "She is an undeserving woman, and she will get her own recompense."

"I did nothing wrong," Christine replied, sniffling. "She is a horrid cat."

He chuckled, the tones of his laugh vibrant and warm. She felt better already. "A cat? You are not fond of felines, then, to put them in the same category as La Carlotta."

"No, I do not like cats. They are sly and arrogant and barely deign to acknowledge one's existence. And when they do, it is as if they are showing you great favor."

She could still hear the humor in his voice when he replied, "Did you have a cat when you were younger, then, Christine? One that did not allow you to pet her?"

"How did you know that?" Her tears had dried.

"It was merely a guess. . . . For you to have such strong feelings about such an innocuous beast, I suspected as much. For what happens in our youth most often molds our maturity." A trace of sadness hung in his voice now.

"Yes, when I was eight, Papa and I lived in Prague for nearly a year. The mistress of our boardinghouse had a cat and she would not ever come to sit in my lap. I chased her and crawled under the furniture after her, dragging her out. She would scratch me when I held her. Then when I cried, she would run away again. She had such dark, soft fur. I wanted to hold her so badly."

"Poor Christine," the angel replied. "You needed to have something to hold, to comfort you."

"Yes . . . I was very lonely."

There was a silence, a hesitant pause before he spoke again. "And now . . . you are lonely still?"

"Not so much," she replied honestly. "I have . . . you."

"Is that why you came here when you were upset?"

"I hoped you would come to me here, *ange*, for this is the place you have come to me most often. And you make me feel . . . less lonely."

"I am glad, Christine. I am glad."

That day seemed to have been a turning point in their relationship. After that, her angel would remark about something that Carlotta, or one of the other dancers, had done that day, and they would laugh or talk about it. He even teased her about her dislike of cats, beasts that he admitted to finding quite intriguing.

He still remained a disembodied voice, and he still made her practice hard, and did not accept excuses. His presence always sent little snaking shivers down her neck and spine, and his voice still raged or soothed . . . but she felt as though he'd begun to reveal more of himself to her. He seemed to know everything about her; she was grateful for any drop of knowledge revealed about him.

Christine realized now, as she lazed in the massive bed positioned in Erik's bedchamber, that those months of sharing their music and conversation had been the stepping-stones to what she felt now. Not just a physical relationship, but a deep, abiding connection that transcended what his hands and lips did to her, that made her feel more than a passion . . . that made her feel as if she knew him, understood him. As if he was the most important thing in her life.

She realized that she'd found what the beautiful woman she'd admired must have had: love and happiness, and no loneliness. But she wasn't wearing a beautiful gown. And she wasn't standing onstage in front of a roaring audience, bathed in the limelight.

She was underground, in the darkness, with her *ange*. And she loved him.

Over the next week, Christine and Erik lived together in his small house by the underground lake, like any other man and woman in love. Erik worked on *Don Juan Triumphant*, the opera he had been composing in stretches for years, and Christine sang when he asked her to.

She loved to look at his writing, the pages of melodic composition: scrawled black notes, in oblong shapes as if they'd been dashed on the paper with little thought. Barely legible lyrics, scratched on the large foolscap, lined up under the notes. He wrote in pulses: frenzied jotting and scratching, and then slow, arrogant, and easy printing.

They laughed and talked and ate; she cooked and washed and cleaned. She learned that, along with his arrogance and mysterious demeanor, Erik had a dry wit and a range of strong opinions on everything from women's fashion to the management of the Opera House. He was well-read and a brilliant engineer who had created a luxurious, if cloistered, living space for himself.

As the week went by, Christine's life at the Opera House was pushed away into the deepest corner of her mind. It became like the memory of a completely different life—competitive, crowded, loud, and superficial. The life embodied by the beautiful lady.

A life to which she was not eager to return.

The only mar on her days was the black mask that Erik refused to remove. She did not know if he even took it off when he slept, for he disappeared after they made love and returned before Christine awoke in the morning.

She did not understand it. She had seen every other part of his body, and it was as perfect as a man's figure could be. Long and lean, muscular without being bulky, golden, and dusted with the right amount of rich black hair in just the right places. What could be so terrible on such a model of perfection that he had to hide it from her?

The one time she attempted to raise the subject, Erik responded with such deep, cold anger and stormed out of the room in such a violent manner that Christine became even more confused and curious. "You can never understand," he snarled, and then locked himself in the music room for the rest of the day and night.

The rabid scratching of his pen over paper followed by discordant clashes and mournful chords came from the room well into the night, and continued when Christine awoke the next day.

Yet, she would not forget it. She could not bear to have something as simple as a tooled piece of leather between them.

And so, when, on the seventh day after he had brought her there, she awoke early in the morning and found him dozing on a chaise in the music room, she knew she at last had the opportunity. Her plan was to carefully lift the mask to see what was beneath, and to show him that it had no effect on her feelings for him. Surely, once the mask was removed and he saw that she still loved him, any annoyance he might harbor would dissolve.

She knew how to turn his attention to more pleasurable things.

Christine approached him quietly, noticing as she always did the way the broad sprinkling of hair dusted his square, molded chest, and trailed into a slender line into his trousers. The column of his neck, wide and long, curved above his throat's tender hollow . . . one area on his sleek body that was as vulnerable as her own.

She reached, lifted the mask, and pulled it off quickly and smoothly.

What she saw was horrible—*horrible!*—and she screamed as his eyes flew open and he launched himself off the chaise.

"Damn you, Christine! Damn you!" he cried, covering his horrid, disfigured face, scrabbling for the mask that still dangled from her fingers as she stared in terrified shock. *"How could you?"* he shouted, snatching at the mask and jamming it back on his face, grabbing her arm and throwing her to the chaise.

She stumbled, fell, crying as he raged and shouted, shoving papers off the piano, sending them cascading over the floor. He was crying, shaking, clutching at his middle as though he'd taken a bullet there, even as he shouted obscenities at her, his eyes wild and wide, his mouth curled in an irate red twist.

"Damn you!" he cried over and over. *"Damn . . . you . . . Christine."*

He collapsed on the floor with great, jerking sobs that came from somewhere so deep they were nearly inaudible. But his entire folded body wrenched with each ruptured breath, and when he raised his flat blue eyes to stare at her at last, Christine knew she'd done the unforgivable.

TEN

Christine Daaé had disappeared more than seven days earlier and Maude knew Erik had taken her to where he might introduce her to more . . . personal tutelage. She smiled at the thought of the pleasure Christine was to receive from Erik's strong body.

Since then, Carlotta had returned to grace the stage with her impossibly high, trilling arias, and the Opera House managers jumped at every shadow or every loud noise.

Maude felt it was her duty to find ways to help alleviate their tension.

She'd been anticipating her own pleasure when she finally got Monsieur Firmin Richard alone and at her mercy, but the moment never seemed to materialize. The man was always surrounded by people—stage managers, singers, dancers, musicians, even patrons. Maude had no choice but to take drastic measures.

It was the seventh night after Christine had disappeared, and the production of *Faust* was in full swell, with music filling the chamber and the dancers swirling about the stage. The Opera House was crowded to bursting—whether it was due to curiosity about the Opera Ghost and his abduction of the ingenuous singer, or desire to see the performance, no one was certain.

Maude wondered if anyone other than Carlotta had realized that, along with Christine's disappearance, the Opera Ghost seemed to have gone away as well.

She stood in the shadows of the backstage area, between two of the five black curtains that hung parallel to one another on each side of the stage, from the front to the back wall. Each curtain was wider than the one in front of it, giving the stage a triangular appearance and affording various passageways where the cast might exit or enter from the performance area.

Beyond the black curtains, off to the side of the stage and beyond the sight of the audience, were the props and scenery from the production. And standing just in front of the large papier-mâché and wood construction that represented Hell was Maude's target.

Firmin Richard was tall and lean, with an equine face, long fingers, narrow wrists, a long bony nose, large, narrow feet . . . and the promise that this tendency would be repeated elsewhere. Maude's quim moistened at the mere thought of what his trousers must hide.

She worked her way between the curtains until she stood in the shadows behind Richard. His attention was focused on the performers, and he stood with his hands clasped at the back of his waist, his elegant foot tapping in off time with the music.

Maude moved closer to him, hiding in the folds of the black curtain carefully so that it wouldn't move and attract the attention of the audience, and so that she could remain out of his sight for the moment. She wanted the element of surprise on her side. Thus, stepping just behind him, she walked right into his clasped hands, aiming her opening right where his fingers twiddled.

When her crotch brushed up against Richard, he fairly jumped forward, and would have blundered into the craggy Hell scenery if she had not grabbed his coattails.

"Now, now, Firmin, you know you have been waiting for this for many weeks," she whispered boldly into his ear, holding him in place, back against her. She tipped her hips toward his ass and felt, to her satisfaction, his fingers take up twiddling again just where she needed it the most. Despite the fact that the little twitching motions were on the other side of three layers of fabric, Maude's nib lifted and stretched there as she pressed forward.

"Now, let us see what you have here . . . ," she murmured into his ear, and slid her hands from behind under his coattails and jacket, and into the front trouser pockets. To her delight, the right one had a hole in it, and it was no large task to force her fingers through the fraying seam and onto the warm, hairy flesh of his thigh.

Richard jumped again when she touched him, and craned his long neck to see behind him. Maude pressed her breasts into his back and slid her hand through the opening of his drawers and found what she was looking for.

Oui, tout à fait!

She smiled, and smiled more as her fingers closed around his slender, pulsing length . . . and slid longer, and longer, and . . . *mon Dieu*, longer!

"*Oui*," she murmured, tears of joy springing to her eyes as her sex throbbed. "*Oui!*"

No one could see Maude and Firmin. Hell stood between them and the audience, and the performers were all in front of the massive set structure.

She slipped around to the front of him, already beginning to unfasten the buttons of her staid black gown. Firmin tried to resist, but no sooner had she opened the high collar and exposed her generous, red-tipped breasts than he was reaching for them.

Those long, elegant fingers closed, one over each breast, and hefted them, thumbs rippling over the pointed nipples. Maude, still smiling, unfastened his trousers and released the longest cock she had *ever* seen. *Mon Dieu*, if it were not pulsing and stretching so straight out, it would hang to his knees!

Liquid flooded her lower lips as she thought about the long, smooth strokes she would get from him. Pulling him toward her, she toppled back onto the orange and red mountains of Hell, and leveraged him off-balance on top of her.

Firmin did not seem to mind that she was in control; he appeared to be as enthralled by the size of her breasts as she was with the length of his cock. He did not wait to be directed; as the music swelled around them, camouflaging Maude's groan of satisfaction, he closed his mouth over one thrusting nipple. Making little circles around it, over the tight, hard wrinkles of her areola, his tongue flicked and twitched against her nubbin. Long-anticipated pleasure washed over her, flowing straight to her belly and then her pip below.

"Ah," she sighed gratefully, allowing her head to tip back onto the papier-mâché ledge behind her. She had not released his cock, and as he continued to suck and lick at her nipples, she felt his member grow harder and longer . . . and *longer* still!

The air around them was cool on her wet nipples, stirred by the activity onstage only *mètres* away. The dancing and the raising and lowering of scenery backdrops sent little gusts of breeze over her flesh, raising every hair and heightening the sensation of his hot mouth.

Her skirts flipped up over her open bodice, sending yet another puff of wind over her heated skin, and Maude felt the relief
of fresh air on her thighs. Firmin was wasting no time, nor did
he fumble with her skirts and crinolines. . . . She closed her eyes
in satisfaction. A man with a wand like that surely knew how to
wield it.

But then, as she felt his warm hands spreading the opening in
her drawers, Maude recognized the music changing around them
and realized . . .

"Non!" she hissed, flipping her skirts back down and grabbing his bony wrist. From his position on his knees, he jerked
away and tipped backward, and would have landed on his ass if
she had not had hold of him. His long reddish cock protruded
quite deliciously from the opening in his drawers, and Maude
had only a bare second to admire its beauty before she pulled
him to his feet.

But it was too late. The scenery on which they had been climbing had already begun to move and in moments, they would be
exposed in all of their disheveled glory, not only to the backstage
runners and waiting dancers, but to the audience as well.

Act II had come and, with it, Faust's descent to Hell.

There was nowhere to go but with him.

Maude and Firmin had the realization at the same time, and
they both scrambled into the back side of the massive structure as
it rolled out from behind the curtains, and slipped into the small
opening at the rear.

When they tumbled inside, Maude landed on top of Firmin.
Under the irregular papier-mâché mountains, it smelled like saw-
dust and paint, and the stage lights blaring through the red and
orange made the interior warm and glowing.

Before she had the chance to react, Firmin slipped out from

under her in the cramped, jutting space, and sidled up behind her. Maude cooperated and raised herself up on her hands and knees, feeling the gentle rumble of the scenery's wheels moving beneath them as it—and they—were hauled to the middle of the stage.

Excitement built in her at the thought of potential discovery. To have the manager of the Opera House, and the proper ballet mistress, copulating inside the scenery just as Faust was experiencing the bowels of Hell . . . how delicious and erotic it would be! Perhaps their groans and moans would be faintly heard by some of the players . . . and the audience . . . and no one would know from whence they came! Her breaths were coming faster now, and she became impatient, ready for that long cock to draw pleasure from her, there in the midst of the performance.

From behind, Maude's skirt lifted, her drawers were yanked down, and her ass was bare and waiting. She wriggled it impatiently before she felt the round tip of his cock knocking at the door. Arching her belly toward the floor, raising her hips and shoulders, Maude waited for that long, sweet length to slip inside.

She was not disappointed; in, and in, and *in* . . . she closed her eyes in deep pleasure as he pushed in as far as he could go . . . and then more. Her labia swelled, closing around him, sucking him into her hot depths.

He pushed up, right up against the inner hub of pleasure, the spot deep inside that never got enough attention. His hands grasped her hips, yet she could not feel his thighs against hers. . . . She reached back to tickle his ballocks and realized he *still had more to go*! He was so long that he could not fit his entire length inside her!

At that realization, Maude came. The orgasm shuddered through her, and she gasped in surprise. The crescendo of music swallowed her reaction, which turned into a long, low moan as he began to stroke inside her before she'd finished convulsing around him.

He reached for her breasts with difficulty, as his cock was so long and rigid that it was difficult for them to get too close. Pinching at her nipples, plucking them, he raised her shoulders so that she knelt upright in front of him, her head nearly brushing one of the wooden beams above.

His breath was hot in her ear as he muttered, "I'll fuck you hard, Madame Giry. You're going to take my whole cock inside if I have to jam it up into your throat." He slammed into her and she nearly lost her balance, one hand coming out in front of her, to catch on the wooden frame.

"You have the longest cock I have ever seen," she replied, turning her head so that her words would go back to him. "You can slam that wand inside me anytime you wish."

"I'm going to tear you apart with my long, hard cock," he told her, pumping faster, grasping her nipples harder. "I'm going to tear your quim apart, I'm going to fuck you so hard. You've never had it like this before. You're going to beg me for more."

Pleasure-pain circled through her at his nasty, biting words. Maude's breath came faster and she tipped her head back. "Fuck me, Firmin. You're the manager. Fuck me. Tear my quim. Rip it up. Make me *come*."

"I'm gonna fuck you until you cry for mercy. I don't care if the whole Opera House hears you. And then I'm going to fuck you up the ass."

Pleasure blossomed suddenly and she moved her hips in time, back and forth, pressing against the wall in front of her. "Harder, Firmin. Fuck me harder! Work . . . harder!" She came again, her nipples tightening to the point of pain, pinched nearly flat by his fingers, and her sex trembling and weeping.

"Good. Now, on your back," Firmin said, pulling his long cock from her. He pushed her to the floor, onto her back, and straddled her belly. "Now, Madame Bitch, you're going to suck me." His cock jutted out so far it nearly touched her chin. She smiled in anticipation.

"I'm going to suck you like a child's lollipop. I'm going to suck you so hard, you're going to scream like a girl. And beg me to let you come." She lifted up and pulled his hips closer, bringing that slender cock into her mouth.

He sighed, closing his eyes, and jammed in as far as it would go. She coughed, choked, then sucked as though she could pull his insides out. She slipped both hands around the exposed length of his erection, working them as an extension of her mouth, trying to encase his entire length.

"Yes, you dirty bitch," he muttered as she worked beneath him. "You're going to drown in my spooge. You're going to choke and cough and I'm going to keep coming and coming. . . ."

The music and dancing around them swelled and ebbed, and there were moments when Piangi's bass voicing of Mephistopheles slipped so low that anyone near the Hell scenery might be able to hear Firmin if they happened to be listening. But Maude didn't care. Her focus was on the long, slick cock that choked her every time it hit the back of her throat.

He played with her breasts, and she could tell he was getting close. She felt his come moving along the full length of his dick, shuttling along toward the head, where it would spurt into her welcoming mouth—and then suddenly he pulled back, out, away.

"I'm going to fuck your titties," he said hoarsely, gathering up her breasts in his hands. In the warm red glow of the Hell around them, she could see the fervency in his eyes. "I'm going to fuck those lovely tits of yours!"

He slid his cock in the valley between them, and reached behind him to slide one hand through the juices drenching her sex. He tweaked her sex, and she jerked beneath him again in a small surprise of an orgasm, and then he took his dripping hand and wiped his cock with her juices. Her smell mingled with his, musky and delicious, and Maude could not take her eyes from his glistening cock.

Then, with his long, warm hands, he pushed her breasts together hard, forming a tight, constricting passage around his cock. And then he started to stroke. Back and forth, the head of his cock bumping into her chin, his thumbs teasing her nipples as he worked back and forth in a heated frenzy. He looked down, watching, never taking his eyes from the slip and slide of his cock between her breasts. Maude had never been fucked like this before, and her labia constricted and swelled, and wanted that delicious wand inside her.

She reached around and found her nib behind his ass, and his cock head banged her chin when she shifted. Firmin was moving faster, his hips pumping, his ass flexing over her belly as he stroked and stroked. . . . She touched her sex, jiggled it, just as he gave a massive gasp and spurted warm, thick come all over her chin and neck and into the pool at the bottom of her throat.

Maude jolted her pip and felt the same shudders sweep over her as she reached with her other hand to smooth the salty, musky come all over the head of his cock.

Then Firmin collapsed next to her and just about that time, they felt the scenery rolling back off the stage.

Moments later, when the scenery had been pushed aside, a very disheveled manager and a very properly buttoned, but lasciviously smiling, ballet mistress clambered out of the back of Hell, and no one was the wiser.

Maude had just found her way back into the stage area where the dancers were preparing for Act III when one of the stagehands hurried up to her.

"Miss Daaé has returned," he announced.

ELEVEN

"Christine! Please!" Raoul begged, holding her slender white hand in his. "Please tell me what happened during those days you disappeared. I've been trying to see you for weeks since your return, and you have been putting me off."

"But I am seeing you now." Christine looked away from his pleading blue eyes.

How could she explain to him that she had given her heart to another, only to have it rent from her? Destroyed by her own foolish choice, her own whim. How could she explain that she felt dead inside instead of alive, as she should feel now that she'd returned to the world of light?

"It has been three weeks since your return," Raoul continued. "You have walked about as if you are no more than a ghost . . . a specter, hardly noticing me when I call after you. Please tell me what

I can do to return a smile to your face . . . color to your cheeks . . . a sparkle to your eyes. Please . . . Christine, tell me how I can help you sing again."

Her belly twisted. "I will not sing," she told him, but she left some kindness in her voice. He could not understand, and she could not punish him for his ignorance. "And I fear that there is nothing you can do but allow me to recover. I am merely weary." It was a lie, but what else could she say to such an earnest face, one that carried the illumination of obsessive love in its eyes?

"I told you I would still love you if you never sang again, and I will. But I feel I cannot allow it when I see how you are so ill. You must sing again."

She shook her head firmly. Her eyes felt parched and heavy in their sockets. She had no idea how many times she'd cried them dry. "Christine, please. I have loved you for so long. . . . You can have no idea what I lived through when you were gone for those days. Please, at least tell me that you were not harmed . . . that he—it was he, was it not?—did not harm you."

"He, yes, it was he. And he did not hurt me. . . ." Her voice choked and broke off. No, he did not hurt her in a way that left ugly red scars, purple bruises, or twisted limbs. A mangled heart, *oui*, but that was buried inside of her where no one could see.

She could never go back. . . . She might yearn for his love, his companionship, his tenderness . . . but she could not go back to that horror . . . that deep, burning anger and those ugly, twisted scars. His fury and hatred still scored her, as if he blasted her with a whip. He'd looked at her with loathing and repugnance, leaving her to cry herself to sleep, dreaming of his rages and his twisted face. When she awoke, she was back in her dressing room. Alone.

That was more than three weeks ago, and she had cried every night. She'd walked through the days in a stupor. She had been foolish, indeed, but Erik had sent her away. After all that they had shared, he'd sent her back.

And he'd not come to her since.

His face was horrible. The sudden revelation of what was under the mask had startled and frightened her, but not nearly so much as the rage and loathing that had followed. How could she live with that?

No. She must make her life here, in what she had come to think of as the World of Light. A world where she could see the man who loved her . . . where she could see and be seen with him. Where it would not be a great feat to walk along the street, hand on his arm, and shop in the shops, and dine with the managers. Where he had nothing to hide.

She could learn to accept that. Perhaps even to love him.

"Christine . . ." Raoul said her name like the whisper of a dying man, and she looked at him. Saw his blond hair and gray blue eyes, and the soulful, desperate look burning in them.

She reached for him, taking his face in her hands, holding it there between her palms. Firm, warm, textured with a day's stubble . . . it was a beautiful face. One that had the power to evoke deep devotion. But it drew only affection from her.

She had learned much in her weeklong disappearance, and even more in the last weeks of mourning and contemplation.

Christine Daaé had grown up.

His lips gentled, slackening into a soft circle, and she bent to press her mouth to them. She felt his swift inward gasp of breath when they met, and she slipped her tongue out to lick over the top of them. Soft, pliant, willing, they were. . . . She kissed him more deeply, there, in her dressing room . . . the one that had not felt the presence of the Angel of Music for nearly a month.

The one that she somehow needed to fill with warmth and emotion, tension and desire again.

The room that she could barely stand to be in alone.

Raoul's hands grasped her hips, pulled her up and against him. He was hard and ready, and she pressed her mound forward. Her body missed the pleasure it had become used to in Erik's lair.

What would it be like to make love to a man who had nothing to hide? Who did not seek to control her?

Raoul's hands were busy, pulling apart the buttons that lined her spine, and Christine let him. The change of air on her bare skin had her shrugging out of the bodice of her gown, eager to bare herself to him. To shed the clothing of her past and open herself to a man who loved her . . . a man, not a monster.

Tears burned her eyes, yet she tore the clothing from her body, helping him to see what he desired. To touch it. To own it.

Perhaps then she could be free of the ownership of another.

Perhaps he could help her forget.

Ah, *oui*, his hands were there . . . on her shoulders, her arms, her breasts . . . brushing gently over her nipples, bringing them to their peaks. His mouth . . . warm, gentle, featherlight, nuzzled over a shoulder, then down her skin to close reverently over her breast. He took care not to hurt her, to draw carefully from her the response he wanted. A gentle tug, tug, and then one long pull with hot, wet suction closing around it.

Her labia swelled, filled, closing together as they moistened and throbbed. Her pip awakened from its three-week slumber . . . twitched, grew.

Already, his cock lifted against her; he'd shucked his trousers as he fondled her breasts with his mouth. Raoul moved his fingers down through the wiry, curling hair of her quim, teasing it away from her skin and sending new rivulets of awareness swimming through her.

Christine moved her hands over Raoul's chest, pulling his shirt away, peeling it from the warm, smooth skin . . . so different from Erik's hairy torso.

She would not think of him.

Raoul dipped his head back to her neck, and drew on her flesh with his mouth in a hard bite that made her cry out. He would leave a red mark, brand her with his ownership.

She was sprawled against the gold brocade chaise longue, her legs spread, her breasts bare and cool from the moisture left by his mouth. Christine turned her head, and she could see the mirror to her left.

The mirror.

No.

She closed her eyes and looked away from the memory, returned her attention to Raoul, whose hands skimmed along her thighs and held them open. The edge of the seat bit into her buttocks; she was half on, half off the chaise, propped by her bent legs, held in place by her feet.

She wrapped her right arm over the back and one side of the half sofa fringed in deep red, her body turning partially toward the mirror, her hair dark against the gold and cream of the sofa. She had a three-quarter view of Raoul's bare ass, the long, lean lines of his pale golden body, his jutting cock, and the swath of smooth tawny hair. His muscled arms held her thighs as he knelt between them.

But Christine could not keep her attention from the mirror, the clean, cold silver that had held her, trapped her, once before. Her breasts, tipped up toward the ceiling, rose and fell as Raoul's face moved between her legs. His nose rode through the dark bush of her hair, his prominent eyebrows dark blond slashes in his fair skin, melding with the thick hair that fell from his head.

She watched, watched herself, as she felt his tongue dive into the wet, warm depths of her quim. Her shoulders twitched, and her breasts shuddered and moved as she drew in long, streaming breaths. She saw the gentle flush rising over her beautiful, round breasts, and realized then, distantly, why men loved such things. The nipples were tight, flaunting themselves as though needing to be kissed and sucked. Her left hand moved, and she watched her movements in the mirror, playing her forefinger over the hard, sensitive nipple of her right breast. Pleasure coursed from the tantalized nipple, spreading down to where Raoul tasted her, murmuring wordlessly into her quim.

The vibrations from his mouth jiggled and burned against her pip. It drew in, tighter; folded out, even tighter. It pitched and throbbed and burned, pleasure rising in her belly and suddenly peaking from her nipple to her sex.

Christine saw herself jolt against the cream-colored chaise. She shuddered, her shoulders slipping, her breasts bobbing, her nipples iron hard. The orgasm poured through her, curling her toes and releasing a great sigh from the back of her throat.

Erik. She wanted Erik.

She swallowed back the sob, the gasp of his name, before it gusted forth.

Raoul did not move. He held her in place, keeping her thighs apart, pulling away just far enough to look up at her.

Desire burned in his eyes; she could see the shiny, purple sway of his cock in the mirror . . . yet he bent his face back to her. He pointed his tongue and traced each fold of her lips, ran it down and around her anus, licking up the moisture that poured from her sex. He dabbed at her pip, where it contracted painfully, still recovering from her orgasm. He was relentless, pulling, sucking, tugging with his pointed tongue until she cried out in pain.

She tried to move away from the insistent plying of his mouth, but he held her firm. The harsh sensations from her overstimulated sex built as she cried for him to stop, to end the torture . . . but his fingers closed tighter over her tender thighs.

"Raoul, please," she begged. This was not pleasure; it was pain. . . . It hurt. . . . It built. . . . Her nib throbbed and suddenly . . . the pain burst into rough pleasure, and the orgasm sent her into uncontrollable tremors, seizurelike. She saw her face in the mirror, the twist of pain and pleasure from her open mouth, the flush over her face as her body quaked helplessly. The angry red tips of her breasts from her own fingers that had never left . . .

And Raoul moved before she could gather herself. He turned her over, quickly and roughly, but with tender hands . . . always a tender touch.

She knelt on the chaise, grasping the mahogany curve that joined the back and side of the half sofa, resting her breasts up against it, pressing her hard nipples into the cold, carved wood that edged the fabric. She watched in the mirror as the length of his body curved up behind her, his hands covering the roundness of her rear.

He massaged her cheeks and then slid his fingers again inside her wet, waiting quim, moving them in the same rhythm his cock strained to do.

The pressure built inside her; she was full, wet, the inside of her vagina moving back and forth with each stroke. She heard his wretched breathing behind her, gusting hot on her bare back. Her nipples jounced into the wood and fabric, more sensitive than ever before.

Her sex burned again, and she reached around to rub her two fingers over it, over her lips, and around to close her hand over his cock. She stroked him with wide, gentle fingers, building his pleasure as her juices drenched his hand.

Now as her breasts banged against the chaise, Raoul slammed his cock into her hand, as his fingers delved into her quim, harder, harder, faster, and deeper.

She was full, swelling—her lips, her ass, her tickler, her quim— and when he finally came, he cried out as though it were his last breath. He pulsed in her grip; she felt her own vibration as he tipped her into another orgasm.

She opened her eyes, looked into the mirror.

And saw Erik.

Erik stumbled away from the image beyond the mirror, tearing down the corridor. Away.

Pain seared through him. His gut burned, his chest twisted, and groans of devastation were stifled in the back of his throat.

Christine. His Christine.

By all that was holy, how would he survive this?

How would he eradicate the image from his mind?

Dimly, he heard her scream behind him, call his name, but he kept going through the corridors that widened, then narrowed, then opened into the vast underground chamber. The sound of water gently lapping mingled with his harsh, horrified breaths.

He stumbled, his eyes blinded, and his hands closed around something . . . hard, rough, damp. The stone of the wall. Dirt and delicate flakes of slate splintered under his fingernails as he grasped at it. He fell against the bricks, sagging, half-collapsed with grief and pain.

He could not bear it.

The roar of pain bellowed up inside him, filling his chest, his lungs, his throat . . . exploding from him and echoing in the brick chamber . . . the sound of a man dying. An animal in pain. A creature maimed beyond saving.

Twelve

adame Giry's costume for the Gala Masquerade Ball was no accident. She had carefully selected the tight, black bombazine bodice that showed a healthy expanse of bosom and fell into wide swaths of red and black from waist to floor. Under the swatches of skirt she wore black stockings held in place with red garters, and high-heeled black shoes. To obscure her face, she had chosen a bloodred mask decorated with four black feathers . . . which she had particular plans for, later in the evening.

To the average observer, she merely looked as though she'd chosen to wear a low-cut gown and a full skirt made of black and red pieces. However, if one looked closely, one would see that she held the handle of a long black whip in one hand, and an article that looked suspiciously like a shiny black cock in the other.

The two managers were walking down the wide sweep of stairs, greeting the attendees of their long-overdue gala, when Maude slinked up behind them. Moncharmin had chosen to garb himself in a Roman toga, complete with sandals, gold bracelets, and a golden mask. Perhaps he fancied himself unrecognizable, but once Maude had held a cock in her hand, she would know its appended man anywhere, in any guise.

Firmin Richard's costume was even less imaginative, a surprise after the creativity with which he'd described what he intended to do to Maude, down to each specific and erotic detail, after the ball. He'd chosen to dress as the English medieval king Richard the Lionheart.

Maude did not have the heart to tell him that *that* Richard preferred cock to quim.

She waited until Firmin had stopped to speak with an ancient, proper, and overly headdressed patron. Then she slipped up next to him and, half-turned away, bumped against his leg and shoved the phallus into the pocket of his medieval tunic so he could feel the size of it.

She snapped open her white fan (painted with little black figures from the *Kama Sutra*) and leaned just close enough to hiss at him behind it: "I'm going to shove this big black cock up your ass if you don't do exactly what I tell you."

Firmin jerked as if she'd pinched him, but he maintained his composure and responded to the elderly woman, who was gushing on about how beautifully La Tressa had sung two years earlier, and why did the new managers not give her leave to sing more often?

"Meet me in the white room in twenty minutes," Maude told him with a liquid promise, and, removing the phallus from his pocket, slipped away . . . and around behind the two managers to Moncharmin.

Her little teddy bear had found a welcome audience in a middle-aged couple dressed as Romeo and Juliet. Maude stifled a yawn at their choice, and managed to pretend to drop her whip in front of Moncharmin.

Gentleman that he was, he bent to retrieve it, and she followed. Their masked eyes met as they crouched to reach for the whip, and she said, "This is for you. Meet me in the white room in twenty minutes."

Then she stood and hurried away. She could only imagine the fiery burst of red that must be flushing her poor teddy's face.

Maude stifled a gleeful laugh. If he was red now, he'd be purple by the time she was done with him.

"But, Christine, why must we keep our engagement a secret?" Raoul asked, clasping her hands fervently. He wore a mask tonight, a fact that deeply disturbed Christine.

Another man in a mask. What secrets did Raoul hide from her?

"If Erik finds out . . . he will be furious," she told him earnestly. "I just wish to give him time. . . ." She toyed with the engagement ring he'd given her, a large square sapphire surrounded by tiny yellow diamonds. Instead of placing it on her finger, where it would be sure to garner attention, she'd chosen to wear it on a chain around her neck, tucked into her bodice.

"Time? Time for what? For him to abduct you again? Christine, you still have not completely recovered from your experience with that monster. You are still pale as a wraith, and you move about as though in a trance. If I did not know better, I would think you were ill."

She was ill. Ill with a broken heart. Ill with the thought of how she'd betrayed Erik. Ill with the knowledge that he'd seen her . . . seen her with Raoul.

And ill with the truth that she was too much of a coward to find Erik and to be with him.

It was easier, much easier to agree to marry Raoul. To become the Vicomtesse of Chagny. To live a normal life with a man who loved her, and who had nothing to hide. And who did not wear a mask every day.

Only at masquerade balls.

She forced a smile and took his hands, clasping them around the bulky ring. "Only for a bit longer, Raoul. When I . . . when I am used to the idea that we are to marry, we will tell everyone. I promise."

They were interrupted in their tête-à-tête alone in a small salon by a costumed young man. "Monsieur *le vicomte*, some of the other patrons have been searching for you."

Raoul turned to Christine. "Shall you accompany me, my dear? I must speak with them on a business arrangement."

"Oh, no, Miss Daaé, I hope you will remain," came a smooth voice. "I wish to have a word with you, if you permit."

Christine and Raoul turned to the man behind them. . . . He had somehow appeared in the corner of the small, lushly furnished parlor room in which they stood. Dressed as a pirate, with a heavy black mask that covered more than half his face, he brandished a long, gleaming sword.

"Ah, Philippe, it is you," Raoul laughed, a bit of a nervous tinge to his voice.

"What? Surely you did not think it was . . . the Opera Ghost?" his brother responded mockingly.

Raoul straightened. "Of course not. And I am glad that you

have arrived. If you would stay with Miss Daaé, I would be most grateful."

He turned to Christine, who suddenly wished for an excuse to leave with him so that she didn't have to be alone with the *comte*. But before she could make one up, the *comte* had taken her arm quite firmly. Raoul gave a little bow and, taking her free gloved hand, brought it to his lips for a brief kiss. "Au revoir." And to his brother, "Take care of her, brother. I shall return as soon as possible."

Christine pulled loose from Philippe's grasp and moved with studied casualness toward the door. She would not let him know how he unsettled her, with those glittering eyes from behind a mask.

Masks, masks everywhere . . .

"What a lovely costume you have chosen, Miss Daaé," the *comte* said. "A close, shimmering Greek-style gown, heavy gold jewelry and headdress, a tiny golden mask. But your identity is not clear to me. Aphrodite, perhaps?"

"What is it you wished to speak with me about?" Christine replied with a steady voice, though her heart was thrumming madly. Why was she so afraid of him, when the fury of a masked man who had the right to be angry merely made her weep?

She imagined he crooked an eyebrow behind his mask. "No conversational niceties, then, mademoiselle? Well, then, let us get right to the point." Philippe's voice was so smooth and low, but not like velvet . . . more like cold, hard silver. It sent unpleasant sensations trickling down her spine. He advanced upon her, tall and hawkish, and her heart pounded madly. She felt the cloth-draped wall behind her, and a chaise to one side. There was nowhere to move, to get away from him.

"First and foremost . . . although I find my brother's interest in you quite amusing, I will not condone his foolish scheme to marry

someone of your class. I have the opportunity to make a much better match for him, and he will comply. So it is just as well that you
have not made the announcement of your engagement."

Before she could react, he reached out and closed his fingers
over the ring Raoul had given her. With a harsh snap, he jerked it
from the chain around her neck and thrust it into her face. "You
will not be needing this."

Before she could react, he jammed it into his pocket.

"Secondly . . ." He moved closer and grasped her chin, his
fingertips digging into the soft give of flesh under her skin. Her
small mask felt ever more stifling under his nearness, yet acted as
a flimsy barrier between them. "I do understand his attraction to
your very . . . titillating . . . person, and I will do whatever is necessary to promote his goal to place you permanently in his bed . . .
among other locations. I am sure he will be quite pleased with that
arrangement. His future wife can produce an heir, entertain guests,
and bear the title of *vicomtesse* . . . while you can serve . . . other
needs."

His face moved closer; she could smell tobacco and clove on
his breath. Their masks nearly touched. His breath was hot, pulsing with desire, and she tried to pull away, but he pressed her back
against the wall, his body pinning her there from the waist down, his
erection most evident. The sword from his costume pressed into the
top of her tender thigh, caught between their bodies. Philippe's free
hand slapped up against the tapestry next to her shoulder, whilst his
other hand kept her chin positioned. Surely he would leave a mark
on her white flesh!

"You should know, Miss Daaé . . . my brother and I share *everything*." He forced his mouth over hers, stifling any cry she might
have made.

Christine struggled, but he was too strong, and he had maneu-

vered her so that the unyielding wall behind her kept her imprisoned under the onslaught. His tongue jammed into her mouth, his
teeth biting at the edges of her lips as though he would take her all
in. His jaw worked, moving over her mouth as his fingers held her
face still and helpless under his attack.

When she was at last able to wrench her chin away from his
grip, he'd already redirected his attention to her bosom. Thrusting fingers down into the scooping gold neckline of her gown, he
slipped his cool hand down and under one of her breasts, folding it
into his palm. He squeezed and fondled it in a rough, demanding
manner, while capturing her wrists in front of her waist with one
strong hand. Her breaths were coming faster now, matching with
his. She felt warm and close and confused.

"We have quite a lot of fun at Château de Chagny," Philippe
told her, tweaking her nipple viciously. Pain-pleasure whipped
down into her belly and Christine gasped in surprise, her eyes flying wide open. She looked up into his and saw dark lust burning
there . . . lust and promise and complacence. "I am quite certain
you will find it very . . . satisfying. And if you should consider
declining my brother's invitation, please remember that we are
the patrons of the Opera House, and as such, we hold your liveli-
hood . . . and that of many others . . . in this very hand." Using
said hand, he squeezed her breast enough to pull a startled, pained
cry from her.

"Do we have an understanding?" he asked, looking down at her
with a mocking smile that told Christine he did not care whether
she understood or not. He thumbed his finger over her nipple,
back and forth, sliding over it, pressing it one way and then the
other. . . .

"No," she moaned, trying to pull away even as her breath
heaved, her nipples tightened, and her labia swelled. *Mon Dieu,*

how could that be? Terrified more by her body's reaction than the man in front of her, Christine tried to twist away. He released her, placing his foot next to hers and causing her to tip off-balance. She tumbled over the side of the chaise next to them and he pushed her, landing on top of her and the slide of golden chains around her neck.

His weight pinned her awkwardly onto the half sofa, and she heard a low, deep chuckle near her ear. "You might be a bit shy at first, Miss Daaé, but I have no doubt you will come around and learn to enjoy our accommodations. Despite your protestations, you appear to be quite . . . persuadable." His heavy legs straddled her waist, his cock pressing down through his pirate breeches into her quim, and he brought her arms up over her head, stretching them long. Her breasts lifted under her gown, her nipples brushing up from under her silk chemise and onto the rough brocade of her bodice.

Looking down at her from behind his mask, his dark eyes glittered with lust. He licked his tongue over his lips. "Although this is not the time or place to sample all of the treasures you have to offer, I cannot resist a bit of a peek."

He yanked her low bodice away, jerking the glittering gold fabric so hard the edges bit into her skin around her shoulders and over the sides of her breasts. Her chemise moved with it, and her left breast was suddenly bare, plumping pink and pointed.

Philippe bent his head, closing his full, moist lips around her nipple. Instead of the harsh suction she expected, he surprised her with a tempting flick of the tongue and the faint nibble of his teeth. Her nipple tightened under his mouth. Christine squirmed beneath him, her breath coming in short pants, her sex brushing up against that strong bulge of erection, sending a spiral of lust curling around her even as she fought to push him away.

Then, suddenly, he froze, his lips opening and freeing her breast. His breath huffed hot on her moist skin, but he pulled away.

Christine opened her eyes and saw a tall, dark shadow looming behind him. Her breathing stopped and her heart plummeted to her belly, and lower. It twittered and flinched and her mouth dried.

"Ah, Philippe, I see that you have not yet learned how to take no for an answer." Erik's voice was as cool and impersonal as the glance he scanned over Christine. "Are you still so desperate that you must take a lady by coercion?"

Erik knew the *comte*?

Christine tried to read her lover's expression, tried to see what was in his eyes . . . but they were flat and black, shadowed by a mask that covered, not just half, but all of the uppermost part of his face tonight. As if he had dressed for the masquerade ball as well.

Philippe muttered something that sounded filthy, but Christine did not understand it. She saw shock and recognition in his eyes metamorphose into bitterness. His mouth curled in disdain as he drew in a deep breath. "And so it *is* you, then, Erik. I should never have expected you would have remained in Paris." Christine felt his hand as it moved toward his waist.

"Erik!" she screamed before she realized she was drawing in the breath; but when Philippe spun with his sword, Erik met it . . . with his own.

Costumed as an English highwayman, Erik whirled with his weapon, and the metal clashed . . . slid and clashed and clanged, and Christine watched in horror from her sprawled position on the chaise.

It soon became clear even to her untutored eye that although Philippe was well versed in swordplay, Erik was the better of the two. He was barely breathing heavily when Philippe dropped his sword and it clattered to the polished wood floor.

Erik placed the tip of his saber in the exact center of the *comte's* chest and paused, tilting his head as though considering how to proceed. The set of his jaw told her he was ready and willing to thrust the blade home.

"Erik! Angel! *Non!*" Christine cried, rushing to his side and grasping his arm. "He is not worth the damage."

He looked down at her and she nearly stepped away. . . . The look in his eyes was blank and removed, as if he'd never seen her before. "This is not the first time he has laid his hands on an unwilling woman." Then his expression behind the mask grew even more chill. "Unless you were not unwilling."

Christine gasped and stepped away. "Erik! No . . ." But she could not find the words; her mouth stopped moving.

Philippe seized the opportunity. "You will not kill me, Erik. You are no more than a weak fool who must hide underground for fear of being seen in the light of day. The only time you are free to roam about is when the rest of us wear masks as well. Do not," he warned as Erik's arm tensed visibly, as if to drive the sword home. "You have too many deaths on your head, and one more would bring the wrath of the city down upon you. Now that I know where you are, you would have no place to be safe."

He stepped away from Erik's saber, reaching to pick up his own weapon. "I will tell you this, Erik, Monsieur Opera Ghost. . . . You have stepped in my way one too many times. This has been . . . what do the peasants say? The last straw in the basket on the mule's back?" His attention flickered to Christine, then back to Erik. "Now that I have found you, I'll have my revenge, and it will be my pleasure to take the woman too. As you well know, Erik, the Chagnys will not be naysaid."

He turned, sheathing his sword with an easy, silvery slide, and turned to walk out of the room.

Christine watched him go, watched as he closed the door with a soft snick behind him, and knew that finality could mean nothing good. . . . Then she turned to Erik.

Oh, *mon Dieu*, to see him. She itched to touch him, to feel his smooth, warm skin under her fingers . . . to press her mouth to his, to taste him.

"Erik."

"Helen of Troy. The face that launched a thousand ships." His voice was wry, and his body language kept distance between them. But his eyes burned.

"You recognized my costume."

"Of course . . . the gold, the chains. The Grecian gown." Disdain colored his words. "And so Helen has chosen the young, handsome Paris, then? What of Menelaus? Does he have no choice but to go to war to regain his bride?"

Raoul had indeed dressed as Paris, the Trojan who had stolen Helen from her husband, Menelaus.

"If Menelaus *discarded* his wife, she would have no choice than to go with Paris—"

"*Discarded?*" Erik whipped toward her, his body tense and tall and powerful, cloaked in a swirl of the black that he favored. "Christine, you—"

But she didn't allow him to finish. Her arms went around him, pulling his head to hers, and she covered his mouth with hers.

She forgot about what the mask covered, about his rage and loathing toward her. It didn't matter any longer what one part of his face looked like, that one small part of him. He was there; he'd forgiven her. He'd saved her from the *comte*.

And *mon Dieu*, he tasted like Erik . . . like Erik . . . warm, slick, sensual. It was a bare moment before he lost his control and wrapped his arms around her. He held her face, kissing her back, moaning into her mouth.

"Christine . . . Christine . . ." His tongue, his lips . . . they ate of her, drank of her. . . . She tasted him in turn, the warm, mellow tongue, the thick, slick curve of his lips. . . . She felt the broad, square edges of his shoulders . . . the heavy thrusting cock between them. She reveled in the familiarity, the comfort, the homecoming.

Before she knew it, her gown was up, her gartered thighs bare. Her buttocks rested up against the arm of the chaise, and her arms braced her torso. Her breasts jounced, bare from the bodice pulled down to her waist, gleaming cream in the low light. Erik slid his thick erection inside her, and tears burned the edges of her eyes. It felt . . . full, and right and familiar.

He lifted her, his hands strong and powerful at her hips, holding her as he drove inside, up and in, up and in, his warm thighs wound beneath hers, his knees pressing into the side of the sofa under her legs. In and out . . . his eyes were closed. . . . Why would he not open them, look at her?

He pushed in and out, faster. . . . Her breasts jiggled, moving up and down, free and chilled in the open air. Her pip swelled, her labia filled, slick and hot with the friction . . . building . . . her sex pounding, wanting it. . . . Erik breathed, the puffs warm and hot, moist, as he worked his hips . . . in and out . . . filling her, the curl of lust building . . . building. . . .

He came. Long, hard . . .

She knew it, because of the way his eyes flew open, his gaze driving into hers with the same intensity as the saber blade . . . naked emotion burning there . . . his jaw tensed and his neck corded, his dragging in of deep, gulping breaths . . . the pulsing warmth inside her as his hips stopped moving.

And he pulled away. Turned away. Gathered up his saber.

Slid it into its sheath.

"Erik!" she sobbed, her quim crying, her heart breaking.

"Helen chose Paris, causing a war led by her husband." He looked at her over his shoulder once briefly, then opened a door she had not known existed. "This Menelaus will not fight for a lost cause."

And then he was out the door.

When Christine reached it, opened it . . . he was gone.

THIRTEEN

*I*n the privacy of the white salon, well away from the partygoers of the masquerade ball, Maude had one thick cock slamming her quim from behind, and another long, slender one in her mouth from the front.

What more could a woman ask for?

Something up her ass, for one. A tongue-lashing on her pip, for another. Perhaps another pair of lips on each nipple . . . if one were to get specific.

All things considered, however, Maude wasn't complaining. No, she had no complaints as her body trembled in her third orgasm of the session. Her groans of delight were choked off by Firmin's cock in her mouth.

The masquerade costumes had long been shed . . . except for the masks. She'd insisted they keep them on . . . as part of the excitement.

Her whip lay coiled on the floor, forgotten in the moment

of two cocks working her, one from each end. One in, the other out . . . one out, the other in . . . as though they were one long rope being pulled in and through her in a smooth, sleek rhythm.

Her heavy breasts dangled, thick, hard nipples brushing over the rough rug as they swayed back and forth with the pulse of their movement, sending little jolts of sensation to her throbbing clit. The slick suction sounds from her pussy matched those from her mouth as Firmin held her face, sliding in and out, long and slow.

"You lovely bitch," he gasped between breaths. "I'll choke you . . . when I come, you'll be drowning."

Oh, *oui, oui,* Maude thought in delight, her lips curving around him.

Behind her, Armand grasped her hips as his thick, round cock filled her quim, settling into its space and holding there, as he began to work the black dildo she'd dropped in Firmin's pocket.

The unyielding column slid in her anus, and Maude had the lovely sensation of being filled, full, tight . . . so tight that every little breath brought pleasure-pain coursing through her body. Armand moved behind her, drilling the phallus deeper . . . and his cock in and out, slowly, full . . . fuller . . . so full, she felt her entire insides shifting with each of his strokes. The cavern of her vagina swelled, the sensation deep inside burning with the need for relief.

Exquis!

Tears stung the corners of her eyes, tears as the pleasure grew to an unbearable level . . . pain-wrapped, the feeling of being trapped, imprisoned by three stiff cocks. . . . She couldn't move, and then, when she thought it could grow no more, Firmin released her head and grabbed for her breasts, holding them in his hands as they swung beneath his ballocks.

She was breathing heavily through her nose, choking on every other stroke of Firmin's cock, her quim so wet that Armand slid all the way out for one glorious moment . . . and then slammed back inside of her, pushing the phallus in ever deeper with his belly. *Pain!* Her pip throbbed so hard it must be bright red, burning with the need for release.

Firmin groaned, and shot himself deep into her throat, filling it with warm, salty ejaculate, choking her.

Maude gulped it back, tears stinging her eyes, and sagged, face to the floor, as Firmin pulled out, Armand still working sleekly from behind. And then, he reached around and touched her shiny, hard sex and she screamed into the rug . . . screamed as the violent burst of relief swept over her. She shook and quaked beneath him, and felt his long, huffing groan of orgasm pulsing inside her as he slumped over her.

When she staggered to her feet moments later, Armand and Firmin were both still lumps of male flesh on the rug. Maude stood above them, in all of her naked glory, her pip and quim still humming . . . her asshole still twitching.

She snapped her whip, and it cracked in the air over them.

Firmin jerked and opened his eye. "Surely . . . Maude . . . you are not . . ."

Armand merely groaned.

"Come, come gentlemen . . . or is it that you already have?" Maude chuckled at her own joke, and cracked the whip again. "The night is still young! The masquerade ball may be winding down, but we do not have to!"

But, to the managers' infinite relief, Maude's plans were suddenly interrupted by a scream in the distance. And then shouts and more screams. "The Phantom!"

A woman, one of the costumiers, had been found near the dressing rooms, deserted due to the masquerade ball . . . and discovered only when one of the stagehands had been sent to locate a specific item for La Carlotta's costume. She had been describing it to the Opera House's patrons, the Chagny brothers, and the elder one had requested to actually see the intricate fan of which she had spoken.

The dead woman, Régine, was only in her late twenties . . . not a particularly pretty girl, but not an unfavorable one either. Her neck was broken; her head sagged awkwardly against her shoulder.

She had been costumed as a shepherdess, and her mask still remained in place over the upper half of her face. Her skirts were jostled up, but it was not clear whether that was because of the way she'd fallen, or because the Opera Ghost had helped himself to her charms either before or after he'd broken her neck.

For it had, indeed, been the Opera Ghost. The one who'd remained silent and unobtrusive for well over a month . . . since Joseph Buquet's death. There was no doubt in anyone's mind that he was the perpetrator.

Christine stared in horror at the lifeless body as it was carried away, draped in a white sheet. Could Erik have done such a thing?

How?

She could not comprehend it.

Pressing her hand to her mouth, Christine staggered down the corridor to the room where she slept. Such violence. Yes, he was capable. She had seen it in his eyes, seen it even tonight when he'd contemplated killing the *comte*.

Had he taken out his rage on Régine instead? Rage directed at Philippe de Chagny . . . and also at herself, Christine Daaé.

A strong hand seized her arm, and Christine whirled, her heart leaping into her throat. Madame Giry stood there, her face settled and foreboding. Her hair hung, not in its neatly scraped-back chignon, but loosely bundled at the back of her head and falling in swaths.

"It is long past time for us to talk, Christine," she said firmly, pulling her into a nearby room. "You have put me off long enough, and now this has happened. If you had spoken with me before now, we could possibly have prevented it. Now there will be no hope for Erik. Do you understand that?"

She thrust Christine away so that she stumbled to a chair, and sank gratefully into it. "But Madame Giry, Erik . . ."

Her words faltered when the ballet mistress turned on her, her dark eyes sharp. "You do not believe Erik has done this, do you, Christine? After all you have known of him?"

Christine sobbed. "I do not know! I do not think he would . . . a woman . . . but, Madame Giry, he has killed before. . . ."

"You fool. You foolish girl," Madame spat, whirling about the room. "Of course he has not. Of course he has never intentionally killed. You do not deserve the love he has given you if you believe otherwise. Foolish, foolish . . . both of you. I warned him that you were not . . ." Her voice trailed off, but the fury in her eyes did not wane. "Christine, the legend of the Opera Ghost is just that. A legend. One that he, with my assistance, has cultivated in order to provide him protection. If it appears that every mishap, every accident or injury, is attributed to the ghost, then he is safer. He is more the fool for not telling you this himself."

She paced the room, the black and red strips of her skirt flying around her ankles, showing Christine a glimpse of well-shaped legs. And, she noticed faintly, a bodice that bared a healthy expanse of bosom.

"Why did he send you away? What happened that he sent you back to us?" Madame Giry demanded. "I thought you would go off together and be happy."

"I . . . I . . ." Christine's voice dried up. "I removed his mask."

Instead of the wrath, the spew of fury, that Christine expected,

Madame Giry stopped. She looked down at her with an expression much more horrifying than what had been revealed under Erik's mask. "You *dared*."

The sobs came anew, wrenching from deep inside her. "I meant only to show him that I loved him, regardless! I did not know. . . . I did not know. I was startled. . . . It was so frightening. His face. I didn't know what to expect, and it shocked me. I screamed, and he became so angry. He hated me. I could see it in his face. He didn't want me anymore." It was such a relief to speak of it, of the horror and the pain she'd experienced.

"You no longer love him," Madame said flatly. "You cannot bear to be with a man so deformed, so you have found yourself a new, wealthy love."

"No, madame. *No!* I—at first I was frightened. And he became so angry. And he brought me back here. He cannot love me any longer, it is clear. He hasn't come to me since then." She couldn't tell even Madame how Erik had seen her and Raoul through the mirror. "But I love him still, madame. I do. His face . . . it is only a small part of him. It is horrible, but . . . he is more than that." Her voice trailed off as she remembered how bereft she'd felt when Erik left her, claiming that he, like Menelaus, would not fight for a lost cause.

He did not believe she could love him.

Perhaps Madame's countenance softened a bit. . . . Perhaps it was just that she moved and the shadows over her face changed. "He will not forgive such a betrayal. It is no wonder he sent you away. And then . . . and then you take up with the *vicomte* of all people. And his brother! How much more could you design to hurt him, Christine?"

She stalked away, red and black fluttering. "Part of it must be my fault, for not telling you. And his too, for not . . . but Christine!

How could you throw away the gift of such deep love, passion—a *truth*, so easily? So ignorantly? I thought you of all the girls here would understand the rarity of such a connection."

Christine stopped crying. "Madame, please, I do not know what you are talking about. What must he be kept safe from? How does he know the Chagny brothers? Please . . . tell me. I did not mean to hurt him. I truly did not."

"Philippe de Chagny will do anything and everything to destroy Erik. They have known each other since they were boys, young men. Always garbed in his mask, Erik would join up in the dark of night with the *comte*, his brother, and others as they roamed the streets of Paris doing what young men do. It was an odd, unsteady alliance, the masked Erik with the titled, spoilt nobility. . . . How they came to be friends, I do not know. Erik held his own, with his . . . athletic grace and sharp intelligence. . . . They respected him and perhaps were a bit afraid of him. . . ." Madame's voice trailed off, and Christine fancied for a moment that perhaps the ballet mistress might have a much more . . . intimate . . . knowledge of Erik than she'd realized.

The thought did not sit well in her churning belly.

As if reading her thoughts, Madame looked sharply at her. "No, Erik and I were never lovers. His mother's name was Amelie, and I was her closest friend. We grew up in the south together near Batéguier, on the sea, where my mother had a ballet school. Amelie's father was a sailor and her mother a beautiful Persian woman he met during his travels and brought to live with him in the south of France. Amelie and I learned to dance together, and we came here to Paris when we were eighteen. She, with her exotic beauty, caught the attention of the old Comte de Chagny, and they had a liaison for a time. She died when Erik was twelve. Because of his relationship with Amelie, the old *comte* found work for Erik, and later, when it became necessary for Erik to go into hiding, he came to me." She hesitated, then added, "There is more to the story, much more. But Erik must tell you, for I have promised him never to reveal it. And, even for you, I cannot."

"Erik came upon Philippe and me this evening," Christine ventured to say.

"He did? So that is what precipitated this evening's events!" Madame's eyes narrowed. "What happened?"

Christine told her, leaving out the fact that her body seemed to respond to the *comte*'s assault, and the fact that Erik made love to her before leaving her in a whiff of anger. "Why does Philippe hate Erik?"

"I am not certain how it began, only that it was long ago, and there is some rivalry between them related to events that happened in their youth. Philippe has threatened to destroy Erik for some secret he knows about him, so Erik remains hidden in the Opera House underground. This is why the legend of the ghost has been created. I do not believe Philippe realized that Erik had become the Opera Ghost until recent events." Her stare pinpointed Christine, and she realized that Madame was speaking of her own interaction with the Angel of Music. "Erik has become careless since he has fallen in love with you, and now that Philippe knows who and where he is . . . it will not be long before he seeks to destroy him."

Madame looked at Christine, waiting until she looked back. "Make no mistake. . . . Philippe is the one who killed Régine tonight, and he did it to make certain the public outcry toward the Opera Ghost is raised. Erik will not be safe for long. And neither are you."

FOURTEEN

"Think of it as having your cake and eating it too. There is no need to wed the girl in order to have her as your own," Philippe told his brother over a glass of claret the next evening. He still burned with hatred and fury for the mangled-faced bastard who'd interrupted his pleasure with Christine, but he was pleased that he had confirmed that Erik was indeed the Opera Ghost.

Now it was only a matter of time before he had his vengeance . . . and that sweet little quim. He sipped and smiled and hardened.

"A wife and a plaything," Raoul was musing, as though the thought had never occurred to him before. Perhaps it hadn't, the fool.

"Your marriage into the Le Rochet family will bring nothing but more power and money to our family, Raoul. And Celeste is most enamored with you. . . . Certainly, she is not as beautiful as

Miss Daaé, but she is rich and she will stay out of your way. You will be able to keep Miss Daaé in your bed, and Celeste in your parlor. In fact . . ." Philippe picked up the phallic-handled ivory whip he'd just acquired, and snapped it experimentally. "I think we could find quite comfortable accommodations for Miss Daaé here at Château de Chagny, don't you think? The estate is certainly large enough."

He cracked the whip again languidly, delighting in the clean, crisp sound it made. From his chair, he shifted so that he faced the spread-eagled, ass-side-up lovely little upstairs maid who was arranged over a chaise. Just as Christine Daaé had been last night. Or would have been, had Erik not interrupted them.

Anger tightened his mouth and he snapped the whip expertly, watching in delight as it scored a thin red mark down the maid's buttock. She jerked, shrieked, and jerked again when he laid another line across her other buttock. Not enough to break the skin . . . no, he had more finesse than that.

"My dear friend . . . Rose? Is that your name?" The whip cracked, and she shuddered, sobbing that he could call her Rose if that was what he wished. "Rose and the others will make certain Christine is well cared for. And you could visit her whenever you wish."

Raoul smiled, nodding slowly, as though he had just worked out the details in his mind. "Perhaps that could work. I could be her protector. She needs a protector, and if it is I, then no one else will dare to touch her. If Christine stayed here, Celeste would have no knowledge of her existence. I could visit when I wish. And I know that Rose and the rest of the staff are discreet."

"Indeed." Philippe nodded. He paid the staff very, very well in order to ensure their discretion . . . and their participation in *all* of the duties he required of them. Rose was a bit new to his private chambers, although she'd been at the château for well over a year, and therefore was still being trained. But he was certain she too would soon fit in rather nicely. And if she didn't . . . well . . . he had several options at his disposal.

And, for the moment, with her long, black curls and creamy white skin, she looked just as he'd imagined Christine would have looked . . . bare to him. Helpless. And, if he was not mistaken, more than a bit moist there between the legs.

He drained his claret and stood, the cock-handled whip in one hand, the other fingering the fringed edges of the braided end. His own cock filled his trousers and his breathing quickened.

"But I am not certain Christine would agree to come here, to Chagny House," Raoul said woefully.

"Do you want that Opera Ghost—what does she call him, the Angel of Music?—to have her? For that is, indeed, what he has planned. He will abscond with her and keep her prisoner in his deep, dark lair."

"*No, not again!* I could not bear it if he should have Christine. She belongs to *me*." This fierce possessiveness was so unlike his brother, but quite welcome, in Philippe's opinion. At last, Raoul had come to see his point of view.

Pleased, Philippe opened his trousers and his erection sprang free. "Never to worry, brother," he told him, standing at the edge of the chaise. Still holding the whip, he shoved a small bolster pillow beneath Rose's hips, pulling her tied arms and legs even tighter as her ass rose. Her plump red lips lifted and opened toward him, glistening in invitation. His cock twitched.

"Never to worry," he repeated, coming around to her face, flushed and wet with tears. Another pillow then, under her chin, raising her face so that it rested on the edge of the chaise, facing Raoul. Damn, she did look like Christine . . . enough that another provoking image filled his mind.

Rose and Christine. Rose on Christine. Christine on Rose. Christine twins. That would be a pretty sight.

He plunged the white dildo whip handle into her mouth so far her eyes goggled and she gagged, coughing and choking behind it. Tears streamed from her eyes and she jerked and twitched as he trickled fingers down her spine, between the globes of her ass, and down into the slick wetness of her quim. He took it, smoothed it over and around her nether lips, delighting in her moans and cries behind the ivory cock.

"Christine will be more than pleased to accept your invitation, you shall see, Raoul," Philippe said, settling himself behind the spread thighs. "I will tell you exactly how to ensure it."

And he slid inside, already quite satisfied.

Erik was back in the damp, foggy corridor. It stretched on forever, and he ran, his feet pounding on the stone floor.

The sounds of pursuit came faster and harder, closer. His lungs burned, his legs ached, yet he ran, pushing himself. A little farther . . . a little farther . . .

His vision shifted, fogging from those horrors many years ago to a new scene. A room strewn with tapestries, bedding, pillows, ornate furnishings.

Christine. Sprawled on the bed . . . was it his bed? Her hair spilling over the sides of the narrow mattress, dark against the rich gold silk. Her breasts, round and full, their curve echoed in the swell of her hips, nipples jutting and moist. As though someone had been sucking on them.

He stood above her, at the end of the bed, looking down. Her legs wide, not like a whore's, not crudely . . . but inviting, beckoning. His cock hardened, lengthened, throbbed.

Then Erik realized he couldn't move. His arms were spread, his wrists bound to the top of the tall bedposts . . . his legs spread, ankles bound at the corners, his feet on the mattress. Suspended at the end of the bed, looking down at the feast below him . . . unable to sample it.

Then Christine was touching herself. She tugged at her nipples, plucking at them with her forefinger and thumb . . . pluck, flick, tease. . . . They tightened before his eyes and he pulled on his wrists, pulled, but there was no give.

She slipped a finger to her lips, over the plump red curve, inside, then out again, glistening. He watched as she moved it in circles over her nipple, around and around, jiggling and shaking her breast, her eyes burning into his.

Then, down between her legs, her hands moved. One opened her lips, holding them wide and red and wet, and the other slipped in and out, around, one, two, three fingers inside the deep, dark entrance. When she brought them out, they dripped, shone with her juices.

He struggled again, his cock straining as hard as his arms. She lifted her hips, inviting, lifted them, lowered, lifted, lowered, in a parody of the rhythm he needed.

Then it changed again. . . . Somehow he was in her place, on the bed. His arms tied, his legs in a vee. His cock straight and towering, twitching as he watched her above him. Her breasts lifted with her arms outstretched, at each bedpost, just as his had been. Her legs wide, as though they were straddling the mattress itself. A shiny trail lined the inside of her thigh.

Then, wide, dark fingers slid from behind, covering her breasts. Lifting them, thumbing over the stark-hard nipples. Squeezing.

Christine jolted, her hips moving, and Erik saw the shadow behind her. Her head tipped back, her long, white throat convulsing as she cried her pleasure. He watched as those rough hands fondled her, covered her smooth white skin, sliding over her belly, her ribs, her hips . . . everywhere. One hand on a breast, pinching at the nipple, while the other slid to cover her mound.

Erik's mouth dried when that thick finger slipped down into the fluff of hair, jimmying there between her lower lips. Christine's hips moved frantically, tipping and twisting, trying to slip that finger in farther . . . but she was as helpless as Erik.

His cock was screaming; he probably was too, but nothing filled his ears except Christine's cries of pleasure. "Please, please," she moaned, "please . . ."

He could tell just when the man's cock slipped inside her from behind. She lifted, rose, and her eyes fluttered. Her chin lifted even more, and the delicate bones at her throat became shadowed as the man's head bent to her shoulder, covering her neck with his mouth as her head dipped to one side. Her long black hair fell like a curtain behind her outstretched arm, swaying as she undulated with pleasure.

The tendons in her arms tightened as she fought with her restraints, fought to gain the movement she desperately needed, the freedom to pump her hips, to push herself closer into his fingers. Her mouth opened into a dark, silent oval, her lips red and wet from biting them. Christine's hips moved faster, Erik's cock surged harder, he pulled futilely at the bonds holding him, and he watched those dark hands . . . those rough hands, holding her hips, pulling and pushing them until she screamed her orgasm, shaking and shuddering from her spread-eagled position.

And then suddenly, she was falling . . . falling from her mount. Her soft, wet body landed on him, her face just off his chest. Her hips at his knees. Her torso next to his needy cock.

He saw the man behind her.

Philippe de Chagny. Not Raoul. Philippe.

He advanced, his face a mask filled with mockery and plea-sure. Christine's arms lay limply across the bed, across Erik's helpless body.

And then she was on her hands and knees, over him, just over Erik . . . but not . . . not where he wanted her.

One leg between his, her knees straddling his thigh. Her breasts hung in front of him . . . moved closer as she shifted forward, over him, still over him, now her belly high above his chest. Her nipples teased, her breasts bumping against each other, just over his face. He could see them, could almost reach up to taste those jutting, red nipples.

Her face rose behind him, above his head, so he could not see her expression . . . but when he looked down along the line between her breasts, to her curving belly and the black nest of hair at the end, he saw another set of thighs behind her. Thick, hairy thighs, and then the edges of thick, dark fingertips, grasping her waist. Just above him, just above Erik's own belly.

Christine's cry of pleasure pierced his ears as Chagny's cock slid inside her. Erik could see his ballocks dangling behind her spread thighs. They moved above him, Chagny swift and sure, in and out, jostling Christine so that her hands, placed on the mattress above Erik's head, brushed against his hair as she shifted to keep her balance.

He watched in horror and fury as that thick dark cock worked inside her, teasing him with what he could not have, and what Chagny took, and took. . . . A long, turgid column sliding into dark, wet lips . . . faint suction sounds, slipping, slick noises . . . in and out, long and short, her lower lips moving together, then apart, as he moved in and out. Those heavy hands moved, cover-ing her ivory breasts, dark and rough, squeezing them, just above

Erik's face. He struggled, kicking at his tight ankles, pulling at his wrists, his hips jostling the bed . . . but nothing put Chagny off his stride.

Christine's body shone above him, moist with sweat and with her own juices, both sliding down her thighs to pool onto Erik's own belly. He was wild, pulling, thrashing, fighting . . . and still, Chagny pumped away, moving those hips teasingly above him, those breasts nearly close enough to touch . . . and then the end, the shuddering, quaking, heaving . . . and the last, worst ignominy . . . when Christine's knees collapsed and she and her lover fell atop him.

Trapping him.

His aching cock dripping and surging, his face wet.

His heart pounding.

Erik dragged his eyes open at last. Perhaps he could have crawled out of the dream earlier . . . but instead he had forced himself to endure. To feel the pain.

Christine had meant pain to him. Only pain.

He'd given her everything, and she had killed him.

His eyes, adjusting to the dim candlelight, saw the parchment curling next to him on the bed.

Maude had written, and he had yet to decide whether to respond.

> The Vicomte de Chagny has moved Christine to a new dressing room . . . one where you cannot visit through the mirror. She is never alone, for the vicomte fears that you will visit her again. She is to move with him to Chagny House tomorrow, Erik. The count has insisted upon it, for he says she is not safe from the Opera Ghost.
>
> To that end, they have laid a trap for you should you at-

tempt to interfere, which, I believe, is exactly what the count anticipates. Whatever you do, have a care for yourself above all.

Erik closed his eyes. His dreams were about to become his life.

FIFTEEN

Christine had not sung onstage since her abduction by Erik, but tonight she returned, singing the role of Scheherazade for the first—and last—time.

Her dark hair had been gathered at the crown of her head, wrapped with gold and purple, and then left to fall in thick corkscrew waves to her shoulder blades. One long curl hung from each side of her temples, wrapped with jewel-laden cords so that they sparkled amethyst and carnelian and topaz. Despite the harem setting, her costume was more French than Persian, with silky, flowing skirts of sheer material that slid sinuously about her legs and brushed her bare feet. The bodice of her gown was heart shaped, the vee cutting well below and between her breasts. The rounded tops of the corsetlike bodice curved down around her breasts, cupping them like the hands of a lover, leaving only a narrow strip of boning thrusting up to cover each of her nipples.

When she stepped onstage alone for the first time, after the scene in which she had married King Sharyar, Scheherazade sang her most poignant aria, knowing that if her stories did not entertain him, he would put her to death. As she sang, Christine stared out into the sea of faces, remembering the way it had felt when she'd sung for Erik . . . when she'd known he was listening for her.

Was he listening tonight?

She sang as if he was, knowing it would be the last time.

It was her farewell to him . . . her last good-bye to the man she loved, but who had rejected her.

The spotlight shone down, sending a faint sheen of perspiration over her bare skin, trickling down between her breasts. Yet she could still see into the crowd. . . . She could see the outlines of gendarmes waiting at the alcove of every entrance and exit of the Opera House.

They waited in the wings too, and in the backstage hallways. . . . She had seen them.

For Erik. They waited for Erik, expecting that he would snatch her tonight.

This would be her last performance, for she would leave with Raoul tonight. He had told her they were to elope. The fear and loneliness Scheherazade must have felt rang deep within Christine as she raised her arms, beseeching the Persian gods to save her.

Her breasts rose as she looked up into the blinding light, her voice true and sweet. Tears spilled from her eyes from the light, and from the loss within her.

The music changed, portending the entrance of Sharyar, her murderous husband, and Christine held her final note, standing alone on the stage.

Suddenly, there was a soft *pop*, and the stage—the entire chamber—was plunged into utter darkness.

Shouts and screams erupted from all around and Christine froze, afraid to move and take the chance of falling into the orchestra pit. The air shifted above, and she felt something *whump* down behind her, just barely behind her. . . . Had she been a step farther back, she would have been crushed under the weight of . . .

Erik!

There was no mistaking those hands, that brush of his face against the side of her jaw, the smell of him, his presence. . . .

His arms closed around her from behind—strong, welcome— and then she felt the whiplike motion of his hand, and then a short step, and then they were falling. . . .

She screamed in spite of herself, as her skirts blew up around her and the cool air rushed over her bare thighs. She saw the faint glow of lights above as they slipped through a trapdoor in the center of the stage, a door that closed immediately behind them, leaving them bundled together in a smooth chute of darkness.

They slipped easily down some sort of slide, Christine caught up against Erik's long, strong body, held against him with one arm. Her heart raced madly in her chest. . . . He had come for her! And he had bested the gendarmes; he'd foiled the *comte*'s plans.

When they reached the bottom of the slide, Erik's feet planted abruptly on something hard, jolting their slide to a sudden halt. Then he was pulling her to her feet, dragging her after him. He had said nothing, and she did not know. . . . She did not know if he had taken her in anger, or because he loved her still.

But it did not matter to her, for she was with him.

She was not going with Raoul.

Christine stumbled after him, her hand captured in his. When he spoke, he said only, "Hurry."

They ran and ran, through dark, damp twisting and turning corridors, taking first one branch and then another. Even in total darkness, Erik moved unerringly, one hand gripping her wrist none too gently, and the other brushing along the wall for guidance.

Suddenly, as they came around yet another corner, he grabbed her shoulders and pushed her back up against the wall. Her panting breath gusted out of her, but she had no time to catch it, for his lips crashed down onto her . . . her jaw, her chin, finally, her mouth.

Warm and sensual, Erik's kiss was nevertheless relentless and demanding, mingled with his own panting breath. Anger and need colored the way he devoured her mouth with his own, pausing long enough to drag in a deep draft of air, then back tasting her again. The deep, familiar flare of lust coursed down to her belly, unfolding and uncurling into tingling heat.

His strong hands pressed her shoulders against the harsh stone wall as her breasts rose and fell behind the confining corset. Gritty dirt and chill dampness bothered her bare back as she was pushed up against it, yet Christine lifted her chin and met his lips eagerly. Slick and hot, deep and strong, they kissed as though starving, legs twined, hips positioned against hips.

Her breasts burst free of the flimsy corset confines, pressing bare, hard nipples against his clothed chest in a slower rhythm and her breathing settled. She shifted her face away, found her mouth on the rough, unshaven side of his face . . . kissed along his jaw in between warm, hard breaths, and slid her hands over his shirt, feeling for skin beneath.

It was so dark, she could see nothing. . . . Her world was nothing but a maelstrom of sensation. The cool air on her skin, the heat of his body in front. The brush of his crisp, woven shirt against her arm. The scraping of brick against her shoulder blades. The dank, musty smell of wet stone. A trickle of perspiration between her breasts, matched with a line of moisture from the wall, sliding down her spine. Her being filled with his presence, his musky, masculine smell. Hot, slick sensations from his mouth. The firm grip of strong fingers at her shoulders. The brush of his eyelashes over her cheek.

"Erik, oh, Erik," she cried, tears leaking from her eyes. Trembling overtook her. "You came for me." She could not see his face, still could not tell if he was angry or resigned, pleased or subdued. But his mouth . . . it ate her; she felt as though it would devour her in the most gentle all-consuming fashion.

He released her shoulders and closed his hands over her breasts, one warm palm covering each. Pinning her against the wall with his hips, he shifted his torso away, leaving her skin bare and cool except where his fingers played with her nipples. Spikes of pleasure jolted through her and she sighed, closing her eyes, tipping her head back. A drip of water seeped into her hair, cold and sharp, contrasting with the deep, pitching arousal in her belly.

"Christine," he murmured into the darkness. "I could not let them have you. You are mine." He brushed his thumbs over the tips of her sensitive nipples, sending her shuddering and her breath jittery, then squeezed and lifted and squeezed again. Christine's labia swelled, moistened; her pip lifted and her hips nudged against Erik's most evident erection. Sharp heat coiled in her belly, the burning, tingling sensation of lust grew, and she reached blindly for his face.

Her fingers brushed his mask, and she felt him still for a moment . . . then breathe again as she combed through the thick dark hair behind it. "Erik, I love you. Mask or no, I love you. I did not mean to hurt you."

She felt his fingers trembling against her, sliding over her skin, pulling the corset away. When he bent, she felt it, and arched her back to bring her breast to his mouth. He kissed the side of it, his lips warm against her chilled skin, his eyes—one masked, one free—brushing over her flesh, wet with warm tears, gentle with fringed lashes. She cried too, relieved at last to be with him.

Then . . . with his head at her breast, she reached down and covered his hair with her hands. He sucked, licked, swirled, his nose huffing hot breath on her skin as she arched against him, breathing in his smell. She stroked her palms down over his ears, brushing the leather mask and warm, stubbled skin. She framed his face, jaw moving as he pulled at her nipple, and she held it there, while he suckled as though he wished to swallow it.

And then . . . holding him, she slipped her fingers under that mask and culled it away.

At her first touch under the formed leather, he stopped, froze, snatched in his breath as though to howl . . . but her insistent hands held his face.

"No, Erik . . . ," she murmured, raising his head from her breast, holding him so he could not pull away. . . . Of course he could, if he'd chosen; he was so much stronger . . . but he did not. He breathed shallowly, carefully, as though afraid to do that, letting her lead him.

The mask skittered to the floor at their feet; she felt it tumble against her skirts as it landed. "Erik . . . I love you . . . all of you. You don't have to hide from me." Still cupping his face, she moved her fingers over the bifurcated halves . . . one warm, covered with the texture of an unshaven chin . . . melding into smooth, moist skin . . .

. . . and the other rumpled and mangled, twisted like plant roots, hard, brittle, smooth.

She covered his face, there in the dark, learning it with her fingers, gentling him to the sensation of being touched by another human. Touching his shame.

Christine was crying for him, sobbing silently for his pain, as she pulled his face to hers, met his stiff, parted lips with her warm ones, and covered them gently. With her mouth, she closed over his upper lip, drawing it in, sliding her tongue over it in a slippery, sensual dance. He trembled in her arms, his own hands moving around to pull her close. He kissed her back, eating again at her mouth as though released from some great restraint. Her tears mingled with his, dripping down to where their mouths met in softer, gentler kisses. Loving kisses. Understanding and forgiving ones.

"Erik, please, I want you inside me," she whispered, aware of the growing throb of her sex. She fumbled with his trousers as he yanked up her flowing skirts, and there against the cold stone wall, he lifted her onto his raging erection.

When she slid onto him, her legs wrapped around his waist; he filled her, nudging that inmost part where the pleasure grew. Erik shifted slowly, so slowly, there against her, his breath ragged, measured . . . his movements matching. As though he wanted to take the time to savor every stroke, every inch, in and out, slowly . . . excruciatingly slowly.

Christine's nipples pinched; her pip ached as the pleasure built . . . so slowly and deeply. It was like a pit in her belly, growing larger and sharper, tingling and burning and sweet. She sighed, tightening her legs around him, pushing him into her with her heels, feeling him bump against the top of her vagina. His fingers gripped her hips; the wall shifted up and down behind her in their easy rhythm there in the dark.

Slowly . . . her slick quim closed around him, opening as he moved back out. Their breaths rose; the shivers pebbled her skin; more tears leaked from her eyes. In and out . . . slippery and hot . . . slowly, easily . . . thick and hard . . . sliding along her bursting pip, sending shivery sensations radiating from her center.

The orgasm, when it came, was long, slow, undulating. She

caught her breath, then let it go, trembling, ending with a jerk as the full force of pleasure peaked and withdrew.

And with that, he let himself go mad. Deeper, harder, faster . . . pumping madly inside her, there, against the wall. In and out, faster and faster . . . his breathing loud and noisy, his muscles trembling, and a sharp wave of lust returning to Christine's sated pip. He thrust and moved and finally slammed into her one last time with a low, long groan that matched the coursing she felt inside of her.

"Christine . . . ," he murmured, his face against hers now. "Never leave me. Never leave me."

"I'll never leave you," she sighed into his ear. "Never."

When the Opera House plunged into darkness, Armand Moncharmin and Firmin Richard were standing in the offstage wings.

"The ghost!" cried Firmin, grasping the jacket sleeve of his partner. "He has come again."

"We shall be ruined!" replied Armand, stumbling out onto the dark stage. He felt the whoosh of air as something heavy moved and swung past him, and turned back to see three of the gendarmes rushing onto the stage from different directions, torches in hand. The gas lamps at the edge of the stage were suddenly reignited, casting warm yellow light over the pandemonium in the theater.

Miss Daaé was gone.

"Miss Daaé! Where has she gone?"

"It's the Phantom! He has taken her."

At that moment, an ominous rumble sounded from above and all of the gendarmes raised their lights at the same time to show the great chandelier, its lights still extinguished, swaying and tipping angrily.

Firmin and Armand looked at each other in horror, recalling

the ghost's joke about bringing down the chandelier. "The chandelier," Firmin shouted. "Run!"

"We are ruined," cried Armand again, stumbling backward, his eyes still on the clinking, clattering, swaying lamp above.

A great tearing noise sounded, and the heavy lamp pulled loose from its moorings as if in a dream, as if every second slowed to more than a minute . . . and then it crashed onto the stage in a great bursting clatter. Explosions from oil leaking onto the gas lamps, shards of shooting glass, and billows of smoke filled the theater.

The audience screamed and panicked, pushing and shoving to get out of their seats. The cast and orchestra—those who had not been injured by the falling chandelier—stumbled and cried as they made their way toward the back of the stage, to get away from the mess.

"We are ruined! We are ruined! How can such a misfortune befall us?" cried Armand as Firmin dragged him away from the wreckage and away from the tearing fire.

In the back, where the dressing rooms were emptying and the dancers were rushing screaming from the building, they turned to see the Chagny brothers standing there, unruffled and unharmed.

"It is the Phantom, the ghost who has done this," cried the *comte*. "Just as he threatened before—he has brought down the chandelier and destroyed the theater. We must stop him. Send the men after him!"

"He has taken Miss Daaé. We must find him!"

"I know where he has gone," the *vicomte* announced passionately. "Through Miss Daaé's old dressing room. Come, we will stop them. Send the men after us with their guns and torches. We will catch him, and make him pay!"

"We will hunt him down," the *comte* said. "Collect the others and bring them."

Maude Giry came rushing around the corner. Her hair straggled from its tight bun in a manner that reminded Armand of the times she'd let it fall loose. Armand would venture to guess that this was one moment that the woman did not have sex on her mind.

"This way! They are hunting for the Ghost. This way!" Armand called, waving the gendarmes over to him. The fire raged out in the auditorium, and the smoke was beginning to seep into the high ceilings back where they stood, but there was still time to find their way back through the dressing rooms.

"But no, he has not done this! He would not!" Maude was crying, her face soot-streaked, a scratch of red along one cheek. "He would not!"

"But he has, madame, and we will not rest until he has paid for this. It is long past time the Opera Ghost should be stopped." The Comte de Chagny looked at her with dark, glittering eyes, then turned and rushed away after his brother.

Sixteen

The lovers walked hand in hand through the darkness.

"Where will we go?" Christine asked, noticing that the corridor had become lighter.

They rounded a corner and found Cesar, the white horse, and a torch. This was not the same place she had been taken before; at least, she did not think it was. The stone hallways looked so much alike.

"I have made plans for our safe trip and refuge," Erik told her. He had retrieved his mask but, in a show of trust, had not donned it. His twisted, angry skin shone tight and brittle, horrible in the low light next to the dark, handsome half she had come to know. "We will leave here tonight and be far away from here . . . and from the Chagnys. They will not be pleased you have slipped away."

It was only a short ride on Cesar before they reached Erik's cot-

tage by the underground lake. Erik pulled her off, and she landed
lightly on the ground, following him inside.

The house was just the same as she had remembered.

Except that the moment he closed the door behind them, they
were face-to-face with the Chagny brothers.

"You must have taken the longer route," Philippe said pleas-
antly. He was holding a gun, and before Christine or Erik could
react, something whipped through the air and settled around
Erik's neck. "The Punjab lasso. Isn't the Opera Ghost famous for
his technique with the lasso? Or, at least, that is what the legend
says."

He tightened the rope and Erik coughed, jerking off-balance as
he tried to pull it away.

"Don't touch it," snapped Philippe, jabbing the pistol at Christine's temple in an obvious threat. "Raoul," he snapped with a flick
of his wrist.

"Raoul!" Christine cried, ignoring the push of metal into her
skin. "What are you doing?"

He yanked Erik to his feet and muscled his arms behind his
back, tying his hands there as Erik stood stoic, coughing faintly, face
dark and twisted on both halves now.

"What do you want?" Erik choked from behind the rope cutting into his throat.

"Christine, for one," Philippe said, twisting her arms behind
her back and dragging her toward him. He replaced the pistol in his
pocket and reached around to squeeze her half-bare breast. She stiffened and tried to pull away, but he yanked her arms back harder,
and she cried out. "Your final destruction, for the other."

Raoul finished his job and walked over to stand next to Christine. Philippe thrust her toward him, and she stumbled before Raoul
caught her arm. "Let me go," she demanded, watching as Philippe

coiled Erik's rope onto the small lamp that hung from the ceiling. His neck strained upward, and his face was darkening red.

"Let you go back to the horrific Opera Ghost? Never," Raoul told her. "We have come to rescue you."

"Rescue me?" Christine's fear eased out of her. It was a misunderstanding. "No, Raoul, I don't need to be rescued. Let him go; he means no harm—"

"No harm?" Philippe stepped toward her, a little smile on his patrician face, the other end of the rope taut in his hand. "I beg to differ, Miss Daaé. In fact, at this very moment, the Opera House is engulfed in flames. Explosions have been heard from every corner of the stage, and the chandelier was rigged to crash down upon the stage. It has killed, I'm certain, at least one woman, and injured many others. Just as you threatened, dear Opera Ghost. I thank you, for not only putting the idea into my head, but also for setting yourself up as the scapegoat by your own words to those stupid managers.

"It was only because of luck, and our fast thinking, that Raoul and I were able to escape from the turmoil . . . and chase down the perpetrator of this disaster." He jerked the rope and Erik's head snapped helplessly as he struggled to breathe. "At least, that is how we shall explain it to the authorities . . . who will be only too pleased to listen to the Chagny brothers."

Christine's heart stopped—surely it did—for a long moment, as black flashes colored the edges of her vision. And then it began racing again, madly, as nausea pooled in her belly.

"He kidnapped you once, Christine," Raoul said. "He's done it again, but this time, he won't get away with it. The mob is already forming. . . . We sent them in the wrong direction, but they will be here soon enough. They are coming after him. And you. If you take his side, you will be torn apart . . . or worse. We are here to take you away to safety."

She stared at him in horror. "How could you do this, Raoul? I thought you loved me!"

"I do love you, Christine. Beyond anything, I love you. I am doing this for you. I've done it all for you. I can't allow you to spend the rest of your days with this . . . this monster."

"The only monster in this room is *him*," Christine spit, pointing at Philippe. "And you, Raoul. You both did this. All of this. And for what? *What?*"

Philippe stepped toward her, and she shrank back into Raoul, for angry and frightened as she was, he was still the better choice in this madness.

"For this." Philippe squeezed her breast. "And this." He reached for her other, pinching the nipple. "And for this." Holding her by the nipple, he reached down and crudely cupped her sex. "And to watch *that*." He turned, pointing at Erik, whose bound arms were struggling tightly as he tried to twist his neck loose. His breaths were gasps of air, desperate . . . but not as desperate as the burning, horrified eyes he turned toward her.

Christine tried to break free of Raoul's grip, but it was too strong. "No! You cannot. I won't go with you. Leave me here. With Erik!"

To her surprise, Philippe loosened the rope enough that Erik was able to breathe easier. "Leave you here? Why, we could not do that to you, Miss Daaé. That would be most unchivalrous. You will want to be coming with us . . . although I must tell you that your arrangement has been altered. You see, my brother, the *vicomte*, cannot be marrying someone of your station. . . . He simply cannot disappoint the Chagny family in that regard. So he will be wedding Celeste Le Rochet, a young woman who, although she does not have your considerable charms, does come from a great family and brings a fortune to ours. You will simply be . . . our guest . . . at Château de Chagny."

"Never! I will not," Christine shouted, struggling anew. "Raoul, you deceived me!"

"Christine, it will be for the best," he told her gently. "You will be very comfortable at Château de Chagny, and I will visit you often. Every day, at least." He smiled, but there was a glint in his eyes that belied his tenderness. "I will be your protector."

"You cannot return to the Opera House," Philippe told her. "For there is no Opera House . . . or there will be none by the morning. And you have already been identified as an accomplice of the Opera Ghost—all of your talk about the Angel of Music has done it for you. You are trapped, Christine. Trapped unless you accept our offer of succor."

"I will not! I will stay here with Erik!" Tears streamed down her face.

"Let her go." Erik's voice, rough and raw, drew their attention. "It is me you want, Chagny. She has nothing to do with this."

"*Au contraire, mon ami,*" Philippe told him smugly. "She is in the very center of this, for she is everything to you. And the best, most painful way to destroy you is to destroy that which you love . . . for you have never loved *anything* before . . . and have never been loved in return. Most especially by our father."

"Father?" Christine gasped, and her attention flew among the three men.

"Ah, yes . . . that is the one secret I am most determined to keep, Miss Daaé. The identity of my bastard half brother . . . the deformed monster that he is, we Chagnys cannot allow him to claim his position with the family. Never have. Never will."

He paused . . . looked consideringly at Christine. "Although, I might . . . might perhaps be convinced toward leniency . . . for a price."

She knew immediately what he meant. His lewd gaze, his las-civious smile, the bulge in his trousers.

"Raoul has had the opportunity to test the wares, of course, but I have not . . . because of your interference. Perhaps we might come to an arrangement of our own, Miss Daaé?"

"No," Erik snarled, fighting anew. "Christine, no!"

"You won't find it so very difficult, will you, Miss Daaé? After all, from our brief interlude at the masquerade ball, you seemed to find me . . . not so very distasteful. Not so distasteful as you might have pretended. It must be the Chagny blood. We all have it. All three of us." He laughed softly, his eyes fastened on hers.

Christine's heart thudded in her chest. "Would . . . would you leave, and let us go free?"

"If I found your performance convincing enough . . . I'm sure we could come to a satisfactory arrangement." His mouth curled and he watched her, waiting. Waiting.

"Christine, nooo . . ." Erik was sobbing now, twisting and turn-ing, trying to break free.

"Tell him to shut up, or I will shut him up," Philippe told her quietly, never moving his attention from her.

"Erik . . . please. You will make it worse." Her words came out rusty, but they seemed to have an effect, for he stopped calling . . . subsiding into heavy, rough breathing behind them.

Ignoring Raoul, who had released her during the exchange with Philippe, Christine drew in a deep breath. Philippe blinked easily, but his attention remained avid and steady. She stepped toward him and lifted her face, pressing her lips to his.

He did not move and she drew back, looking up at him.

"Surely you can do better than that," he told her. "I said the performance must be *convincing*."

Refusing to look at Erik, she stepped forward again. Pulling in a deep breath, she lifted her arms, and felt her breasts rise from behind the corset as she slid her fingers around the back of Philippe's neck. Bringing his head down, she rose on her toes to kiss him, moving her lips over his in sensual, sleek strokes. From the shift of his breath, she knew she had been successful, yet he did not move.

She kissed more frantically, thrusting her tongue into his mouth to taste his tobacco and wine-scented tongue, and bringing her hips forward into his, where his erection told her she'd had an effect.

Christine stepped away again, breathing heavily, and his hand lashed out to grab her wrist. "That was an adequate beginning, Miss Daaé." He yanked her back up against him. He looked down at her, forcing her wrist straight down along his thigh, and sliding his other hand between them to fondle her breast. "Why stop now?"

"I thought . . . I thought we could move somewhere more comfortable," she said, trying to make her voice and expression coy. She did not want to do this in front of Erik. "To the boudoir."

"That would be nice, wouldn't it?" Philippe smiled down at her, twitching his finger over her nipple in a rough rhythm that sent little sparks to her belly. Christine swallowed, shocked that her body would respond so quickly . . . so easily . . . in such a situation. "But we wouldn't want my brother to miss the show, would we?" He glanced back over his shoulder to where Erik stood, then smiled back down at Christine.

Her throat dried. "You are evil," she whispered into his face, even as the languid stroking over her nipple caused her quim to swell and burn with arousal.

"Not evil," he told her, "merely obsessed with beauty. And determined to get what I want. Now, off with your clothes. You are wasting time."

Christine cast a glance at Raoul, who appeared to be little affected by his brother's orders, despite his pronouncements of affection for her. In fact, his eyes seemed to glitter a bit brighter.

She did not dare look at Erik. If she did, she couldn't go through with this. But she would do this for him, for them. It was only sex. She could do it.

"*Now*, Christine," Philippe said sharply. He tautened the rope around his wrist, giving a threatening yank. Erik gasped and coughed, and Christine spared him a brief look.

"I will. . . . Please . . . let him breathe," she begged. She met Philippe's eyes and drew in another deep breath, then placed her hands over the top of her corset and pulled it down suddenly.

Philippe moved slightly, and Erik's horrible choking stopped. But his tortured breathing rasped in the air, and she could not look at him.

Her breasts were bare, and Philippe smiled as he looked at them. He sat back in his chair and waited, and Christine felt Raoul behind her. Before she could react, Raoul gripped the back of her neck, holding her in place under the long curls of hair, tight enough that she hardly dared breathe. With a swift, rough motion, he pulled at the laces Madame Giry had done up only hours before and yanked the corset down and off, whipping it away. Her skirts and crinolines dropped to the floor, leaving her bare to everyone.

Raoul hissed in a deep breath, and positioned her wrists behind her so that he could cover her lips with a harsh, passionate kiss. Christine closed her eyes, kissing him back, feeling the shameful way her nipples tightened and moisture pooled between her legs as she was held prisoner.

As Raoul kissed her, his fingers tight on her jaw and her hands clasped behind her back, trapped between her ass and his bulging erection, she felt a movement in front of her. Philippe's teeth closed over one of her breasts, tight enough to hurt, but not hard enough to break the skin. Pinching and fondling her other breast, he teased her nipple with his teeth, nibbling over the very front of the sensitive part, then using his tongue to slide over it.

She twitched and jerked as the pleasure-pain caused her body to tighten and moisten and swell. Raoul's hand—at least, she thought it was Raoul's hand—slipped down between her legs, sliding through the growing wetness there as she trembled inside. Her breathing was raspier, and her eyes closed. . . . She couldn't think about what was happening. She just had to get through it.

Philippe moved to her other breast and sucked gently, as though to contrast with his rough attention to her first nipple, and she reacted to that by arching her back, pushing into his face. Raoul had finished kissing her, leaving her mouth to open and gasp when he bit at her shoulder.

Erik was still half-hanging by his neck, his arms still pinioned behind him. His eyes were closed, one with dark lashes marking his cheek, and the other with the lashless lid hanging awkwardly to one side, drawn into an obscene shape. His chest rose and fell rapidly, his nostrils flaring as though to drag in as much air as possible.

Christine jerked her attention away, relieved that Erik was not watching . . . although he could hear. He could hear every sigh, every lick and suck, and the moist sounds of fingers sliding through her sex, the shifting of skin against clothing.

"You! Open your eyes!" Philippe shouted, and Christine realized he was talking to Erik. "Open them and watch. . . . Watch everything, or I'll cut her throat when I'm done with her."

"It wouldn't be the first time," Erik managed to growl, his eyes bloodshot red and burning with deep fury.

Christine braced herself for Philippe's response, expecting violence, but he merely laughed. "Ah, you still have some spirit. It must be getting difficult for you, Erik. Well, just wait. It'll only get worse." He pushed Christine down onto her knees before him.

Raoul moved closer. He'd opened his trousers and his cock roared free, red and purple, and glistening at the tip, at her eye level. He took her by the back of her neck and brought his cock to her mouth. "Open up, my dear. It's not as if it's the first time."

Christine opened her mouth. He slid in, all the way, and she could barely hold her jaws open wide enough. He touched the back of her throat and she gagged, coughing around him . . . and then he began to move slowly in and out, never fully withdrawing, but enough that it was a long slide back in . . . and out . . . in . . . and out until he came with a low moan.

"Now, Raoul," she heard Philippe say.

And before Christine knew what was happening, she heard a scuffle, and looked up to see Erik, standing in front of her, where Raoul had been moments before.

His hips were eye level with her, and his trousers open, displaying his lovely, throbbing cock. She tipped her head back, horrified, and saw that he was looking down at her with wild eyes, the good side of his face tense and drawn, the rope biting into his neck, and Raoul standing behind him, pushing him forward.

"Do it, Christine," Philippe ordered, his voice strained. "Do it, *now!*"

She closed her eyes and opened her mouth, and Erik slid in.

Mon Dieu . . . it was Erik. Warm, thick, full . . . she tasted him, focused on him instead of what was happening around her.

He slid frantically in and out, her saliva easing the way, as Raoul grabbed her breasts, pushing them up against her, knocking her off-balance so that she grabbed at Erik's thighs to hold herself steady.

Erik gave a long, choking cry and shot his seed into the back of her throat.

She dropped to the floor, exhausted, sore, drained.

Raoul stuffed his sagging cock back into his trousers. Philippe looked down at her from his position against the wall. His eyes glittered with lust and she feared for a moment he would demand she come to him.

Christine looked up, hardly daring to see what condition Erik was in.

He half hung against the wall, his marked face more stark than ever before. His cock hung, sated, to one side. His expression was bleak, defeated. He did not look at her.

Christine struggled to her feet, her knees and legs trembling. She clutched at a chair to gain her balance, and looked for something to draw over her body.

A blanket . . . she saw one, and reached for it, pulling it over her shoulders. Then she staggered to Erik's side, wrapping her arms around him, trying to pry the rope loose from his neck.

"Please . . . let us go now," she said to Philippe.

He cocked his head, listening . . . and a smile curled his lips. "Do you hear that?"

She listened, and heard, in the distance, the sounds of shouting. Horrible sounds, angry ones . . . and her blood chilled. "What is it?"

"They are coming for him." His smile broadened. "I did not expect them so soon, but at least we had finished our business first. Now, Christine, you have a choice."

"A choice?"

"I'm afraid after that performance, my brother and I aren't quite willing to let you be torn to pieces by the mob. Nor are we quite willing to allow this murderer to be set free. After all, he is a very dangerous man."

"But you agreed—"

"I said that we would come to some arrangement that would be agreeable to both of us. And I think we still can. Listen . . . they are coming closer. Raoul, why do you not go and find them . . . bring them here? Then things will be over very quickly."

"No!" Christine shouted, tears swimming in her eyes as she clutched at Erik, frantically trying to pull the rope loose. "No! Please!"

Philippe looked at her, raised his gun again in a threat, pointing it straight at Erik's head. He was close enough that he would not miss. Christine stopped pulling on the rope. "Much as I love to hear you beg, I don't think you wish to have those angry men hear you at this time. Or they might find their way here even sooner. Raoul, wait one moment. . . . Perhaps we can come to an agreement."

"Let her go," Erik croaked, his chest rumbling next to her. He was so weary, so empty. She felt his absolute stillness . . . as though he had given up. "She's done what you wanted."

"I'm happy to let her go . . . in exchange for turning you over to the mob. Christine can leave here and do as she wishes." Philippe looked down at her. "Or . . . she can come with us. And be safe."

"What do you mean?" But she was sure she already knew.

"This is your choice, Christine. Yours to make. Not his. You come with Raoul and me, back to Château de Chagny . . . and we will allow him to leave now, before the mob comes. I'm certain he will find a way to rid himself of those ropes . . . just as I am certain that he has a secret way out of this underground lair. He might escape from them . . . but if he doesn't, at least he will have had a fighting chance.

"If not . . . then you may go free, and we will lead that angry group of citizens here, and ensure that they do as they wish with your lover. It is long past time for him to have his due."

"You . . . you intended this all along," Christine choked.

He inclined his head. "Perhaps. I will say that your performance sealed the bargain. I am not willing to walk away from such passion and energy so easily. Now! Your time is running short. . . . They will be upon us in a moment. *What is your decision?*"

Erik was struggling again, heedless of the gun. "Christine, no, you cannot! You cannot. Leave me. . . . Go free while you can. Get far away from these men!" His voice was rough and scratched, with emotion and from the cut of the rope.

She looked up at him, tears blinding her. "Erik, I can't leave you to your death. I can't! At least if I do this, there is the chance we will be together . . . the chance. I love you. You have had so much pain. . . . Erik, I love you. I'm sorry."

She brought his face down for a hard, passionate kiss, crying between gasps and tastes of him. He kissed her back helplessly, hungrily . . . as though trying to argue her out of her folly by using his lips . . . but she backed away before she could change her mind.

"I love you," she said.

"I will come for you, Christine. *I will come for you.*" He turned his face and looked at Philippe, who'd been watching their tearful parting with that same mocking smile. "I will hunt you down, and I will kill you, Philippe. I promise you that. . . . I will not die until I do." His words broke at the end.

Philippe laughed. "Of course. Now that I have your complete humiliation, and the woman you love, instead of letting you die and putting you out of your misery . . . I set you free. Go. Go, Erik, and remember these images of what occurred here tonight. Let them torture you, day after miserable day. . . . Remember her cries of pleasure, her ecstatic expression. . . . Remember the feel of her mouth on your cock . . . because every day, every night, every morning, every noontime . . . that is what I will have. Wonder if she will learn to love me. Wonder if she will forget you. Live it and remember it and wish for it . . . but you will never have it again. And I will. After all these years, I have won."

He grabbed Christine's arm, holding the gun at her temple—"Just to ensure you do not try anything foolish"—and untied the rope from the lamp. Erik was free to move now, the rope loose around his neck, but his hands were still bound behind his back. "Go, now, go . . . before I change my mind and put a bullet in her head."

The voices of the mob were closer, reverberating angrily in the underground cavern, sending shivers of fear into Christine's belly. They would tear him to pieces. "Go, Erik, go! Save yourself!"

He backed away, back toward the rooms where he'd composed music, where they'd made love . . . where she'd removed his mask for the first time. . . . "Christine, I will come for you. I will come. Never give up on me."

And he was gone.

Part II:

The Prisoner at Château de Chagny

SEVENTEEN

"You shall find it quite comfortable here," Raoul told her. "You shall have everything you need or want."

Everything except for Erik.

Christine walked numbly into her room at Château de Chagny. She was still dressed in her Scheherazade costume from earlier that night. Or perhaps it was from the night before; she had no concept of time anymore.

Only that she had let Erik go.

It had been to save his life. But she had let him go.

I shall come for you.

Those words, the stricken expression in his eyes that had given way to determination, had burned into her memory during the last . . . hours . . . half a day . . . however long it had been since she'd been hustled from the depths of the Opera House to this opulent estate. It hadn't been a long ride from Paris, well less than half a day.

She had cried silently in a corner of their carriage and spent most of the journey in a half-sleeping, half-waking stupor, while Philippe and Raoul conversed quietly.

She'd been sleeping when they turned in to the drive of the estate, and woke only when the carriage jerked to a halt and the shouts of servants greeted her ears. She had the impression of a large building made of gray brick, flush with windows across its square, imposing facade, and a large expanse of lawn, but little else. She was too numb.

The interior of the château was nearly as opulent and ornate as the Opera House. She noticed gilt furnishings, high, mirrored hallways, and thick rugs as Raoul ushered her up to her chamber.

Through it all, she could comfort herself with the fact that at least the *comte* had kept his word and allowed Erik to go free. While Raoul had kept Christine hidden as she dressed, Philippe had met the raging mob that had come for Erik.

"He has gone. Escaped," the *comte* told them. Even from where she watched through a crack in the wall, Christine could see the murderous rage on their faces. The flickering of the torches they carried, and the glint and gleam of pistols and swords. She shivered, glad that she had made the decision to save Erik from them.

It had been the right decision.

She watched through the crack when the *comte* really did send them off in a different direction from the one Erik had gone. And only then had she allowed her shoulders to slump from their drawn-up tension, and her eyes to close in relief.

Erik would be safe.

"And you," the *comte* had said, thrusting his face into hers after the mob had left, "shall be very grateful to me for saving the life of your horrific lover. I shall make quite certain of your gratitude, Miss Daaé. Or perhaps I may be permitted to call you Christine?"

The glitter in his eyes made her stomach roil, and Christine found herself pressing back into Raoul's arms, where he'd held her still and quiet. She could stomach the younger brother's touch, but never the *comte's*. Never.

Now, as she looked vaguely at the sumptuous room at Château de Chagny into which she'd been led, Christine heard the door close behind her. She turned and found that she and Raoul were alone.

"Christine . . . you must understand. It is for your own good." He stepped toward her, his handsome face earnest yet determined.

"My own good?" She managed to form the words even as bitterness swelled inside her.

"You had no future with . . . Erik. He would keep you prisoner; he would keep you hidden away. You could never see the light of day, interact with people, or drive in a carriage. You would be destined to darkness and subterfuge. Here . . . here you will be cared for, in comfort."

"For the pleasure of your brother? You heard his threats!"

"No, he said those things only to drive Erik away. No, Christine, no . . . you are here because I love you. Philippe has nothing to do with this. In time you will forget that—that beast, and come to realize that you belong with me."

Christine stared at him, his image going blurry as tears filled her eyes. "I love Erik. He is my life! I cannot be happy here, without him."

Raoul's hands seized her shoulders, dragging her up against his body. "Don't say that," he said fiercely, his face close to hers. His words fanned hot over her lips. "You are so beautiful, so perfect and pure . . . you cannot love a man such as he." Shaking, he pulled her closer, covering her mouth, wet with salty tears, kissing her deeply.

Christine sagged in his arms, twisting to pull her mouth away. "Raoul, no."

"Christine," he said at last, when she'd freed her lips. "Trust me. You will come to thank me in time. You will realize that I was right to help you escape from him. You belong with me. I love you. I will take care of you."

She shook her head, the word *never* billowing up behind her lips. But she could not say it, for Raoul brought his mouth to hers again, covering her lips and her breath with his, absorbing her being into his so strongly that at last she acquiesced.

Yet the word *never* echoed in her mind.

Erik felt hollow and worn, his soul more pitted and scarred than he'd thought possible.

But the morning after he left Christine, after a long night of dodging through the streets of Paris, he began to fill that hollowness with anger and determination, and self-recrimination.

He'd lived the last ten years in darkness. He'd cowered behind the threats of his brother, a brother who'd carelessly wrought evil on those he came in contact with. He'd let Philippe control his life.

And now he'd let Philippe take the most important thing in the world from him.

His thighs bunched around Cesar, and Erik prodded him faster with his knees. They fairly flew through mud-and-snow-mixed streets, through a graveyard on the outskirts of Paris where he'd found a place to hide while the mob was looking for him.

He was desperate to be on his way to the estate at Chagny, where he knew Philippe had to have taken Christine. But first he had to find Maude, find out what happened at the Opera House, and whatever else she could tell him.

Philippe, damn him, had been right—Erik *had* carefully

planned an escape for him and Christine, and last night, he'd used it. For himself. Only for himself.

Although every nerve and muscle in his body rebelled, his brain won out: Sick to his very bones, he had left Christine with his two half brothers, knowing that it was the only chance for both her and himself to survive.

And he wanted to survive. For her. With her.

He couldn't live in the dark any longer. It had made him more weak and vulnerable than his face ever had.

Erik felt the chill February wind rush over the bare half of his face as Cesar galloped. He greedily gulped in the daytime breeze. His fingers were holding the reins so tightly that they were cramped, bloodless. His body was so tense and stiff with anger and devastation that it felt frozen.

He hated himself for the weak fool he was. His mouth burned with bile that she'd had to save him, when he should have been saving her. He'd left her, when he should have found a way to take her too.

Allowed her to make the choice . . .

His throat still ached from the rope Philippe had flung around his neck. Erik had spoken to no one, but he knew his voice would be rough and scratchy . . . perhaps permanently damaged.

Just as he was. Permanently damaged.

Erik closed his eyes. It had begun to snow, and the icy flakes bit into the lids of his eyes, as Cesar kept on. He would hear the news from Maude—what they were saying about the Opera Ghost, and the fire; whether they were still looking for him; and whether there was any word about Christine. Only then could he make his plans.

"Ahh, Christine, you look lovely tonight," said the *comte* as she entered the drawing room her first evening at Château de Chagny.

"None the worse for wear after your . . . adventure last night, I see. May I pour you some sherry? My brother has been detained in town. I am sure he will join us shortly with news of the fate of the Opera House."

How very civilized Philippe sounded. How perfectly normal this must be for the upper class—to meet in the drawing room for drinks before dinner, to provide excuses for the tardiness of one of its members.

Except for the fact that Christine had no desire to be in the drawing room, in the *comte*'s presence, or even in the house at all. And most definitely not alone with him.

Philippe spoke again as he offered her a small pink-tinted glass that held a golden liquid. "We do not stand on ceremony at Château de Chagny," he added with a mocking glance. "I shall call you Christine, and you shall call me Philippe." He stepped closer, so that his shoes bumped against her slippers and the wing of his jacket brushed against her bosom. "I look forward to hearing you say my name . . . in many ways."

Christine stepped away, her heart pounding. She had not wanted to come down for dinner; she would have preferred locking herself away in the elegantly furnished ivory lace bedchamber Raoul had given her. But the threat had been made: Dress and prepare for and attend dinner, or welcome a personal visit from her host. And with Raoul being absent from the château, she dared not antagonize his older brother.

Despite Raoul's protestations that Philippe was merely offering her sanctuary, Christine was fully aware that the *comte* had much more than that in mind.

"I was rather hoping that you would have preferred a . . . private . . . dinner tonight," Philippe told her, confirming her fears.

Where was Raoul? Why could he not be here?

After Raoul had brought her to her chamber, she had spent the day alternately crying, sleeping, and worrying about her predicament.

She had done what she had to do to save Erik; she had no regrets in that. She had hurt him once before by removing his mask, and baring his deepest secret, his greatest pain, to her. Choosing this . . . captivity in order to assure his freedom was a small price to pay. And she believed him when he said he would come for her.

He would.

But until then . . .

"Where is your *comtesse* this evening?" asked Christine, her voice rusty. She sipped the golden sherry, surprised at how warm it felt cascading down her throat, burning gently into her insides. But then, when had she ever had anything better to drink than cheap wine or ale? This was even better than the wine she'd had at dinner after her debut. She drank again, a larger sip this time.

"I am glad you like the sherry; please, drink. It will help you to . . . shall we say . . . relax. And Delia will be joining us shortly. She is not one to keep to her rooms, unless there is a reason for it. Ah, and here she is now," Philippe added as the door to the drawing room opened.

In walked the *comtesse*, and Christine nearly dropped her glass. The blond woman was tall and beautiful, her hair piled high on her head with corkscrew curls brushing her bare shoulders. But her gown . . . if one could call it a gown . . . it was enough to make Christine blush.

The gown had no bodice. The woman's breasts sat perched in two gentle cups of corset, edged by lace, completely bare to the air and anyone who cared to look. The sides of the corset hugged her breasts, rising to just under the arms and then around low in the back. Her nipples jutted dark pink and pointed, jouncing delicately as she glided across the room to her husband, who waited with a glass of the same golden liquid he'd given Christine.

"Ahh, my lovely. You look delicious this evening," he told her, handing her the drink. "Delia, meet Christine, Raoul's . . . guest. I'm certain you two will become intimately acquainted during her stay here."

When Delia turned to look at her, Christine felt her belly tighten. The woman's gaze passed appraisingly over her, her lids half hiding her expression. "I look forward to it," she replied in a throaty voice that left no doubt about her meaning.

Christine did not care to contemplate that thought, and she put down her drink. "I must excuse myself," she said, starting toward the door. "I find that I am not feeling so well."

"Oh, no," Philippe said, barring her way firmly. "I think not. After all, you are a guest here, and we must ensure you are properly entertained. In fact, I do believe—ah, yes," he added as he tipped his head toward a faint chiming sound, "dinner is served. This way, please."

"I find I am not so very hungry—"

Philippe took her arm, and suddenly Delia was at her other side, grasping her other elbow. Christine's bare arm brushed against the side of Delia's bare breast, and the woman turned to smile meaningfully at her.

"You will join us for dinner," Philippe said, "or I shall find myself very offended. I am certain Christine does not wish to offend me, does she, Delia?"

"Indeed not," Delia replied. "Although I rather hope she does . . . so I can *watch*."

Christine was thus prodded toward an ornate door at one end of the parlor and, taking deep breaths, decided she was better off in the dining room with servants about.

She could force herself through a meal with the *comte* and his half-clothed wife, and their lascivious looks and unsubtle double entendres.

She expected to be led into a dining room as vast as the other chambers in this massive château, but to her surprise, the room was not at all what she had expected. In fact, it hardly looked like any dining room she'd ever seen, or imagined. Instead of chairs lining a long table, illuminated by a crystal chandelier and a multitude of candles, the seating choices appeared to be large cushions and hassocks. There were several of them, perhaps a dozen, of all shapes and sizes. Some of them surrounded a square table set low to the ground, so that one sat on the large pillows in order to reach it. Candles burned in sconces along each of the walls, and a candelabrum was perched on the center of the table. Some odd scent hung in the air; it was nothing that she'd ever smelled before, but it permeated the room in such a way as to be not too cloying, yet impossible to ignore.

Her heart began to beat faster when the doors were closed firmly behind them, and the *comte* paused to look at her with an odd smile that made her heart lob awkwardly to one side.

"Have a seat, my dear. Anywhere you like."

Christine stepped reluctantly into the room.

The *comtesse* had chosen a generous blue velvet hassock in the shape of a flattened ball. Her breasts jounced as she settled herself next to the table, arranged on one hip and propped on an elbow. As Christine watched, she selected a small purplish fruit from the table and bit into it.

Philippe noticed her interest, and steering her firmly toward another cushion near Delia's, he said, "That is a fig, my dear. Very soft and velvety on the outside, and moist within. I find them quite delicious . . . as they remind me of other, more earthy delights."

She was feeling very warm, and suddenly aware of every one of her five senses, and what they were experiencing: the sight and texture of the luxurious, low-lit furnishings; the incense that made her want to draw it in more deeply as it pervaded her being; the spread of food over the low table—everything from fruit to wine, cheese, and bread, and even rich pastries and dishes of crème.

Christine's knees gave out and she sank slowly onto a soft, plush pillow that seemed to embrace her. With her heavy skirts wrapped around her legs, and the malleability of the cushion, it was difficult for her to move and she feared she would be unable to rise out of the deep hassock without assistance.

Philippe, who selected a firm square-shaped cushion between the two women, seemed to understand her predicament, for he sent her a knowing smile. "There, now . . . is this not cozy? As I said, the sherry helped to relax you, for it was laced with something special . . . as is our incense as well. Now, I am sure you are hungry. Please, eat. You will need your strength."

Although Christine's belly lurched at his comment, sending an uncomfortable queasiness and apprehension barreling through her, she recognized that she was hungry. And that, as disconcerting as his words were, Philippe was right. . . . She would need her strength.

Because, Christine decided at that very moment, though her mind was a bit dim while she watched Comtesse Delia's generous breasts lift and sway as she reached for another fig, she was going to escape from the Château de Chagny. She must escape and somehow find Erik. And they would be together again.

Until then, she would have to take care of herself . . . and she would have to suffer the hints and innuendos . . . and, please, God, nothing else . . . from the *comte*.

And Raoul. *Mon Dieu* . . . she did not know how to feel about him. He loved her, she believed that . . . but he had forced her to come with him to this place. He claimed it was for her protection—

perhaps he truly believed it. He was a kind man, a gentle one; she cared deeply for him.

Or, at least, she *had* cared for him.

If she thought Raoul might have gone along with the *comte's* plan in the underground house only to allow Erik to escape, and to assuage his brother's taste for vengeance, that thought had dissolved earlier today when he'd kissed her in her room. He had no intention of letting her go back to Erik.

What if Erik never found her? What if he never came for her?

The pit of her stomach felt deep and empty. No. He would come. Erik would come. . . . He loved her; nothing would keep him from her.

But until he came, or until she found a way to escape, what would she have to endure?

Her thoughts swirled, her senses heightened; she felt sluggish and aware at the same time. Philippe watched her, his attention heavy and obvious, and Christine felt the upswing of her heartbeat as it jolted through her body.

She forced her attention to the table in front of her and reached for a stem of grapes. They were crisp and juicy, and slid sweetly down her dry throat. The *comte* offered her the plate of figs, and Christine took one of the odd-shaped dark purple fruits, lifting it by its stemlike protrusion. It was indeed soft, soft as velvet, and the skin slightly shriveled. She felt as though she were holding a heavy, yet delicate, organ. A male organ, for though it was the wrong shape, it had the same weight, the same heavy, velvety feel.

The thought startled her, and when she looked up, her face warm, she found Philippe watching her, his dark eyes glittering beneath heavy lids.

"I see you find the same intrigue in these little fruits as I do," he said, lifting another fig and cupping it in his palm like a small breast. Christine felt her nipples tighten as he gently rolled it around in his palm, tilting and tipping it, and then lifted it by the stem to bring it to her lips.

Her heart pounding, Christine opened her mouth enough to take a small bite, surprised at how smoothly her teeth cut through the velvety skin. She hadn't expected it to yield so easily, but it was just as delicate as it seemed.

"Now feed me," Philippe commanded.

Christine lifted her own fruit to his lips, and could not draw her eyes away from his teeth as they surrounded the fig and then gently bit. She felt as though there were nothing in the room but his mouth and that fruit and the way it crushed between his teeth.

She offered the fruit again, and this time, his mouth moved along the edge of her palm as he took in the rest of the little fig. The warm touch of his lips on the side of her hand sent an unexpected tremor along her arm. Philippe let off a soft groan as he chewed, and his eyelids dropped farther.

That was when Christine realized that the *comtesse* had somehow moved from her own hassock and her hands were busy in her husband's lap.

Christine started to pull away in surprise after she glanced down and saw a flash of dark red flesh in Delia's slender white hands . . . but Philippe caught her wrist before she could move away and pulled her face to his.

His mouth, tasting of fig and wine, closed over hers. She was trapped by his warm, slick lips as they ground onto hers, held in place by strong fingers jammed into the back of her hair. Her mouth opened and she was invaded by the full sensuality of the moment: the taste of sweet fruit, the erotic scent on the air, and, suddenly, hands on her breast, lifting it free from its bodice.

One of them had grasped her other hand, and she had no way

to prop herself up; she half fell against Philippe, who held one wrist, and felt her other hand being directed down, down between them . . . until her fingers brushed against something turgid and warm. The fingers that held her were small, but strong, and through the haze of sensation—at her mouth, at her nipple, now, suddenly, tingling between her legs, deep beneath her skirts—she realized Delia was forcing her fingers around the hot swelling length of the *comte*'s erection.

Christine couldn't pull away; she wrapped her grip around him, her fingers beneath Delia's, and together they stroked up and down, using the gentle drip from the head of his cock and from the *comtesse*'s mouth to lubricate their way. Philippe had released Christine's lips and in a sort of dizzying shift, she found herself half-fallen between the *comte* and *comtesse* while he had turned his attention to his wife's breasts.

There in front of her tilted world, as her fingers rose up and down the length of his erection, Christine saw those same lips that moments before had devoured her own, open and close around the entire tip of Delia's breast. She could not look away as he sucked and licked and bit, drawing her thick red nipple long and straight into his mouth. He pulled and tugged until it must hurt . . . but her own breasts were tight, and her own nipples throbbed as though they too were being teased. Her sex pounded and she felt the moisture between her legs as Philippe breathed faster, and she and Delia stroked harder and longer, and the little juices from his head leaked wetter.

Faster, faster they stroked, and through the rhythm she heard ruptured breathing, slippery suction, quiet moans, and felt the jolt as someone pulled at her own nipple . . . the room shrunk to those sounds and sensations. Suddenly Philippe jerked his face away with a groan and Christine felt the warm, wet spill pour over her fingers.

Delia released her and Christine fell back onto her cushion, wiping her hand on a piece of cloth from the table, her heart pounding, her forehead moist, the room spinning, her arm aching from the unrelenting back-and-forth motions.

When she pulled herself back to a sitting position, hefting awkwardly up on an elbow, Christine was confronted by Philippe's complacent expression.

"A most delightful repast," he commented, his dark eyes scanning lasciviously over her. He reached suddenly toward her, and before she could react, he'd plucked at her breast, where it sat, exposed, from her drooping bodice.

She jerked away, but her movements were sluggish, and did not save her from the practiced tweak of his fingers . . . which sent a chitter of pleasure-pain into the pit of her stomach. Christine quickly tucked her breast back into her bodice as well as she could, but somehow it would hardly stay put. Her gown, corset, and chemise had been loosened during the fray, and they all gapped in the front, leaving her nearly as exposed as the *comtesse*.

"Delightful, *oui*, and her reluctance is just enough to be endearing. But it won't be long before she is begging for you, my lord," added Delia. The nipple on one of her breasts was bright red, and swollen, and thrust up at an angle, hard and sharp, from where it had been fed upon.

"Or you, my dear. Do not underestimate your own appeal."

Christine's throat dried as she found her gaze caught in Delia's snapping blue one. A sly smile on her face, the other woman slid her attention back to the table before them. "I look forward to that opportunity. But for now . . . I find that I am hungry again." She reached for a small block of cheese as if their dinner had not just been interrupted by sex play.

Just then, the door opened.

"Raoul!" Christine couldn't hold back her relieved greeting. She would have struggled to her feet, regardless of her confining, twisting skirts and the quicksand-like cushion, but Raoul came to her side immediately.

She fancied she saw a flash of annoyance in his eyes when he looked at his brother, but she was not certain, for the room was not well lit. When he turned toward her, there was nothing there but delight. "Have I interrupted your meal?" he asked, sinking onto a hassock next to her. "You look beautiful, as always, tonight, Christine."

Before she could reply, Philippe spoke. "We have just begun. I am so glad you are here to join us. I believe Christine was becoming lonely."

Raoul flashed him a glance as he reached for a thick slab of bread. "And am I to assume you made her feel welcome in my absence?"

Delia giggled and sipped her wine as her husband responded, "But of course. However, to my dismay, I do believe she would have preferred you to join us before now. She seemed a bit . . . reluctant to fully engage in our . . . meal."

"I'm certain Christine will feel more at ease now that I am here. Of course, I would have been here before now, but I was detained in the city," he replied, reaching toward Christine.

At first, she thought he meant to tug her bodice back into place, but when he slipped his fingers down and inside to smooth over her breast, she didn't know how to react. Little tingles lifted the fine hairs on her skin and her nipple tightened again; she wanted to ease away from his touch, yet she did not want to antagonize him. She was certain Raoul was the only reason Philippe had not been more forthcoming with his advances thus far.

"I was meeting with Le Rochet, of course," Raoul continued.

"Ahhh . . . yes," Philippe replied in a knowing voice. "And have you completed the arrangements?"

"We have nearly done so. I am quite pleased with the way they are progressing." Raoul's fingers continued to stroke over Christine's breast, easy, sensual, nonchalant. Her skin tingled and tightened, and she took a deep breath. "But enough of business." He used his other hand to lift Christine's chin so that she looked bashfully into his eyes. "You have missed me, then?"

An odd light of desire burned in his gaze, and she tried to look away.

"Christine?" His voice tightened.

"I did miss you," she said, forcing herself to look at him. "I . . ."

But the rest of her words trailed away as he moved toward her, swallowing up everything in the room but himself, and the way his mouth took over hers. Christine was overwhelmed by the intense onslaught of his lips and teeth and tongue delving into hers as his fingers grasped her bare shoulders.

She struggled to breathe, to keep herself from being pressed so far down into the depths of the plush cushion that she smothered under the fabric and his weight. She was drowning, caught in a whirl of sensation. Warm lips, slick, probing tongue, questing fingers . . . the heavy, hard prodding between her legs, through her skirts, where her sex was already swollen and wet . . . the bursting feeling of her nipples under the pads of his fingers . . . suddenly, somehow, her reluctance faded into something altogether too familiar. Her breathing became soft gasps and little sighs around his mouth. . . . Her eyes closed.

Raoul knew how to kiss her. She might not agree with what he'd done, but in this frightening place, he was familiar to her. An oasis.

She might not love him as she deeply, painfully needed and adored Erik . . . but he was strong, and handsome, and he knew her body; he loved it, loved her. . . .

There was an edge of obsession to his touch, but Christine, already titillated by her experience with Philippe and Delia, and half-aroused from the aphrodisiac sherry, could match it. She had her own desperation, her own obsession.

Somewhere in the recesses of her mind, where sanity and clarity still reigned, she knew that in order to preserve herself, she needed to keep Raoul happy. To make him believe she would be content with him . . . all the while holding back from giving him everything she'd given Erik.

She kissed him back, biting the edges of his mouth gently with her teeth as she lifted up, closer to him, openmouthed, to let him know she was with him. Her hands moved awkwardly between them, and when he realized what she was after, he shifted his weight, pulling her half up toward him so that she tilted sideways on the cushion. Her breasts were free, falling to one side, suddenly cool in the open air. Her thrusting nipples brushed deliciously against his shirt as Christine fumbled blindly with the buttons of his trousers down where her gown mingled with his legs.

She drove her hand into the heat of his drawers, this time willfully seeking the hard, heavy cock buried there. He sighed next to her mouth when she lifted it free, sliding her fingers over the fig-velvet skin and through wiry hair, cradling the heavy sac below it. Raoul moved away, pulling her with him, tipping back so that she came with him, up on her knees.

The hassock surged around her, soft under her, as Christine knelt into Raoul's lap. She opened her mouth and formed a soft O with her lips, sliding down along the full length of him as he gasped in pleasure.

Rocking gently up and down, Christine fondled and licked, sucked and stroked, her breasts jolting and swaying enticingly. He dripped from the end, and she tasted the bare salt, closing her lips tightly, then loosening them as she closed her eyes and thought of Erik.

Suddenly, she felt someone behind her, kneeling at her feet. Two hands cupped her breasts and squeezed them back up against her ribs, and began to roll her nipples between thumbs and forefingers. Sharp pleasure surprised her, shooting down to her engorged pip, as the nimble fingers teased and taunted expertly while she matched the strokes of her mouth with the curl of her fingers around Raoul.

The weight against her back was not heavy; she knew it must be Delia who now curved over Christine's spine, her lips against the side of her neck. Her consciousness narrowed down to one of sensation and rising need. Raoul moved his hips beneath her and she rose and lowered faster to match his rhythm as the teasing of her nipples made her sex wet and slick, made her want to grind it into something . . . anything . . . for relief.

A sudden jolt behind her shoved Delia into Christine, sending her forward and nearly gagging her with Raoul's ready cock. Delia's sudden moan of delight just behind Christine's ear sent more peals of need coursing through her; she felt a different rhythm behind her now as Philippe stroked inside his wife while she fondled Christine from behind.

Delia's lips opened and her tongue slipped out, curling into Christine's sensitive ear, sending a hollow roar down her neck and spine as the four of them jolted together in mismatched rhythms, with Christine trapped between them all.

She felt Raoul stiffen, ready, and the little tingle move along his cock before it splurted into her mouth, echoed by his groan of release. At last she could close her sore jaws, pull away, and slip to the side. Delia rolled with her, and suddenly Christine's head was against Raoul's chest, and she was looking up into Delia's flushed, glaze-eyed face as her husband pumped her from behind.

Raoul was beneath Christine, the rhythm of his breath shifting her up and down as his hands slipped around from behind and cupped her breasts. Delia's red mouth, open, panting, her dangling nipples just in front of Christine as though insisting she touch them. And Philippe, behind his wife, his handsome face taut with concentration and lust; his eyes, not dull with pleasure, but sharp and black, pinning Christine there as if it were he who held her instead of his brother.

He watched her and she watched him, their gazes connected as his pupils tightened, his breathing came faster, his mouth narrowed cruelly . . . and when he finally gave the last thrust inside his wife, his expression told her it was Christine he wanted, and Christine he would have.

And as soon as he rolled away from Delia, Philippe was reaching for Christine. His hands grasped at her, crumpling the skirts and underskirts as they slipped up beneath the heavy material.

"No," she cried, twisting against Raoul's chest, flinging one ankle up and narrowly missing Philippe's head as she clamped her knees together. His hands were hard and clawing as they pulled up her thighs, dragging her toward him. "Raoul!"

At the invocation of his brother's name, Philippe stopped, his face just above hers, panting, his shirt gapping open, his fingers loosening on her legs. His dark eyes settled and his breathing edged into normal. "No, Christine? No?"

She tried to turn, to curl into Raoul's bare chest, but his brother's grip held her still. He looked up at Raoul; she could see the expression passing between the brothers.

"See how she plays coy, brother?" Philippe said, easing back, not hurriedly, not as if he'd been reprimanded . . . but as if he'd changed his mind.

"Philippe . . . ," Raoul said, stroking Christine's hair. "She is not ready for this. She must be willing."

Her heart rammed in her chest. *Willing.* She would never be willing to spread her legs for Philippe. Christine pressed a small kiss to Raoul's warm skin, but said nothing. She felt as though the very moment was tenuous.

Philippe gave a low, easy laugh. "Then I—we—shall do our best to ensure her *willing* participation." Christine felt his gaze fall to her again, and she found herself looking back at him, caught. "I do not think it shall be a great hardship . . . for any of us."

Eighteen

"Raoul, please," Christine told him, her hands braced against his shoulders. "Promise me."

He'd escorted her to her bedchamber in an ironic gesture of propriety, and now they stood in the hall outside the room as though it were imprudent for him to breach its threshold. Christine's knees trembled with exhaustion and relief, and her breasts had been tucked back into her gapping bodice enough that her nipples were hidden.

As though he'd been spared her lips all night—which couldn't have been further from the truth—Raoul bent to her again, covering her mouth with his like he could never get enough of her. "Christine," he sighed her name, slipping his hands over her bare shoulders. "You belong to me . . . only to me."

"But Philippe—"

"My brother knows that," he said, grasping her shoulders more firmly. Now he was looking down at her in the dimly lit corridor. "He knows you are mine. Only mine."

Christine sagged back against the wall, held upright by his grip, as he bent to kiss and suck along her throat. Warm prickles skittered over her skin, and the tension of pleasure and need balled up in her belly, tightening again.

"He . . . he wants . . ." She could barely form the words during the sensual movement of his lips along her tender skin; any touch, any slip-slide, any gentle squeeze, brought back all of the tension, the built-up lust, she'd kept under control, tried to ignore, through the evening . . . but it burned to be loosened.

Her sex pulsed with every step she'd taken up the many stairs and along the hall, and now burgeoned between her legs. Her breasts, nipples taut and free again, jostled against the boning of her corset, aching in permanent arousal. Her fingers trembled as she pressed them into the wall behind her as Raoul sipped along her throat.

"He wants you . . . ," Raoul murmured against her skin. "Of course . . . who would not, Christine?" His mouth formed the syllables as his teeth closed over the edge of her neck. "Who . . . would . . . not?"

Just when she would have allowed her knees to sag, he moved back and looked down at her. "He will not force himself on you, Christine. And I do not wish to share you . . . in that way. You have nothing to fear. I will keep you safe. Always." He kissed her full on the mouth, no tongue, just a gentle buss of lips that—had it come from Erik—would have brought tears to her eyes. But from Raoul . . . it was just a reminder that her response was as superficial and automatic as the contraction of her heart, the blink of her eyes. "Always, I will keep you safe."

Christine slipped away from him, her hand on the doorknob. "Good night, Raoul," she said, her voice trembling. For how could he say such things after what had happened tonight . . . and last night, when they were in Erik's lair?

She wanted to believe him, but she could not trust him.

"Good night, Christine."

He didn't follow her and she closed the door quickly.

Pressing her palms against it, Christine bent her forehead to the solid oak door and let her lids close in relief. Her knees shook; her belly felt tight and empty. Tears burned the corner of her eyes.

What was to become of her? How could she stay here, even one more day?

Raoul's promise that his brother would not force her held little weight; she saw the look in Philippe's eyes and knew it would be only a matter of time before he got what he wanted.

And the light in Raoul's eyes . . . the glinting, sparkling odd one that appeared whenever he looked at her, whenever he spoke of his love for her . . . it was nearly as frightening as the cold, calculating one in his brother's. It frightened her in a different way.

Christine pushed herself away from the door; her body was so weary, taut and tight as though strung from the ceiling to the floor.

When she turned into the chamber, lit only by the coal fire in the grate, she realized with a start and a drop in the pit of her stomach that she wasn't alone. Her hand flew to her mouth to cover the gasp, and she saw that the figure wore a gown, and not trousers.

"Madame Giry?" Christine whispered in disbelief, recognizing the woman's profile.

Madame moved from the shadowy corner of the room and into the orange glow from the grate. "Be silent," she said, her words barely audible.

"But what . . . how . . . ?" She let herself be tugged by two hands toward the bed.

Madame Giry sat, and pulled Christine next to her. "You must be silent. They do not know I am here," she whispered into her ear. Her voice was low and her breath warm, the brush of her lips moving against Christine's skin. "The Opera House has been greatly damaged by the fire; the officials are looking for the arsonist. They believe it is Erik."

"No," Christine told her. "No, it was the *comte*."

"So I thought."

"But how are you here, in the château?" Christine asked, her voice rising enough that Madame shushed her, pressing three fingers to her lips.

"Erik sent word that the *vicomte* had taken you."

"Erik? Have you seen him? Oh, *mon Dieu* . . ." She began to sob silently, her face suddenly burrowed into Madame's bosom. "*Mon Dieu*, I had to leave him. . . . I . . . had . . . to. . . ."

"I have not seen him myself," replied the older woman gruffly, her hands smoothing along the sides of Christine's face. "He came looking for me, but I did not see him. He left word that I should meet him nearby. What has happened? Tell me all and stop your weeping."

Christine clutched at the ruffled silk of Madame's bodice, which, instead of covering her bosom, inexplicably left a large expanse of skin exposed. She sniffled and composed herself enough that her voice, rusty and rough, at least came out audibly as she explained what had occurred since Erik snatched her from the Opera House stage the night before. *Mon Dieu*, only one night ago!

"Raoul claims he loves me, but this is not love." She began to sob again, scraping her hand across her nose and eyes. "He will keep me here. And—and the *c-comte* . . ."

"Yes, I know of the *comte*. He is a nasty one." There was relish in her voice that Christine could not understand; but somehow, with Madame present, she felt as if things were no longer so hopeless.

"How did you come to be here in this house?" Christine asked again.

"The third upstairs maid was once in the ballet corps," Madame told her quietly. "Pansy, but she goes by 'Rose' now. She injured her leg almost two years ago and could no longer dance, and the *comte*'s housekeeper offered her a place here. I came here on the pretense of visiting her, and seeking employment. She writes to me of the happenings here, and I have given the news to Erik over the years."

"But surely they do not believe that Madame Giry, the famed ballet mistress, would seek household employment!"

Madame's soft laugh brushed her ear. "No, indeed, they would not . . . if they knew that I was the dance mistress of the Opera House. No, Rose has merely said I am an old friend of her mother's who is in need of a position. How should they know otherwise? None of the staff here has ever seen me at the theater; even the *comte* himself would not notice me when he comes backstage, for I am no longer one of the young, beautiful dancers who would capture his attention. And as a low-level member of his staff, I can assure you, he would pay me no attention at all. Thus, my position here is quite secret. But on to more important matters, Christine. Surely you know by now that Erik is the *comte*'s brother, which was what I was sworn not to tell you before. But now you know."

Christine nodded, smelling lily perfume as her nose bumped Madame's throat. Her tears had dried. "Yes, they are brothers. How can that be?"

"The old *comte*, of course, had the same wandering lust that his sons do—*oui*, even Raoul, Christine, for all of his naive ways, he cannot resist a beautiful woman and expects to have what he wishes—and he got my cousin Amelie, who was working here on the estate, with child. Thus was born Erik, with all of his imperfections."

"So he was born with his face like that?" Christine asked.

"He was. The moment the *comte* laid eyes on the poor babe, with his horribly twisted cheek and sagging eye, he vowed never to look on him, never to recognize him. But shortly before Amelie died, he changed his mind and found a use for him. There are times I wonder whether it was heartbreak for her son and his future that caused her death."

"Was he raised here, then? At the château?" These were things Christine could perhaps have asked Erik . . . but he seemed so reluctant to answer her questions about the past. And talking about him now made her feel as if she was doing something for him, even if she was only assuaging her curiosity.

"Yes, after Amelie died, and not as a brother, you understand. Erik knew he was the old *comte*'s son, but Philippe did not until later. They were of an age, you see, born within a month of each other, if you can believe the fate of it." Madame sighed, and beneath their bodices, Christine felt the press of her breasts against her own.

The strangeness of being breast to breast, bare collarbone to bare collarbone, reminded her all too much of Delia and her plump little hands on Christine's nipples, and she moved away. "Why does the *comte* hate Erik so?"

"I do not know all of it, only that the two were often together when they were young men, and that the *comte* and his friends would allow Erik to come with them when they went out in the evenings, only his face had to be covered, and he must do what they ordered. He lived with ridicule and castigation by them and by the entire household. He slept in the corner of the stables and was brought slop from the kitchens."

"But why would Erik go with him?" Christine's heart squeezed in her chest as she thought of the terrified, repugnant young boy he must have been, how he must have tried to be normal.

"Because his father ordered it. Because he required Erik to be Philippe's shadow, to follow after him and to clean up any untidiness the young *comte* might have left in his wake. And Philippe resented Erik's presence, of course, and so he created increasingly foul and disturbing predicaments for his half brother to attend to."

Christine was shaking her head. "I do not understand, madame."

The older woman gave the gust of an exasperated sigh. "I am not speaking of the messes of a young boy when he tears his trousers, or steals off to ride his father's best horse without permission and causes the beast to strain his leg—although that is how it perhaps started. Philippe has always been a man who likes his pleasure, and fine expensive things at any cost. Even as a young man, before the age of twenty, he took what he wanted and left behind what he did not."

"And the old *comte* required Erik to clean it up?"

"Indeed. To dispose of the young girls his brother deflowered, or injured, or worse. To pay for the damages wrought by him and his friends when they had drunk too much wine and cavorted throughout Paris or here in the town of Chagny. To hide the evidence or to provide another scapegoat for the crimes. Even to try and force him to ravage the girls that Philippe liked to play with. He thought it great fun to watch them scream and cry when he threatened to let Erik touch them. And Erik had little choice in the matter if he wished to live at all."

And at last it all became clear to Christine. "As he has done now, at the Opera House. Erik is the scapegoat, not only for his brother, but for anything terrible that happened at the Opera House."

"At last you understand. He has spent his last ten years in hiding because he has been so often implicated in the *comte*'s actions. He dares not show his face, not only because of its hideousness, but also because he is held to blame for much of what Philippe de Chagny has done."

"His face is not hideous!" Christine cried, louder than was prudent. "It is not. It is *not*." She was sobbing again; perhaps she would never see Erik again. Perhaps she might never touch that beautiful mouth, nor feel the raggedness of his deformed skin, nor the comfort of his embrace. She could not bear the thought of it.

She could not bear the thought of his pain, his never-ending pain.

"It is not so hideous as Erik has been taught to believe, Christine, that is true . . . but you see it now with real love, and nothing will naysay your opinion." All trace of annoyance was gone from Madame Giry's voice now, and it sounded kinder than it ever had. "Perhaps I have misjudged you. Perhaps you are worthy of the love of a great man like Erik de Chagny. He is a brilliant musician, you know, for even though Amelie was with him such a short time, she recognized his talent and encouraged it. If only she had not died so young, and he had not been made to live with the *comte*, and then to hide away." She sighed. "If only."

Christine sucked back her sobs and straightened from the huddle she'd slipped into with her tears. "How long has he—"

"Shhh." Madame stiffened, and she slapped her fingers over Christine's lips again. They sat in silence for a moment, and Christine felt her companion strain as though listening for something, but Christine herself heard nothing. "I must go; I have been here long enough," Madame said at last, her words barely audible, with none of the whistling hiss of a whisper. "Do what you must to stay in Raoul's good graces. He is your only chance."

"My only chance—" Christine started, but the other woman clapped her palm over her mouth, shaking her head so vehemently that Christine saw it in the dim light.

With one last abrupt shake of her head, Madame shifted away from Christine and moved to a door opposite the one that led to the corridor. She opened it and slipped into what Christine thought was a closet.

But by the time she reached the door, which had closed after Madame, and she figured out how to open it—there was a clever little latch that needed to be moved just so—Madame was gone. The closet was empty, and it was too dark to know how and where she'd disappeared.

Christine closed the door and turned back to her bed, weary, aching, and disconsolate.

And feeling very much alone.

NINETEEN

*P*hilippe pulled away from the tiny hole and turned to look at his companion. "So our guest has had a guest," he said. "Do you recognize her?"

"Ah, *sí*, indeed," replied La Carlotta in her affected Spanish accent. "It is as you suspected, the ballet mistress Madame Giry."

"The woman did not think I noticed her earlier this evening, when she was doing her duties in the upper chambers . . . but it is rare that I forget a face, even when it belongs to a new servant of my household. Although," he added, mostly to himself, for Carlotta did not need to know much of him, "it seemed that I did not recall my first meeting with Miss Daaé, those years ago at the seashore, for I needed my brother to remind me of it."

Philippe placed his eye back at the peephole and felt the shuffle next to him as Carlotta did the same, peering through a different opening well concealed among the brocadelike wallpapering near the ceiling.

The ballet mistress, whom he had perhaps laid eyes on once or twice during his visits to the backstage lounges at the Opera House, had disappeared into the closet, where, obviously, she had made use of the hidden passageway. This was after she had had a whispered, inaudible conversation with Christine. It was to Philippe's great annoyance that, not only could he catch only a random phrase here and there, but the elder woman did not do what she had clearly wished to do—or at least, what he wanted her to wish to do—and assist the younger woman in disrobing and slipping into bed.

But now, as he peered owlishly through the largest of the peepholes, he watched in the room lit only by firelight, which gave it an orange glow, as Christine struggled out of her half-laced corset and loose gown. Her beautiful breasts—truly, he'd seen none better in all of his years—tipped and swayed gently as she unrolled her stockings over long, slender legs.

Damn Raoul for a weak-kneed boy. If not for him, for his misplaced sense of chivalry, Philippe would be in that bedchamber, assisting Miss Daaé.

Philippe drew in his breath in a sharp hiss when Christine sat on the edge of the bed, just perfectly across from where his eyehole was, her thighs spread in a most unladylike manner, bathed no doubt by the warmth of the fire. He could see everything he'd imagined—her sex, wide but shadowed in the low light, at last open to his view—her breasts lilting up as though offering themselves to him at his elevated perch.

His mouth dried and even after all he'd had this night, his cock hardened. He was barely aware of the shifting and shuffling of Carlotta next to him, but he felt her breathing change when they saw Christine slip her fingers down between her parted legs. Though it was impossible, he swore he heard the gentle lap as her hand slicked through the wetness there, the shine of which was evident even in the firelight.

One hand played there, in the dark red haven he *must* have, as the golden orange glow of flames was cast over it; her other fingers nibbled at her breast, stroking a nipple to what had to be an iron-hard point.

Philippe licked his lips, pressed his erection against the wall in front of him. His fingers curled into the wall and he pressed his eye so close to the hole that his socket matched the opening perfectly.

Her head was tipped back, that long dark hair cascading over her milky skin and onto the coverlet, and her lips were parted in a delicious O that made him want to jam his cock into the warmth. . . . Then the fingers between her legs moved faster, and her hips shifted. She collapsed backward onto the bed, her hand working her sex busily, now slipping about so much that he wondered how she could control it.

Christine's hips moved; her legs jerked and shuddered as her body arched beautifully. Even one of her legs moved, straightening and trembling in the air as she came.

Philippe watched, his mouth hard, his cock harder, his determination ironclad. Neither Philippe nor Carlotta moved until Christine pulled herself from her crumpled position on the bed and slid under the coverlet. Then, when at last she was concealed from their sight, the two watchers turned away from the peephole wall.

"An enjoyable display," Philippe commented, moving away from the vantage point with a nonchalance that he didn't feel. His cock was steel beneath his trousers.

"Indeed, although she was quiet about it all. I prefer to *hear* it." She turned toward him, and Philippe was startled to see that she held a long red whip in her hand. Carlotta looked at him with an odd smile on her face.

"As do I," he replied. "In fact, I consider it a requirement that all new members of my household—you included, my dear—be quite voluble in their praise . . . or pleading." He opened one of the cabinets in this, his largest playroom.

"Am I now a member of your household?" asked Carlotta, sliding the whip along her palm, watching him judiciously, a smirk over her plump lips.

Philippe considered his choices, then settled upon the cat-o'-five-tails with pearls braided into the tails. It was white, the color of purity and innocence. Perfect for his stand-in for the touch-me-not Miss Daaé.

Aside from that, white showed blood very nicely. Always an added benefit.

Turning back to face her, he replied, "The Opera House is burned, and there will be no performances for the foreseeable future. You may feel free to extend your visit here as long as you wish."

"It will be my pleasure, *comte*. I shall take a short holiday while the Opera House is rebuilt, or is moved. They will be mad for La Carlotta's return by then." Her lips curled in a self-satisfied smile. "Now that Miss Daaé has disappeared again, right from the stage of the Opera House's last performance, the rumors have begun to fly. She is crazy, they say. She thinks the Opera Ghost is her father come to visit her."

She stepped toward him, the cherry red whip in a generous arch from one hand to the other. "Of course, it was I who started such rumors, even before the Opera House burned last night. I could not suffer such a rival. If anyone should ask about her disappearance, all will say the girl is crazy and that the Opera Ghost spirited her away." With a quick snap of her wrists, she dropped the whip around his shoulders and gave a surprisingly hard yank on it.

Philippe jerked toward her, nearly stumbling in his surprise. A shocked, uncontrolled smile sprang to his face at her boldness, but then he regained control of himself and let his own whip fly. He would not allow a woman to have the upper hand.

His pearl white whip curled around Carlotta's waist, making a band over her brilliant green gown, and there they were, face-to-face, body to body, each lightly captured by the other's whip.

"I will make you scream," he said, bending his face toward her, wanting to bite those full, glistening lips, wanting to squeeze and twist her bountiful breasts, wanting to rip into that red, hot sex that he knew burgeoned beneath her skirts.

"I think that I should prefer to hear your screams, *comte*." She tightened the whip, managing in one quick motion to pass both ends into one hand, and to reach for his straining erection with the other. Her hand closed over the generous package beneath his trousers, her fingers tightening in a pleasant . . . painful . . . way.

His cock shifted under her touch, and Philippe felt his muscles tense all over. "No, I think . . . not," he managed, keeping his breath steady. No one had dared . . . ever . . . but his cock tightened, hardened, so that he imagined it was past purple and near to bursting. Pain laced with pounding lust throbbed there beneath her palm.

"Oh . . . yes, you would like it, I think," she said, squeezing again, looking at him with a knowing, arrogant smile. "I will make you beg like I did my other men."

He reached toward her, shoving one of his hands down her low bodice, easily finding a thrusting nipple. With a nasty pinch that caused her face to blanch and her eyelids to flutter, he twisted.

She gasped and released his cock, twisting away, freeing the tail of her whip so that it slithered into place alongside of her gown, but he came after her.

He no longer had the whip in his hand; he didn't need it for now. Philippe clamped his fingers over Carlotta's upper arms, feeling the slip of her flesh as he dug in toward bone. His vision was edged with red, his breathing so hard that it gusted noisily between them. "Oh, no, Carlotta. It is you who will scream."

With a great shove, he sent her flying across the room. She stumbled, tripping over one of the stools, but caught herself at the edge of a sofa. She looked up at him, the crafty look gone from her eyes, shock blazoning there instead.

"Of course, if you insist, I shall scream for you." She tipped her head, a glint of suggestion coloring her gaze. "It is—"

But she never finished whatever it was she was about to say, for Philippe grasped the front of her bodice and jerked her toward him so hard the fabric roses on the bodice corsage separated from its short attached jacket. His hand whipped out and cut across her cheek with a satisfying slap.

Carlotta staggered back, then straightened, wiping the back of her hand over her mouth, looking at him with wide eyes. She had dropped the whip in a red snake at her feet. "I didn't mean to offend ye, *comte*," she said, her Spanish accent evaporating, and a tremulous smile on her face. She reached up and tugged away the rest of her torn bodice, exposing a low-cut corset fairly bursting with breasts. "I was just pretending. If you've a mind to be the one in command, then I am happy to oblige."

Philippe stepped toward her, his hand snaking out to close over her throat. "Foolish bitch. I am always the one in command. Now take off your clothes."

He bent to pick up the red whip at her feet and, when she didn't immediately respond to his command, flicked his wrist and snapped the leather toward her. As it cut into her arm, she cried out, whirling away toward the door that led to the hallway.

She would have opened it, but Philippe grabbed her before her fingers closed over the knob, his grip slipping a little in the blood from the whip cut. With a curt movement, he propelled her away from the door, shoving her toward a narrow bedlike structure with four tall posts.

Carlotta sprawled backward as he'd intended, her knees buckling beneath twisting, sagging skirts. Philippe moved quickly to stand between her legs, pushing her back down onto the bed with a strong hand over her windpipe. She choked and coughed under the pressure, but he held steady as he captured one of her flailing hands. The little cuffs at each bedpost were specially designed to be fastened quickly and easily with one hand . . . and Philippe heard the satisfying click of one restraint before Carlotta realized what had happened.

But then she began to struggle anew. She kicked and her hips bucked; her gown was full enough that she could swing her legs freely despite the fact that he stood against her skirt. Philippe had not made a sound but for the reflexive grunts and sighs of exertion as he subdued her.

He fitted her second wrist into the cuff with a bit more difficulty, and her legs were becoming bothersome, but they would soon be taken care of.

Philippe had had two beds created especially for matters such as this; one he had here, in this room he used to spy on whoever happened to be in the chamber Christine now occupied, and the other was in his private chambers, which also held many other furnishings and accoutrements for his pleasure. The bed's shape was that of an inverted Y with the juncture of the V-shaped angles perfectly positioned to accommodate spread legs. Thus, Carlotta lay on the straight part of the bed, her wrists fastened just above her head . . . but her legs spread, and the opening of the vee was ideal for him to stand in so that he could mount her there.

He subdued one of her kicking feet and restrained the ankle on one narrow "leg" of the Y. That left one limb free, and she frantically fought with that one appendage as if it would help her escape.

His initial anger having subsided, Philippe stepped away to admire his handiwork.

Carlotta's walnut-colored hair, which wasn't nearly as thick and long and beautiful as Christine's—but would do for tonight—had sagged to one side during their altercation. It was plastered to the perspiration along her throat and over her shoulders, caught in the little rolls of flesh at the side of her neck. Her breasts had slipped free from the corset and burbled up awkwardly and unattractively over the scalloped edge. The green dress was torn and off-center. Parts of it were hanging by stretched threads, so Philippe decided it was time to put it out of its misery.

But first . . . he easily grasped her flailing leg and firmly slipped the last little cuff over it. Carlotta was subdued, the heavy cloth of her gown and underskirts falling in a neat swing between her spread legs. Still she struggled, tried to kick, rolling her head from side to side.

"Let me go," she cried in a ragged voice, straining, tears rolling from her eyes. "How dare you!"

"I dare." He was in no rush at all. Philippe stepped toward her and began to deliberately tear the gown from her person. The fashions of these times were rather convenient in such situations, for the gowns were made of several pieces of fabric sewn together almost like a puzzle. It was a matter of three jerks of his wrist, and Carlotta was wearing nothing but her stockings and chemise.

Her breasts quivered under the fine lawn garment; her hips shifted and startled as he came to stand between her legs. "What are you going to do?" she asked, her voice raspy, her eyes wide.

But before he could reply, a knock sounded at one of the doors—the one that led to the main corridor and not to any of Philippe's other pleasure chambers, as he liked to call them.

He hesitated, and the knock came again, more stridently. "My lord?" called a voice.

It was François, likely bearing the good news he awaited. Philippe cast a last look at Carlotta, then turned to the door. The confirmation that his orders had been carried out would only serve to heighten his enjoyment.

But when Philippe opened the door and François came in, he knew immediately that the news was not what he'd anticipated.

"What is it?" he demanded. "Is he dead?"

François, a burly man with quick fists, stood near the door but met his eyes squarely. To his credit, he did not even glance toward the trussed-up, spread-eagled Carlotta, who obviously was either too frightened or too intelligent to beg for help. "No, my lord *comte*, he ain't. We followed the orders you gave us, even followed the trail from his underground hideaway, but the bastard got away. We never even saw him."

"You do not know where he is? You have not even seen him?"

"No, my lord."

"*Find him.* I do not want to see you until he is found!" Philippe turned from his man, his fingers shaking with rage. He had sent three carefully selected members of the mob after Erik last night, intending to have them put an end to the man once Christine believed he'd escaped . . . but somehow he'd eluded them.

And now Erik, the half brother of the Chagnys, was loose upon the world, out from the darkness, and bent on revenge.

Philippe turned toward Carlotta. The expression on his face must have spoken for itself, for when she saw him, she began to cry and struggle anew.

TWENTY

*I*t was well past sunset on the second day since Erik had lost Christine, but the rising of the full moon had given him plenty of light to ride from Paris, where the Opera House still smoldered and stewed in its remains, to the estate where he'd been raised.

As he approached the edge of the vast Chagny holdings, Erik watched the southwestern horizon closely. In the distance, he saw two riders leaving the estate, and quickly directed Cesar toward a clump of trees that edged a thicker forest. He couldn't be certain the riders were looking for him, but they were coming from the direction of Philippe's home, and it was an odd time for anyone to be out.

If they weren't looking for him now, they would be soon.

Cesar had been traveling for several hours with Erik on his back, but he still responded to the urgent press of his master's knees and kicked up his speed to a low canter. It was too dangerous for a full-out gallop through an unfamiliar wood, but Erik knew he must put as much distance as he could between himself and the possible pursuers, while circling around to the village of Chagny.

He was to meet Maude Giry at midnight behind the stable at Le Vache Dormante, the only inn located in the small town spread beneath the château's bump of a hill.

Upon reaching their meeting place, Erik positioned himself and Cesar behind a cluster of trees near enough that he could watch the stable and see who came and went. He was cold, and hungry—he'd eaten nothing but a stale hunk of bread since leaving his little house two nights ago.

The orb of the moon cast a full, bluish glow over the fields. After a long while, Erik saw the erect figure in a dark cloak walking quickly toward him. He recognized her right away despite the heavy coverings. Thank God she'd come.

When Maude came near enough to the stable, Erik tossed a rock from his hiding place so that it landed near her. When she looked over, he peered around the edge of the brush to signal her.

"This way," she said, and walked past him as if she'd not seen his gesture. Erik followed and she led him away from the inn and its stable, down a little hill, and to a small structure. "We'll be safe here," she said, opening the door as he approached, and gesturing him inside.

The little hut was hidden from the main road, and looked as though it had not been used for some time.

"One of the girls at the château told me her brother left his house when he went to join a merchant ship. At least you'll be out of the cold here and not be seen," Maude told him, pulling Cesar in with them. "He will have to stay in here with you for a bit, for that white coat will be seen anywhere."

"Christine? Have you seen Christine?" Erik asked the moment he was in the house, even speaking over Maude's explanation.

"I have seen her and spoken with her. She is well. Your hands are freezing, Erik, and you look as if you are ready to collapse. Sit." Maude pushed him toward a small pallet in the tiny one-room building.

When she would have gone to the fireplace, Erik stopped her. "No. The smoke will alert them that this house isn't empty; I don't need a fire. Now tell me of Christine." He knew he didn't want to hear it, but he must.

"She is not injured or hurt in any way," Maude told him, reaching under her cloak. "Here. Eat something, you foolish man. And here is some wine too. You'll be no good for her if you're weak from hunger. Why did you not take anything with you when you left Paris?"

She produced a packet of cheese and beef, wrapped in cloth, and then a hunk of bread along with a small bottle of wine.

"Thank you for meeting me," he told her, forcing his attention to the matter at hand now that he knew Christine was uninjured. He would suffer through the details later. "You have had no problems?"

"Indeed, no. All has gone smoothly. The morning after the fire, I left Paris as we'd planned, and came here to the town. I sent word to Rose and she met me, then brought me back to recommend me as an upstairs maid."

"You did not tell her why," Erik said.

"No, no, she knows only that the Opera House burned, and that I was in need of a position, at least for a time."

"Other than Rose, no one knows who you are?"

"Not at all. I have been very discreet and quite busy," she added, looking at her red hands with obvious annoyance. "I'm not used to such work. But, Erik, we will have to move quickly. Philippe will not be held at bay by his brother for much longer."

"Raoul has been protecting Christine?" A mixture of relief and jealousy poured through him. Christine with Raoul was hardly a better image to dwell on than Christine with Philippe; although with Raoul, she was at least likely to remain free of scars.

But what else might she give to him, the Vicomte de Chagny? Her heart? What would become of her love for Erik now that she was away from the Opera House and her poor accommodations, now that she was housed in the luxurious château with all of her wants and needs attended to . . . maids, clothing, all the food she could wish for, a chamber to herself, jewels . . . a man who could walk the streets in the day, and escort her to parties and soirees and to the shops in Paris . . . a man who did not let fear make him cower in the darkness for a decade?

The cheese crumbled in his fingers, scattering on the floor before him. It would be much easier for Christine to choose a man of light. Better for her. What sort of future could she have with a man who remained in the dark?

"Stop it, Erik," Maude snapped as though reading his mind. "You have come too far to give it up now. I vow to you, she is the stronger of the two of you at this moment—much to my surprise. I thought she would be wailing in the corner, frightened like a little kitten—but no, she is determined to do what she must until you can come for her. She truly loves you."

Maude was right, of course, and he was annoyed with his momentary lapse. "I know she does," he said quietly, suddenly desperate for Christine. Erik forced himself to take a bite of cheese. It tasted little better than paper, but it was sustenance. And he trusted Maude like he trusted no one else, for she'd been as much of a mother as he'd had since his own had died nearly fifteen years ago.

It was Maude who'd helped him find sanctuary in the depths of the Opera House when he'd finally had to get away from the Chagnys. She had been against his love for Christine from the beginning; if she was supporting it now, it was the right thing.

Maude touched his hand; her fingers were warm on his skin. "You've been so used to hiding from the *comte* and his threats that it's no wonder you hesitate."

"But it has been ten years since he forced me into hiding—ten years of living underground because of something I didn't do. The images of the bodies of those three women—no, girls, for they could not have been more than fifteen—have never left my mind. It was abominable what he did to them."

"What proof does the *comte* claim to have that would implicate you for those crimes?"

Erik shrugged, taking another bite of the cheese. "I have not seen it, of course, but who would believe the innocence of a hideous monster over the wealth and power of a Chagny?" he said angrily. "I've wondered every day whether I should step out into the world and take my chances, try to take back even the mean life that I had and at least be able to call it my own, instead of cowering in the darkness because of my wicked half brother. I think of these years I've lost because of my fear of him and his wealth and power and I berate myself for my weakness."

Maude closed her fingers around his wrist, her touch so comforting to a man who'd had little affection. "Strong in mind and heart, so strong in so many ways, you are, Erik . . . but one great weakness, one thing you haven't been willing to risk—your freedom, or going back to a life of ridicule, and loss of yourself. That's not so surprising, nor is it a great failing. Who among us would not do what we must to keep our persons free?

"You were young, then, remember, Erik? You could not have

been more than seventeen, perhaps eighteen, when you had to take refuge. And what was your life like before then? Full of derision and pain . . . it's no wonder you made the choice you did. No wonder."

"Even now, when the thing I love more than anything is at risk, I hide. I scuttle in corners like a beetle and rely on you to bring me news, and on you to speak to her, to soothe her."

Maude looked at him, an unfamiliar glint in her eyes. "Erik. Do you need me to tell you that you are doing what you can? No, I don't think so," she said, shaking her head. "I help you because I love you, and because I want you to have something *right* in your life, after all the years of anguish. When the time is right for you to come out of the darkness and fully into the light, you'll do it."

He had finished the cheese and now took a drink of wine to soothe his suddenly tight throat. No one had ever spoken to him with such kindness or confidence. "Thank you," he said, with a short nod. Then he threw off the mantle of doubt and darkness that had come over him, and put his agile mind to work.

"I know all of the ways to enter the château, but I'm certain my brother will be expecting that," he said. "He'll be watching for me. We'll have to find some way to get Christine out. Tell me . . . does she spend most of her time . . . alone? In her chamber? Or . . ." He took another drink of wine, his fingers tight on the smooth glass bottle.

"She dined with the Chagny brothers and the *comtesse* last evening, but today she has spent much time in her chamber, alone. Although I do not expect that will last for long, for as I said, Philippe is becoming impatient."

"The moment Raoul's back is turned, he will do what he wishes." Erik bit into the last of the bread. "Christine must escape before then. . . . There must be a time when Philippe will be busy or otherwise distracted from her presence."

"I heard mention that he expects visitors tomorrow. Perhaps when he is busy meeting with them—"

Erik was already nodding. "Yes, yes. That will be a good time. Philippe will make the grand gesture; he and Delia will dine with them . . . but what of Raoul? If he is there, Christine will likely be on his arm at the dinner table."

"Raoul must return to Paris tomorrow morning, something related to his enlistment and upcoming voyage."

Which meant that Christine would be without her protector. "Then we must do it tomorrow," Erik said. "Do you know when the guests are to arrive?"

She was glancing out the window. "Late in the morning, I hear. The *comte* directed the staff to prepare a large dinner for them."

Erik nodded. "Good. Raoul will be gone and that will make it easier. I'll need you to make a distraction that will call the guards' attention away from her escape—a fire in the barn would do it. The horses will be out to pasture, but the fire will be a threat nevertheless."

"I can attend to that," Maude agreed.

Cesar nickered nervously, his ears cocked and flickering, his feet prancing in the small cottage. Erik reached to pat him on the haunches. "Easy, boy," he murmured, wondering if he'd sensed a wolf. "Take care on your return to the château; there have always been wolves about, and they have little fear."

"I will indeed."

He turned his mind back to the details. "If the fire is begun in the stable during dinner, that will pull Philippe from his meal and his guests. Start it a quarter hour before the meal is to be served, back in the upper loft. By the time it's noticed, it will be a full-fledged blaze. Have Christine slip from her room through the passageway I told you of, and she can leave the estate on the south side, farthest from the barn. Cesar and I will be waiting there for her."

"I'll do that." Maude took his face in her hands, something she'd never done. Her fingers were cool on his bare skin and, on the other side, pressed the leather of his mask into his nerveless face. "Have a care, Erik."

He nodded, and allowed her to draw him into an embrace. "Thank you, Maude. Thank you for all you've done."

At the door of the cottage, he stopped her, listening. The faint rustle he thought he'd heard wasn't repeated, and after a long moment of watching and waiting in silence, and noting that Cesar remained calm, he said, "Go now and beware the wolves."

"Au revoir, Erik," she said. And she was gone.

TWENTY-ONE

"Christine."

The sound of her name wavered through the lull of sleep, and Christine opened her eyes, her heart pounding when she realized someone was in the dark bedchamber with her. It was a frightening moment before she ascertained that it wasn't Philippe, or even Raoul. She smelled lilies.

"Madame?" Her voice was low by design and from sleep, but before she could say another syllable, a hand was pressed over her lips.

"It is I, *oui*. . . . Now listen closely. I have seen Erik—this night, in the village." The hand tightened when Christine would have spoken to demand how he was, and where he was, and every little detail she craved. "Hush! He is well, and nearby. We have planned for you to escape tomorrow."

"Tomorrow?" Her voice was crushed by the hand, but Christine's lips formed the word in delight, nevertheless.

"While the *comte* is visiting with his guests, there will be a fire in the stable. As all rush to battle it, you will go through the door through which I have come, there in the closet, and make your way to safety."

Christine pulled the woman's hand from her mouth to whisper, "You will not come with me?"

"I cannot. . . . I dare not be complicit, in the event that I am still needed within these walls after. Erik will be waiting for you on the far side of the château, away from the fire. You shall flee to safety. Do you understand?"

Christine nodded, the hand holding her mouth easing away.

"Now, I shall tell you the path you must take for your escape." Madame's voice remained low and smooth as she described the route Christine would take through the secret passageways and out near the servants' entrance, which was on the opposite side of the château from the stables.

"If there is a secret way out, why can I not go now?" Christine whispered, pulling herself half-upright.

"The château is guarded on all sides because the *comte* expects Erik to come for you. That is why tomorrow, when the stable is burning and the *comte* is busy with his guests, will be the best time for you to escape unnoticed. The guards will be busy with the fire, and you will slip from the small entrance near the side."

Christine nodded, but she had another concern. "But if the château is guarded, how did you come to meet with Erik? Did the guards not stop you?"

Madame's low laugh was rough. "They have no interest in the comings and goings of a servant. It is you, or Erik, that they watch for. And, indeed, there are enough servants who venture into town in the evening to have a drink at the inn that it is no cause for speculation."

"And so tomorrow, I shall leave this room through the secret passageway." Christine smiled in the dark. Tonight will have been the last night she must hope that Philippe would be denied his obvious desire. Tomorrow, she would have no more worries of it. She would be with Erik.

"Indeed, and none will know you are missing until much later. And then you and Erik will leave, and start a new life somewhere where his face will not give cause for horror or hatred or accusation."

"Thank you, madame," Christine said, squeezing the woman's hands. "Thank you."

The ballet mistress slipped from the room soon after, and Christine rolled to her side in the large bed.

Tomorrow. Tomorrow she would be with Erik again, and away from this house of eroticism and salaciousness and danger.

Sunlight streamed through the window, and Raoul was standing, tall and gilt-haired, next to her bed when Christine opened her eyes again.

"Raoul," she gasped, awakened from a lush dream with a raven-haired man, a very different man from the composed, elegant one who looked down at her.

"Good morning, Christine," he murmured, his eyes glinting with an expression she'd become much too familiar with. "How lovely you look, all tumble-haired and rumpled in your bedclothes. But there is dark under your eyes, *mon ange*. Have you not slept well in your soft, large bed?"

"The bed is very comfortable, Raoul," she replied, looking up at him and trying to recall, trying to *find*, the kind young man she'd befriended those years ago . . . the one who'd dashed into the surf for her scarf. Not the one who looked at her as though he wished to devour her completely without taking a breath. Not the one who'd brought her to this place against her wishes.

Not the one who'd forced her to choose captivity to save her lover.

He sat, and his slender weight rocked her ever so slightly toward him; then his fingers moved, sliding up along the bare arm that she'd curved, fist toward her throat, on top of the bedding. The dream of Erik had left her aroused, and wanting, and her heart was still slamming from being pulled so abruptly from that sensual world to this . . . this room that crackled with apprehension and uncertainty.

He positioned a hand on either side of her shoulders and his fingers pressed into the pillow next to her, causing him to tilt closer. "A bed is much more comfortable when it is shared," he murmured, his face moving toward her.

Christine's breath caught as she resisted the urge to push him away. Last evening, he had attempted to seduce her after dinner—which had been served at a regular dinner table, unlike the night before—but she had managed to hold him off by claiming an aching head.

Raoul hadn't argued, but Christine had not missed the knowing expression on Philippe's face as he watched from his chair in the parlor. He clearly knew what she was about, and his countenance told her that such prevarication would not work on him. The determination in his face had made her even more apprehensive, particularly after Raoul announced that he would be leaving the château the next morning.

Today. Leaving her alone with Philippe.

Suddenly, Raoul's proximity was the lesser of two evils.

"When will you leave?" Christine asked Raoul, closing her eyes against the hungry expression on his face. Would there be time between Raoul's departure and the arrival of Philippe's guests for the *comte* to visit her bedchamber?

"Do you miss me already?" he asked, lifting his foot to straddle her body trapped beneath the bedclothes. Before she could reply, he lowered himself toward her, kissing the exposed flesh of her shoulder.

His lips were surprisingly hard, mauling her sensitive skin, causing Christine to twitch and jerk away even as his touch pulled desire from her. He followed her, his hands moving to cup her shoulders and keep her in place, and his breath coming faster against her shoulder, moist from his mouth. "No," he murmured, his voice shaky. "Christine, I need you."

He nibbled her shoulder with his lips, the edges of his teeth grooving into her skin, and she felt his weight settle closer to her. Trapped beneath the heavy bedclothes, she was in a cocoon between his legs, unable to kick or shift away.

"Raoul . . ."

"My ship sails in two days. I'll be gone for a year, and I'm not going to leave without you as my wife," he said, raising his face so that she could see his eyes. "I love you." He dipped toward her, covering her lips with his, sliding one hand down to move the blankets from her breast. "My brother wanted me to marry the Le Rochet girl, but I cannot. I will make a short trip to her father today to break the betrothal, and then I will come back for you."

When his fingers touched her nipple, still sensitive from the arousal of her dream, Christine felt the jolt of pleasure; and as he kissed her, his tongue slick and strong, tangling with hers, her eyes closed. She felt the memory of desire rise again, and then his hands sliding over her breasts, pulling the lace of her night rail away, releasing them to the cool room. Her lower body was still trapped, and Raoul had moved, lowering his hips so that his cock pressed down into her sex through all the layers of blankets.

He was breathing heavily, and when she opened her eyes she saw that his were glazed and odd, determined in a way that caused her a pang of nervousness. Still, he kissed her, holding her shoulders in place again, arching his back so that he could move his lips along her jaw and down over the delicate skin of her throat. His mouth was light and wet and harsh and sensual all at the same time, and Christine couldn't move away from the sensations, the unending trickles of his lips. She felt jumpy and achy all at once, and her eyes fluttered as she fought to keep them open, to focus on the ceiling above instead of the feel of his mouth on her skin.

He sucked hard and long at her neck, and she gasped as the sensation poured through her body, tingling in her belly and down into her throbbing sex. With one smooth move, Raoul had a nipple in his mouth, and she could hear his labored, rasping breathing as he sucked and sucked, drawing it into a point at the back of his mouth. The incessant tug of pleasure-pain was so unbearable that she cried out, and Raoul lifted his head.

"You'll marry me, Christine," he said, his lips full and red, his eyes blazing with determination, his words choppy with emotion. "You'll marry me . . . and you'll forget about that monster. I don't care . . . what my brother says. You'll . . . marry me."

He was rocking against her, his breaths coming faster and faster until his eyes rolled back up into their lids and with a soft sob of release, he shuddered against her, bowing his head against her chest, dampening her skin.

When he looked up, his face was wet with tears, and when she tried to roll away, he grasped her wrist, pulling himself up. "Christine," he said, "tonight, when I return, you leave with me. You are *mine*. Do you understand?"

Tonight she would be gone, with Erik.

"Raoul," she began, scrambling for something to say. The gentle boy was gone, completely gone. His fingers around her wrist hurt, enough that she wanted to gasp with it, but she saw that oddness in his eyes and dared not. She dared nothing but agree with him.

"I'll protect you from him, from all of them," he said, sitting up next to her, still grasping her wrist. "I'll make you forget what that monster did to you, and you'll be with me, Christine."

Holding her wrist, he pushed his other hand under the bedclothes, far down beneath them to the juncture of her legs. Before she could move, he covered her with his palm, slid his fingers up and into the folds of her sex and began to stroke with long, easy movements.

She was more than ready for it, and the surprise of his sudden movement caught her off guard so that the pleasure consumed. Her world centered there, between her legs, and rose and fell. Christine gave herself up to it, let it go, and focused everything on the sleek rhythm of his hand.

She felt Raoul next to her, heard his raspy breathing and the strange low sobbing in the back of his throat. She knew he was the one touching her, bringing her to the body-wrenching shudder she knew would come.

But it was Erik she thought of. Erik she yearned for.

And Erik she wept for when at last she came, and her body convulsed in relieved tremors beneath the fingers of another man.

Tears leaked from the edges of her eyes as she prayed, prayed that her escape today would go as planned.

When she opened her eyes, after a long moment, it was to see Raoul standing there, his eyes focused on her. "You'll marry me, Christine. You are one thing my brother will not keep from me."

He left the room with a silent swish of the door.

Twenty-two

Two hours after Raoul left her, just after the midday dinner was being served below, Christine heard the shouts of alarm that portended the burning stable. She was ready, and without hesitation, she left her chamber through the passageway in the closet.

Only moments later, after meeting no one, Christine emerged from the small servant door at the back of the château. The sunlight over the patches of snow was blinding, but the crisp winter air was refreshing and biting, tinged with smoke from the burning stable—but it was the air of freedom.

Though she wasn't free from the Chagny brothers yet, she was closer to Erik than she'd been for days. She knew he was out there, just beyond the trees past the low stone wall. And over that stone wall and beyond was true freedom with him.

Wrapped in a dark cloak, Christine moved away from the château. A shout in the distance caused her to freeze, her heart filling her throat. But after a moment of gaping around from behind a large oak, she realized it had come from the direction of the stable, on the other side of the château.

A glance up over the top of the house's square tower told her that whoever'd set the fire had done the job well. A tall spiral of dark gray smoke billowed up, and with a small gust of wind came a shower of ash over the peaked château roof and the stronger smell of burning wood.

Hoping none of the horses would be injured in the fire, Christine gave one last look at the cloud of smoke and hurried toward another tree. Madame Giry had warned her to move quickly from tree to tree, ending at the clump of scrubby pines next to the wall. There would be a pile of stones there for her to use to climb over the wall, and Erik would be waiting for her just on the other side.

Erik.

Christine hurried her steps, the cloak flapping about her legs as she dodged toward another tree. Even though it was winter, the branches were thick enough, and the pines close enough, that anyone looking down from the upper windows of the château would be hard-pressed to see her.

There—she saw the trio of pines and, as she darted forward, the pile of rocks. The wall was no higher than her chest; the flat-topped stones that looked as though they might have been left over from the building of the wall or the château would give her enough of a boost to make climbing the wall simple, even in her heavy skirts.

Christine stepped up onto the pile of stones, holding the top of the wall, and swung her foot up and onto the ledge, looking for a sign of Erik. Beyond the wall, trees were scattered over low, rolling fields patched with snow, and in the distance, a line of trees curved around the edge of the estate. Far to the left, along the wall onto which she hoisted herself, were the massive iron gates to the lawn she'd just crossed, and beyond them was the dark curl of smoke from the burning stable.

At first, there was no sign of any life. All was silent and still. But then she saw him, near a cluster of trees.

"Erik," she said softly, hardly daring to believe he was there, coming toward her on Cesar. His heavy dark coat flapped over the horse's dirty white haunches, his face shadowed by a wide-brimmed hat. He sat tall and strong in the saddle as he and the stallion followed the line of trees, out of sight of the château and its burning stable.

Bringing both of her feet to the other side of the wall, she launched herself over and ran toward him.

"My, what a welcome surprise." He swept off his hat and Christine staggered back in shock. "But I hope you are not leaving so soon."

"No!" she cried, and turned to stumble away, but Philippe was too fast for her. He raced up on Cesar and swooped an arm down to snag her around the waist, lifting her to slam her belly onto the saddle in front of him. The wind knocked out of her, Christine gasped for breath as she tried to slip from under his grip.

"A case of mistaken identity, I presume, based on your reaction," he said, his hand grasping the back of her neck and holding her in place as her stomach jounced painfully against the saddle. "Forgive me for interrupting your plans, but I would not want you leaving the château so soon, my dear."

She could not squeeze away from under his hand, but with the bit of breath she had left in her, Christine managed to say, "Erik?" She knew something had befallen him. How else would Philippe be riding Cesar?

Philippe had wheeled the white horse back around and Christine was able to lift her head enough to see that they were going toward the gates at the back of the château.

"Your beloved Erik is unable to help you now."

No.

Christine squeezed her eyes closed, blocking away the gloating in his voice, the satisfaction in his words. Philippe would have no qualms about it, none at all . . . but, no, *no* . . . she wouldn't believe it. Not yet. Not until she had proof.

They galloped to a halt near the same servant door through which Christine had emerged only moments before. Without loosening his grip on her neck, Philippe slid off Cesar and moved to clamp a stifling hand over her mouth as the other closed around her arm.

She fought and kicked, but he was taller and stronger than she by far, and he easily maneuvered her into the building. Once inside, he stopped in the narrow back hallway, and still gagging her with his hand and keeping her pulled up tightly against his body, he fumbled around with his other and produced a gleaming knife.

"Now," he said, breathing heavily, "you'll not make a sound, or I'll cut your pretty throat. I'd hate to damage such a lovely songbird, but as with Carlotta, I've no qualms about doing so if necessary. Walk this way."

He released her mouth but held her upper arm with a grip so tight that her fingers tingled, and with the other hand, he held the tip of the knife to her throat. Christine walked as he directed, but when she thought to turn toward the chamber she'd occupied, he steered her in a different direction.

"No, my dear. I have much more comfortable accommodations available for you now where the walls are thick and padded. It is in my private quarters."

Her stomach pitched and a wave of fear swept over her. He

must have seen her wide eyes and panic-stricken look, for he smiled. "I'm sure you'll be pleased to know we won't be disturbed."

For a moment, Christine thought she would prefer the knife slitting her throat to the certainty of being locked away in the *comte*'s private chambers, but then she remembered Raoul. He, despite the obsessive light in his eyes, at least meant her no harm. He wouldn't allow his brother to hurt her; he wanted to marry her.

Philippe wouldn't dare to keep her from him. He wouldn't dare hurt her. Much. Christine's stomach churned, but she swallowed back the nausea. And, if there was a chance that Erik was still alive, she would find out. She'd endure anything, make it through anything, if there was a chance to see him again.

But when Philippe opened the door to his chamber and thrust her in so hard she stumbled to her knees, Christine felt another wave of panic. She saw things that made her want to take the knife to her throat herself.

A row of ugly-looking whips, neatly arranged on the wall.

Three abnormal pieces of furniture: one in the shape of a Y, one X, and a board slanting from ceiling to floor—each with dangling cuffs.

A tall pole, studded with spikes, and decorated with two cuffs hanging far above her head.

A table with metal and wooden implements in long sleek shapes, pointed lethal ones, and round studded ones.

And a naked young woman chained to the wall, legs spread, mouth stuffed with a large white ball, and bulging eyes.

Christine couldn't breathe, and the room began to close in on her. She heard a low chuckle, then the clink of metal, and she let herself slide into black.

"I so hate to be the bearer of bad news, my dear brother," said Philippe as he stood in front of Erik. "But I don't believe it's fair to allow you to hold on to lost dreams. You see, the woman you love, the one you've risked everything for, has made a most pragmatic choice."

Erik said nothing; he reacted not at all. Not a hitch of breath, not a flicker of an eyelid. Most of all, he dared not lift his face to meet his brother's eyes, for fear the man would see the deep hatred there and cut him down right at the moment. He had to prevent that. As long as he lived, there was the hope of escape and finding Christine.

"She's come to her senses and decided that her fortune would be better served by aligning it with the *vicomte* instead of the bastard Chagny brother. They ran away to marry early this morning. So, you see . . . there is really no reason for you to hold out any further hope. You can crawl back into your dark dungeon and wallow there for eternity. Oh! But forgive me. . . . You already are in a dark dungeon, aren't you?"

He laughed and Erik gritted his teeth, felt them grind dully near the edge of his jaw. His arms were numb from the tight metal around his wrists, attached sturdily to the stone wall above his head. His legs had been treated in the same fashion, manacled near the floor so that he had to alternately stand on his toes to relieve his arms or hang by his wrists to rest his feet. His mask was long gone and the fact that his face was naked only increased his sense of vulnerability.

He'd been this way since late last night, not long after Maude left the small cottage. Perhaps a quarter of an hour after her departure—which gave him the hope that she'd gotten safely back to the château unseen—the door burst open and five burly men stormed in, attacking with fists and feet and clubs.

Even then, Erik would have escaped but for a sixth man waiting outside the window he tumbled through, hands grabbing for his hair, ready with a large stick to slam across his shoulders with a force that sent him driving into the ground. Moments later, in a whirl of blows and kicks, he succumbed to the pain and the world went black.

When he regained consciousness, he found himself here, chained in the damp cold cellar of Château de Chagny. He recognized it immediately; his initials had long ago been carved into the stone, remnants of days spent here when he angered his father or brothers.

A bitter thought, that he'd come so far only to return to this hell.

This was the first he'd seen of Philippe, although he'd been brought food and water—in an effort, he supposed, to keep him strong for the pain that was sure to come.

Erik wasn't altogether certain how many hours had passed, but from the numbness in his arms and the roaring pain encumbering his body, he knew it had been many. The pain always waited, gathering its forces, after a beating like that.

"What is it, dear brother? Have you nothing to say? No gratitude to me for taking you back in, now that you've been left by your true love?" His voice sneered at the last words. "She very much enjoyed her stay here; Christine was quite vocal about it. Ah, yes, we quickly moved to a first-name basis, my dear brother. She spread her legs so quickly, I thought the breeze would put out the candles." He laughed.

And then Erik heard it. The sound that still had the power to set his stomach to roiling. The light, sharp crack.

"It's not befitting the son of a *comte*, even a bastard, to keep his eyes downcast in servitude. Even with a face like yours."

This time, the whip snapped near his ear and it was all Erik could do to keep from flinching. But he did. . . . With a grim sense of smugness, he didn't move. That first time, or even the second, third, fourth . . . even when the bite of the sleek leather cut into his arm, his thigh, his ribs, his good cheek.

"Still stoic as ever, are you, dear brother? Or have you fainted?" There was the barest hint of annoyance in Philippe's voice; it was betrayed by the harsher, more stinging whipcrack that he laid across Erik's torso. This time, he couldn't contain a low groan.

"Ah, *bien*, still conscious, I see."

Erik braced himself for another stripe from the leather, but whatever Philippe's intention, it was interrupted by the arrival of another person.

Awash in the reverberating pain and his own dull confusion, Erik didn't hear their whispered conversation. When Philippe returned his attention, Erik heard his words with relief. "It is your good fortune that I'm called back to my guests. Sleep well, my brother. I'll be back as soon as I can."

Philippe moved soundlessly away, and Erik hung, miserable and aching, sweat and blood dripping from his skin. He pulled on the chains, with the only result low clinks and clanks and more strain to his muscles.

At last, he gave in to his body and allowed himself to sink into oblivion, for only there would the pain ease.

TWENTY-THREE

Before Christine opened her eyes again, she remembered where she was. Even in her sluggish state, she knew. Dread made her heart thump sharply as she opened her lids and looked around, afraid of what she would see.

But the goggle-eyed girl had disappeared and she was alone. Unfettered. Sprawled on a large bed she hadn't noticed before.

And then she realized she wasn't alone. Someone had awakened her.

"Madame," she whispered in amazement. "How did you find me?"

Madame Giry had a guarded look on her face, and she held a finger to her lips. "Rose told me," she whispered. "She is one of the few who have access to these quarters. It is a secret that you are here. I brought you this." She handed her a warm, wet cloth and Christine used it to gratefully wipe her face and hands.

"What of Erik? Philippe said he was dead!" Christine asked as she washed.

Madame shook her head. "He is in the dungeon. The *comte* has made him his prisoner. He is hurt, but by no means dead."

Her heart swelled with relief. "Thank God he's alive! How badly is he hurt?"

"Come, quickly. I will take you to him while the *comte* is busy with his guests. We haven't long, and you must be back—"

"Back?" Christine reared away in fear. "No, if I leave here, I won't come back! Erik and I will leave."

"I hear he is in chains; no one knows where the key is. No doubt in Philippe's pocket. Rose has dared to bring me here, and will guide us to the dungeon—but is too frightened to do more to help us. If you do not come back here and pretend you know nothing, you will not have the chance to find the way to free Erik. Do you understand?"

She understood. And . . . Raoul should return soon. If Philippe was busy with his guests for long enough, there would be no chance for him to come to her.

"Take me to Erik."

Rose was waiting for them in the hall, her delicate features pinched with worry. Christine recognized her immediately as the girl who'd been hanging on the wall, with the ball in her mouth. It was no wonder she knew Christine's whereabouts.

They hurried like silent wraiths along the corridors and through servant passageways down four floors to well beneath the ground, where it was damp and dark.

"He is down there," Rose said, pointing down another flight of stairs that led into darkness. "Now I must go. I am leaving this place, and I will never return." She disappeared back the way they'd come.

Madame gave Christine a little push. "I will wait here and signal you if someone comes."

Christine barely heard Madame's last words; she hurried down the rest of the stairs and around the corner—and there he was, manacled at wrists and ankles, sagging against the cold gray stone. Blood streaked his torn shirt and along the sinewy muscles of his bare forearms, drawn tight from their fastenings high on the wall.

"Erik . . . oh, my dear Erik," Christine cried softly, rushing toward him.

He lifted his head at the sound of her voice, struggling to hold it upright as her hands cupped the sides of his face, and she brought her mouth to his lips.

They were dry, cracked, bloody, but it was Erik. She softened his brutalized mouth with hers, fitting to him as she stroked her fingers over his jaw and neck.

"Christine, no," he murmured against her kisses, "you should not be here." But his mouth mauled hers with tenderness, as though he knew he'd never taste her again, and she heard the dull clank of metal as he reflexively attempted to hold her. "He told me you'd gone off with Raoul," he said, nudging her aside so that he could press his lips to her cheek and huddle his face into her neck, breathing deeply, shakily, and then releasing a long exhale in a low shudder.

"I thought you were dead," Christine replied, pulling away from him and, despite Madame's warning, tugging at the heavy iron cuffs, shaking and rattling them in search of a weakness. "He told me you were dead, but I would *not* go with Raoul. I never will, Erik. Even if you were gone."

"Thank God," he murmured, bending his face toward her. "I thought perhaps . . . it would be so much easier for you, Christine," he told her. He brushed his good cheek along hers, rubbing gently like a cat, caressing her in the only way he could. Over the dampness of the dungeon, amid the must and gloom, she smelled his familiar scent mingled with sweat and blood and breathed it in as their faces cuddled. "I cannot—"

"Do not say it," she told him, pressing her fingers against his mouth. "I would rather live in the darkness of danger with you than in the sunlight with anyone else. You've taught me what no other has . . . how to really love, how to bring my music back . . . how full life can be. How not to be lonely." She looked up at him, looked into both of his eyes—the thick-lashed one, the sagging, half-hooded one—and took both sides of his face into her hands again, feeling the scrub of his whiskers, the stickiness of oozing blood, the unyielding texture of mangled skin. "I love you, Erik. I'll find a way to set you free."

"Save me again, will you?" he said, pulling away with sudden force. His voice was low, raw, as he buried his face in his shoulder, only the angry, mutilated side showing. "Why must you always be the one to sacrifice, to risk, to choose? Why can I not take care of you?"

"Erik . . . don't! Don't, my love," she said, smoothing her hands over his beloved shoulders, up onto the strained, smooth rope of his biceps. "You are so much stronger than I. You've risked your life coming here. . . . I've done so little in comparison."

"So little?" He heaved in a great breath, turned his face to look down at her. "The giving of your person, of your very most intimate self, to my brothers is a greater sacrifice than this dark life. I'd eagerly give my life for you, Christine . . . but you've given so much more. And I cannot think that I deserve it, for I've done nothing but pull you into the middle of this. You should never have gone with them that night, Christine. *You should have let them take me.*"

"Erik, Erik," she said, blinking away gathering tears. "You are a fool. You've lived too long alone. Do you not know that this"—

she slid her hands down along the ridges of his torso, then up and around as she pulled herself flush to him—"means nothing without love?"

"Christine—" But she stopped whatever foolishness he was about to say with her mouth, standing tall on her toes so she could kiss him full on the lips. She gently told him how much she loved him, how much he meant to her, and how much she trusted him, with the adoring slip of her tongue over his half-open mouth, with the soft nibbling on his upper lip and the bare brush of lip against lip.

So easy, so sweet and slow, the kiss was, as if they were learning each other for the first time. As if they had all the time in the world, and there was no danger of being discovered, separated.

Christine felt the welcome swelling of deep lust, real love, move through her body, tightening her nipples and spiraling in a tingling curl down past her belly. She moaned, pressing her hips against his, shifting her arms around the back of his neck to bring his face to where she could really taste him, and pull his mouth close to tangle her tongue with his hot, greedy one.

Again Christine heard the clink of metal as Erik moved, and the groan of frustration vibrating through his chest when he could not touch her. She removed her hands from his neck, sliding under the ragged, dirty shirt to feel the sleek muscle, smooth skin, and wiry hair.

He could do nothing but breathe and tremble as Christine pulled away the edges of his shirt, scratched her nails gently down along his chest and down to the sagging waist of his trousers. She kissed him on one tiny, hard nipple, bit at the edge of his pectoral, and then sank to her knees on the floor in front of him.

"Christine," he said in a tortured breath when she pulled at the fastenings of his trousers. "Nnn . . ."

She felt his powerful thighs trembling next to her, warm and solid against her arms as she pulled apart the sagging breeches to free his erection. Taking him in both hands, she kissed the soft head, licked around it, and slid him deeply into her mouth, once, twice, then back away to love the tip again.

Erik was breathing as though he'd run for miles, his muscles tense and shaking from effort, from being slung up by them for hours. Christine stroked her hands along his massive legs, around to the back, and up to his buttocks, fitting her fingers between muscle and rough, damp wall. She couldn't get enough of touching him, of the solidness of him, of the smell and the taste.

Despite the always-present danger, she took her time; she feasted, licked, stroked, scratched, sucked, beneath torn shirt, ragged trousers, around manacled legs and wrists. Her breathing matched his; they both sounded, there in the cavernous stone room, as though every last bit of air was being taken from them.

"Christine, please," Erik murmured in the voice of a man dying and out of time.

She slid up his body, pressing flush against him, still completely clothed. She smiled, kissed his neck, sucked for a moment as she flipped up her skirts, and, opening her legs, straddled one of his thighs. The pressure of his leg eased the throbbing of her pip for a moment; she was dripping and she eased her way up and then down, holding on to his wide, square shoulders for support and leverage as her pleasure built.

Then the roar in her ears, the heat between her legs, became too much. "Erik . . . help me," she said, her own voice thin and needy. "I want you inside me."

"Hold on to me," he managed. His eyes were dark, black; his face was twisted on both sides—one by nature, one with desire. "Hold . . . on."

Christine used his shoulders to lift herself so she could straddle his waist. "My love," she gasped as his dripping cock brushed wetly against the inside of her thigh, beneath the mass of skirts and crinolines. He could do nothing to hold her, nothing to help as she looped an arm around his neck, levered her feet against the wall behind his hips, and scooped her skirts away.

The desperate grunts and sighs, the moisture of slick skin, the driving need, kept her frantically moving and shifting until at last . . . they found the place and she slid forward, filled.

A sigh that was half-sob, half-moan came from the back of her throat. Tears stung her eyes. Erik's deep, rasping breaths huffed against her neck.

Carefully, she positioned her feet flat against the wall, fingers clamped on his shoulders, and she moved, flexing her knees, feeling the long slide in and out, up and down . . . as the beauty built, there in that dark, angry dungeon. Her pip swelled, her stark, hard nipples jouncing gently against her chemise, while the telltale tingle in her belly built, ready to shoot through her body.

She worked, her muscles trembling; he moved as much as he could to meet her, the slick suck of moisture between them the only sound beyond their channeled breathing. Faster she moved; more urgently he tilted back and forth, back and forth. Her fingers slipped and she almost lost her grip, but she held on as the desperate rhythm built unbearably, then, finally, blossomed into uncontrollable shudders throughout her limbs.

He surged against her then too . . . metal clanking, shoulders bulging with effort, and a long, husky breath ending in a moan.

"*Dieu, Dieu*," she breathed after a moment of stillness, of satiation. She slipped away, allowing her legs to fall, her fingers still gripping his sweaty shoulders.

"Christine . . . ," he whispered, trembling against her, trying again to bury his face against her. "Ah, Christine."

She kissed him again, a slumberous moment of lips and tongue, heat and tenderness. "I must go," she said, smoothing her hands over his chest again. She would never tire of feeling that sleek plane, the power and heat of it. She kissed him beneath the hollow of his throat, bumping her nose into its little curve.

"I love you, Christine," he said, the glazed look of lust, the dullness of pain, gone from his eyes, replaced by clarity. "Do not endanger yourself to save me. Promise me. Allow me at least that comfort."

She looked at him, purposely chose to stroke the gnarled side of his face. "I promise to take care. I love you."

And she slipped away before love won out and drew her back to his side.

Still breathing heavily, still tingling, Christine came around the corner where she'd left Madame.

"Such a lovely display, my dear," said Philippe, stepping from the shadows. "You are much more accommodating to him than you are to Raoul or myself. I look forward to remedying that situation in the very near future."

Christine couldn't move at first; she couldn't speak. Her eyes darted around as the *comte's* hand whipped out to grab her arm, and she saw the huddled form on the ground. A long, heavy chain led from the wall to under the bundle, where her arms might have been. "Madame!" Her automatic surge toward the still figure was halted as Philippe jerked her back.

"She tried to stop me. . . . The voyeuristic bitch attempted to stop me," Philippe said easily, tugging Christine after him, back toward the alcove where Erik was imprisoned.

"No!" she cried, trying to pull away, seeing the glint in his eyes. "Let me—"

His other hand moved, flew through the air, and cracked against the side of her face, leaving her ears ringing and her cheek throbbing. "I'm beginning to believe that I should have left you to my brother from the beginning, but it is too late for me, Christine Daaé. You have become my obsession and I'll have you. There's nothing to stop me now."

Erik was looking at them, horror plastered over his face, as they came back around the corner. Philippe thrust Christine ahead of him while his heavy fingers grasped her arm.

"Raoul will kill you if you touch me," Christine said desperately, blinking back tears from the pain of his blow. "He intends to marry me; he'll not let you touch me."

Philippe chuckled, shoved Christine forward so they were standing directly in front of Erik. "Raoul is on his way to Paris. He believes that you and this monster have run off together . . . and he is hell-bent on stopping you. I tried to prevent him, tried to tell him it was a folly. But he would not listen." There was false pity in his voice.

Christine's stomach suddenly felt like lead. Her lips formed the syllable of negation, but she could not speak it. She hadn't the breath, nor the energy.

Philippe had no such handicap. "So, my dear brother, you see that I told you a little white lie—just as I told our other brother— but in the end, it works out for the best that you know the truth. For now, as you wait for me to turn you over to the constable here in Chagny—you know the townspeople have never forgiven nor forgotten that monster who ravaged and killed those three young girls—you'll have something more to think about.

"You'll be able to contemplate the fact that, a mere five floors above your very cell, I'll be enjoying that which you'll never have again. And . . . ah, that makes your last moments of intimacy so much more poignant, doesn't it?" He *tsk*ed, his fingers tightening over Christine's arm as his other hand jammed down the front of her bodice, yanking it away to expose her breast.

Fondling it roughly, he tweaked and pinched as he continued his taunts. "Quite lovely, isn't she?" He hefted the weight of her breast in his palm, and Christine could do nothing but try to rear away from him. But the small movement she was able to make only sent her back into his embrace, closer to him.

"And you, my dear . . . it will be best if you cooperate. Truly. For there will be no Raoul to interrupt, and your lover isn't going anywhere. Nor is that slut you call a ballet instructor. In fact, if you don't cooperate and make this enjoyable for me—us," he amended with a low chuckle, "I am sure I can find ways to make things even more uncomfortable for my brother here."

He looked down at her. "So, my dear, shall we repair to above? If it weren't so drafty and cold, I might have been persuaded to remain down here in sight of your lover . . . that way he could participate vicariously. But . . . ah, well, you know . . . comfort is a great thing for me. I have many different . . . mm . . . places to recline that will suit our needs much better than the cold stone floor."

With one last look at Erik, Christine felt herself being dragged away. Their eyes met, his dark with shock and regret, burning into her. She thought for the first time she saw resignation there, and felt her own wave of despair crawl horribly through her body.

There really wasn't any way out, any hope of rescue or reunion.

She wondered if she would live through the night.

TWENTY-FOUR

*P*hilippe's private chambers were as she'd left them—empty, remote, and horrifying. He thrust her into the room ahead of him as he'd done before, and closed the door behind with a snap of finality.

He said nothing for a long moment, simply looked at Christine as she pulled herself up from her trembling knees. When she was standing, she backed away from him and watched warily, heart ramming in her chest, as he appeared deep in thought.

"Oui, ma chère," he said at last, "I am unable to choose. Shall we play the game of pursuit, after which I shall have you as you kick and scream and fight . . . or shall I make you comfortable"—at this, he gave a brief nod toward the Y-shaped bed—"so that I can play with you until you beg me to take you?" He stepped toward her now, his salacious expression sending renewed fear tumbling in her belly. "Or, perhaps, a combination of both?"

Christine took her eyes from the *comte* just long enough to look around for something she could use as a weapon, then returned her attention to him as he came toward her, stalking, as if he were the sleek barn cat that lived in the Opera House's stables and she but a mouseling.

There was no one to help her.

Raoul was gone, ostensibly to save her from what he perceived as a horrible fate. Erik was beaten and chained, and Madame, if she was alive, was also chained to the ground. Even Rose, who might have helped, had run off to the village, leaving Château de Chagny well behind her.

"What is your choice? You wish to fight?" Philippe asked in an indulgent voice. "You do not wish to make use of my comfortable furnishings? I promise you, if I wish you to have pleasure, you will do so. All of my women do."

"And then you kill them," she spit, having spied her weapon of choice. The entire arsenal of whips hung behind Philippe, out of her reach . . . but there was one long, slender dowel lying on the edge of a table nearby. She dared not contemplate what that dowel might be used for in Philippe's warped chamber; instead, she lunged for it as he replied to her taunt.

"That is only when I have become bored with them." He lifted a brow as she turned back, wielding the stick. "My, how enterprising." He gave a little laugh. "But do not worry yourself. I do not expect to become bored with you for quite some time, Miss Daaé. It has been quite the chase, and I mean to make the most of it now that it has ended. And then there is, of course, the *comtesse*, my wife. She found you most enticing during our lovely dinner the other night. Unfortunately, she is off to visit her sister for a bit, so she won't be able to sample your charms until she returns, but I do know that she intends to. Did you perhaps think she might be of assistance in helping you run away? No? Surely the thought crossed your mind, Christine." He stepped to one side, his eyes never leaving her. "You must be frantically considering all possibility of escape."

He looked at her again. "And perhaps you had hoped your dear friend the ballet mistress might help you. Well, *ma chère*, she has helped you enough. I have been spying on her visits to your chamber since her first, and it was she who unwittingly led me to your lover Erik."

Christine braced herself, holding the dowel in front of her like a clumsy sword. The closest she'd ever come to wielding a weapon was when she and Franco had played at sword fighting one day whilst he was putting away the props from *Don Carlos*.

Philippe turned and she saw that he had a whip in his hand. It lashed out and she ducked away, but the snap of leather did not cut into her skin. Instead, it easily wrapped around the edge of her own weapon and with a flick of his wrist, Philippe jerked it out of her fingers. Then he threw the whip behind him and advanced another step toward her.

"Let us keep this to what they call hand-to-hand combat, *ma chère*," he said with an easy smile. "I want to feel you fighting me with your nails and teeth. . . . I want our bodies to roll together on the floor, or the bed, or wherever, as you kick and struggle beneath me, your heart pounding, your lungs screaming as they heave."

He lunged and snatched at her arm, his fingers closing over the silky fabric of her sleeve. Christine shrieked and jerked away, and the sleeve tore from her gown.

She whirled and bumped into the wall, and felt him coming after her again, easy and calm as if he were indulging a playful toddler. The wall was behind her, and to her left the corner of the room where she would be trapped—and to her right, a narrow space through which she might pass.

Philippe was grinning wider now, and he canted to one side, giving her an even larger space through which she might slip past. "Come now, Christine. I had expected more from you than to see you cowering in the corner. Why, you are making this no fun at all. Erik would be quite disappointed in your lack of ferocity. After all, you are the only thing standing between him and a very unpleasant trial and execution."

She ducked and dashed toward freedom, staying as close to the wall as possible, but his arm reached out when she'd nearly gotten past. He grabbed her wrist and used her momentum to jerk her toward him, pulling her off-balance so that she fell into his person.

He grabbed her other wrist and pulled her arms straight down, bringing her body flush with his. Christine knew he wanted her to struggle, that her helplessness aroused him, but she couldn't stop herself. She tried to kick out under her heavy skirts, but succeeded only in driving her foot between his wide-legged stance and falling toward his body even more.

His greedy smile filled her line of vision as he swooped down, pulling her closer by her arms, and seeking her lips with his. Twisting her face away, Christine struggled to pull free even as his mouth slid across her jaw and cheek. Hot, moist breath blasted her skin as he mauled her face, nipping at her tender earlobe, then sliding across her jaw as he forced her backward with the brunt of his mouth until he at last covered her lips with his.

She tried to bite him, tried to kick out, but he crushed his mouth harder against hers, laughing into her as her foot swung clumsily, harmlessly between his legs. She tasted blood, felt the invasion of his slick tongue and the sharpness of his teeth at the edge of her lips as she tried to twist away.

Tears streamed from the outer edges of her eyes, and her arms and wrists had gone numb from his relentless grip. She jerked at the hips, slamming into the bulging arousal that was horrifyingly evident even beneath the many layers of clothing between them, and felt his groan of pleasure when she did. At last she pulled free from the kiss, turning her face away, and felt the scrape of teeth and the slickness of his lips and tongue over her cheek.

Suddenly, the grip on her arms loosened, and she was falling backward, tumbling to the floor. She landed sharply on an elbow and a hip, her hand slapping so hard on the wood that her fingers tingled. Tangled in a mass of skirts, Christine rolled frantically to one side, watching the shiny black boots as they stood, planted wide, just out of her reach, and she tried to scramble to her feet. Her gown was not made for fighting or running, or any sort of quick movement, and she tripped again as her foot caught in its hem.

"You seem to be having quite a bit of trouble with your gown, Christine," Philippe said. His voice was still easy, but she heard the deeper gust of his breath. When she dared to glance up, she saw that his lips were full and moist and red, and that his blue irises had shrunk as his pupils swelled. "Perhaps I can help you with it."

He dived toward her, and she felt the tug on her skirts, and then heard the tear as he yanked the fistful of fabric away. The front two pieces of her gown came loose, and the lace and tulle from her crinolines tore in a long, white froth. She felt the weight lifted from her legs, now nearly bare, covered only in stockings and a light lawn chemise, and when she twisted away, the fabric tore even more.

Christine rolled on the floor, her skirts pulled from her bodice, her feet able to move more freely. Using the cabinet next to her, the one with the long, slender, pointed objects of ivory, to pull herself up, she turned and saw, not Philippe lunging at her again as she'd expected, but him standing there, watching her, a large frothy mess hanging from his fist.

The door was just to his right. He hadn't locked it. If she could just slip past him . . . Christine looked in the opposite direction and saw a large, studded club, leaning against a chair leg. She pretended to stumble, throwing herself toward the club, and she managed to grab it before she fell.

Hearing him behind her, she pushed to her feet, clutching the nasty weapon, and swung blindly as he lunged toward her. Amazingly, it connected with flesh—she didn't see where, for she was already turning toward the door. Without looking back, she darted toward freedom.

Carlotta crept along the narrow, jagged hallway at the back of the château—the passage that connected to the lowliest of the servant quarters. The lowliest of the servant quarters, where she, La Carlotta, had been banned for two days, barely conscious and hardly able to move. No one had dared nurse her other than to bring her clear broth and tea, and a bare crust of bread, so she had no use for any of them.

Her legs were still weak, her arms bruised and aching, one wrist screaming with pain, and her throat . . . she dared not think about it, dared not let herself think that she'd never sing again. Instead of the terror of having no voice, having had it squeezed from her by the violent hands of the Comte de Chagny, she made herself focus on the anger, the terrific, blinding, galvanizing anger she felt for the man who'd dare use her so. How foolish she had been to accept his invitation to the château after the Opera House had burned!

But there would be time to grieve and mourn later. Now she would have her revenge.

There'd been enough whisperings among the servants for her to guess what had occurred. Despite the *comte*'s claims of secrecy, there were certain things that did not go unnoticed or unseen. Perhaps his pathetic brother might have believed that the *comte* had allowed

Christine Daaé to escape, but Carlotta was not so stupid. After all, she had been there, watching him as he watched the girl through the small hole in her room. She'd seen the crazed light of obsession and salaciousness in his eyes.

The *comte* had been careful not to let the servants know where he kept the keys to the dungeon, but Carlotta knew. She'd seen him put them in a small cupboard in the room in which he'd tortured her after they'd spied on Christine. He thought she was unconscious when he hid the keys beneath one of the lewd paintings on the wall, but she'd been watching him through slitted eyes.

Yes, he'd hurt her, but she'd had worse at the hands of her father, growing up in the dirty streets of London. She'd learned how to feign unconsciousness, and how to bury her screams deep inside so he'd stop hurting her.

No one would have thought to look in that room, anyway, for it was not the chamber the *comte* usually used for his sexual activities. The room from which he and Carlotta had spied on the Daaé girl wasn't used as frequently, although he'd outfitted it with a small clutch of instruments—as Carlotta had cause to know.

She saw no one as she walked awkwardly along the hall on trembling legs, then to the small door that led to the dungeons. She at least knew where the captive was, the man called Erik. It had been a shock to learn that the so-called Opera Ghost was actually the natural brother of the *comte*. Chagny's vitriol and hatred toward the man had spewed forth during that horrible night she'd spent helpless and abused under his hands and body, and she'd learned enough to know that whatever sins Erik might have committed at the opera, the fact that his brother both hated and feared him meant that he was her most obvious ally.

———

Christine had the knob in her hands, smooth and cool, before Philippe's grasping hand jerked her back. Not hard enough that she tumbled to the ground, but enough that she lost her grip on the metal and jolted backward. Another shove from him and she spun around, this time keeping her balance as there were no heavy skirts to set her off-kilter or trip her.

But he came toward her before she could celebrate that little victory, his eyes ferocious and his hands reaching toward her. "So you want to play with the club, do you, Christine?" he asked. "I'd be most happy to accommodate you. But first . . ." He didn't grab at her arms as she'd expected; no, again, he surprised her, his fingers sliding into her cleavage and rending away the triangle of her bodice in a loud tear.

Christine pulled away, whirling, but he came after her again. It appeared the game was over; her blow, however ineffective, had angered him. His footsteps were hard and fast behind her, his breathing more harsh. He grabbed at her shoulder, pulling her back with a head-jolting snatch, and suddenly she felt herself falling.

Unable to control a surprised screech, she tried to brace herself for the fall. But instead of hard floor, she found herself slamming onto something soft. Before she could roll away, Philippe's heavy weight was there, over her, stretching her wrists above her, as she lay on the bed, or whatever it was she was on.

His hips jimmied between her legs, which somehow had become splayed beneath him, and he paused to look down at her. His mouth was twisted in a combination of pleasure and greed, one side tilted up and curled—reminding her of Erik for a bizarre, horrific moment. He breathed heavily, but it was not from exertion. As he looked down at her, pinning her with his violating gaze, one of his hands moved from where it had held her wrist, to slide down over her throat.

One hand free, Christine slapped and scratched, dug her nails into his other arm, the one that held her wrist so tightly her fingers began to tingle. But he ignored the pain; perhaps he reveled in it, for his pupils swelled and his free hand slid down . . . slowly, excruciatingly slowly, over her sweat-moist skin to cover her breast, thumbing her nipple back and forth contemplatively. Then he fitted his palm over the whole swell, like a lover, molding, lifting, squeezing through the protection of her corset.

Still she batted at him, struggling on, though she was becoming weary and out of breath. He moved his hand from her breast and slid fingers down between corset and skin and gave a sudden pull that nearly jerked her shoulders from her neck, making the edges of the corset cut into her skin. Her breasts fell free, but the corset stayed in place, rubbing against her tender skin.

Christine moaned, kicking in earnest from under his weight and grasping a handful of his hair as he bent to suck roughly on her nipple. She gave a hard yank, twisting and bucking beneath him, and Philippe pulled up suddenly, his eyes glinting angrily. Grabbing her free wrist, he pulled it above her head and captured it with his other hand, leaving her pinned by the arms, and one of his hands free.

"Now, my dear," he gasped, pressing his weight into the vee between her legs, his face glistening with moisture, "kick and cry all you wish. . . . It's better that way." He bent to her breast, his breath rasping against her skin as he rammed his hips against her. She fought him when she felt his hand slide down between them, where he ground into her; she felt him pull at his breeches even as he kept her nipple between his teeth. The pain stung, down from her breast to the heavy weight on her, and though her legs shook from fatigue, and his grip above her head numbed her wrists, she roiled and rolled beneath him, gasping for air, tears streaming from her eyes.

His hand brushed against her sex; she felt the shift as his trousers opened and fell away; then his pounding cock was free against her chemise-covered thigh. His breath was out of control, his eyes closed and face tight with pleasure and concentration. He moved against her; she struggled to pull away, her legs and hips moving frantically against him, trying to keep him off-balance. Suddenly, he stiffened, stopped, and groaned against her chest. Something wet and warm seeped through the light fabric of her chemise, soaking through to the sensitive skin of her inner thigh.

Puffing with exertion and release, Philippe lifted his head and looked at her. "Now," he told her, "that we have that out of the way . . . let us move on to something more interesting. I've a mind to hear you beg." He released her, stepping away to refasten his breeches, his eyes watching placidly as she rolled from her position and staggered from the bed.

He allowed her to reach the door again before his fingers closed over her shoulder and he pulled her back. Roughly, he dragged her across the room and shoved her into the narrow vee of the elongated Y-shaped bed. She stumbled backward, and before she could catch her balance he was upon her, thrusting her onto the structure so hard her teeth snapped together. Firm hands closed around an ankle, and suddenly it was clamped into place down on one of the legs of the Y.

Screaming and kicking anew, Christine struggled harder, but he was too strong. Her second ankle was locked in place and then she had only her hands and nails to claw and strike with.

But Philippe stepped away, around to the top of the Y, and grabbed her hair from behind as she bent forward, trying to free her legs. He yanked, and she fell back, her head slamming into the hard surface beneath. Stunned, she could only blink and fight feebly as he locked her left wrist into place, far from her head and other arm, in a terrible echo of Erik's own position five stories below.

He left one arm free, and came to stand between her wide legs. She tried to twist and roll her hips, tried to close her legs, but of course she could not. He watched her for a moment, a delighted grin stretching his lips. "I do love to watch a woman struggle. It's not so unlike watching one find pleasure: the same writhing motions, the same groans, the same expressions."

She tried to stop, tried to still her body, but she couldn't cease fighting. She couldn't succumb.

At last, reaching behind him, he produced a long blade and said, "Now, then, let us see exactly what you've been hiding."

Starting with her left foot, he delicately cut away the flimsy slipper. With a long, straight slice from her foot, under the imprisoning cuff, up along her calf, over the bump of her knee, to the top of her inner thigh beneath the crumpled and stained chemise, he slit her stocking. It fell away, leaving her leg bare and chill, and with nary a scratch.

One hand closed around her leg and slid all the way from ankle to thigh in a possessive caress as Christine lay sobbing quietly, no longer struggling. Her free hand was useless; a tease. She could do nothing but flail with it, wipe her tears, clutch it over her chest, try to bat him away from between her legs.

He unclothed her other leg in the same manner, then stood again between her legs, this time with the knife in hand. Her breath caught as he bent to her chest, and she felt the insistent tugs as he skimmed the blade under the ties of her corset, slicing through them like a cobweb. The corset loosened and fell away in two clam-like halves, and now there was nothing left but her chemise.

The blade was cool and sharp against her skin, and he drew it slowly, so slowly she thought she would scream . . . but she dared not move, dared hardly to breathe . . . as he drew it slowly down between her breasts, down, down past her ribs and over the slight swell of her belly, nicking the edge of her navel, down, down to the rise of her mound and the fluff of sensitive hair that grew there . . . down and around, dipping between her legs, so close there to her most sensitive part, just a breath away, and then, a sudden fast, sharp rending as he sliced from there to the hem.

She heard him drop the knife, felt the parting of the chemise as it fell away, leaving her naked, bare, spread, with only one useless limb to cover herself.

His hands were on her then, everywhere. Shoulder to arm, down over the rise of her breasts, along her ribs and waist, cupping her buttocks, lifting her hips, they swarmed everywhere as she tried to cover herself, to push them away, to scratch and hit and punch. He remained always just out of reach, his hands heavy and hot, damp and groping, grasping, grabbing, probing, pinching.

At last he lifted them, grasped her free wrist, and snapped it into its place beyond her head. And now she had nothing with which to cover herself.

Nothing.

Down, down . . . the steps were agonizing to Carlotta's injured legs and sprained wrist. She wasn't certain how far beneath the ground the prisoner was kept, but she knew to keep going until there were no more stairs. There were spiders and cobwebs, rat turds, and, more than once, the skitter of tiny feet on the stone, the quick dart of little shadows at her feet. Carlotta gritted her teeth and kept going. It had been a long time since she'd been so low that she must make her way through such filth, but she'd not come so far that she'd forgotten it.

At last she came to the bottom of the steps and turned to follow a crude passageway. Just around the first corner she was startled by a figure crumpled on the floor, too small to be Erik, but she paused to look anyway.

The ballet mistress! So that was what happened to her. She appeared to be unconscious, but was breathing steadily, and would be of no assistance to Carlotta, so she hurried past.

When she came around the next corner, she knew she'd found her quarry.

He sagged between two iron rings set in the wall above his head, which was bowed in abject defeat. His knees buckled, his clothes filthy, torn, and streaked with blood. He didn't move when she approached; perhaps he was unconscious too. But then—it must have been when her feet came into the view of his bowed head—he raised his face.

Her breath caught at the sight of his mangled flesh, but she did not hesitate. She had seen worse. Carlotta met his eyes, dark ones, weary but still filled with challenge, and held up the key.

"Where did you get that?" the man called Erik breathed, his eyes widening as she stepped toward him.

"Before he did this to me," she gestured toward her arm, "I saw where he kept the key ring. In a place separate from his private chambers, in a room he used to spy on others like the Daaé girl." Her voice came out warped, raspy, ruined, and devastating to her ears. It was the first time she'd spoken aloud to someone. Her hand went to her throat, and for a moment, she saw pity and then understanding flare in his eyes.

"Thank you."

But when she reached up, she realized she would never reach his manacled wrists, and in that moment, she remembered the Giry woman.

Without explanation to Erik, she hurried back to where she was crumpled on the floor. "You! Wake up!" Her voice came out again, rougher than the pebble-strewn floor on which she knelt. She crouched next to the bag of bones, shaking it until it stirred.

With a groan, the woman opened her eyes. Carlotta had to give the woman credit: She recognized her right away and as soon as Carlotta figured out how to unlock her, she staggered to her feet.

Swaying, she grabbed the wall. "Erik?" she managed to say. "Christine?"

"Come," Carlotta rasped.

Erik was watching as they came around the corner, and hope lit his face as they rushed toward him. Giry took the keys from Carlotta after watching her fumble with the fingers of her useless arm and had his ankles unlocked in a trice. But now they had to reach his wrists, high above their heads.

Carlotta fell to her hands and knees, propped up on her good arm, and leaned against the wall next to his leg for support, making of herself a stool on which Giry could stand. The other woman did not need to be told; she was smaller and slighter than Carlotta.

Erik groaned in pain and relief when his first wrist was released, and Carlotta crawled to the other side, sweat beading her forehead, pain screaming throughout her body as she steadied herself, ready for Giry to climb on her again. This one seemed to take longer; it was agony for all of them . . . but at last, she heard the clink of freedom, and felt the sudden lurch of Erik's body next to hers.

He didn't fall, but he staggered away from the wall, nearly collapsing on his knees. Tears of pain clouding her vision, Carlotta used his empty chains to pull herself to her feet.

"Thank you," Erik said to her, now standing upright with a slight sway. She noticed that he kept the bad, scarred side of his face angled away, even though he met her gaze. He began to rub his wrists and test his feet, obviously trying to get his body to work properly.

"You do not have to hide your face from me," Carlotta told him in the voice that did not belong to her. "I've seen much worse." It was an unfamiliar sense of compassion that prompted her to speak unnecessarily in the horrible voice.

Erik looked at her in disbelief, one of his hands going automatically to touch his tortured skin. "Thank you," he said again, letting his fingers fall away. From the expression on his face, she knew he meant this perhaps more than he'd meant the previous thanks. He turned to the Giry woman. "But now . . . Maude? Are you badly hurt?"

"Not so badly as you, I'd say," she replied, and Carlotta agreed.

The handsome side of his face sported a long oozing scar, and what was left of his shirt and trousers was split with obvious whip marks. Bruises colored his high cheekbone and around his good eye, and she'd seen the massive purple and green marks on his torso when his hands were still raised. Still, despite the fact that he was battered beyond comprehension, he had a body that she would have enjoyed exploring as much as she'd enjoyed Guy's. It was no wonder Christine Daaé had spent a week alone with him, and had returned hollow-eyed and quiet.

"I am much better than I would have been after another day at Philippe's hands," Erik said, starting to move away from the small alcove of a prison. "I am alive, and free. But now . . . I must find Christine," he said, even as he was using the wall to support his weight.

"I can show you the *comte*'s private chambers," Giry told him, but she looked as though she could barely stand herself. Indeed, she clutched at the wall with white fingers and knees sagging.

"Unfortunately, I am well aware of their location," Erik replied.

Carlotta eyed the labored breaths he was taking, and noticed the trembling that accompanied his every move. "You'll be no match for him in your condition; we must plan a better way. I wish to see him dead."

Erik paused at the edge of the wall, turning to look back at her. The expression on his mangled face was frightening. "You will."

She couldn't stop writhing and twisting, despite the fact that she was spread-eagled and helpless. The cuffs on her wrists and ankles just barely allowed her to twitch and jerk, and as Philippe bent to her, pinching, sucking, stroking, grasping, Christine fought, uselessly, to get away from his touch.

And she tried to escape into the recesses of her mind, away from the reality . . . remembering Erik's touch, the love and reverence in his hands and coming from his lips . . . not the repulsive possessiveness of the *comte*.

When he bent between her legs, his fingers closing over the tenderness of her spread thighs, and his hungry mouth latched on to her, she screamed and writhed, tears streaming from her eyes. It was an invasion, a horrific invasion, and it was unbearable.

But she had no choice but to bear it; the sliding, thrusting rape with his tongue and teeth was relentless. Christine's cries ebbed into keening sobs as she twisted and turned her head, bucked her hips until his fingers dug into the soft skin above them to hold her down, so that he could all the better ravage her.

When he lifted his face, his lips full and glistening, she knew the worst was yet to come. Wiping his mouth on his sleeve, he settled between her legs, pulling on her hips to bring her bottom just to the edge of the table, her knees slightly bent, and then belted her into place. The leather strap fitted over her hips so tightly she could not move and she began to struggle with renewed fear, whimpering.

He looked down at her, breathing hard. His eyes showed no blue; they were black and glittering and frightening. His hands began to move at his waist, his eyes focused on hers.

Suddenly, there was a loud crash, and Philippe looked up, behind her head. Christine could not see what had happened from her position, but when the *comte*'s face turned ashen, hope lifted within her. "You!" he choked.

"Get away from her," came Erik's voice, and Christine nearly cried with relief. She was saved. Somehow, somehow a miracle had occurred.

"You are in no position to give orders," sneered Philippe, turning from Christine. "You can barely walk, you miserable *beast*." He stalked away, over to the array of whips hanging on the wall, but before he could reach them, something barreled across the room, knocking him to the floor. Erik.

Christine could barely see what was happening, but she heard the grunts and punches, the slapping of flesh to the floor, the slams of feet and boots on the walls and furniture. She saw arms raised in blows, a shoulder, the rearing, then ducking dark head of her beloved followed by the glint of Philippe's lighter hair, all accompanied by the sickening sounds of battle.

All at once, there was a heavy thud that jolted into the bed on which she lay, and suddenly Philippe was leaping to his feet. He whirled toward the line of whips, his fingers closing around the longest, thickest, blackest of them all as Erik struggled to his feet next to Christine.

"Erik!" she cried softly, wanting more than anything to reach to him, to touch him and assure herself that he was alive, and here . . . but of course she could not—she could not move, and she could not distract him from what was surely the battle of life and death for them both.

He spared her a bare glance, but that was enough for her to see his face. This face, his warrior face, she'd never seen before. This face was more horrible, more twisted and dark, and it fairly burned with determination and loathing.

She could see them now; they were standing, braced and facing each other, and Philippe had his ugly whip.

"You always seem to come back for more of this," he sneered with a flick of his wrist. The leather cracked through the air, so loud and sharp that Christine gave a small, involuntary shriek as it snapped next to her, laying into Erik's flesh.

She saw it close, right in front of her eyes. Saw the way the thick black striped over his muscular arm, the way he jolted, and the wide red cut it left in its wake. Tears clogged her throat. How could he bear it? How could he fight such a weapon?

The whip cracked again, but this time Erik moved. She saw the leather flick angrily around his wrist, and saw the way he grunted, accepting the pain, but gave a great jerk at the right moment, pulling on the leather that had wrapped around him. Philippe's eyes widened in shock as he was pulled off-balance.

Suddenly, the whip became the rope that bound them together. Philippe did not release the handle, pulling and twitching it, and Erik held his end, the leather still draping over his muscular wrist. They struggled, Erik dragging on the leather as if reeling in a fish, and Philippe drawing away, trying to loosen his weapon, his face tight with fear and hatred.

At last, the *comte* released the handle, whirling back toward the rest of his weapons. Erik stumbled a step back at the sudden release, but he kept his wide-legged stance and, with a great swish of movement, pulled the whip toward him.

He didn't wait for Philippe; there was no mercy in his face. The black whip snaked out, just as his brother turned, holding a smaller one with several tails, and cracked into Philippe's arm. He howled in pain, but did not release his weapon . . . but before he could raise his arm to strike, Erik brought his own whip around and caught him on the other side, the other arm.

He'd said nothing during this entire time, and Christine saw the way his fingers trembled; his knees staggered when he moved. Sweat and blood mingled over his body, glistening on his dark skin where the shirt had been torn away. He breathed with effort, nearly gasping at times, but he didn't waver. He didn't miss.

And when his whip flashed out again, this time, it wrapped around Philippe's upper arms. For all the *comte*'s skill with the whip, he was not so skilled at defending himself from one.

Erik jerked, and Philippe came toward him.

Then Erik released his whip, and in a quick, smooth movement that happened in the blink of Christine's eye, he had the black braid coiled around his brother's neck, crossed at his throat. One end of the whip in each hand, Erik pulled.

From her place on the table, still bound and belted, Christine watched Philippe's face turn red, his fingers grasping futilely at the two strong hands that pulled relentlessly at the whip. He wasn't yet choking; Erik was playing with him. . . .

"Erik, *no*!" she screamed, watching in horror. "No! You'll be no better than he!"

Erik looked at her, his face still a hideous expression of darkness. "He deserves it," he told her. But she saw that the whip had loosened slightly. "I could snap his neck with one movement."

"No, Erik. No. You cannot. You will become a murderer in truth . . . not only in legend. *Don't do it*."

With a sudden movement, he released the whip, and Philippe staggered away, hands clutching at his throat as he tumbled backward.

Erik turned at last toward Christine, quickly unbuckling the belt that had held her in such a vulnerable position, and one of her ankles, before Philippe pulled himself to his feet and came after him again.

Christine screamed, but Erik had already turned to face him again. This time, Philippe had something long and silver that glinted in his hand, and though he was struggling for breath, a thick line of red welting over his throat, he came after Erik like an enraged bear.

Erik ducked and Philippe whirled past him, nevertheless managing to slice through his trousers with the knife.

Christine watched, her heart choking her, and at first she didn't notice the movement behind her, beyond the fracas between the two brothers. But when Raoul came into her view, moving silently and quickly, she gasped and would have cried out if he hadn't placed a hand over her mouth.

A tight hand.

"Quiet," he said, quickly unfastening her wrists. He removed his hand from her mouth and, grasping one of her arms, moved to unlock the foot that Erik hadn't been able to release. "Come with me," he said, pulling her none too gently off the table and toward the door through which he'd come.

"Erik!" she screamed. "Help!"

"Christine!" He glanced away from Philippe, and she saw the flash of the blade come down just as Raoul yanked her out of the room.

"They can battle to their death," Raoul said, manhandling her down the hallway.

Christine screamed again, struggling to free herself from his tight grip, but he was too strong for her. Her fingers tingled, and her bare breasts jounced unpleasantly as he forced her along.

"Let me go!"

He spoke carefully, steadily, as if to a young child as they made their way down the stairs. "You belong with me, Christine. You know you do. Ever since we met years ago, I've needed you. Wanted you. My brother cannot have you. Neither of them. Now," he said, pushing her into a small alcove, "cover yourself. We are leaving Château de Chagny and will be traveling to board a naval ship. We'll be wed on board, and you'll join me on my journey to the Antarctic for the rescue mission. We won't return for years, and by then . . . my brothers, if they are still alive, will have forgotten all about you."

He pulled out a gun and pointed it at her. "Now, let us go."

TWENTY-FIVE

*E*rik watched in horror as Raoul pulled Christine from the room, and as he shouted, "Stop!" the slice of Philippe's blade caught him along the torso.

Burning pain arched through his battered body, and he stumbled, dark spots alternating with bright lights to obscure his vision. It was getting harder and harder to stay upright, to stumble back into the fray with his gasping brother, who was now bent on slicing him to death.

But Christine . . . she was being taken by Raoul. He had to go after them.

Summoning all of his consciousness, every last bit of his strength, he turned and charged toward his opponent, heedless of the knife. If he didn't stop Philippe now, he'd lose Christine. Again.

The knife raged through the top of his shoulder as Erik rammed into Philippe, but then the metal clattered to the floor as Philippe was propelled backward by Erik's charge.

With a roar of victory, Erik shoved his brother again, onto one of the horrific pieces of furniture he used for torture. Philippe struggled, kicking and fighting, but Erik forced one of his legs down, lining up his foot with a cuff, even as fists pummeled him at his back and an arm slipped around his neck, tightening until those black spots swelled to fill his sight.

Focus. . . . focus. . . . He held the foot in place, straining to breathe, and at last—*snap!*—the cuff locked into place. Philippe screamed with rage, struggling anew, tightening his arm around Erik's throat as he pulled at his hair.

Erik wrenched at the arm choking him, pulled it away just enough that he could swallow and catch a desperate breath, then released the arm again and fought to subdue Philippe's other leg. This one was easier, because the other foot was already cuffed.

When Erik clipped it in place, he stepped away from the vee his brother's legs made on the Y-shaped bed, and stood panting, sweating, bleeding. Philippe was already bending toward his legs, trying to unlock them, and Erik would give him no more time.

He smashed a fist into his brother's face, stunning him enough that he could grab his arms and pull them up behind his head, lining them up with the main line of the Y.

Just as he was clipping them into place, the door opened again.

Erik looked up as Philippe cursed and struggled to free himself, but he had made the restraints so well that there was no way to escape.

Carlotta and Maude had at last come through the door; it must have taken them much longer to come up from the cellar and find their way to the private chambers. They looked at Erik, and then at the confined Philippe.

"Where is Christine?" Maude asked.

"Did you see her?" Erik said at the same time. "Raoul has taken her."

The women shook their heads, and Carlotta moved toward Philippe, a determined look on her face. "So you have not killed him yet," she said in her ruined voice, looking at Erik, who was trying to catch his breath.

Only a moment, only a minute, to rest, to try to fight back the waves of pain that threatened to lay him on the floor. But he could not give in. Not yet.

He had to stop Raoul and get to Christine. But he was so weak. . . .

"No," he panted. "I saved him for you."

Carlotta grinned and looked at the array of whips, the long ivory dildos, the knife, and then the helpless Philippe. "It will be my pleasure."

Christine sat across from Raoul in a small carriage that rumbled along on the muddy, snow-patched roads. She was fully dressed now in a gown and all of the appropriate undergarments.

Raoul had played maid and helped her as their vehicle trundled down the drive of the château, Christine swaying and tipping as she tried to remain steady for him to dress her. He'd put the gun away once she was safely inside the carriage.

She didn't know how long they'd been traveling. The sun had been low in the sky when they came out of the château, Christine wrapped in the blanket he'd given her to hide her nudity. Now the sun had been gone for quite a long time, and there was nothing to see but the very occasional lamp from a house they passed by.

Christine had no idea which direction they were going. She

just knew that every turn of the carriage wheels took her farther and farther from Erik.

If he was still alive.

That last slash of the knife . . . she shivered. Philippe might have killed him.

And if Philippe had killed him, would he come after them? Would he come after his own brother, his true brother?

He would. She was sure of it.

Christine could hardly believe how narrowly she'd escaped the brutal rape Philippe had planned for her. A moment later . . . just a moment.

And how had Erik escaped the dungeon? She hadn't had the chance to ask him.

She might never.

"Raoul, please, please let me go," she begged again, breaking a silence that had stretched for a while.

"You belong with me, Christine. How many times must I tell you that? I am the only one who really loves you. I adore you! No one will take better care of you than I."

"But I love Erik," she said, again. She'd been saying it over and over, pleading for her release, asking him to take her back.

And each time, he replied calmly, as if he'd never heard her say it before. "No, Christine. I love you. You belong with me."

"Raoul. Please!"

"No, Christine," he said. "You are trying my patience. Do not ask me again."

She turned her face toward the padded wall and tried not to cry. Tried to think of a way she might get out of the carriage . . . but then what? Where would she go? How would she get there? She had no money, no one to contact.

Her thoughts were interrupted when the carriage rolled to a halt, and she looked out of the little window. They were in the yard of a small inn.

An inn.

"Are we . . . stopping here?" she asked.

Raoul gave her an odd look as he unlocked the door. "Of course. We'll stop for the night and then move on in the morning. My ship is awaiting us. Come. And," he said, pausing at the door, "don't make a scene. There is no one to help you here, nowhere for you to go. Don't be foolish."

Christine was weary; she could hardly believe what had happened this day. It was only early this morning that she'd tried to creep out of the house and escape . . . and now here she was, heaven knew where, with Raoul. And she had no idea where Erik was.

Sooner than she thought possible, Christine was following Raoul up a set of narrow, dark stairs in the inn, dreading what would happen once they found themselves behind the closed door.

She prayed she did not have to fight off yet another Chagny brother tonight.

"Raoul," she said after the innkeeper left, and they were alone. She knew she was looking at him with wide, frightened eyes.

He turned to her. "Get into bed."

The look in his eyes made her shiver deep inside, but she dared not refuse. He, at least, would not hurt her.

"I . . . need help," she said quietly, turning her back to him. He unbuttoned her gown and unhooked her corset. His hands strayed over her shoulders, brushing the light linen of her shift, and she braced herself.

As her gown slid away, and the corset fell to the ground, he turned her in that pool of fabric until she faced him. Tipping her head up firmly, he bent to kiss her.

Christine tried not to pull away as his lips touched hers, but she wanted to. Instead, she let him kiss her, let his lips trace hers and his tongue slip into her mouth. She closed her eyes and let him touch her, on her shoulders, grazing over her throat and down to cup one of her breasts, now free and loose under her chemise.

At last he pulled away, his breathing unsteady. She stepped back, warily. Waiting.

"Get into bed," he said again. And he turned and left the room.

When the door closed, Christine leaped toward it, looking for a lock, but there was nothing to keep him out.

Shivering from the chill and from nerves, she climbed into the bed. This night would be filled, not with the abuse and pain she'd expected from Philippe, but with its own price and its own torture under the hands of a man who believed he loved her.

As Erik did.

Raoul would come to her as Erik did, with tenderness and love, and she would lie there and allow it. She had no choice.

At first, she did not believe she'd sleep. She kept waiting for the sound of returning footsteps, of the soft click of the door when the knob would turn and open.

Once, she heard steps, and her heart began to pound so hard she felt her entire body reverberate with it. She held her breath, listening for the turn of the knob . . . but nothing. It became silent again, except for the voices of the people in the pub below the inn.

She must have fallen asleep at some point, for the next thing she knew, a heavy weight jolted the bed next to her. Christine's eyes flew open and she gasped in her breath to scream, automatically, not even thinking about how Raoul would react . . . but before she could, his mouth covered hers.

The room was dark, lit only faintly by a sliver of moon shining through the window. There was nothing but shadow and the long body over her, the hands holding her, the mouth seeking hers.

She tried to twist away, tried to push off the heavy weight that lay half on top of her, over her legs, unreasoning panic blaring through her. He held one of her shoulders, the other hand smoothing the hair away from her face. He fitted his mouth to hers with a tenderness she hadn't expected, and she felt his face brush against her cheek, and it was wet.

And she tasted him, at last, the rampant panic receding, and she felt the tremors in his chest as he breathed, and moved his lips with hers, their mouths equally desperate and their tongues slick and long.

Tears leaked from her own eyes, trailing down along her temples into the pillow beneath as her breathing rose, quickening. His hands had left their hold and now moved along the length of her body to touch her in an echo of his brother's greed earlier . . . but now with reverence, and familiarity, and comfort. She arched up when he pulled the chemise away, bringing her breasts up to him to touch.

Her areolas gathered tightly, ready, as he brushed over them. She closed her eyes and sighed as he moved his mouth from her lips to press kisses all along her throat, sending dusky shivers down to her belly. He kissed a nipple with the slow, sensual swirl of tongue and lips and gentle teeth, making her twist beneath him, pulling desire from deep inside her with great, moving tugs.

Christine sighed, her breath becoming uneven as the delicious build started. Her hands moved through his thick hair, brushed over the broad, strong width of his shoulders as he made her moan and need. Made all of the ugliness dissolve.

Then he moved, shifting under the bedclothes. His hard, muscled legs, covered with a soft brush of hair, slid against hers as he lifted himself over her, raising his face to look down at hers. She gazed into the darkness, up into the shadow where his face was, and over the breadth of his shoulders to where the moon shone in. He touched her with long, confident fingers, and she was ready, swollen and wet.

His breath came out in a long warm gust, a homecoming sigh, as he spread her legs, shifting between them, and at last . . .

"Oh," she cried softly as he eased in, rested his face against her cheek, head bowed and shoulders raised, and moved. Slowly, oh so slowly, as though to savor the moment, to permanently imprint it on his mind, to draw out every bit of beauty in their joining.

Christine gently rocked beneath him, her eyes closed again, her hands in his hair, her body as full as it could be. She brushed her hands over his chest, felt the warm hair, the unevenness of his muscles moving beneath, the square edges of his shoulders.

"Christine," he cried low and deep in her ear as he came, his great body trembling against her. She quivered her own release beneath him, the flush and bloom spreading from her pip up through her chest and arms.

She drew him down onto her, taking his weight with pleasure, the heavy body warm and comforting there in the dark room.

After a long while, she spoke, loath to break the peace, but the question clear in her tone. "Raoul?"

"He's confined to the carriage. They'll find him in the morning, after we're gone."

"He's . . . not hurt."

"No. A bump on the head. He never meant you harm, Christine. He couldn't help but love you. As I do. And will."

She smiled against him, moved her fingers over the two parts of his beloved face. "You are the man I love. The only one."

"I want only to be with you, Christine. It's nearly time for us to leave."

She glanced toward the window. "The sun will be up soon."

"I know. Our life together will begin in the sunlight, Christine. I'll not hide in darkness again."

"My angel."

The Comte de Chagny was found in his private chambers four days after the great fire at the Paris Opera House. The cause of death was uncertain, but he was discovered in a most lewd position, his unclothed body spread-eagled from the waist down on an unusual-looking piece of furniture.

His bright red, well-used cock was erect; his body showed signs of whip marks and restraints, even a dark red line around his throat. But he had a lascivious smile frozen on his face, and although common rumor had it that he'd died a happy man, the official word put out by the Chagny family was that he drowned in a tragic accident.

Raoul, Vicomte de Chagny, disappeared from the family château, never to be seen again. The story the servants told was that he and the beautiful Christine Daaé had run off to marry, against the wishes of the *comte*, and they were bound for his ship to take to the sea.

La Carlotta, the prima donna of the Opera House, and Madame Maude Giry, the mistress of the ballet corps, created a strange alliance, and opened what became one of the most celebrated brothels in turn-of-the-century Paris. Their girls were known far and wide as the most beautiful, most accommodating, and most talented prostitutes in Europe, rivaling even those of Marcel Jamet's establishment at 122 rue de Provence. Some of their most frequent visitors included Messieurs Richard and Moncharmin, who, after the fire, gave up on opera theater and went back to their original, lucrative business of trash disposal.

According to her journals, Christine and Erik used the funds he'd saved from his years of salary paid by the Opera House managers, and sailed for America. They lived happily in New York City, where Erik wrote music and Christine performed onstage with the likes of Sarah Bernhardt.

Those patrons of the theater and music in New York became familiar with the man who wore a cream-colored mask covering half his face with the same flair a pirate might wear his eye patch. The women found him mysterious and dangerous, and half the men wished they had an excuse to don such an intriguing article.

Eventually, Christine and Erik would move to a newly thriving city called Hollywood, where they would use their musical talent to work on some theatrical productions known as moving pictures. Erik and Christine became friends with a young man by the name of Lon Chaney, who would eventually star in a film called *The Phantom of the Opera*.

But that is, perhaps, best saved for another volume.

A Letter from the Author
Regarding Her Next Work

Dear Reader,

Not long after I finished compiling the documentation that became *Unmasqued*, in which was revealed the true story of *The Phantom of the Opera*, I was fortunate enough to acquire some personal effects that shed new light on another familiar tale: that of *The Count of Monte Cristo*.

Alexandre Dumas's novel of betrayal and revenge tells the story of the horribly wronged Edmond Dantès, and his bid for vengeance against the villains—his friends—who sent him to prison for fourteen years. The tale has been adapted for film and television, and has been translated and republished, abridged and dissected in numerous ways since its initial publication.

However, through my acquisition of the personal diaries and letters of one of the most pivotal players in the narrative, I've discovered that the story told by Dumas—along with its other adaptations—is incomplete and misleading.

I have had the pleasure of studying and organizing into a fleshed-out, chronological tale the journals of Mercédès Herrera, the first and true love of Edmond Dantès, who is as much a victim of the events told by Dumas as Dantès was. Perhaps even more so.

Her diaries and personal letters bring to light a much different and more accurate chronicle about what occurred during the years of Dantès's imprisonment, and what really happened when he came back to Paris as the wealthy, learned, and powerful Count of Monte Cristo.

In addition, her story reveals that there is much more that came to pass in her life and that of her lover after the pages of Dumas's book have run out.

Thus, my next project will be to make public the true story—with all its explicit details taken directly from her personal effects—of Edmond Dantès and Mercédès Herrera, a pair of lovers separated by greed, jealousy, tragedy, and revenge.

It is the story of *The Count of Monte Cristo* as it has never been told before.

—Colette Gale
August 2007

About the Author

Colette Gale is the pseudonym of a historical novelist. She lives in the Midwest with her family.